Praise for

The Suitor

"The romance, passion, and love . . . will thrill all readers and keep them hooked from the start. This is a great romantic novel."
—*Rendezvous*

"Delightful, well-written Regency twist on Shakespeare's *Taming of the Shrew*. A superb job."
—*Old Book Barn Gazette*

"*The Suitor* starts out as a romp . . . then, in a surprising twist, the lighthearted tone of the beginning chapters falls away and the story becomes one of adventure and epic romance."
—*All About Romance*

"Ms. Hingston uses touches of humor and a devilish hero to enchant readers. Her skillful writing makes for a compelling read. Four stars."
—*Romantic Times*

"Riveting adventure romance . . . it's an entertaining read."
—*Booklist*

Turn the page for more rave reviews . . .

The AFFAIR

Sandy Hingston

BERKLEY BOOKS, NEW YORK

THE AFFAIR

A Berkley Book / published by arrangement with
the author

PRINTING HISTORY
Berkley edition / March 2003

Copyright © 2003 by Mary Sandra Hingston.
Cover illustration by Leslie Peck.
Cover design by George Long.
Interior text design by Julie Rogers.

For information address: The Berkley Publishing Group,
a division of Penguin Putnam Inc.,
375 Hudson Street, New York, New York 10014.

ISBN: 0-425-18907-4

BERKLEY®
Berkley Books are published by The Berkley Publishing Group,
a division of Penguin Putnam Inc.,
375 Hudson Street, New York, New York 10014.
BERKLEY and the "B" design
are trademarks belonging to Penguin Putnam Inc.

PRINTED IN THE UNITED STATES OF AMERICA

10 9 8 7 6 5 4 3 2 1

For Caroline and John, the whippersnappers

So well I love thee, as without thee I
Love nothing.

—MICHAEL DRAYTON

Prologue

"I'm so very, very sorry, Miss Finn, to hear about your loss," Mrs. Treadwell said, in precisely the warm, sympathetic tone that her role as headmistress of an academy for girls dictated.

"Thank you kindly," Claire Finn replied, her head lowered, her voice a bare whisper as she twisted her hands.

Her uncle, Gannon Finn, Lord Carew, cleared his throat. "In this difficult time, Mrs. Treadwell, as you can imagine, what matters most to me is my niece's comfort—which is all we can hope for, since happiness is beyond imagining."

"Oh, yes," breathed Greer Delaney, the stunningly buxom blonde perched on the settee at Carew's side. "No happiness. No indeed."

Mrs. Treadwell, despite her years of experience in dealing with such creatures as Miss Delaney, could not quite suppress a sniff. "Young people are so splendidly re- silient," she said stoutly. "Let us trust that Miss Finn will prove so. We at the academy will certainly do our best to provide lessons and distractions that may move her mind from this dreadful tragedy."

Claire, a slight, dark-haired girl of seventeen, showed no reaction to these inspiring words. But her uncle, a very tall, somewhat dangerous-looking man in somber but fash- ionable black, nodded agreement, and Miss Delaney chipped in: "Oh, yes! Oh, yes!"

"You are, of course, encouraged to visit her whenever you please," Mrs. Treadwell said soothingly, suppressing a fleeting urge to slap the idiotic blonde.

For the first time since the start of the interview, Claire's pale, pretty face became animated. "Uncle Gan- non," she whispered, her voice as frail as her figure, "don't do this to me. Don't abandon me here."

Before her uncle could respond, the blonde leaped in: "Abandon you? What could you be thinking, Claire? It is hardly abandonment on Lord Carew's part to see that you are to be well cared for by Mrs. Treadwell, and to be amongst friends your own age."

"I have no friends here," Claire said, with a spark of spirit.

"Well, I'm sure you will have, very soon," Miss De- laney declared, her fingers, including one bearing a very sizable ruby betrothal ring, twining through His Lordship's much larger hand.

Lord Carew looked across at his niece and pushed his waving black hair back from his forehead. "Claire," he said very gently, a broad tang of Irish to his voice, "I only want what's best for you."

"I want to stay with you," the girl said plaintively.

"That's just not possible," Miss Delaney said, helping herself to a treacle tart from the tea tray.

"Why not?" asked Claire.

"Why, your uncle is a very important man! He has re- sponsibilities—"

"Am I not one of his responsibilities?"

"Of course you are," Lord Carew said, his voice suddenly husky. "But, Claire—"

Mrs. Treadwell felt compelled to interject. "I do wish you would give the academy a try, Miss Finn. We have so much to offer. I don't think I flatter myself when I say our curriculum is as fine as any in England. From what your uncle has written me, you have a good head on your shoulders."

"My niece is exceedingly clever," Lord Carew said proudly.

"I don't know a soul here," Claire declared, her voice very small.

Mrs. Treadwell sighed. She was all too well acquainted with Lord Carew's notoriety as a rakehell, and she knew in her heart that Claire Finn would fare far better at her academy, under her wing, than in his care. She was particularly sure of this because of the behavior of Miss Delaney, who was clinging to His Lordship in a most indecent manner. A forty-year-old bachelor with a heady reputation for seducing young women was hardly a fit guardian for a tender thing like Miss Finn. Especially considering the difficult circumstances. . . .

"Perhaps," Mrs. Treadwell offered, "if you were to meet a few of our students, it would ease your mind." She rang the bell at her elbow, and a maid in crisp black and white appeared at the door. "Clarisse, would you be so good as to ask Miss Carstairs and Miss Boggs to join us?"

Clarisse bobbed a curtsy and vanished on her errand. A few moments later—moments filled with an awkward silence in which Miss Delaney caressed Lord Carew's sleeve and smiled up at him in the manner, Mrs. Treadwell thought privately, of a besotted cow—there was a clatter from the stairway. The headmistress smiled. Her girls, she was sure, would rise to any challenge she set for them.

"Ladies," she declared, "this is Miss Claire Finn, a new and rather hesitant student. Miss Finn, let me present Miss Elizabeth Boggs and Miss Gwendolyn Carstairs."

"Unfair," Bess instantly announced. "Absolutely unfair. She is far too pretty. We won't have her. She'll only make us look bad. Don't you think so, Gwen?"

"She is certainly lovely," Gwen replied thoughtfully, "but she seems quite glum."

"Miss Finn's parents were murdered in an attack upon their coach only a fortnight past," Mrs. Treadwell mentioned.

"Oh, dear God!" Gwen cried in shock. "How awful for you, Miss Finn. I'm so terribly sorry."

And Bess, too, instantly let go her insouciant air. "Forgive me, please, for making jests. I had no idea." And somewhat to Miss Finn's astonishment, she crossed the room and wrapped the dark-haired girl in a sturdy hug. "It is hard to understand what God has in mind at times, is it not?"

"Oh, it is!" Claire cried, burying her head against Bess's shoulder. "Everyone tells me I must be stalwart and strong and have faith, but I *have* no more faith! And why should I?"

"No reason at all that I can see," Gwen noted thoughtfully.

Miss Delaney, apparently somewhat peeved that the girls were paying no attention to her despite her peak-of-ton clothes and hat, cleared her throat. "It was a dreadful loss for all of us," she put in.

Gwen looked at her. "Who are you?"

Lord Carew let out the briefest snort. "This is Miss Delaney, my fiancée," he noted.

Bess looked him up and down. "And who," she asked, "are you?"

"That is my uncle Gannon—my father's brother," Claire explained, still within the circle of Bess's arms. "My guardian."

"Ah," said Bess. And something in the way she spoke it brought a flash of animation to Claire Finn's sad, lovely eyes.

"Uncle Gannon says he cannot keep me with him because he is such a busy man," she noted.

"Really? My papa says the same thing," Gwen told the newcomer. "It infuriates me. Does it infuriate you?"

"Now, see here!" Lord Carew said abruptly, pulling at his short black beard. "The fact is that I am a man of the world, a man of affairs—"

Now it was Bess who snorted, with a pointed glance at Miss Delaney.

"What I mean to say," Carew recovered hastily, "is that I have any number of obligations weighing on me—"

Obligations, Gwen mouthed at Claire. "That's what Papa pleads, too."

"Now, girls," Mrs. Treadwell cautioned—though in fact she was wholly in their corner. It seemed quite shameful to her that Lord Carew would leave his niece here against her wishes so soon after her parents' tragic deaths.

"Have you debuted yet?" Bess inquired of Claire, who shook her head.

"No. Mama and Papa meant for me to come out next season."

"Neither have we," Gwen told her. "Not officially. Though we have been to country balls and such. Have you?"

"My late brother kept Miss Finn rather sequestered, at home in Ireland," Lord Carew put in, still attempting to gain the upper hand. "Which is only one more reason why I thought Mrs. Treadwell's academy would serve her well."

"Oh, yes. Oh, ye—" Miss Delaney began, but stopped as both Bess and Gwen looked at her with biting scorn.

A smile crossed Claire Finn's face.

"I can only tell you," Gwen said, addressing Claire, "that if you are to be abandoned by your family—"

"See here!" Lord Carew roared. "I am not—"

"There is no finer place for it," Gwen went on clearly and firmly.

"I'll vouch for that as well," Bess put in.

"So if your only other choice is being a fifth wheel at home—" said Gwen.

"She is *not* a fifth—" her uncle began.

"Better at least to be someplace where you are appreciated," Gwen finished calmly, ignoring Lord Carew's furious glare. "And you *will* be appreciated here."

Claire Finn looked to Mrs. Treadwell. "I like them," she told the headmistress.

"Oh, I do, too," Mrs. Treadwell said warmly.

"Well, I am not at all certain that I do!" Miss Delaney cried. "They seem quite cheeky to me!"

"You've spilled something across your bodice," Gwen observed. "Treacle, if I'm not mistaken." Miss Delaney glanced down at her bosom in horror. Claire snickered. And Mrs. Treadwell, her eyes trained on Lord Carew, thought she glimpsed a grin before he hid it behind his teacup. Really, this was a most unusual interview! She felt the need to restore propriety.

"My dear Miss Finn," she began, "perhaps you'd care to accompany Miss Boggs and Miss Carstairs on a tour of the premises."

"I'd like that very much," Claire announced.

"Shall I come with you?" Lord Carew offered.

"There's no need for that," Miss Delaney said curtly.

"What are you most interested in, Miss Finn?" Bess asked, as the three girls headed toward the door.

"I scarcely know," Claire allowed. "I am not at all well educated."

"Mrs. Treadwell will see to it that you know all you need to know before you debut," Gwen told her confidently, leading the trio into the corridor.

Lord Carew was stroking his beard. "They're very . . . outspoken, your students, are they not? Sure of themselves," he noted to Mrs. Treadwell.

"Why shouldn't they be? We provide the finest education for young ladies in all of England. We teach Latin, mathematics, the sciences both general and specific, literature, French—"

"Do you never worry about raising up a bunch of blue-stockings?" Miss Delaney inquired airily. "I myself had no more than six years' schooling from a tutor in my parents' home, and I daresay it has served me well enough."

"I couldn't agree more," Mrs. Treadwell purred, utterly flustering the blonde.

Lord Carew stroked his beard again, but this time it might have been to hide a smile. "I'm impressed with the caliber of your young ladies, Mrs. Treadwell."

"Well, I am not!" Miss Delaney declared.

"Do hush, Greer," His Lordship told her. "This is none of your concern."

"I daresay it is!" she countered huffily. "When we are married, Miss Finn will be my ward as well. And since I am to be the one charged with introducing her to the ton, I would much prefer she not acquire pernicious habits and attitudes that it will be my task to erase!"

Lord Carew leveled his gray gaze at her. "Perhaps, then, it would be best after all if I kept her with me, so she could absorb your influence more readily."

"Good God, no!" Miss Delaney declared, so vehemently that she recognized the need to explain. "As you have said yourself, milord, you are a man of the world . . . you have so many interests and pursuits. Not to mention the tangle of your brother's estate . . . I think it best all around that she attend a school, as you have suggested. I am simply not convinced that Mrs. Treadwell's academy is the *appropriate* place."

"Well, I am," Lord Carew said briefly. "So long as it suits her, of course—and I begin to think it will. We did not touch on fees, Mrs. Treadwell, in our correspondence. In what amount shall I make out a cheque for the first semester?"

"Our fee, which of course includes room and board as well as all curricular materials, is—" Mrs. Treadwell broke off as the door to the parlor opened. A petite woman with a tumble of black curls beneath a cunning leghorn hat that made Miss Delaney's bonnet resemble a cart-basket burst through, slamming the door shut behind her.

"Honestly, Evelyn," the woman declared heatedly, shaking out her yellow-and-white-striped silk skirts, "you would not believe the time of it I had convincing that stupid ass Forrester that Petra's aptitude for mathematics is to be celebrated rather than—"

Mrs. Treadwell cleared her throat emphatically. "Lady d'Oliveri, we have guests. Permit me to make introductions. Lord Carew, this is—" Then she stopped again, this time because the petite woman with the tousled black curls had frozen still as stone, her pert red lips slightly parted, her dark eyes round in disbelief.

"You," the Countess d'Oliveri breathed, making the word bear so singular a freight of loathing and revulsion that poor Mrs. Treadwell was quite lost as to how to finish the niceties.

"You," Lord Carew answered from where he'd risen from his seat, with just as great a weight of loaded meaning as he stared at the woman in the striped silk dress.

There was a moment of utter stillness. Then the countess gave a little shake of her elegant shoulders, as though shrugging off a vexsome pest. "I do beg your pardon," she said in quite a different tone, smooth and controlled and cultured. "No one took the trouble to inform me, Mrs. Treadwell, that you had visitors. I think it best I withdraw."

"Just one moment, if you please." Carew's voice was like low thunder, ominous, if distant. "Surely, Mrs. Treadwell, *she* is not employed at your academy."

"Who is she?" Miss Delaney inquired avidly, pulling at his sleeve again. "I must get her milliner's name!"

Mrs. Treadwell shot the countess a glance that clearly indicated she needed rescuing. She needn't have worried. "I *am* engaged here, as it happens," the countess declared coolly, and then leveled her gaze at the blonde who was clinging to His Lordship. "Is this your daughter that you have come to enroll?"

Mrs. Treadwell nearly swooned. "Come, come, Lady

d'Oliveri, don't be foolish. This is Lord Carew's fiancée, Miss Delaney."

"Fiancée? Really? Fancy that," the countess said, her lip curling. "Well, I suppose it is fitting for a man to seek a wife of his own level of maturity."

"Christiane!" Mrs. Treadwell blanched.

"I must say," Lord Carew noted, the thunder barely controlled, "there is no place on earth I would have thought it less likely to encounter you again, Miss Roxell, than in a school for girls."

"I am no longer Miss Roxell," the countess shot back. "And have not been for quite some time."

"You mean to say you actually found a man to wed you?"

"Damn you," Christiane spat at him. "I'll have you know I am the Countess d'Oliveri."

Lord Carew nodded, *his* lip curling. "A foreigner. Of course."

"He was extremely cultured and well mannered—a striking contrast to the *Englishmen* of my acquaintance."

"What every woman longs for in a husband—that he be cultured and well mannered," Lord Carew said, with what struck Mrs. Treadwell as amazing impudence. "I don't suppose he happened to be old as well, and heirless, and to possess a considerable fortune."

"You *bastard!*" Christiane fairly snarled, coming forward with her hand raised as though to strike him.

"Christiane! Lord Carew! That's enough!" Mrs. Treadwell cried, leaping from her chair to step between them, utterly bewildered at the venom being flung about.

"I have no more to say to him," the countess announced, turning her back pointedly.

"Well, I have more to say," Lord Carew declared. "I would no sooner leave my niece in a school to which this—this—this—"

Christiane whirled on him. "This what, milord? Go ahead; find your tongue."

"Lord Carew," Mrs. Treadwell put in desperately, "the

countess is my partner in the academy, it is true. But you wrote me yourself that it was Miss Westin's mother who recommended us to you. I can assure you, Mrs. Westin is fully aware of the countess's connections here, and approves of them. What's more, it was solely due to the countess that Miss Westin and Lord Fanning managed to make a match of it. I can give you the names of a number of other satisfied parents—"

"Carew, I don't understand. What is going on?" Miss Delaney asked in her soft, breathless voice, batting wide blue eyes at him.

" 'Carew, I don't understand. What is—' " Christiane began in devastating imitation.

"Shut up, Greer," Lord Carew commanded, then glowered at the countess. "You shut up, too."

"Make me," Christiane said, sounding for all the world like a belligerent five-year-old.

Mrs. Treadwell had had enough. "Now see here!" she declared sternly. "I should think we would all be sufficiently mature and selfless—"

"Hah!" Carew barked.

"To see that what matters most," Mrs. Treadwell plunged on desperately, "is Miss Finn."

"Who the devil is Miss Finn?" Christiane demanded.

At which precise moment the door to the parlor opened once again, to admit Bess and Gwen and Lord Carew's niece, who was looking far less pale and unearthly than she had half an hour before. "Oh, Uncle Gannon!" she cried, running toward him, completely oblivious to the crackling tension in the room. "It is the most marvelous school that ever existed, I am convinced of it! There is a scientific laboratory where the students perform experiments. There is Latin and mathematics. The girls put on plays—Shakespeare, even! There is a riding stable. And the dancing master is Monsieur Albert, who taught Mama so many years ago. I remember that she admired him so."

Lord Carew had stiffened at her embrace. "There's been a mistake, Claire, I'm afraid," he told her, glaring over her shoulder at the countess. "I could not possibly in good conscience allow you to remain here."

She pushed back, looking up at him, laughing. "You are such a funner, Uncle! Why, it was all your idea that I should come!"

"But that was before I knew . . ." He stopped. Christiane had left them, slipping through the door.

"Knew what?" Claire Finn demanded.

"Who was that woman in the striped silk, Carew?" Miss Delaney asked in a dangerous tone.

Gwen, always sensitive to nuance, had caught the friction as she entered on Claire's heels, and had seen the countess's furious face as she'd fled the room. "Some folk," she said slowly, evenly, "have a prejudice, Miss Finn, against one of the teachers here—a woman we call Madame. Many, many years ago, she was unfairly driven from the ton by a conniving debutante who envied her, and who took extreme measures to stain her reputation. It seems your uncle is one of those who believed the sordid lies. But Miss Boggs and I are witness, Madame's lessons in life are worth ten thousand times those of any other instructor here—begging your pardon, Mrs. Treadwell."

"Oh, no, not at all," Evelyn hastily concurred. "I quite agree. It was the countess who convinced me of the necessity of this academy. It was her dream, not mine."

"Madame," Bess put in, quite intractably, "is the most marvelous person I have ever known. And I'll skin the soul who dares imply otherwise."

Carew started to speak, then stopped himself. He seemed to be weighing something in his mind. His niece stared up at him, eager and hopeful. Miss Delaney nudged him, drew him down to whisper: "It would be such a *bother* to have her about!"

Lord Carew trained a truly terrible look at her, and she shrank back to the settee. "Claire," he said then, and pushed his hair back. "Claire, I don't know what's best. I don't know what to do. Certain . . . certain factors have arisen—"

"Lies. Jealous lies," Gwen said stoutly.

"It's not that simple, young lady," Lord Carew told her. "When you are older—"

"I don't need to be older," Gwen declared, her eyes flashing, "to know that before I came here, nobody cared about me, truly cared about me, or took the time to discover what I was good at, what I loved, what made me me. Go on, if you like. Take your niece to some school that turns out simpering, well-mannered misses who marry the first man who offers for them, without a thought as to whether the match will suit. There are those amongst the ton who feel Miss Boggs and I are failures because we have not yet snagged husbands. What they don't realize is that we are content to wait for the best man, the right man, to come along. And until that happens, we will go on learning and absorbing the invaluable lessons Madame and Mrs. Treadwell have to teach us, and be grateful for the chance!"

"Well spoken, Gwen!" Bess said, somewhat awestruck.

"Uncle Gannon, *please!*" Claire begged.

"Let her stay and be done with it, for God's sake!" Miss Delaney hissed from the settee.

Lord Carew put a hand to his forehead. The three girls stared at him beseechingly, and Miss Delaney glared. Mrs. Treadwell, when he looked to her, returned his gaze steadily, with her chin raised.

He sighed, reaching again for his chequebook. "How much did you want for the first semester, then, Mrs. Treadwell?"

"Hooray!" Bess and Gwen and Claire cried, as Mrs. Treadwell hid her smile behind her teacup.

"It's just two hundred and seventy-five pounds, milord," she said complacently.

When Claire had been settled, with her belongings, in the room she was to share with Gwen and Bess, and when her uncle and Miss Delaney had made their good-byes—the former still with obvious misgivings, the latter with none at all—Mrs. Treadwell returned to her parlor, poured herself a sherry, swallowed it in a gulp, and went in search of her partner in the academy.

She found the countess in the kitchens, barking out numbers to a somewhat baffled-looking Clarisse as she counted the plates lined neatly on the shelves along one wall. "Forty-three dinner," Christiane snapped out. "There's one broken; I want to know who did it. Only forty-one fish—*three* broken! I'll not have this sort of laxness among the staff; have you any notion what crockery costs?"

"But, m'lady," plump old Cook, who was setting out cinnamon rolls to rise, tried to interject.

"No excuses! Only look at this serving platter—chipped in three places!"

"Christiane," Mrs. Treadwell said sharply.

The countess waved her off. "Not now, Evelyn. Can't you see we are busy? I noticed just today at breakfast that the china is in a shocking state."

"Christiane," Mrs. Treadwell said again.

"Only three-score bread plates—are you using them as bowling pins, Clarisse?"

"Clarisse, you may go," Mrs. Treadwell declared, earning an extremely grateful look from the maid.

"I'm not finished here, Clarisse!" Madame countered.

"Yes, you are. Go to bed, Clarisse. As for you—" Mrs. Treadwell crooked a finger at the countess. "In my parlor. *Now*."

"I'm not one of the girls, that jumps to your beck and call," the countess noted angrily, a splotch of color high on each of her cheekbones. Clarisse, meanwhile, had edged her way to the servants' stair and ran up it at a clatter.

"Very well. We'll have it out right here, if you prefer," Mrs. Treadwell said evenly, without the slightest hint of how greatly she would have preferred being within arm's reach of another sherry.

Cook, her task accomplished, settled her girth on a

stool, planted her elbows on the table, and rested her chin in her hands, making it plain she had no intention whatsoever of missing the upcoming brouhaha. Christiane glanced at her over her shoulder. Cook beamed benignly. "In the parlor, then," the countess muttered gracelessly, and started for the door.

Mrs. Treadwell threw a wink at poor disappointed Cook and followed Christiane into the hall.

She was prepared to offer her partner a sherry, but Madame had already poured herself a small whiskey. Mrs. Treadwell beat back the urge she always had to remind the countess that it was just such irregularities in her behavior—only men drank whiskey!—that precluded any possibility of her ever being welcomed back into society's fold, and instead refilled her sherry glass. "You came within a hairsbreadth of costing us a student this evening, Christiane," she said, taking care to keep her voice steady and even.

"Pity I didn't succeed," the countess answered darkly, sipping her whiskey straight.

"I would very much like to know what touched off your revolting display of bad manners."

"Would you?" The countess's eyes flashed. "Well, I would very much like to know why God created brambles. Apply to Him for both answers, and let me know what He says."

"Was it not just last week," Mrs. Treadwell went on, undaunted, "that you mentioned to me that our enrollment was still somewhat below your initial projections? And that unless we managed to attract several more students to the academy, we faced the prospect of dire financial straits?"

The countess made no answer, simply staring into her glass.

"And now along comes Miss Finn, a girl desperately in need of love and attention in the wake of the unspeakable tragedy that has befallen her—"

"What tragedy?" the countess interrupted.

"Well, perhaps if you had been less busy spitting at Lord Carew—"

"Dammit, Evelyn! What tragedy?"

"I can't imagine where you might have been for the past fortnight. It has been all the buzz," Mrs. Treadwell said a bit smugly. "Her parents were murdered by a highwayman while riding in their coach as they started back to Ireland from London. And Claire, heaven help her, was there to see it all."

The countess's cold, set expression underwent a sudden shift. "Dear God. That was she?" she asked, in quite a different tone. "The poor wee thing."

"Precisely. And of course, once her uncle brought her here and I realized how utterly inappropriate he would prove in the role of guardian—"

"We are in agreement there!" Madame said vehemently.

"I determined to see her safely enrolled, and to do my best to provide her with the care and guidance she so desperately needs at this most difficult crossroads in her life," Mrs. Treadwell finished, with a hint of triumph.

The countess had set down her whiskey glass. "I do wish, Evelyn, you might have informed me of these events before—"

"Before what? What opportunity did I have? You came charging in here haranguing Petra Forrester's father without so much as a by-your-leave, and the next thing I knew, you and Lord Carew were at one another's throats! I believe that under the circumstances, *you* owe *me* some explanation!"

The countess's expression was guarded. "You are quite right to remonstrate with me. I beg your pardon. I'll be more careful in the future."

"I did not ask for an apology—though I accept it. I want an explanation."

The countess turned away, shaking her head so that her lavish curls rose and settled again. "No point in it," she said briefly. "Thanks to you, it's all settled and salvaged. Miss Finn is enrolled, and I'm certain she will profit by it."

"Nonetheless, her uncle made it plain to me that he intends to visit—on a regular basis—to look in on her progress," Mrs. Treadwell noted. The countess flinched a bit. "If I am to act as umpire in an ongoing series of verbal bouts of fisticuffs between the two of you, I would like to know why."

"Because he is an idiot," Christiane said briefly.

"That may be," Mrs. Treadwell replied, her voice dripping patience. "But a bit more background would prove helpful."

Christiane crossed to the window and stared out into the darkened courtyard. "I knew him in France," she said at last, grudgingly.

"*Knew* him?" Mrs. Treadwell frowned. "In the biblical sense?"

"I didn't sleep with every man I made the acquaintance of, if that's what you're implying!"

"I wasn't implying anything. I am simply trying to understand."

The countess sighed. "He came to Paris on his grand tour. He was an *infant*. It was twenty years ago. He made his way to the Maison de Touton. And he was . . . trouble."

Mrs. Treadwell nodded encouragement, sensing that at last she was getting somewhere. The Maison de Touton was the gambling house Christiane had founded abroad after she'd been driven out of England by the gossip of the ton. "Did he cheat at cards?" she inquired.

"Worse," Madame said briefly.

"Seduce the young ladies you employed?"

"Worse."

"The young *men*?" Evelyn's eyes were saucers.

"He . . . took a fancy to me."

Mrs. Treadwell could not help it; she laughed. "For heaven's sake, where's the offense in that? Half of Paris was in love with you in those days!"

"But none with so single-minded a passion as Lord Carew," the countess said mutinously. "I cannot possibly convey to you what a *pestilence* he made of himself!"

Mrs. Treadwell chuckled, pouring herself a tad more sherry. "I find it rather touching, you know. The young man and the older woman—"

"Not so much older!" Christiane said hotly. "At least, not in age. He was only three or four years younger. But oh, my God, in terms of experience . . ."

"He *is* Irish, of course."

"He was a maniac. He was insufferable. He would not leave me alone! There I was, perfectly happy as Jean-Baptiste's mistress, well set up in the world, raking in money hand over fist, and he would not leave me be!" The countess groaned at the memory, still staring out the window. "He wanted to rescue me."

"Oh, this gets better and better," Mrs. Treadwell declared. "Rescue you from what?"

"From my life of sin. From that den of vice—that den of vice," Christiane said, voice rising, "that I had devoted five years of my life to building up, and that was finally paying off handsomely for me! He would not leave me be, I tell you! He was there every day, a great callow hulk of a thing, begging me: 'Let me take you away from all this. Let me save you from this. Let me love you the way you deserve to be loved.'"

"And what," Mrs. Treadwell inquired astutely, "had Jean-Baptiste to say to this?"

"What do you expect? At first he was amused—at first *I* was amused! It was so patently ridiculous. Carew was such a—a vulture! Each night he'd sit at a table in the corner and moon at me with those big gray eyes while I went about my business. His own friends tried their best to dissuade him, but he wouldn't listen. He was like a millstone around my neck, following me with his gaze, absolutely *oozing* disapproval—of my gowns, of my manners, of the company I kept."

"Do you know," Mrs. Treadwell put in, "I find that rather curious, considering that he is known nowadays as one of the greatest rogues in England. I cannot tell you the number of 'fiancées' he has disappointed."

"This latest one seems daft enough about him."

"I daresay it will come to naught, just as the others have. I thought myself that he was laughing at her through his beard."

"She is just what he deserves," Christiane said with distaste.

"But what you describe is no more than a simple case of puppy love," Mrs. Treadwell said soothingly. "One can almost pity the poor man for having such grand notions. After all, he is only an Irish lord."

"If you listened to him—and believe me, I had to again and again, or else he would have created even more of a ruckus—his title goes back much further than any king of England's. I tell you, Evelyn, I have never in my life met such a vexsome creature! It got so that I dreaded going downstairs to work, knowing that I would see his great, gaunt, disapproving glare day after day after day."

"Well," Mrs. Treadwell noted much more cheerily, "whatever you did to turn him from his affection for you certainly proved effective in the end. I have never witnessed such complete loathing as he harbors for you now."

"Aye, but you don't know at what cost. When, despite all my rebuffs and the pleadings of his acquaintances, he would not leave me in peace . . ."

"What? *What?*"

Christiane took a deep breath. "I told him precisely what I thought of him."

"And that discouraged him sufficiently." Mrs. Treadwell nodded understanding.

"Oh, no. That was when he challenged Jean-Baptiste to a duel."

"Surely Jean-Baptiste didn't accept."

"Of course not. He flung Carew's glove back at him, told him civilized men did not behave that way. But Carew was impossible. He *insisted* that Jean-Baptiste fight him."

"It would not have been fair," Mrs. Treadwell said worriedly. "Your Jean-Baptiste was a master swordsman—the finest in all the French army, you told me once."

"And so he was. He was terrified he'd murder the fool. He tried in every way he could to avoid the duel—he even paid Carew's friends to spirit him away from Paris. To no avail. Carew was dead set on killing Jean-Baptiste and carrying me off in triumph as his bride."

"Dear me," Mrs. Treadwell said avidly, sipping sherry. "What happened in the end?"

"They met at dawn. In the Bois de Boulogne. And he damned near killed him."

"Jean-Baptiste nearly killed Carew?"

"No, no, Carew nearly killed Jean-Baptiste! Oh, I will never forgive him so long as I live. It took me three months to nurse him back to health. Another inch to the right, and that bastard would have pierced his heart."

Mrs. Treadwell stared into her glass. "See here, Christiane. Are you certain you didn't encourage him?"

"I never did in the least! I did everything I could to *dis*courage him!"

"Sometimes men misread what women mean."

"He could hardly have mistaken *my* meaning. On my soul, I never treated him as anything but a silly boy."

"I wonder . . ."

"What?"

"Whether that might have been where you erred. In not taking him seriously, I mean."

The countess waved her hand. "God forbid I had. According to you, I'd now be married to one of the grandest rogues in all of England. I'm sure he'd be having pert little Miss Delaneys on the side all along. Besides, it was the *certitude* of the man that I found so unbearable! He was so sure I needed salvation, when I was so far from needing any such thing."

Mrs. Treadwell, who had her own tight-held convictions about the countess's past and its repercussions, wisely stayed her tongue. "I suppose one could say he meant well," she ventured.

"One could *not*. He is a monster of ego," Christiane said tartly. "He simply found it incredible that I would prefer another man to him."

"He must be quite a swordsman, nonetheless, to have landed so grave a wound."

"A lucky stroke is all," the countess said loftily. "Jean-Baptiste said so himself."

Mrs. Treadwell tipped a bit more sherry from her glass. "Well, I am glad to have a full accounting. And I must say, I hope you shan't allow your feelings toward Lord Carew to color your behavior toward his niece, who needs us so desperately."

"As though I ever would!" Christiane replied indignantly.

"I imagine," the headmistress went on, "that despite his vows to check in often on Miss Finn, he has no intention of doing so. And Miss Delaney will do her best to convince him that she is better left to our care. So perhaps you and he won't be seeing one another very often after all."

"Nothing could make me happier than never seeing him again," the countess declared curtly.

"In that case, let us hope for the best, eh?" Mrs. Treadwell said hopefully, and drained her sherry glass.

One

"Well!" **Mrs. Treadwell** said, settling herself at her parlor desk. "I must say, the first month of this semester has gone very smoothly, don't you think, Christiane?"

"I suppose one could conclude so. Though I am slightly concerned about that wild little Nora Buck. Is Mrs. Caldburn still complaining of her?"

"Not so much now. It always is the younger girls who have a hard time making the adjustment. Nora did quite well in her last examination on precedence in table-seatings, Mrs. Caldburn says."

The countess d'Oliveri suppressed a shudder. "Jolly good for Nora."

Mrs. Treadwell shot her a sidelong glance. "They have to learn such things, you know. It can't all be higher mathematics and poetry—not that I am denigrating such pursuits. But it would hardly reflect well on the academy to produce young ladies who cannot run a household properly."

"I know, Evelyn. And I do appreciate the work you do to ensure their preparation. I only wish . . ."

"Well, you may as well stop wishing, because the lot of women isn't going to change in our lifetime, no matter how subversive you make the curriculum."

Christiane smiled at her old friend. "You are very patient with me."

"We have the same goals in mind," Mrs. Treadwell noted, returning the smile. "Only you are in far more of a rush than I am. What is the latest news on Petra Forrester's father?"

"He continues to insist that we discourage her mathematical ambitions. Honestly, what a nitwit! She could be the next Newton, with the proper encouragement. I've written to an old friend at Oxford—"

Mrs. Treadwell blanched. "Petra cannot go to Oxford!"

"No, more's the pity. Simply asking for suggestions for further texts and reference works. She has far outpaced anything we have to teach her. She needs new challenges."

Mrs. Treadwell cocked her well-coiffed gray head. "I find it fascinating, don't you, how different young minds are in their interests and proclivities? How is Bess getting along in her playwrighting?"

"Her work continues to grow in depth and intricacy the more she reads. Oh, I do hope she will someday find a young man who shares her love for words."

"I'm quite sure she will. By the by, Dr. Caplan reported to me last week that Gwen assisted at the birth of Mrs. Meecham's baby."

"Don't scold, Evelyn. You should hear her describe it! She was quite helpful, too, Leon told me. The boy was breech, and Gwen helped turn him in the womb."

Mrs. Treadwell's brows knitted. "I really don't see how such talents are to pay off for her when it comes to finding a husband."

"Don't you? I do. Competence—in any field, in any subject—is precisely what these girls need to feel secure in themselves. Without it, they risk falling prey to the first smooth-talking man who walks into their lives."

"I suppose you are right. Still, we must guard against turning out bluestockings, or our reputation will suffer horribly."

"Thinking of Miss Delaney?" Christiane asked, and was then sorry she had.

"I wasn't, actually. But since you raise the subject . . ." Mrs. Treadwell consulted a file on her desk. "What do you make of our Miss Finn?"

"I know that all the instructors report she is quite dreadfully behind what they expect in terms of education. Which is no more than *I* would expect, considering her background," the countess said darkly.

"You mean that she is Irish."

"Dash it all, Evelyn, I don't! And I wish you wouldn't make such broad generalizations. I have known plenty of learned Irish in my life."

"Lord Carew attended Oxford, did he not?" Evelyn asked innocently.

"And you can see all the good it did him."

Mrs. Treadwell let her pince-nez drop on their chain. "I quite liked the man, you know, despite your prejudice against him."

"Did you?" Christiane's dark eyes flashed. "He has not exactly been forthcoming on his promises to visit his niece. It has been four weeks."

"You can blame him for that," Mrs. Treadwell said evenly, "but you might just as well look to yourself."

"I?" The countess was indignant. "How could I be at fault?"

"You admit that what went on between you happened two decades past. Yet when you saw him, you ripped into him as though the wounds were still fresh. Considering the way you mocked and attacked him—"

"I gave no more than I got!"

"I can hardly blame him for staying away—despite the cost to his niece," the headmistress continued calmly.

Christiane stared. "You don't truly think I intimidated him! Oh, you don't know him at all, Evelyn. He isn't the sort of man to be intimidated, by me or by anyone. If he cared about Claire, he would brave seeing me again. He is simply too wrapped up in himself—and in that simpering fiancée of his."

"Gwen has told me Claire suffers from nightmares."

The countess sighed. "That's to be expected, isn't it? After all, she witnessed the murder of her parents. Have the attackers been arrested?"

"Not according to the accounts I read in the *Gazette*. The trail has gone quite cold."

"What could Claire tell the Crown about the attackers?"

"She remembers nothing at all."

"It's shocking how dangerous the roads have become," Christiane reflected. "More than likely, it was discharged soldiers. The regent has been quite neglectful in seeing that pensions are paid. Still, it's rather peculiar, isn't it, that they'd have left a witness?"

"The *Gazette* said they were frightened away by someone arriving on the scene."

"Someone who?"

"It didn't mention. A drover or farmer, I assume. Well, we must have extra patience with the child. What has she shown an interest in thus far?"

Mrs. Treadwell consulted her notes. "Not much of anything. Mrs. Caldburn reports that she is disgracefully ignorant of household management. Says the chit cannot even properly rank dinner guests."

"That's the Irish for you."

Mrs. Treadwell stared. "And you accuse me of prejudice!"

"That's not what I meant. I was simply thinking of her uncle, always insisting that he had no need to learn English ways, since those of his homeland were superior. No doubt her father thought the same. How is she faring in literature?"

Mrs. Treadwell frowned. "She seems to be scarcely literate."

"Mathematics?"

"She has gone no further than simple addition and subtraction."

"Good Lord. What could her parents have been thinking? Science? Latin? French?" Mrs. Treadwell shook her head dolefully. "Dancing?" the countess assayed in desperation.

"Monsieur Albert reports that she does a fine Irish jig."

The countess shuddered. "That will hardly suit at Almack's! There must be some bright spot, though. There always is."

"If there is, we haven't found it," Mrs. Treadwell said worriedly. "Then again, it could simply be that her grief over her parents' deaths makes her unable to concentrate. Still, she seemed so happy to be left here, once Gwen and Bess had taken her in hand." She chewed on her lip. "I've tried talking to her, Christiane, but I have gotten nowhere. She is perfectly polite and sweet, but we just don't have a meeting of minds. You are ever so much better with the hard cases than I am. I wonder if you might—" She broke off, seeing the countess's expression of distaste. "He is only her uncle, for heaven's sake! You cannot punish her for whatever went on between the two of you twenty years ago!"

The countess flushed and bowed her head. "Perhaps you are right. Perhaps I have been selfish."

"She is just a child," the headmistress fretted. "And a very poorly prepared one at that. If we can't think of some way to draw her out of her shell, I daresay we shall have another wild renegade on our hands."

"Claire Finn, wild?" Christiane seemed amused by the thought.

"You must remember—blood is thicker than water."

"Whatever that means," the countess muttered.

"But you'll speak to her."

"I will," the countess said with a sigh.

*   *   *

"Well, Claire!" Madame said heartily, nodding to indicate that her guest should have a seat. "We haven't had much opportunity thus far this term, have we, you and I, for tête-à-tête?"

Claire Finn looked up blankly from the settee in the parlor. "For what?"

"Ah. It is a French term," Christiane clarified. "Tête-à-tête. 'Head to head.' Private discussion."

"No. We haven't," said Miss Finn, appearing slightly alarmed.

"Mrs. Treadwell and I believe in tailoring the education of each of our girls to her special interests. Yet more than a month has gone by, and we have not, I am ashamed to say, discovered yours."

"I really . . . haven't any."

"Everyone has special interests," the countess declared warmly, "even those who haven't yet found them. Perhaps you could begin by enlightening me as to your prior education."

Miss Finn blinked. "I have already said . . . there wasn't much of it. I had a governess—Miss O'Toole—who taught me numbers and letters. Mama—" She hesitated, and seemed on the verge of tears. Then she began again. "Mama wanted to send me to school in England. But Papa was adamant that I should stay at home."

The countess contemplated that. "Have you any brothers or sisters?" The girl shook her head. "Are you—pardon the question if it seems intrusive, but we really ought to have asked it before. Are you Roman Catholic?"

"No. Church of England."

"I was only concerned that perhaps being at school might have caused you to miss mass."

"The services here are what I am accustomed to."

Christiane nibbled her lip. There was a strange stiffness to this young woman, a self-containedness that was unsettling. With what she had witnessed, had been through, had lost, one would think she would be more eager for human connection.

"How do you find your lessons?"

"They are very edifying," Claire said. "I have always regretted that my education wasn't more extensive. And I am most appreciative of the opportunities afforded me here."

"Is there any particular subject that engages you?" Christiane asked hopefully. "Science? Music? Literature?"

"They are all interesting."

"But none grips your soul," the countess murmured.

The girl looked up at her. "I beg your pardon?"

Christiane sighed, settling into a chair. "What do you think the purpose of education is, Miss—Claire?"

"Why—to prepare one for life, I suppose."

"And for what sort of life would you like to be prepared?"

That startled Miss Finn. Her gray eyes widened. "I . . . don't know, I'm sure. The sort of life that everybody has."

"And what sort is that?"

"Ordinary. Regular."

"With a husband? Children? Mistress of your own house?"

"I suppose so."

The countess leaned toward her. "But what if it were just for you? Say you were shipwrecked on a desert isle. What would you want there with you? What would be most important to you to have?"

Miss Finn laughed a little. "What a peculiar question!"

"Well?"

"I don't know. I can't imagine. A Bible, of course. Someone to cook for me; I'm hopeless in the kitchen. A stout pair of brogues."

This was very hard going, the countess thought, but fought to remain patient.

"Oh!" Miss Finn said suddenly. "And my uncle Gannon, of course."

"You're fond of him, are you?" The countess kept her voice warm and even.

"Exceedingly fond!" Claire declared, with a flash of animation in her gaze. "He has always been my favorite relation. Well . . . he was always my only relation, actually."

"Dear me. No grandparents?" The girl shook her head. "Cousins?"

"I . . . I think there may be a few somewhere, back in Ireland. But not close cousins. My father and Uncle Gannon were the only children born to Grandfather and Grandmother, who both died ages ago."

Christiane chewed at her lip. She was walking a fine line here, she recognized. The last thing she wanted was for Claire, if her uncle Gannon ever *did* show up at the academy, to report that the countess d'Oliveri had been asking questions about him and his family. It would be just like Carew to take such information entirely the wrong way, conceited as he was. And yet she had a duty to press on.

"Can you tell me what your parents were like, Claire?" she asked briskly.

The girl looked downright alarmed. "What they were *like*?"

"What I mean is, what goals did they hold for you? Were there directions in which they steered you? Were they, perhaps, great readers? Did they enjoy riding, or hunting? Dancing? Did they play the pianoforte? Did your mama sew?"

Claire thought about it. "I . . . don't know. Papa was always very busy with his estates. He spent a lot of time visiting them, going over the accounts . . . that sort of thing. Is that what you mean?"

"Partly. What did he do for amusement?"

"I've no notion. None at all. Oh, wait! He bred wolfhounds. He was very fond of wolfhounds. We always had a throng of them about."

Christiane suppressed a shudder, imagining a dank Irish castle filled with huge, smelly dogs. "And your mama?"

"She just . . . she just *was*," Claire said, with some bewilderment.

There were a host more questions on Christiane's tongue: Was happy? Was busy? Was morose? Was flirtatious with the stablehands? But she quelled her curiosity. "I see. I don't mean to make you think of painful subjects, Claire. I know that you must miss your parents terribly. You have nightmares, I believe?"

"Who told you that?"

"Gwen and Bess are as concerned as Mrs. Treadwell and I that you find your way in life, *chérie*. They are only looking out for your interests. Everybody is."

"I wish," the girl began, and then bit the words off.

"Wish what?" the countess asked gently. But Claire Finn only shook her head, averting her gaze. "That your uncle would visit you?" Christiane said, making a stab in the dark.

Claire's head whipped back toward her in surprise. "Yes. Yes. I do. Why do you suppose he doesn't? Is it because of you?"

"Me? Oh, I hardly think—"

"You knew him once, didn't you?"

"That was a very long time ago."

"You don't like him." Her tone was faintly accusing. "I could tell that."

"Well, I . . ."

"Most women seem to like him very much," Claire Finn declared.

An exceedingly fine line . . . But Christiane could not help herself. "Miss Delaney certainly is very fond of him."

The girl rolled her eyes. "Miss Delaney is an idiot."

"Now, what makes you say that?"

"Oh, because of the way she simpers around him. Uncle Gannon isn't the sort to be attracted to simpering."

He seemed comfortable enough with it when I saw them together, Christiane reflected. Though he had told his fiancée to shut up. Of course, he had told Christiane to shut up, too. "I'm sure she is everything he wishes in a wife," she told Claire smoothly. "After all, they are betrothed."

"He has been betrothed plenty of times before. It never comes to anything."

Really, this was too delicious not to pursue. "Why do you suppose that is?"

"I haven't any idea. I only know he brings—he used to bring—the women 'round to Aerfailly—that's the castle—and introduce them, and you'd congratulate them and wish them well, and then next visit, it would be a different one." Claire pursed her lips. "I overheard Mama tell Papa once that Uncle Gannon could not be happy because his heart had been broken."

Christiane's own heart skipped a beat. "By whom?" she breathed.

"She didn't say. Or rather, I didn't hear it if she did. Miss O'Toole caught me eavesdropping and hauled me off upstairs."

Christiane pondered this. It was ridiculous to suppose that she herself was the woman who had set Lord Carew's love life off course. Still, the notion was seductively flattering—that he had been so besotted by her during that interlude in Paris that he had never been able to find true happiness with anyone else.

But she was losing sight of her objective in this interview. She shrugged off the frisson that Claire's words had caused. "Have you written your uncle and asked him to visit you?"

The girl's face fell. "Of course not. It is not my place. I know how very busy he is. I am nothing but a burden to him."

"I daresay that's not true," Christiane said crisply. "And I must tell you, I find it unconscionable that he has not yet made good on his promise to be frequent in his visits. Suppose I were to ask Mrs. Treadwell to write him and suggest that he come by to see you?"

Those gray eyes, so much like his, slanted toward her. "I don't like to put her to the trouble. And I don't suppose that it would make much difference. Uncle Gannon comes and goes as he pleases. That is what Papa always said."

"Nonetheless, I think that I will do so," Christiane decided. "In the meantime, I urge you to apply yourself with all your heart to your lessons. And to seek within yourself for what it is that will bring you peace and joy in life."

Claire Finn looked highly dubious. "Peace and joy?"

"There's no sense in dwelling on the past, Claire," the countess said gently. "I'm quite sure your mama and papa would have wished for your happiness more than anything else."

"If that's so, they never gave a hint of it while they were alive."

Christiane stared at the girl on the settee, aghast. But she had already pushed the edges of propriety in this discussion. And clearly, some outside advice was called for. That the only source for such advice appeared to be Gannon Finn was highly unfortunate. Still, there it was. "I'll have Mrs. Treadwell write your uncle straightaway," she assured Claire.

"If you think that best."

"I do." Indeed, the countess thought it *vital*. "Now, as I said, do take care that you apply yourself, *chérie*."

"Why do you call me a cherry?"

Madame winced. "Not 'cherry.' *Chérie*. It is French for 'my dear.' "

"Oh," said Claire. "Imagine that. Good night, then."

"Good night," said the countess, fighting off an urge to take the frail, ethereal student into her arms and hug her ferociously.

Two

"Here I am," Gannon Finn said gracelessly, looming in the doorway to the parlor, scanning the room with a frown. "Where in hell is Mrs. Treadwell?"

Christiane bit off the response she was dearly tempted to make. "I'm afraid she is otherwise engaged at the moment. She asked me to speak with you. Won't you sit down?"

He hesitated. "I really think I ought to go see Claire. I've been away so long. . . ."

"That is part of what Mrs. Treadwell asked me to discuss with you, Lord Carew. I believe that when you enrolled your niece, you made assurances you would be a frequent visitor?"

Standing in his dusty black riding clothes, he pushed his hair back with both hands. "You needn't chide; I know I've been remiss. I've been in Ireland the past month, trying to make some sense out of my late brother's affairs. I came the moment I arrived back in London and read Mrs. Treadwell's letter." He looked at Christiane with a curious combination of arrogance and apology. "How *is* Claire?"

"I do wish you'd sit down. And perhaps you'd care for something to drink?"

"Tea or orangeade are my choices, I suppose," he rumbled.

"We also have claret, brandy, sherry, whiskey—"

"I might have known."

Christiane stood ramrod straight in the elegant but chaste silk daydress she had chosen, after rather lengthy contemplation, for this meeting. It was a deep copper, high-throated and long-sleeved, but admirably fitted through the bodice and waist, thanks to the French couturiere who'd fashioned it for her many years before. The skirts rustled as she smoothed them with her hands. "You cannot have it both ways, milord," she told him coolly. "If you wish for tea or orangeade, say the word. But if your busy schedule, not to mention your long ride, has raised a thirst in you for something stronger, then don't cavil when I offer it."

"You haven't changed a bit, have you, Christiane? Still as supercilious as ever." He crossed the room, very suddenly, and she fought back an impulse to shrink from him. Despite his disheveled attire, he was an imposing man— far more so, in truth, than he'd been at age twenty. He'd been so slender then, not yet grown into his great height. He had since filled out admirably; for someone who led, according to repute, such a life of dissolution, he seemed extraordinarily well muscled. And the beard lent him an aura of dignity that had been sorely lacking in his youth.

To her relief, he moved past her to an upholstered chair and settled into it, crossing his long, black-clad legs. "I'll have whiskey and water," he announced. She could feel his eyes on her as she mixed his drink—and then another just like it for herself.

"Cheers," she offered, tipping her glass toward his.

"It really does seem most remarkable to me to find you ensconced here in this corner of Kent, catering to a coterie of schoolgirls," he noted, and took a long swallow of the whiskey.

"Does it?" she retorted. "I don't see why. I believe I made perfectly clear to you in Paris my strong belief that the female sex is poorly served by English society."

"I put that down to sour grapes."

"How so?" Christiane asked, through gritted teeth.

He waved a hand. She remembered those hands very clearly. "Since the ton had driven you from its midst . . ."

"I count that the most fortunate event in a most fortunate life." She took a seat on the settee, across from his chair.

He cocked his head. "You know, I almost believe you."

"Almost." She could not keep the sneer from her voice. "Is it so remarkable to you that once freed from the strictures of the life that faced me here, I rejoiced in my emancipation?"

"It is, rather, since you have turned up in your homeland again, teaching Latin and dancing to a passel of hopeful misses."

"Latin and dancing are only a part of our curriculum at the academy," Christiane said obliquely, noting that the sun from the window was hitting his hair and making it gleam blue-black. "If you can bear, though, Lord Carew, to put aside insulting me in favor of the subject at hand—"

"Insulting you? Is that what I was doing?"

He really was infuriating. "I think the needs of your niece ought to take precedence over your pathetic attempts to achieve some sort of belated triumph over me."

He extended those long legs. "Of course," he said gravely. "We must keep Claire's needs uppermost in our minds at all times."

Christiane looked at him suspiciously, but his handsome features were arranged in a solemn expression of concern. She took another sip of her drink, then set it aside. "The fact is, Lord Carew—"

"It's fairly silly, isn't it, in light of all that has gone on between us, for you not to call me Gannon?"

"I disagree. I prefer to maintain the social niceties. As I

was saying, *Lord Carew*, Mrs. Treadwell and I are greatly concerned about Claire's welfare."

"Is she not settling in?" he asked quickly, edgily. "Not making friends?"

"We have no concerns on that account," Christiane said truthfully. "She is a delightful girl, and gets on very well with her mates. Our qualms have to do, rather, with her education." She paused. "Or lack of it."

"Oh, really." There was a note of blithe dismissiveness in his voice that raised Christiane's hackles. "What does a girl need to know to get ahead in this world? How to curtsy prettily, and smile at the proper times, and ask prospective suitors about their interests. I should think two hundred and seventy-five pounds a term ought to cover that."

Christiane was hard put to restrain herself. "Your attitude toward the education of the fairer sex, were it shared by your brother, certainly explains Claire's lack of knowledge of even the *fundaments* of civilized life."

To her astonishment, he grinned. "Your long sojourn on the Continent is showing, I'm afraid. That word is only used nowadays to refer to what the common folk term one's backside. Be that as it may, Claire doesn't know a thing about faro or vingt-et-un; I'll acknowledge that."

"You bastard," the countess said evenly.

He grinned at her. "Touched a bit too close to home, did I?"

"You only wish so. Did you never pause to wonder, Gannon—"

"Oh, we are back on a first-name basis."

She forged on, "How it happened to be that I, an unknown English miss, was able to build up a successful gaming house in a foreign land within a few years of my arrival there?"

"From the moment I made the acquaintance of your paramour, the renowned General Jean-Baptiste Vouillard, that was quite clear to me."

Claire, Christiane reminded herself. *This is about Claire, and not about me.* . . . "I had established the Maison de Touton before I ever met Jean-Baptiste," she said evenly, calmly. "I was able to do so because my parents had the foresight to ensure that I had an education in mathematics, and finance, and foreign languages, and the classics, and—"

"None of which availed you much amongst the ton," Lord Carew noted.

She allowed herself a small smile. "That is just the sort of comment I would expect from a man betrothed to Miss Delaney."

She was rewarded by seeing him flush. "Let's leave Greer out of this, shall we?"

"As you wish, of course. But since she is the sort of woman you find worthy of assuming your illustrious name, I can only surmise that your brother's wife was cut from much the same stuff."

To her astonishment, his mouth went taut, and so did the muscles at his temples. "Watch what you say of Georgina," he said sharply—so sharply that Christiane paused, surprised by how the blithe comment had riled him.

"I meant no disrespect," she murmured, as she wondered why his hackles would rise so at the mention of his brother's wife. Georgina . . . She recalled suddenly how Claire had said of her mother, "She just . . . *was*."

"I came here to talk about Claire," he noted curtly.

She took a giant step backward. "The fact is, Lord Carew, we at the academy pride ourselves in tailoring each girl's studies to her interests. And we have yet to discover Claire's."

"I warned him of this," Gannon Finn murmured, almost to himself. "I warned Georgina as well. But he would not listen to me. And she . . . would not stand up to him on it." Then he looked at her, his gray eyes troubled. "Is it hopeless, then? Will she never fit in? Be—be marriageable?"

For a moment, she almost felt sorry for him. "We never consider any of our charges hopeless," she said slowly. "But she faces rather a harder course than girls who have been more properly prepared for what they face in the world." She hesitated, then used his given name again—for Claire's sake. "She is such an enigma to us, Gannon. We need something on which to peg her education—some special interest, some talent, some cause. We understand how greatly she must be grieving. . . ."

"Do you?" His voice was gruff. "Does anyone?"

"No. I don't suppose we do. But we only have the . . . the tools we are given to work with. Any information you might have—"

"I don't know her that well myself."

"She told me you were her favorite relation—almost her only relation."

"More's the pity, I am." He hesitated, thinking. "See here, Christiane. We have gotten off on the wrong foot, haven't we, because of—because of the past? But I do appreciate your efforts on behalf of Claire." He stopped again, then looked straight at her. "May I be frank with you, and be assured that what I say will be held in confidence?"

"I hope you will, for Claire's sake."

He took a long swallow of whiskey. "My brother's marriage was not a happy one," he said, with some difficulty. Christiane waited, making certain her expression was non-judgmental. "Georgina should never have married him," he went on finally. "And she surely shouldn't have stayed with him. He was . . . beastly to her. He was beastly to everyone."

"To Claire?"

"Oh, no. Not . . . not in any nefarious way. He thought the world of her. She was his only child. The heir of a Finn, of the line of Finn. He'd rather have had a son, and he made no bones about that. But Georgina . . . was delicate. There were miscarriages before Claire was born. I think he had resigned himself . . . that she would be the heir."

Christiane nodded. "But with Georgina—"

"He blamed her for the weaknesses . . . the lost sons."

"Is it such a burden, then, to be the heir of a Finn?"

"You would laugh, I recall, in Paris, when I spoke of Ireland's honor, and the glories of her past."

"I was very young when you knew me in Paris."

His smile flashed. She had almost forgotten that smile, broad as a church-door, bright, without a hint of mockery. "And you are older now. Well, so am I. I suppose what I am saying is that Claire's early years were difficult. Filled with conflict. With no particular effort at her education beyond a morass of tales about Ireland's past glory and the need to recapture it on her father's part, and nothing on her mother's. Georgina, I think, believed that her own considerable education only served to make her more aware of her misery." His gray gaze found her face at last. "You will say I ought to have stepped in."

"From what you say, you tried. But there is nothing on earth so difficult as intervening between parents and a child. However well-meant one's attentions, such efforts are bound to be read as interference."

"Mine certainly were," he said ruefully. "But I could have been more forceful. More persevering. As you are, I gather, in the matter of Miss Forrester's proclivity at mathematics."

"Now, how would you know that?"

"It was the first thing I heard you say after twenty years of absence—that her father was an ass for demanding that you and Mrs. Treadwell discourage her interest in the subject." For a moment, with his acknowledgment—wistful, surely—of how long it had been since they'd known one another in Paris, she warmed to him. Then he took a swallow of whiskey and water and said, "That's rather arrogant, isn't it, to go against a parent's stated wishes?"

The warmth vanished instantly. "In a good many cases," Christiane said frostily, "Mrs. Treadwell and I find parents mired in outdated notions as to the worth and abilities of women. We consider it our duty to our sex to remedy that."

"I've made some inquiries, you know, back in London," Gannon Finn noted. "It is true that the academy has its admirers, not least of all Mrs. Westin. No doubt it will shock you to learn that it has its detractors as well."

Christiane caught her breath. The son of a bitch . . . "I appreciate the mention of your inquiries, milord. At least I will have been forewarned when we have a rush of withdrawals."

He laughed. "Never fear, Christiane; I do have some discretion. I made no mention of *you* to the ton tigers. But I gather there was some unpleasantness concerning one of your girls a few years back—a Miss Hainesworth."

"She is deliriously happy, living in Strathclyde with her husband and their twin babies."

"And another, more recently—Lady Katherine Devereaux."

"Mrs. Treadwell and I had a letter from Katherine just last week," Christiane said evenly. "She has no regrets about the course her life has taken."

"Her parents might, though," Carew said shrewdly.

"Ask them, if you think so. You might be surprised."

He looked at her. "I did, as it happens. I have not been so negligent a guardian as you seem to think."

"And?"

"Her stepmother is perfectly contented. Her father the duke . . . is coming around."

She opened her hands, palms upturned. "I'm not sure I see your point, milord."

He leaned toward her from the settee. "Don't you? There seems to be a pattern at your academy of encouraging headstrongness—even, one might say, rebelliousness."

"If by 'rebelliousness' you mean taking care that a girl gets to know herself before she takes a husband, I plead guilty. And that," Christiane said firmly, "brings us back to your niece. Can you give me no clues as to where her particular interests and talents might lie?"

"Ask her," he suggested.

"Do you think we haven't?"

"What does she say?"

"That she longs for an ordinary life."

He stared at her. "Oh, God."

"Precisely. I was hoping you might cast some light on her response."

He rose from the chair, putting his drink aside. "I think it best I see her now."

Well, thought Christiane. That was singularly uninformative. But the news that he'd been asking about the academy in London provided the germ of an idea. She and Evelyn were altogether too isolated here in their corner of Kent to keep up with the *on-dit*. Perhaps it was time she herself made a sojourn to London. She rang the bell at her side.

Clarisse appeared so promptly that Christiane could have sworn she'd been eavesdropping. "Would you conduct Lord Carew to the courtyard, Clarisse, and let Miss Finn know he is waiting for her there?"

"Of course, mum," the maid said, with a curtsy. "Won't ye come this way, m'lord, if you please?"

Lord Carew started to follow her, then paused, glancing back. "I appreciate your concern, Christiane. I want you to know that."

"See to Claire," she said shortly, refusing to acknowledge the illogical skip in her heartbeat as she met his grave gray gaze.

A better woman would have let it go at that. But the Countess d'Oliveri was aware of her deficiencies, and did not overly bemoan them. The drapes at the parlor window were drawn. She went to the window, parted them imperceptibly, and peered through the gap into the courtyard. She saw Clarisse conduct His Lordship there and take her leave. She saw Carew light up a cigar as he waited, and then cast it aside as Claire came flying toward him through the courtyard door. She watched as they embraced, saw the way Claire clung to him in joy, saw him, after a moment, push her away and look at her, making what she gathered was a jest. Claire laughed. He did as well, but Christiane caught the sober expression in his eyes. They turned their backs to her then, strolling arm in arm across the grass, heads close together. Halfway to the far end, Claire stopped, catching him by the sleeve. He turned to her almost reluctantly, Christiane thought, and listened while she spoke. When she had finished, he shook his head. The girl argued a bit more, heatedly at first and then pleadingly. Was she asking him to take her away? Christiane wondered. Was she that unhappy here? In the course of her career at the academy, she had seen any number of homesick girls. But Claire did not appear homesick, exactly; her movements, her words, seemed too intense for that.

In the midst of his niece's impassioned importuning, Lord Carew abruptly raised his head and stared straight at the parlor window. Though she knew, though she was certain, that he could not possibly have seen her, Christiane nonetheless let the curtains fall together across the minute gap, with a strange flood of shame. I was only concerned for Claire, she argued to herself, finishing the whiskey in her glass, fighting back an urge to part the curtains once again.

There was a knock at the door, and Mrs. Treadwell entered. "Well!" she declared. "He has come at last—thank heavens! What excuse did he give you?"

"That he has been in Ireland, settling his brother's estate."

"Hmm. Well, that could be true, I suppose. And seeing him is bound to make Claire happy."

"No doubt," Christiane agreed, with more hopefulness than she felt. Something about that tableau in the courtyard made her fear that Claire Finn's happiness would not be so easily achieved.

Three

"*Oh, it's on* everyone's tongue," Violet Westin said eagerly, delighted to be the conduit of information to her old friend the countess. "Cake?"

Christiane accepted the plate she was passed and took a Hessian tot. "But what does everyone say?"

"There are a million stories," Violet confided. "You would not believe the theories being bruited about. That he arranged it all, as a sort of suicide, because of gaming losses. That *she* arranged for *him* to be killed, because he'd kept her hidden away in his decrepit Irish castle for so long, but that the robbers she'd hired got greedy for her jewels. That it was political—I can't quite follow the logic of that; it has something to do with Hibernians and the Home Office. And, of course, that the daughter did it."

"Claire?" Christiane's old friend nodded sagely, biting into a lemon-curd tart. "But that's absurd!"

"It is *all* absurd," Violet opined. "Why there should be so much surprise over yet another highwayman attack escapes me. The roads are impossibly dangerous anymore.

But the background of the brothers does lend itself to speculation, does it not?"

Christiane forced herself to sip her tea and return the dainty cup to its saucer without the least hint of clatter. "By that, I suppose you mean," she began, and counterfeited a very realistic fit of coughing that swallowed her words.

"Precisely," Violet declared. "Why, we were all perfectly astonished when she chose him over him."

The Countess d'Oliveri wished, not for the first time, that her old friend might be more precise in her casting-about of pronouns. "Chose . . ." Another timely coughing fit. "Terribly sorry," she apologized. "Inhaled a bit of sugar."

"Take more tea," Mrs. Westin advised, refilling the countess's cup. "After all, Gannon had offered for her first."

"I hadn't known that," Christiane confessed.

"Oh, yes! It was ages ago, of course. Not long after Georgina debuted—she made quite a splash, by the way. Did you ever know her?" Christiane shook her head. "One of those long-limbed blondes, very pale and fragile. And green eyes, like a cat. She was positively striking to look at. Her mother—I'm sure you do recall Lady Fothergay . . ."

The countess screwed up her nose. "A very haughty old biddy? Given to silly hats?"

"That's the one. But she wasn't really old, you know—at least, not older than we are now. It only seemed that way because we were so young. Oh, those were the days, weren't they, Christiane?" Then she recovered herself. "Only not for you, of course. Not in the end, I mean. But before that—when we had all the swains after us, and it was naught but flirting and parties and dancing . . ." She trailed away in a sigh.

"I'm much happier now than I ever was then," the countess told her.

"That's because you have something meaningful to do—the molding of young lives."

"As do you. You have your grandchildren."

"I do — and all the agony of watching as Martha and Kit and James and their spouses make perfect muddles of their upbringing, while I bite my tongue. You would not *believe* how this generation coddles its offspring!"

Christiane smiled. "I daresay that's a complaint made by every grandmama since Eve. Tell me, Vi, is there a date set for Lord Carew's marriage to Miss Delaney?"

Violet peered at her old friend across the rim of her teacup. "Now, why on earth would you want to know that?"

"Don't go imagining things," Christiane said dryly. "I have already had one bout of being the object of His Lordship's affections. I long for another about as much as I long for chilblains."

"I'd forgotten about that! You wrote me of it from Paris. He dueled with your French general, did he not?"

"He did. It was dreadfully embarrassing to all concerned."

Mrs. Westin pursed her lips. "That could not have been very long before he first became enamored of Georgina. Yes, yes . . . it is all coming back to me now. He came back from the Continent in mid-season, and all the girls made such a fuss over him because he was new to the scene. If I'm not mistaken, at the time Georgina was thought to be well on her way to wedding Jumpy St. Martin — you do remember Jumpy?"

"Oh, yes," Christiane said warmly, patiently, aware that at the end of such lengthy meanderings Violet was capable of delivering trenchant information. "Who did marry him in the end?"

"Belinda Ingham — and a merry dance he led her, too, once the deed was done. She ended up having the marriage annulled on the grounds it had never been consummated."

"Hard to imagine, having known Jumpy."

"Not so hard after all; he's living now with a former priest somewhere near Cambridge. Their house is said to be perfectly outrageous — all Oriental, from tip to toe. And

Belinda moved on to marry that nice Todd Farmleigh and have six sons by him. Strange, very strange . . . but where was I? Oh, yes, as I say. Lucky for Georgina that Gannon Finn came along when he did!"

"So it is. Was the other brother in London as well?"

"Hugh? Oh, yes."

"And what was he like?"

"Very moody. Quite the opposite of Gannon. In fact, I distinctly recall thinking there was something off about him. Handsome, naturally, just like Gannon. But with a darkness to him. He was one of those fatalistic Irish types, you know—full of blather about English injustice and Irish superiority and the evils of the Plantation. Some girls find that sort of stuff romantic. I suppose Georgina did. And the Finn brothers were so striking—very dark, like Indians. Spanish blood, my father said, from when the Armada went aground in Elizabeth's day."

"Were they close, the brothers?"

Violet shot her another glance. "For someone who detests chilblains, you are certainly asking a great many questions about Gannon Finn."

"If so, it is your fault, for recommending the academy to him for his niece. The poor thing is totally unprepared to debut—and what is worse, neither Evelyn nor I can get any sort of grasp on where her interests lie. And so I thought, naturally, if I could understand more of her family background . . ."

"Hmm. I'm not a bit surprised to hear you say that she is unprepared. Georgina more or less dropped off the earth once she wed Hugh. Only came up in the early years to see Dr. Driscoll—you know, the one who treats the royals for their reproductive failings. We all gathered there was something amiss. Once Claire was born, though, we never, ever saw Georgina. Sad, really. She had been so lively, once upon a time."

The countess made mental note of Dr. Driscoll's name—he was, she knew, an acquaintance of the academy's physician, Dr. Caplan, who happened to be her good friend—and then said shrewdly, "But she did come to London, didn't she, two months ago?"

"So she did," Violet agreed. "But no one thought it peculiar, since Claire was of an age to debut. We assumed Georgina and Hugh were simply preparing her for the ordeal to come."

"Were they seen out and about?"

Mrs. Westin considered the question. "Now that you mention it . . . I can't say that they were."

"Do you know where they put up?"

"I *ought* to. I'm sure I heard it. . . ." She screwed up her eyes, then opened them in triumph. "The St. Pierre! I am sure of it! I remember distinctly that Lady Calhoun mentioned she'd seen them at breakfast there the very morning of the tragedy."

Lady Calhoun, the most daunting of the ton tigresses, was off-limits to Christiane, alas. "Had she any observations on their behavior?" she asked delicately.

"I swear, you are behaving like a gendarme! I'm sure I don't know. Or perhaps I do. She mentioned some sort of contretemps with the waiter over the tab. But Hugh always was impossibly tight."

"I don't suppose Lady Calhoun remarked on Georgina's appearance?"

Violet burst out laughing. "As if that old she-cat wouldn't! She said Georgina looked quite dreadful, if you must know. But then, what else would Theodora say?"

"Quite so," the countess agreed, and retired her teacup for the last time. "I am sorry, Vi, to have spent so much of our visit together on such a dreary topic."

"I am beginning to think it must be quite fascinating, actually, considering that you are so intrigued by it," Mrs. Westin declared, her eyes sparkling. "What on earth do you imagine went on during that carriage ride?"

"I haven't the least notion," the countess said frankly. But she did, she thought privately, have some idea of where to begin looking for answers. After two decades of isolation in Ireland, Georgina Finn had come back to her beloved homeland—and had promptly been murdered. Perhaps it had been, as Violet believed, mere coincidence, another instance of the increasing lawlessness on the nation's highways. On the other hand—in her mind, she pictured again the interview between Claire and her uncle Gannon that she had observed through the parlor window, and the way the girl had seemed to plead with him.

Where Gannon Finn was concerned, nothing ever turned out to be simple, Christiane reflected, taking her leave of Violet and promising not to be so much a stranger. She would have bet her stake in the academy that in the end, the circumstances of his brother's murder would prove more complicated than they appeared.

Dr. Leon Caplan, Christiane happened to know, was also in London, for a meeting of the Royal Academy. As a Jew, he was not, of course, a member, but he had a number of good friends who were, and who were glad to meet him afterward over cigars and whiskey and keep him abreast of the latest scientific and medical breakthroughs. She ought, she thought, to be able to catch him before dinner; he always stayed at a rooming house owned by one of his fellow Jews, Mrs. Mordecai, in the Holborn section of the city. She took a hired carriage there, and was warmly received by the proprietress.

"Why, if it isn't the countess!" Mrs. Mordecai declared, opening the door herself to Christiane's knock. "Ooh, that's a striking hat, that is. But you look peaked, dear, indeed you do. Busy day of it?"

"Very," Christiane confessed, then grinned as a darkhaired child of perhaps five peeked out from behind the landlady's voluminous skirts. "That can't be Rachel, can it? Why, the last time I saw you, you were only this big!" She held her hands a few inches apart, and the girl giggled shyly.

"Not that small, was I, Mama?" she piped.

"Not ever, pet. Can you stay to supper, then, milady?"

Christiane sniffed the air, which was scented with roasting chicken and the exotic spices Mrs. Mordecai employed so adroitly—cumin, coriander, hyssop. "I hope so," she said. "Is Dr. Caplan here?"

"Indeed he is. Suppose I show you up to him, and then you let me know if you've a mind to join us at table. Rachel, do stop looking so beggarly."

"She has peppermints. She always has peppermints," Rachel declared stoutly.

Christiane laughed and dug into her reticule. "Quite right, Rachel! Here you go."

"What do you say, then?" the girl's mother prompted.

"Thank you!" Rachel bobbed a curtsy, taking the foil-wrapped sweets. Mrs. Mordecai shook her head fondly and led Christiane to Dr. Caplan's room on the upper story. "Doctor?" she said, knocking at the door. "It's the Countess d'Oliveri to see you."

"Christiane!" The doctor promptly threw the door open. "You didn't tell me you were coming to London."

"I didn't know I was," the countess said.

"Something to drink, then, the two of you?" Mrs. Mordecai inquired.

"Esther lays in a very fine Spanish sherry, you may recall," Leon Caplan noted.

"I do recall it, and I'd love a glass."

"And you, Doctor?"

"I never miss the opportunity, Esther, thank you." The landlady bustled off, and Leon Caplan, a small, neat man with red hair and deep-set brown eyes, ushered Christiane to an upholstered chair, while he perched on the ottoman. "She is making that extraordinary chicken with almonds," he observed. "The smell has been tormenting me all day as I did my best to read up on dropsy. I'm quite certain I shall accidentally prescribe it for my next suffering patient: 'Take one half of a fowl that has been roasted for six hours with coriander and almonds—' "

Christiane laughed. "You could make far less efficacious recommendations, I'm sure. You look well, Leon.

City life always has suited you; I cannot understand why you are content to sequester yourself away in Kent."

"Nor I you," he said, and grinned. "I suppose the answer is that neither of us is *de bon ton.*"

She returned the smile. "But the ton loses more by snubbing you than in disdaining me."

"I'm not so certain of that. All I can do is cure the occasional malady. Whereas you — is that a new chapeau?"

She touched the bonnet she wore. "Mrs. Mordecai remarked on it as well. Like it?"

"I adore it. And I pity the city's misses, who will never have the chance to admire and emulate it as they should."

"Oh, one or two may have glimpsed me as I rode. See here, Leon. I have a few questions to put to you before that chicken with almonds." Just then, Mrs. Mordecai arrived with the sherry, waited until it had been duly complimented, and again withdrew. "In your confabulations with your colleagues, have you ever heard the name Georgina Finn mentioned?"

"How odd of you to bring that up," he said, and took an appreciative sip of his sherry. "Just last night, Henry Driscoll was going on about her at length."

"Would it be a violation of your doctorly discretion to tell me in what context?"

"I don't think so — not now that she is dead, poor thing. She came to see him a month or so ago, suffering from extreme pelvic discomfort. He made a diagnosis of advanced cancer. Said there was little he could do beyond recommending opiates to ease her pain."

"That would hardly lead to a lengthy discussion," Christiane noted.

Dr. Caplan laughed. "You are as shrewd as ever. It was her past history that was so involved. Driscoll had previously treated her for an inability to maintain a child in the womb. She suffered three miscarriages in all. One was a set of twins."

"Poor thing indeed," Christiane murmured, and took a sip of the very fine sherry.

"The subject of the general discussion was whether the miscarriages might somehow have presaged the cancer, or even caused it in some way."

"Did Dr. Driscoll think so?"

Leon Caplan pursed his lips. "He did not contribute much to the general review, beyond setting out the facts."

Christiane smoothed back a wayward wisp of hair. "You found that unusual, I gather?"

He flushed. "Trust you to go to the heart of it. I did, yes. Driscoll's a bit of a blowhard, always anxious to toot his own horn. But in this case, he didn't. I had the sense . . ."

"What?"

"It is difficult to explain. That he . . . that he had his own theory for what had happened, but was hoping to be dissuaded from it."

"Yet he gave no hint what that theory might be."

The doctor shook his head. "None at all."

"But you suspect something." He started to demur, and she frowned at him. "Don't try it, Leon; I know you too well. What is it?"

He laughed, reluctantly. "There were certain unusual circumstances surrounding the birth of the surviving child, Miss Finn—"

"What circumstances?" she asked eagerly.

"See here, Christiane." He looked quite serious. "Why are you asking about all this?"

"Miss Finn is a new student at the academy. She is a most unusual young lady—very bright, clearly, but with very little formal education. Mrs. Treadwell and I are merely attempting to understand her better, so that we can discover her special needs and strengths."

"Hugh Finn committed her to your care?" He seemed surprised.

"No. Hugh's brother, Gannon. After her parents were murdered."

"That makes more sense. I cannot see Hugh allowing her to study in England, from what Driscoll said."

"Which was?"

"That he detested all things English."

"His wife was English," Christiane said, after a pause.

"*All* things English," Dr. Caplan repeated meaningfully.

"Don't hint, Leon, if you please," the countess said tartly. "Too much depends on this. Are you saying he despised his wife?" The doctor was silent, clearly warring with himself. "Well?"

"I'm unwilling to speculate about a situation I don't know intimately," he said slowly. "And I abhor gossip."

Christiane sighed. "Within the limits of your honor, could you perhaps relate to me the speculations of the other physicians present at your discussion with Dr. Driscoll?"

He leaned toward her intently. "What makes it so difficult, you see, are the circumstances of Miss Finn's birth."

"Which were?"

"During the entire laying-in for that last pregnancy— the one that came to term—her mother was in residence at her brother-in-law's estate."

"At *Gannon's* estate?" He nodded. "Was there an intimation that he was the girl's father?"

"No. No, it isn't that."

"Well, what the devil is it, then?"

It was rare for plain-spoken Dr. Caplan to look embarrassed, but he did now. "See here, Christiane. You know how people will talk—"

"Everyone but you, evidently! I should hope you know me well enough to recognize I am not given to idle tittle-tattle."

"I do know that. Nonetheless . . . the man is dead. So is she. I hardly see the point in dragging up unpleasantness that may or may not be true."

"If you saw the girl, Leon—if you witnessed how *unanchored* she is—"

"Then Gannon Finn has shown excellent sense in entrusting her to you."

"But how am I to help her when I know so little about her? Her past, her family affairs—"

"Ask her," he suggested.

"I have. Do you know what she told me? That her father was always very busy with his estates. And that her mother was 'just . . . there.' Meantime, she suffers from nightmares. On a nightly basis."

"Those should subside in time. Don't be angry, Christiane. Why don't you apply to Lord Carew for more information? Surely he is a more proper source for it than a crowd of half-drunken physicians with no intimate connection to the family."

"Dr. Driscoll has—had—an intimate connection," she said stubbornly.

"And as I already mentioned, Dr. Driscoll showed uncommon reticence in discussing the matter. Oh, Christiane, do leave it be!" He looked so uncomfortable that she took pity on him.

"Very well," she said, and threw him a smile. "I suppose, with all you know of me, I should be grateful for your aversion to gossip."

"I can't imagine what you mean," the doctor said, so completely deadpan that Christiane laughed. Then he said, more naturally, "If the girl should ever show overt symptoms of some illness, some distress, that would be different. But from what you tell me, she is simply a young lady adrift—not so much to be wondered at, when one contemplates what she has lived through."

It is what she has lived through that I am trying to pin down, she wanted to tell him. But she could see it was no use. Blast him for being so upstanding! Of course, she never would have asked him to be the academy's physician were he anything else. "I did well in choosing you, Leon, didn't I, to serve our girls?"

"I like to think so." He grinned, the tension between them eased. "Now, how about tackling Mrs. Mordecai's chicken with almonds in my company?"

"I'd be honored," the countess told him, and rose from her chair to let him lead her downstairs.

Four

She had one trick yet up her sleeve.

Among the countess's acquaintances in London was the publisher of a broadsheet, the *Weekly Guardian,* that was generally considered an utterly scurrilous and unreliable source of the city news. It was also, of course, very heavily subscribed. After a most pleasant meal in the company of Mrs. Mordecai and her family and boarders, Christiane hailed another hired carriage and told the driver, "Four Meekin Lane."

He looked at her askance. "That ain't no proper neighborhood for ye, mum."

"I am calling on an old friend," she said demurely, and settled back against the seat. She was weary, but her curiosity had only been tweaked by the tantalizing hints Dr. Caplan had let drop regarding Georgina and Hugh Finn's family life.

The driver took her to the address, but tried again to dissuade her as he handed her down. "Rough here by the docks," he cautioned, glancing both ways along the darkened street. "No place for a lady."

Christiane pressed a pound note into his hand. "Wait for me, will you, please? I won't be long."

He was impressed by her largesse—but not so impressed that he would guarantee it. "If there's trouble—"

"Of course I don't expect you to stay on in the case of danger," she assured him, and went to knock on Matthew Darby's door.

He took a long time answering; she could hear the driver fidgeting at her back. But the light was on in the upper window, and she knew what that meant. At last the door opened, just a crack, to show a glimpse of Darby's round, pale face. When he saw her, he threw the door wide. "My dear countess! What a delightful surprise!" He started to hug her, then stopped as he realized his hands were blotched with ink. "Beg your pardon. Come in—and bring me everything you've got! What's the latest juicy scandal?"

"Now, now, Matthew, you know I have reformed."

"Aye, more's the rue. I miss those tantalizing tidbits you used to send me from Paris—'What wealthy scion has presented his mother's prized emeralds to a common streetwalker?' 'Which peer's Cambridge-educated son has been accused of cheating at cards in a decidedly second-tier establishment?' Ah, those were my salad days!"

"You are aware, I hope, that my purpose in delivering such news to you was simply to impress upon English parents their duty to keep tighter reins on their sons during tours of the Continent."

"And my purpose in publishing them was absolutely the same," the gazetteer noted, so solemnly that the countess burst out laughing.

"You dreadful liar!"

"One could say the same of you," he said, utterly undiscomfited. "Who would blame you for wreaking some revenge on the cosseted, corseted hypocrites who'd driven you from their midst?"

Christiane took off her bonnet and ran a hand through

her curls. "Still, it was quite petty of me, and I am thoroughly ashamed, in retrospect."

"Does that mean you haven't any *on-dit* for me?" Darby gestured her to a chair in the disorderly sitting room.

"Quite the opposite. I am here to at long last demand payment for my past reports."

"I owe you quite a tidy sum, then, for you gave the *Guardian* its start. But I understood you were now happily ensconced as the silent partner of a very exclusive academy for young ladies down in Kent."

Christiane blanched. "Good God! Where did you hear that?"

"It isn't true?"

"Oh, no. It is completely true. But were the fact known, the academy would instantly see all its students withdrawn."

"Well, of course. That's why I haven't published it." He grinned at her, eyes twinkling behind his thick spectacles. "Does that pay down some of my debt?"

"Absolutely. In fact, it may turn the balance in your favor."

"I doubt that. Though if you would ever care to impart—anonymously, of course—any choice tidbits concerning your students . . ."

"Not a chance, Matthew. I did say I'd reformed."

"You were more fun when you were outraged at society," he grumbled. "Still, I reckon I remain more beholden to you than you to me. How can I be of help?"

"What do you know about the murders of Hugh and Georgina Finn?"

He whistled between his teeth. "Now, why in the world would you be asking about that?"

"I assure you, my motives are utterly philanthropic." And she sketched out for him, briefly, how Claire Finn had come into her care. "I am convinced that helping Miss Finn depends on understanding her family background," she concluded, "and am seeking any information that might achieve that end."

"I haven't run a word about the crime—which isn't to say I haven't got a file on the family. Hold on, and I'll run upstairs and fetch it. Pour yourself a drink if you like." He gestured to the sideboard, then grimaced. "Damn. There's nothing left, is there? Some blasted manservant from Carlton House sucked me dry last night as he reported on the regent's latest indiscretions."

"You aren't publishing such stuff as that, are you?" she asked in horror. "You are sure to be shut down if you do."

"Naturally not. But in knowledge lies power, doesn't it?" He winked and vanished up the narrow staircase, returning a moment later with a black file tied with cord. He sat across from her, turned up the lamp at his elbow, settled his glasses lower on his nose, and pawed through the file. "Which aspect interests you most?"

"All of it," Christiane said frankly. "What have you got?"

"Well, there's a lot of old stuff from when Georgina threw over Hugh's brother to marry him. Various biddies' comments on the relative worth of the two brothers, that sort of thing. Oh, and some pert young misses expressing their delight that Gannon was still to be on the scene."

"I gather he was generally considered more eligible?"

Darby snorted. "Was? Still is, ain't he? If I believed in such nonsense, I'd almost think she broke his heart. It's been—what, twenty years? And he has never married."

"But he is betrothed to Miss Delaney."

"The man's been engaged to marry half a dozen misses, and I don't yet see a wedding band on any of their fingers."

"Do you know him, Matthew?"

"Can't say I do. You did, though, didn't you, in Paris?" He looked up through the thick lenses. "Sent me a lovely little snippet about him, as I recall. Something about a duel at dawn in the Bois de Boulogne, and how a French officer had gallantly declined to slice the young idiot's head off when he had the chance."

Christiane flushed slightly. "Is that what I said?"

"It sticks in my mind," Darby told her dryly, "because

his family solicitor came 'round to visit after it appeared and demanded a retraction. Claimed he had half a dozen witnesses who'd swear Carew won the fight."

"I see. Did you print the retraction?"

"Not a chance. It would have set a dreadful precedent. I merely pointed out to the solicitor that considering the national temperament at the time, losing to a Frenchman was likely only to enhance Lord Carew's reputation. After all, everyone else was losing to the French as well, and garnering considerable sympathy for it."

The countess burst out laughing. "You are irrepressible, Matthew, are you not?"

"I like to think so. Let's see what else I've got here." He returned to the papers, drew one out. "Hugh's Irish estates weren't doing so well, according to this. From a banker friend of mine who'd turned him down for a mortgage a few years back."

"How fare Gannon Finn's estates, pray tell?"

"Damned well. Damned well indeed." More rustling of paper. "He invested what he inherited—his mother was a Varner, you know—in the New World. Warehouses, ships, and textile mills in New England. Quite a portfolio."

Christiane pondered that. "Any scandal surrounding him, besides the succession of fiancées?"

"Not since he lost to—or conquered, depending on the source—your French general. Strictly lady stuff with him."

"No gambling?"

"Not beyond what a gentleman must do to maintain appearances."

"Any gossip concerning Hugh?"

Matthew Darby settled his pince-nez, paging through the file. "Nothing other than the rumors about the estates. He kept himself to himself, once he'd gone off with Georgina to Ireland."

"You haven't heard of any reason why someone might want him dead?"

He shrugged. "Sorry I can't be of more help. If you ask

me, he and his family just happened to be in the wrong place at the wrong time."

Christiane glanced through the smudged window. The carriage driver was craning in his seat, clearly growing more agitated as the hour advanced. Reluctantly, she rose. "I must be going, Matthew. If you *should* hear of anything concerning the case, let me know, won't you?" She opened her reticule and drew out a card.

"With pleasure. And in return, should you ever run across any tidbits you can push my way—without, of course, compromising your young ladies—"

"You have my word on it. Take care, Matthew. It was lovely seeing you again."

"And you, my sweet. Mind your carriage doesn't get lost down here." He saw her to the door. The driver let out an audible sigh of relief as it opened. Matthew Darby kissed her cheek. Their shadows fell onto the street, commingled.

"For God's sake, let's be off," said the driver, hurrying to lift the countess in.

She looked back as they drove away, waving through the window. But Matthew Darby had vanished from the doorway, back to his press and his scandal-sheet.

She was tired; her head was swimming. She leaned against the seat-back, closing her eyes, surrendering to the jolting rhythm of the wheels over cobbles. She had more questions now than she'd had at the start of her journey, And none of what she'd learned seemed helpful in regard to Claire.

Perhaps I am making mountains out of molehills, she thought, as the carriage turned safely back onto the High Holborn. Would I go to such lengths if Gannon weren't involved? What was it, exactly, that she hoped to accomplish with all this poking about? To expose him? Impress him? Make him suffer more for what he'd done to Jean-Baptiste?

Her confusion was exhausting. Her head nodded down. The wheels bumped and turned, bumped and turned. Her reticule slipped from her hands, unnoticed. Her eyes stayed shut.

Paris. The way the city shone at night, reflected through the mullioned windows that the maid wound out to catch the breeze from the Seine. The savor of rich bordeaux, and the sweet, unearthly scent of muguets du bois *in the vase at the side of the bed. His hands, his long, slender hands, reaching for the buttons at her throat. His touch, so delicate, almost womanly. The look on his face, of awed discovery.*

His voice, a whisper: Show me what to do. How to please you. *His hair spilled over the linen-clad pillow, black against white. The wash of sweat on his forehead; his scent, more pungent than the lilies—leather and wine and good clean English soap—as he stripped off his shirt, peeled it over his head. The hair on his chest was lighter than his queue. He bent to kiss her breast, so hesitant, so gentle, like the breeze off the river that scarcely lifted the gauzy white curtains. And there was music, very faint music, from the rooms downstairs. There was music, too, in how he whispered her name:* "Christiane. Christiane..."

She jerked awake. The carriage had stopped; there was some sort of commotion. Remembrance of the dream overtook her, and she blushed. How odd that she should dream of him. . . .

And then, as though the dream had merely been overtaken by another, she heard his voice once more, clear as day, only outraged this time, stripped of any emotion but fury: "Christiane!"

Dazed, she straightened in her seat, reached up by instinct to adjust her hat. Blinking in the glow of gaslights, she saw the driver staring back at her over his shoulder, reins gripped in his hands, his eyes gone wide. And beyond him, blocking the roadway, was Lord Carew atop a huge dark horse, a silver pistol glinting in his hand.

She said the first thing that came into her mind: "Are you robbing me, Gannon?"

"Told ye the docks was dangerous, didn't I?" the driver blubbered.

"Are you robbing *me*?" he countered, still in that wrath-whipped voice, paying the driver no heed.

"Robbing you . . . of what?" she asked, bewildered, even more convinced that this, too, was a dream.

"What was your business with Matthew Darby?"

"Give him yer reticule 'n' have done with it!" pleaded the driver.

"I don't want her bloody reticule," Carew snapped, just as Christiane, finally recognizing that this was reality, came to her senses—and gathered them swiftly. Outrage overwhelmed her.

"Have you been following me?" she demanded, rising in her seat.

"And what if I have? It's an interesting day you've spent in the city, isn't it? First Mrs. Westin, and then that hanger-on of the academy, and then the greatest gossip-monger in all of London—"

"How *dare* you follow me!" she raged, and hurled the closest thing at hand, which happened to be the reticule.

"Aye, there's the ticket," the driver said, greatly relieved.

Carew batted it away. "I have a right to protect my niece," he said, his gray eyes hard as granite.

"As though I ever would do anything to harm her!"

"Ye've got the purse, there," the driver mentioned to the horseman. "Mayhaps ye'd like her jewels, too?"

"You'd have me believe your visit to Darby didn't concern my family?"

Only Christiane's rock-hard faith in Matthew Darby's discretion—a man did not become the greatest gossip-monger in London by not knowing when to keep his mouth shut—emboldened her to declare with utter sangfroid, "It did not!"

Carew's upper lip curled. "I see. It was a social call, then?"

"He is an old and dear friend."

"Fine friends you choose, for the matron of a girls' school."

"Matthew has never once betrayed a confidence I laid on him," Christiane said tautly.

He laughed, confusing the driver even more. "You've as much as admitted I've no reason to believe what he said of your visit."

"Which was?"

"That you are his old and dear friend."

"Perhaps," she suggested tartly, "the world is not so full of conspiracies as you seem to imagine, milord."

He sat back in the saddle, though he still held the pistol cocked. "I suppose Mrs. Westin and Dr. Cohen are old and dear friends of yours as well."

"As it happens, they are."

Around the next corner of the street, a night watchman appeared, striding slowly, smacking his club against his palm. The driver's eyes darted toward him, then back at the countess, then to Lord Carew, who had his mouth open to say something more. But before he could, the driver suddenly screamed at the top of his lungs: "Help! Murder! Mayhem!" The watchman, startled, broke into a trot. Lord Carew never moved.

"Here now, wot's it all about?" the watchman gasped, pounding up to the hansom.

"This man accosted us," the driver announced, equally breathless. "Pulled a pistol on me. Demanded the lady's reticule. There, ye can see it lyin' on the street."

The watchman bent down slowly to retrieve the purse, his gaze steady on Carew. "If he's a robber, he's a rum sort, that don't run from the law."

"I'm no thief," Carew said shortly.

"Well, what are ye, then?"

Christiane waited for him to say it: *Gannon Finn, Lord Carew.* But he stayed mum, his gaze trained straight at her, as though daring her to confirm the driver's claims. She decided it was in her interest, and Claire's, to do so.

"He is an old and dear friend of mine, as it happens," she told the night watchman, and laughed charmingly. "Having a bit of fun. I am sorry the driver was frightened." She looked reprovingly at Gannon. "You really must curb your tendency to play such tricks. I was sound asleep, you know. Had the driver been armed as well, heaven knows what would have ensued."

The watchman took a long, hard look at Carew, and then another at the lady in the cab. "We don't hold with such goings-on here in London," he said sharply, before tossing Christiane's reticule back to her. "Now both o' ye, be on your way."

"My apologies, Officer," Christiane said with a dazzling smile. "Do get along home, milord, and behave."

"I'll be calling on Claire this weekend."

"Good. I'll inform her. Mind you don't disappoint her."

"Mind *you* don't," he retorted, and turned to spur off into the night.

$\mathcal{F}ive$

For several days following this encounter, Christiane simply *stewed* over the fact that Gannon Finn had been tracking her movements on her visit to London. But somewhere around midweek, her fury began to soften. That he would go to such immense trouble on behalf of Claire began to seem touching instead. He had to care about his niece to have spent so much time shadowing Christiane about—and really, it must have been immensely boring, lurking while she dined with Mrs. Mordecai and took tea with Violet Westin.

And then another course of thought overtook her: How had he even known she was *in* London? She hadn't made any great secret of her presence there, but then again, she didn't move among the elite. He had to have been keeping close tabs on her to have been aware of her journey. That prospect was quietly thrilling. She was reminded of what Claire had said about his heart having been broken. Was it possible, after all, that she had been the cause of his life-long disappointment in love? *Greer Delaney could not have been any too delighted to have been deprived of his company while he tracked me here and there,* Christiane thought, with private satisfaction. Not that she cared about the oaf; no, not a whit! Still, there was consolation in contemplating the buxom blonde tapping her toes as Gannon careened all over town in her wake.

She found herself spending an inordinate amount of time wondering what she should wear for his promised weekend visit. Would it be better to match Greer Delaney's modishness, or to affect a simple country air? Back and forth, back and forth she went, before finally deciding on a hybrid of the two styles: She would play the bucolic role, in her charming periwinkle-blue muslin. But she would have the bodice altered by Mrs. Tattersall, in the nearby village of Hartin, so that it was more décolleté. *I may be twenty years older than that Greer,* she thought to herself on Friday morning, standing before the seamstress's mirror and watching as the change was effected. *Still, I daresay I can give her a run for the money.*

Mrs. Tattersall had moved around to the back of the bodice, her mouth full of pins. "Biddagaydere," she mumbled to her patron.

"What's that, Mrs. Tattersall?" Christiane asked grandly, admiring the way her breasts, still taut and firm, swelled against the lowered muslin.

The seamstress removed the pins. "I said, bit of gray in your hair there."

"What?" Christiane cried in horror. "Where?"

"Right here, then." Mrs. Tattersall pointed. Christiane craned with a hand mirror to see.

"Impossible," she murmured. "It must be something else. Dust. Pollen. Flour! I was in the kitchens this morning, helping Cook to—agh!" Mrs. Tattersall had reached up and yanked out the offending hairs; now, wordlessly, she placed them in the countess's hand. From root to tip, the curls were white as snow. Christiane stared at them, aghast.

"The 'pothecary, Mr. Simmons, makes up some very

nice dyes," Mrs. Tattersall mentioned, resuming her pinning. "Ever so natural-looking, they be."

Hair dye. Christiane shuddered. What would be next? Pince-nez? Rheumatism? Gout? She averted her gaze from the image in the looking glass . . . and then, like a moth drawn to flame, glanced back. Those were the start of wrinkles at the outer corners of her eyes, weren't they? And a light dust of freckles marred the once-perfect whiteness of the bosom she had only just been admiring. Was she *sagging*? Surely she was. Undeniably, she was.

She had an urge to run screaming into the street, crying out: *I am growing old!* How had this happened? *When* had it happened? And what had she been doing as it had?

Mrs. Tattersall must have observed her sudden tension, for she withdrew the pins again, mouth curved in a grin. "Aye, well, happens to all of us, don't it?" she said cheerily. "No other choice, is there, 'ceptin' to die, and who would wish for that?"

But that was precisely what Christiane was thinking: *God. I would sooner die.* Far better to expire than to wither away, turn bit by bit into some wretched, crippled, white-haired crone. *I don't* feel *old,* she mused, testing her muscles as she stood, noting that her arms and legs still seemed to function in the way to which she was accustomed. How could three white hairs cause such inner turmoil? She had an ocean of black ones still.

"I could talk to Mr. Simmons for ye," the seamstress offered. "Use his dyes myself, I do. And I fancy I don't flatter myself that no one notices a whit."

Mrs. Tattersall's hair was—and had been, for as long as Christiane had known her—a very odd, lurid shade of red. "Thank you ever so kindly," she managed to say, "but I hardly think that's necessary."

Mrs. Tattersall barked a laugh. "Well—not yet, perhaps! But just ye wait and see!"

Wait and see. With an effort, Christiane tore her gaze from the image in the mirror. "Perhaps . . . perhaps the bodice should be up another inch or so after all," she murmured faintly.

The seamstress nodded sagely. "Aye, I was thinkin' that myself. More fittin', isn't it, for a lady of yer age?"

A lady of your age.

All the way back to the academy, Christiane heard that doleful pronouncement ringing in her head. *I am only forty-three,* she told herself in an attempt to beat it back. *That isn't old. Why, it's scarcely middle-aged!*

But "middle-aged" had just as distasteful a sound as "old"—more so, perhaps, since it implied a limbo between the passage of youth and the advancing onset of senility and uselessness. "I am still the same person I was at eighteen—at twenty-five. At thirty-five!" she said aloud, causing old Stains to turn about on the driver's box.

"What's that, then, mum?" he shouted, cupping his ear and leaning back toward her.

Christiane shuddered. "Nothing, Stains!" she shouted. "I was only talking to myself."

He grinned, his mouth a gap-toothed maw. "Ach, first sign o' decrepitude, that is—talkin' to yerself!"

"Shut up, Stains," she said, but beneath her breath, so he would not hear.

"Eh?"

"I said, you're right, no doubt," Christiane told him from between gritted teeth.

She did not have to see Lord Carew when he visited, of course. She could simply arrange to be elsewhere. And that, she decided with relief, was precisely what she'd do.

But what would he think if she wasn't there?

That I was up to something on my journey to London, she recognized, with a sinking sensation. *That I was guilty of all he accused me of.*

She would have to face him. She had no choice.

Oh, but how could she bear to, knowing that when he looked at her, he must see what Stains and Mrs. Tattersall did—a middle-aged woman, albeit "well-preserved" (God, what a dreadful term that was!)—who had, after a life of minor adventures abroad, come home to teach manners to schoolgirls?

She pictured him again in her mind as he had looked atop the dark steed, potent and furious. No one would call *him* middle-aged! Lord, she thought mournfully, life doesn't get one whit more fair for women as they grow older. It only grows worse. Perhaps, instead of tending to the girls, she should open an academy for middle-aged widows.

Oddly, that thought gave her a scant bit of hope. What would she teach at such an academy? she mused, as the carriage jolted her toward home. To rely on one's advantages. And what were those? Experience. Wiles. Wisdom. A dearth of Greer Delaney's self-centered vapidity.

But could wisdom and wiles and experience—and even lack of silliness—stand up in any man's eyes to the sort of careless beauty Greer held in spades? Did men ever think with anything but their cocks? She had grave doubts of it.

She wished, briefly, that she could discuss the subject with Mrs. Treadwell, who was, after all, the same age as she. But the headmistress, she knew, had given up all claim to youth, and seemed perfectly contented to go gray-haired and matronly. Granted, that suited her role as titular head of the academy. But Christiane had a nagging sense that something more ought to be expected of the former proprietress of the Maison de Touton, a woman who had claimed lovers from three different countries (four, if you counted that very brief fling with the Russian), and who held herself out to be a sort of model for the girls at the academy as to what was bold and dashing and brave.

Could I get him? If I tried?

She recoiled from the notion. Claire was her student, consigned to her care. Her responsibility was toward the bereft, nightmare-tormented orphan.

Then she considered again how the paths to information

she'd pursued in London, while tantalizing, had ultimately
led her no closer to understanding her charge. The key to
what had befallen Hugh and Georgina Finn, everyone she
had consulted agreed, lay with the surviving brother. Perhaps she could combine the two missions—the challenge
of determining what lay behind Claire's peculiar malaise,
and the task of proving, to herself if no one else, that she
was not yet a complacent matron. That she still had something to offer even so renowned a rake as Gannon Finn.

Of course, she would never allow it to go too far. She
knew the limits, and she would not transgress them—especially not with the man who had nearly cost Jean-
Baptiste his life. It would be a scientific experiment, that
was all. With the added benefit of aiding Claire.

The idea seemed irresistible. What could possibly go
wrong? Greatly heartened, she sat up in the carriage seat
proudly, with the perfect posture that had made her the
envy of the girls who had debuted with her.

She had a mission. It felt grand to have a mission all her
own.

Six

"I thought you detested the man," Mrs. Treadwell said in bewilderment, watching as Christiane oversaw the laying of a private supper table in the parlor.

"I told you before, Evelyn, I would not let my personal feelings interfere with our efforts to steer Claire toward happiness. We'll need the oyster forks, Clarisse."

"Very good, mum."

"Oyster forks!" Mrs. Treadwell sniffed. "The last time I looked, oysters were three shillings the dozen."

"You wouldn't have me stint for Lord Carew of all people, surely."

"What else is on your menu?" the headmistress asked suspiciously.

"Nothing so very grand. Pâté. A crab bisque. Tomatoes gratin. Quince tart. And Stains shot us some lovely woodcock. I'm having Cook do them in a sauce Robert. You can't quarrel with the cost of those."

Mrs. Treadwell contemplated the countess. "What's that you've done to your hair?"

"This?" Christiane touched her curls, which were swept

to one side and caught up in bespangled Spanish combs. "Just something new I'm trying. Don't you care for it?"

"You haven't changed the way you wear your hair since I don't know when."

"Quite right. I was falling into a rut."

"See that's all you fall into," Mrs. Treadwell muttered.

"I beg your pardon?"

"I'm not stupid, Christiane. And I've known you for a lifetime. All of this—" She indicated the candle-bedecked table, the arrangement of spicy-scented phlox and sweet peas in the center, the spread of polished silver, the gleaming china. "It appears to me that you are setting some sort of trap."

"That's precisely what I'm doing," the countess acknowledged, to her old friend's surprise. "My trip to London, my inquiries there, my interviews with Claire and her uncle—none of this has gotten us any closer to understanding what underlies Claire's peculiar state. So I am going on the offensive. I hope, with the help of superb food and wine and conversation, to loosen both her tongue and that of Lord Carew."

"Seems like a great deal of bother and expense, if you ask me."

"It was you who applied to me for help in this matter, you'll recall. You can't blame me for employing all the weapons in my arsenal. If you'll excuse me, it is nearly eight. I must go and dress."

Mrs. Treadwell cast another disapproving glance at the table. "One would almost think you were trying to seduce him."

"If I were," Christiane said blithely, "it would only be to suit our cause."

The headmistress tittered. "Come now, Christiane. What would Carew see in the likes of you?"

The countess froze, halfway to the door. "What do you mean by that?"

"Well, really! You must face the facts. He *is* betrothed to Miss Delaney."

"Who is, we both agree, an idiot."

"She may well be. But she is also twenty years your junior."

"You say that as though it were a foregone advantage."

"What the devil else would you call it?"

They stood squared off against each other. The countess faltered first. "Of course I'm not so simple as to imagine I can rekindle the ardor he once held for me."

"But you are willing to give it a try, with the candles dim enough?"

"Evelyn! How callous!"

"I don't like to see a woman of your age make a fool of herself over any man—least of all the likes of Lord Carew," the headmistress said shrewdly. "What are you planning to wear—something in gauze?"

"I resent your trying to intimidate me the way you might the girls," Christiane snapped in reply. "I would think you'd trust me to behave in an appropriate manner."

"And I am beginning to wonder why I should. I notice you haven't asked me to join your cozy little supper."

"Would you care to?"

"No, I wouldn't. For I very much fear I would be treated to the ludicrous display of a woman of a certain age behaving like a senseless schoolgirl."

"Just because *you* are content to grow old and fat—"

"I am not fat!" Mrs. Treadwell screeched. "I am only buxom!" And she stomped off into the hall.

God, Christiane thought, somewhat shaken. There are ten million ways in which we women deceive ourselves.

She hoped, as she mounted the stairs to don her renovated gown, that her dinner with Lord Carew that evening would not prove to be ten million and one.

He arrived precisely on time, and was shown in by Clarisse to the parlor, where Claire and the countess were waiting. "Good to see you again, pet," he told his niece, and kissed her before glancing at Christiane. "How do you do?"

How do you do. The cold, formal greeting shot her high-blown hopes from the sky; she felt every bit the poseur Evelyn had accused her of being. She hated her sideswept curls, the gown she'd chosen, her jewels, her shoes.

But she rallied. She had to. "Very well, milord. And you?" she answered, equally coolly.

He nodded, handing Clarisse his hat and pushing back the dark waves of his hair in a negligent gesture she remembered very clearly from his sojourn in Paris. "Can't complain. I've been working hard. I trust, Claire, you have, too?"

"I . . . I have tried to, Uncle."

"Is that a new gown?" he asked.

She colored, tugging at the waistband of the violet-patterned silk. "I made it myself. Well, I had a great deal of help from Miss Boggs and Miss Carstairs, actually. But I did all the finishing work. Do you . . . is it dreadful?"

"Quite the contrary," he said gravely. "I like it very much indeed." And Christiane, who a moment before would have wished the compliment her own, flushed and was glad he'd given it to Claire instead.

"Won't you sit down, Claire?" she said quietly. The earl held the countess's chair, then Claire's, and then took his own seat, eyeing the flowers and candles and china and crystal. "I thought to make the occasion festive," Christiane said somewhat defensively.

"It looks lovely," Claire quickly noted. "Doesn't it, Uncle Gannon?"

"Lovely indeed," he said dryly. "Miss Roxell—I mean, the Countess d'Oliveri—always did have exquisite taste."

"Serve the bisque, Clarisse," Christiane said briskly. "Sherry, Lord Carew?"

"Please."

"And for you, Claire?"

"I . . ." The girl hesitated uncertainly.

"It's to go in your soup," Lord Carew said kindly, passing her the decanter. "Try it. I'll wager you like it. Just a drop or two." She followed his directions and took a tentative sip from the tip of her spoon.

"Oh, it's very good!" She glanced apologetically at the countess. "Mrs. Caldburn hasn't gotten to sherry in soup yet, I'm afraid."

"Well, now you know." Christiane took up her own spoon.

"Been to London lately, have you?" asked Lord Carew.

She coughed on her soup. His gray eyes were innocently wide. She steeled herself; apparently, he meant to be as unpleasant as possible. "You know I have, only last weekend," she retorted, "for you saw me there."

"Fancy that," said Claire. "Were you at a rout? A ball?"

"No," said the countess, "it was more . . . in passing. Is the city still so unseasonably warm, milord?" For the rest of the bisque and through the oysters and pâté and cheeses, they spoke of the weather, of Claire's studies, of the meteor shower that the science instructor, Dr. Barker, had taken the girls up to the rooftop one midnight to see. Claire did not say much—she was paying great heed to her table manners—but she seemed happy to be in her uncle's company. His Lordship was gentle and teasing with her, and to the countess fairly civil, though there was nothing whatsoever in his demeanor to indicate that the care she'd expended on her toilette was anything but wasted. When Claire asked politely after Miss Delaney, he said that she was well and sent her best regards, then changed the subject very naturally.

The arrival of the woodcock, gleaming in their silken drape of sauce, occasioned compliments from Lord Carew that sent Clarisse blushing and giggling back to the kitchen. Claire stared at the bird on her plate. "Papa was very fond of woodcock, do you remember, Uncle Gannon?" she said softly.

"Aye, so he was. Many's the time I went out traipsing after them with him."

"And then he'd make Mama clean them. How she hated that! 'The poor wee things,' she'd say."

Gannon glanced at Christiane, who hadn't quite managed to hide her surprise at the notion of a noblewoman plucking woodcock. "My brother held the opinion that it was the duty of the woman of the house to see to the fruits of the hunt."

"We at the academy are all in favor of practical education." She looked at Claire. "You needn't eat it if you don't care to, *chérie.*"

The girl smiled. "Oh, I have had *that* lesson from Mrs. Caldburn—on how to push food about on your plate so it looks as though you devoured it when you really can't stand it."

Lord Carew laughed. "A practical education indeed! I never have that problem, though. I like everything." He dug into his bird cheerily.

Cook had done a lovely job with the tart. His Lordship had two helpings, then pushed back his chair with a sigh of contentment. "When I went to school," he noted, "we never ate like this."

The countess was surprised to see Claire shoot her a conspiratorial smile. "Actually, this wasn't even Cook at her best. Was it, Madame? We usually have far more courses."

"I was aiming for that simple, countrified effect," Christiane responded, making the girl giggle again.

Her uncle looked at them suspiciously. "Well, I know damned well you don't always have crab bisque with sherry!" Clarisse brought coffee and brandy. "Mind if I smoke?" he asked the ladies.

"I love the scent of your cigars," Claire told him. "But it is up to Madame."

"I've seen the countess smoke cigars."

"Gannon!" she cried, without thinking.

"You haven't!" Claire's eyes were wide.

"I was very young when I knew your uncle," the countess said demurely—then added, "and so was he. You are welcome to smoke if you like, Lord Carew."

Claire straightened in her seat. "Oh, I nearly forgot! I

have a gift for you, Uncle Gannon. May I go and fetch it, Madame?" Christiane nodded, and the girl skipped out of the parlor, with her uncle staring in her wake.

There was a moment of silence. Christiane sipped her coffee. Lord Carew took out a cigar, nipped off the end, lit it, sucked, and sent a perfect ring of smoke sailing toward the ceiling. "I tried to teach you that," he said then, watching it disperse in the candlelit air. "I daresay you don't recall it."

"I do recall it. You never succeeded."

"I would have, given more time. You appear to be succeeding with my niece, though—doing wonders with her," he said gruffly. "How are the nightmares?"

"She's still troubled by them. But Dr. Caplan—he is the physician I went to see in London; I believe you described him as 'that hanger-on of the academy'? He says they should subside in time."

He had the grace to look ashamed. "See here, Christiane. I made a bit of a fool of myself in London, didn't I? But this business with Hugh and Georgina . . . it's been damned unpleasant. There are all sorts of whispers and innuendos. And then to have you visit Darby—but it wasn't worthy of me to suspect you of . . . what I suspected you of."

"Which was?"

"I'm not certain. Taking advantage of Claire somehow. But it is clear to me that you only have her best interests in mind—far more than my brother ever did."

Christiane was hoping *she* wasn't looking ashamed. She *had* been taking advantage of Claire, hadn't she, in setting up this dinner to see if she could still attract Lord Carew after all these years? And all because of three gray hairs—hardly cause to toy with the future of a poor orphan who'd witnessed the trauma Claire had.

He sent another smoke-ring swirling. "Time seems scarcely to have touched you," he said softly, his eyes on hers. Startled, she stared back at him—just as Claire came tripping in through the doorway again, parchment in hand.

"Here you go, then," she burbled, pressing the paper on her uncle. It was curled in a roll, and he unfurled it.

"Oh, very nice. Very nice indeed!" he declared. "I think this may be your finest effort yet."

"Do you really? I thought so too, but I wasn't sure . . ."

"What is it?" Christiane asked curiously.

"Just a sketch I did. Of you."

"Of *me*?" In horror, the countess grabbed for it. Gannon Finn, his gaze teasing, raised it over his head, out of her reach.

"It is a gift for me," he said solemnly.

"*Don't* be an idiot. It's not a suitable gift."

Claire blinked. "It's not? Mrs. Caldburn says sketches and artworks we make should go to our families, to be displayed in our homes. She says they encourage suitors to think us well rounded."

"I shall have it framed and displayed prominently, to that purpose," Lord Carew declared. "I do so admire the way, Claire, you have captured your subject's mood."

"Let — me — see — that," Christiane ground out.

Still grinning, he handed her the parchment, which promptly snapped back into its roll. She stretched it out with a sense of dread.

"Good God, Claire," she said then.

"You don't like it?" the girl asked anxiously. "I worried so about the eyes. Eyes are the hardest, I think."

Christiane stared at the pencil sketch. "How long have you been doing such work?"

"Oh . . . forever, it seems. Papa said it was a waste of time. But Mama encouraged me."

"No wonder!"

"*Do* you like it, then?" Claire sounded perplexed.

Christiane turned on Lord Carew indignantly. "You knew about this, and you never thought to mention it to Mrs. Treadwell or me?"

"Don't all girls sketch?"

"Not like this. Claire, you have art lessons with Monsieur Battier every week. You never told me you particularly enjoyed them."

"He has us doing landscapes," she explained. "Such a bore, landscapes. I like to draw people. Animals, too. But I don't understand. Do you like it or don't you?"

"I'm in awe of it," Christiane said honestly, contemplating the few simple swirls of lead with which the girl had captured her so adroitly. "You have a remarkable talent—one that deserves to be nourished and fed!"

"It is only a hobby," Claire murmured, but her cheeks glowed with pleasure.

Christiane stood and went to her desk, bringing forth a pencil and a clean sheet of her writing paper. "Can you make another? Can I watch as you do it?"

"Another of you?"

"No, no. Of anyone. Of Mrs. Treadwell. Of Clarisse."

"Oh, Clarisse is simple."

The maid had just come in with more coffee. "Beg yer pardon?" she said, with some resentment.

"Hush, Clarisse. You are about to be immortalized," the countess told her, watching in fascination as Claire went to work. The maid came close, standing at the girl's shoulder as, in deft strokes, her neat white cap emerged, and then the hair pinned beneath it, then the line of her square chin, her nose, her mouth—pursed up in resentment, as it so often was—and last of all her eyes, complete with the impertinent spark they so frequently held.

"Gor!" the maid declared in wonder.

"Gor indeed," Christiane echoed.

"Can I have that, then?" Clarisse demanded.

"If you like." Claire handed it over.

"Would ye sign it?"

"Would I what?"

"Sign it. That's what artists do, isn't it, Madame?"

"Indeed they do. In the lower right-hand corner, generally."

With some embarrassment, Claire scrawled her name on the paper. "It is only a rough likeness," she demurred.

"It looks just like me, it does!" Clarisse marveled, turning the sketch this way and that.

The countess fetched another sheet of paper. "Do Gwen," she urged. Claire obliged, capturing the dark-haired student's fierce, focused intensity so perfectly that Christiane gasped.

"Oh," Clarisse marveled. "It's like the paper is a mirror!"

"I believe I haven't credited you enough, Claire," Lord Carew noted, contemplating the sketches. "These really are remarkable."

"And now we have a starting point," Christiane murmured.

Claire looked at her. "A what?"

"I shall speak to Monsieur Battier at once. No more landscapes for you, young lady!"

"Well, I shall be glad of that!"

"Have you ever worked in paints? Oils? Watercolors?" the countess asked.

"No, never. I don't know that I could."

"You wouldn't, until you try." The countess felt like bursting into song, like laughing out loud. All the worry and fuss she and Evelyn had exerted over how to engage the girl, and the answer had been right there under their noses all the time! She beamed at Claire, who returned her smile more shyly. Lord Carew was watching them, his gray eyes narrowed. Christiane rolled up the sketch Claire had made of her and slipped her napkin ring around it.

"That belongs to me," said Carew.

"Oh, I really don't think—"

"Claire presented it to me," he said stubbornly.

Reluctantly, she drew it from the ring and handed it over. "You'd best have her sign it, at least," she mentioned. "Otherwise, it might be difficult to explain away."

"To whom?"

"Why . . . to Miss Delaney, among other folk."

"I don't see why Greer would object to my possessing a portrait of the matron of my niece's school."

Christiane felt every freckle on her bosom, every hint of crow's-foot at the corners of her eyes, intensify and deepen. That made it plain enough what he thought of her. *Matron.* God, what a hateful word.

"Unless," he went on, and released one last, perfect ring of smoke, following it with his eyes as it swirled toward the ceiling, "it would be because she is so very beautiful."

She stared at him, utterly disconcerted.

He grinned, stubbed out the cigar, and rose from his chair. "It's late. I must be getting back to the city. Shall I come again next weekend, Claire?"

"Oh, yes, please do!"

"Countess d'Oliveri?"

She recollected herself. "We always encourage visits by the families of our students, milord."

He glanced at the maid. "See if you can convince Cook to reprise that tart, won't you, Clarisse?"

She giggled with pleasure at his use of her name. "I'll make sure of it, m'lord," she promised, with a coquettish wink.

"I'll take my leave, then. Milady." Christiane extended her hand, and he bowed over it. His mouth brushed her skin. "Claire." He kissed his niece fondly. "Until next Saturday."

"I'll see you to the door," Clarisse offered eagerly.

Christiane watched them go, her emotions such a tangle that she feared it might take an eternity to sort them out.

Seven

Later, in her rooms, she stepped out of her shoes, took the Spanish combs from her hair, unclasped the diamonds at her ears and throat, and unfastened her ribbons, letting the muslin rustle to the floor. Then she stood in her unmentionables, trying to make sense of the evening she had just lived through.

Discovering Claire's totally unexpected and quite extraordinary talent for caricature, her ability to capture not only appearance but *soul* in a few swift pencil strokes, was tremendously encouraging. Now, at last, she and Evelyn had something to praise in the Irish girl. Any attempt to improve someone's opinion of herself, Christiane knew, could only be successful when it was based on honest appraisal; to try to convince Claire that she was worthy when she could see herself that she was *not,* at least in terms of literature and mathematics and science and household management, was hopeless. But with the emergence of this hitherto unglimpsed burst of brightness, they could set to work! She pictured it in her mind—private sessions with Monsieur Battier, who despite his fondness for landscapes

would surely be excited by Claire's talent; the chance at
house parties and such for the girl to pull out her pencil and
sketchbook and amuse fellow guests; perhaps even, in the
future, an exhibition in London of her works. Portraiture
was extremely popular; if Claire's native ability could be
developed more fully, there was no limit to what lay ahead.
And the work clearly *engaged* her, in a way nothing else at
the academy had.

But there was a deep undercurrent of discontent in
Christiane, even as she reveled at Claire's blossoming, and
it came from the way Lord Carew had dealt with her that
evening. *He was toying with me,* she thought abjectly,
reaching for her hairbrush. He had shown an uncanny ability to elevate—and plummet—her mood with no more
than a few offhand words: He told her she was beautiful,
and her heart exalted; he threw her trip to London in her
face, and she crumpled. Why should he have the upper
hand?

She pulled the brush through her curls, slowly, thoughtfully. Twenty years before, in Paris, she had been able to
affect his moods every bit as easily, and just as whimsi-
cally. When she'd paid a scrap of attention to him, he had
glowed with pleasure; when she'd ignored him or made a
jest at his expense, he had deflated like a spent wineskin.
What had caused the shift in power?

Age, she realized, as she found herself examining the
face of the brush for white hairs. He was still considered a
highly eligible bachelor, ripe for establishing a household,
beginning a family. Whereas she . . .

For more than a year, her menstrual periods had been
erratic. She had rejoiced heartily at the prospect of forever
being done with the monthly ritual of cotton rags and spot-
ted linens and the contrariness that rose in her when the
"curse" was due. Now, though, she felt a strange nostalgia
for that curse. She might not be old, but she was unmar-
riageable to anyone but a man whose inheritance was already assured by sons and daughters from a previous wife.

Jean-Baptiste had had a wife, and children. The Comte

d'Oliveri had been old, just as Lord Carew had surmised, and his first wife had proved infertile. He'd had hopes of settling a son on Christiane, of course. But in the three years of their marriage, until he'd died, she hadn't conceived.

She'd never considered not having borne children a calamity. She had enjoyed her life immensely—the freedom, the ability to go where she wished when she wished. But now, as she contemplated her flat belly and trim breasts, she felt a pang of regret at not having given birth to a child before her time was past.

Though there was a great deal more to it than giving birth, she thought, briskly resuming her brushing. All that waiting for them to become interesting—and the entire time, you had the terror some misfortune would strike them. Pox, scarlet fever, plague . . . there were a million paths to tragedy. The foreign minister of France had told her once, when he was visiting the Maison de Touton, that fully half the children in that country's rural counties never lived to adulthood. It was a harsh world indeed for the young. And then the dreadful pressure for girls to marry well and produce heirs began the dangerous cycle again. A dozen of the young ladies with whom she'd debuted had died in childbirth. Christiane shuddered, letting the brush drop to her dressing table. All in all, she was satisfied with the decision she'd made in that regard—or, rather, that had been forced on her by circumstance.

Still, it irked her no end that a woman should be considered washed up at the same age that a man was deemed primely marriageable. It seemed to point to a certain arbitrariness in God's Great Plan.

Gannon Finn *had* paid her that compliment, though—had said she seemed untouched by time.

And what was that, anyway, but a backhanded way of saying she didn't look as old as she was?

A suspicion began to form in Christiane's mind that Lord Carew might have engaged in his dizzying alternation between compliments and veiled insults to show her that he, too, was aware that the relative positions they'd held two decades past in Paris—he, the callow, moonstruck youth; she, the suave, experienced sophisticate—had, in effect, been reversed. She had not been terribly kind to him then. Should she really expect *him* to be, now that the balance of power had shifted so?

Let Greer Delaney have him, she thought wearily, pulling her nightdress over her head. She'd forgotten how exhausting coquetry could be. And, frankly, she was past the point in life where she could successfully feign interest in the boastful minutiae of masculine life—the horse races won, the animals shot dead, the hands of cards played with such steely nerve, the business deals concluded triumphantly. The plain truth was, most of the men she'd known had bored her to tears, except in bed—and very few hadn't been dreary there.

No, Evelyn was right. Best to slip comfortably into old age, into gray hair and creaking joints and knit caps and tea by the fireside. It was so much easier that way.

Courting was a game for the young, the foolish, those still naïve enough to trust in happily ever after. Perhaps that, in the end, explained why an unmarried man her age was still a bachelor and an unmarried woman was just an old maid. No *female* who'd seen so much of life, she reflected, pushing down her pillows, could ever believe that love could conquer all.

Eight

The countess's newfound conviction made planning for Lord Carew's next visit a good deal easier. "Another private supper?" Mrs. Treadwell sniffed, observing Clarisse setting the parlor table on Friday evening. "What's it to be this time—lobster and champagne?"

"Actually, we're having what the rest of you are having—corned beef and cabbage."

"What a pity Lord Carew proved so impervious to your last supper's enticements."

"You really should curb that tendency to gloat, Evelyn; it is most unattractive."

"I just thank God you've come to your senses. Bad enough to be surrounded by all these boy-besotted girls without you going silly on me, too."

"Even you must admit that uncovering Claire's talent at drawing was worth the cost of the oysters," Christiane noted dryly.

"Oh, you're quite right there. Who would ever have imagined she had it in her? Did you see the sketch she did of me?" the headmistress asked, preening.

"I did. I thought it very flattering."

"So it—I beg your pardon!"

Christiane laughed. "Would you care to do the honors with Lord Carew this evening in my stead?"

"No, no, you go right ahead. Who knows what abilities you may discover this evening, over corned beef and cabbage?" Mrs. Treadwell noted complacently, and went out with a cheery wave.

Clarisse was fussing over the napkins. "He'll be disappointed, he will, over no quince tart," she said worriedly. "I did as good as promise."

"If he is, I trust he'll have the manners not to show it. We are what we are, Clarisse. Why pretend?"

"The tart's as much Cook as the corned beef."

Christiane looked at her in surprise. "That is a very philosophical statement."

"I'm not sure what that means, mum. I only know it never hurts to show yourself to best advantage in this life."

The countess glanced down at her sprigged-muslin gown. She'd chosen it purposefully, determined this time not to give in to false hopes. Still, there was something to what the maid said.

She checked the clock. A quarter to eight already—and Lord Carew had been prompt last visit. Should she bother to change into something more fashionable, or should she stick to cabbage?

Claire turned up just then, knocking at the open door. "May I come in?"

The countess made up her mind in a moment. "Please do, *chérie*. And when your uncle arrives, will you entertain him for me, and tell him I am running just a tad behind schedule? I won't be but a few minutes, I swear."

She was late.

Gannon Finn detested a lack of punctuality, and as he sat and talked with Claire in the parlor of Mrs. Treadwell's academy, he found himself growing more and more irritated. Really, was it too much to expect of women that they make themselves available at a preordained time? Claire had managed to dress and coif and whatever the hell else it was that females did and still be here to greet him upon his arrival. What the devil could be keeping the countess?

He glanced impatiently toward the door. Claire clasped her hands in her lap, chewing her lip. "She did say only a few moments."

"It doesn't matter," Gannon declared, and discovered it was true as he smiled at his niece reassuringly. The Countess d'Oliveri was nothing more than a ghost from the past. Claire was the future. "You were saying Monsieur Battier has been encouraging your drawing?"

"Oh, most marvelously! Do you know, he told me he himself has never been overly fond of landscapes and prefers portraiture. He also told me, however, that I must apply myself to every facet of art. He even wants me to take up sculpture. Native talent, he says, is wonderful, but it must be honed."

Gannon contemplated her eager, piquant face and smiled. God, it was good to see her engaged in her studies here. Eight weeks before, he would never have believed it possible.

It was a pity he had Christiane to thank.

Just then, she appeared in the doorway. He jerked to his feet. She was wearing something silky and smooth, in maize yellow, that caught the light from the candles and shimmered delicately, like fireflies. Her black curls were arranged in the way he remembered them from long ago, held back at her temples with some sort of pins, then tumbling in a cascade. He hadn't liked the way she'd worn her hair the last time. Had she known? How could she have known? Why should she have cared?

"Lord Carew," she said, her voice still faintly French-tinged. He would have thought that an affectation had he not known her in Paris, seen how effortlessly she moved in the foreign milieu. She had seemed to him then some sort of magical chameleon—how could any woman raised in the strictures of the ton have acquired such worldliness? "I kept you waiting," she apologized, coming to him and extending her hand. He took it, kissed it. She smelled of lilies of the valley. For an instant, memory overtook him. He shook it off physically, tossing his head like a startled stallion, his queue whipping the air.

"I was glad for the time to be alone with Claire," he told her.

"I thought you might be. Has no one made you a drink?"

"I don't know how," Claire explained, sounding guilty.

"Mrs. Caldburn will get to that," the countess assured her, smiling. "Whiskey and water, milord?"

"Please."

She went to the sideboard in a rustle of yellow. She always had moved in an extraordinarily graceful way. Her waist was narrow as a girl's. Those glistening black ringlets danced as she walked.

He tore his gaze from her, staring at his boots. "Claire tells me Monsieur Battier also dislikes landscapes," he said, so that he would be saying something.

"He is most impressed with your niece. Here you are." She brought him the glass. As he took it, their fingers brushed. To Gannon, the encounter was electric; he could see lightning leap from her hand. Dammit all, he had to get a grip on himself! Two decades had passed. He'd had so many women in those years. It wasn't logical—or fair— that she still should hold such sway over him.

But simply being in the same room with her reduced him to the state of forlorn longing that had made him suffer so in Paris. *She is a middle-aged matron*, he told himself firmly. *She is Claire's teacher. She is no chameleon. There is nothing magical about her.*

"You must be starved," she said, her black eyes gleaming.

Gannon Finn felt his manhood stiffen.

"Shall we move to the table?" she asked, with an inviting wave of her hand.

"By all means," he managed to say.

She rang a bell at her place. The maid—Clarisse, was it?—entered, wearing a mulish expression. "We dine rather inelegantly this evening, milord," Christiane declared as Clarisse plunked down a tureen before her. "We have a potage of leeks, to be followed by corned beef and cabbage. It is one of Cook's specialties."

"It sounds a delightful meal," Gannon pronounced, clearing his throat. "Very rustic. Befitting the setting." God. He sounded like some stuffy Oxford don.

"Papa loved corned beef," Claire mentioned.

"Did he?" asked the countess, ladling out soup.

"But Mama detested it."

Gannon suppressed a shudder. Christiane wasn't stupid. What would she think of such pronouncements?

"I find individual preferences in food so interesting," the countess said, without blinking an eye. "My grandmother could not abide venison. I can't stand the stuff either, even though my mother and father relished it. I have often wondered whether such tastes are somehow passed down through families the way eye color or hair color may be—sometimes skipping generations, sometimes surfacing unexpectedly. But you said, I believe, Lord Carew, at our last supper, that you enjoy all foods."

Fancy her remembering that. "So I did," he allowed. "But the truth is, I lied. There is one food, and one food only, that I cannot abide."

"Really? And what is that?"

"Asparagus."

"How curious, Uncle!" Claire exclaimed. "Nor can I! Do you know what Gwen says about asparagus? She says that Dr. Caplan told her there is a certain percentage of the population that, having eaten asparagus, experiences a—" She suddenly broke off. "Dear me. I never should have brought this up at table."

The countess nodded encouragement at her. "Go on, *chérie*. Scientific knowledge is never to be scorned."

"Well . . ."

"Let me guess," Lord Carew said, grinning. "Something about the consumer's . . . uh, effusions?"

"Exactly!" Claire said in delight.

"I have never heard of such a thing." Christiane looked perplexed. He enjoyed seeing her look that way. "Whatever do you mean?"

Claire glanced at her uncle. "May I say 'urine' publicly?"

"You must apply to Madame for the answer to that."

"You already have," the countess noted, frowning.

The girl wrinkled her nose. "So I have. I may as well go on. Gwen says that when some people eat asparagus, their urine takes on a peculiar odor. But it has no such effect on other people—or if it does, they don't notice. Perhaps, Madame, it is like what you said about food preferences— passed down from generation to generation, skipping some, sometimes surfacing unexpectedly."

Gannon Finn was trying hard to keep from laughing, watching the countess war with her reactions to this speech. On the one hand, he could tell, she was intrigued. But on the other—

"I think, Claire," she said carefully, "this topic of discussion is better suited to the science classroom than to the supper table." Her gaze flitted to Gannon. "As for you, you should know better than to encourage her."

"Why, when she has brought up precisely what I can't stand about asparagus?"

She blushed. He could swear she blushed. But she rallied to declare, "Well, it certainly has no such effect on me!"

"You can't be sure," Claire observed. "It could only be that *you* don't smell it. I smelled Bess's quite plainly, even though she swore she couldn't tell a thing."

Gannon let his smile flash. "Isn't scientific inquiry marvelous?"

"We are ready for the corned beef, Clarisse," the countess told the wide-eyed maid.

The arrival of the entrée occupied some time, what with

carving and saucing and handing plates about. Gannon happened to be exceedingly fond of corned beef and cabbage, though he never would have admitted it to the countess. Simply looking at his plate of boiled potatoes and onions and green cabbage and shimmering pink beef in its puddle of horseradish sauce put him in an expansive mood. "I always wonder what it is turns beef this color," he mentioned, sawing off a hearty bite.

"Salt," Claire answered promptly. "Mrs. Caldburn gave us the recipe. It's called 'corned' for the corns of salt that make it pink. And did you know the curing was originally intended for beef that had turned a bit? Mrs. Caldburn says it's quite useful for that."

Gannon, who was chewing, glanced up.

"I can assure you . . . ," the countess began.

"Oh, I've no doubt," he said, after swallowing.

"Dear me," said Claire. "Have I done it again?"

"Turned meat and bodily excretions," Gannon noted, stabbing a potato. "What a very interesting academy you have here." He saw the countess's dark eyes flash. "I mean that as a compliment," he added hurriedly.

"It has always been our opinion—mine and Mrs. Treadwell's—that there's no sense in shielding young women from the realities of life."

He paused, his fork halfway to his mouth. "And just what are those realities?"

Her breasts rose and fell within their cocoon of yellow silk. She hesitated.

Claire jumped in. "Mrs. Treadwell says we must learn to manage an estate because the men we marry will be too busy to do a decent job of it themselves."

"Really," Gannon said. "What the devil are we busy with, if not our business affairs?"

"Carousing," Claire said briefly.

"I see." Gannon took a long draught of his wine.

"What Claire means, I believe," the countess put in, "is that men tend to be preoccupied with their standing in the world."

He laughed out loud. "And women aren't? Why, then, do they spend their husbands' money on fripperies like bonnets and gowns and boots in attempting to outdo one another?"

Those black eyes looked straight at him. "Because men have made women's realm so very circumscribed."

"Come, come," he said, and recognized that he sounded Oxford-stuffy again. "Women's natural interests lie in affairs of the home. Children. Fashion. Gossip."

"Nonsense," Claire declared, sounding eerily like the countess. "You would not say that if you met my schoolmates. Petra is an utter wizard at mathematics. Gwen knows everything there is to know about medicine. And Bess writes sonnets as fine as Shakespeare's."

Gannon stared at Christiane. "What exactly is it that you hope to accomplish here?"

"To provide our charges with satisfactions outside of children, fashion, and gossip," she retorted promptly.

"But to what purpose? Do you imagine such pursuits will make them marriageable?"

"They will know how to corn beef as well."

"But they will . . ."

"Will what?" Those black eyes were dancing; she was enjoying this, by God! Gannon shook his head, uncertain how to reply.

"They will be misfits in society," he finally answered.

"If that is so, the loss will be society's," the countess declared implacably, and reached for the carving knife. "More beef, milord?"

It was what he had loved most about her in Paris, even more than her curls and shining eyes and sly smile—that unshakable core of conviction at her center. How could anyone, he remembered wondering time and again, be so self-assured? The men with whom he'd traveled to Europe—boys, really, and she'd known it—had hated her for that, for the fact that they couldn't touch her with their sneering insinuations and coarse insults. Christiane Roxell had been like a boat solidly anchored, blithely riding the storm.

He had never met such a woman then. He still hadn't, other than her, after all these years.

She was waiting for his answer. He nodded, unable to speak as he watched her small, lithe-fingered hands on the carving tools.

The boys had told him all about the scandal that led her to Paris—the way she'd been discovered, shamelessly compromised, in a cheap Kentish inn. He had asked her about it, in one of those conversations they'd shared as he sat stubbornly at a table in the Maison de Touton, covetously watching her ply her trade while he sipped French wine. He'd believed what she told him—that another debutante, jealous of her, had arranged the assignation, telling her the man she loved wanted to meet her at the inn for an elopement. The boys had laughed when he defended her to them, declaring him a fool.

He'd been a fool, perhaps. No, he certainly had been. But he had spent the past two decades searching for a woman, any woman, who could evoke the same emotions in him that this one had.

Tenderness. Hopelessness. A longing so physical that he had only to think of her to find himself erect. Joyousness. Despair.

He gazed at her now, covertly, as he listened to Claire tell about her riding lessons. She still had that tranquil, solid center—and that same flashing fire. She was like a hurricane, a typhoon, all swirling chaos and brightness surrounding an eye of utter calm. He had only ever tasted the chaos. He had no notion how to touch her core, doubted that any man had.

He'd been horrified to discover her here, and terrified to leave Claire in her care. But he'd been even more concerned that taking his niece away after the plans for her enrollment had already been made might arouse the countess's suspicions.

He'd been afraid of her. He still was.

"And so," Claire concluded, "I *did* ride the bay, even though I was ever so frightened, as he seemed so wild. And do you know what happened, Uncle?"

He trained his gaze on her. "No. What did happen?" The words came out so soft and gentle that the countess glanced at him in surprise.

"I triumphed," Claire declared proudly. "I bent him to my will. I made myself the master. That is what Stains says one must do."

"Then Stains is very wise," Gannon noted.

"Mastery," the countess put in, "is a vital part of our curriculum. In whatever our girls attempt, we push for them to attain it. Nothing else, we find, provides such satisfaction."

I would have liked to master you in Paris, Gannon Finn thought, meeting her eyes with reluctance. *By God, I still would.*

But he couldn't allow those feelings to surface. Too much was at stake.

The maid, Clarisse, came and cleared. "I want ye to know, milord, I argued hard for that quince tart ye asked for," she announced belligerently as she took his plate. "But Madame said it wouldn't suit to rile Cook with extra work again, so there's only a cherry buckle with whipped cream."

"Why, I adore cherry buckle!" Gannon assured her, and saw her beam. Dammit all, women everywhere catered to him, took care of him! Why was the countess the exception?

And why should it matter to him still that she was?

Clarisse sashayed out. "It seems even your help partakes of the general attitude encouraging mastery," Gannon noted. There was a faint wisp of white in the countess's black hair, quite close to her left ear. He saw it plainly. He found it alluring.

"Each of us has our sphere in life," the countess declared, taking a sip from her wineglass. "I should not care for servants who did not aspire."

If Georgina had but once met the countess, Gannon thought, how different her life . . . and her death . . . might have been.

How Hugh would have detested such a notion!

As if she'd read his mind again, Claire spoke up. "Papa always said that encouraging inferiors only leads to trouble. Don't you worry, Madame, that Clarisse will get too big for her britches?"

"I believe," the countess said, with a slow, broad smile, "that most britches can be let out very wide. What concerns me more is those whose unmentionables are too constricting."

Gannon Finn's, at that moment, were causing him suffering.

"Cherry buckle," Clarisse announced proudly, coming through the door from the kitchens, bearing the sweet.

Nine

On the whole, Christiane considered, watching Lord Carew enjoy his cherry buckle, the meal had gone rather well. She had not let him cow her with his questions about what the academy's curriculum would mean to society. And, more valuably, he had displayed the same sort of brusque male superiority that had made her dislike him so in Paris. "Misfits in society" indeed! What did he think women were *now,* for heaven's sake? She wondered, not for the first time, at how threatened men were by female education. She thought of the dismissive letter she'd only yesterday received from that Oxford professor of mathematics, in response to her inquiries about Petra: "I cannot see the sense in encouraging the pursuit of higher mathematical learning in a female." And why not? Because if her sex was ever given the chance to prove itself on an equal playing field, men would only suffer in comparison, the countess thought darkly. They have so very little now on which to pride themselves, men do, and they guard it so closely. . . .

Claire had addressed some remark to her. The countess

smiled apologetically. "I beg your pardon, *chérie*; I was preoccupied. What were you saying?"

"Only that I'm quite sure Papa would never have allowed me to attend the academy. Don't you think so, Uncle Gannon?"

He coughed suddenly. "Pit," he said, and withdrew it with his spoon. "It's true, my brother held a low opinion of the value of female education."

"Mama was quite learned, though, wasn't she?" Claire asked, her face screwed up. "I know that she read Latin and Greek. She had books hidden in her rooms. She showed them to me. But then Papa—"

"I hardly think, Claire," Gannon Finn said quietly, "that the countess needs to hear about private, familial affairs."

The countess had edged forward in her chair. "On the contrary, Lord Carew, I have been encouraging your niece to tell me about her upbringing. Here at the academy, we hold the strong belief that—"

"Well, you've no bloody right to," he fairly snarled, making Claire and Christiane stare.

There was a moment's pause. Then the countess folded her napkin beside her plate. "Claire, I see you've finished your buckle. I know you are looking forward to some private time with your uncle. Would you mind terribly if I had a few words alone with him before you do?"

"Of course not, Madame," the girl murmured, pushing back her chair. "I'll be in the courtyard, Uncle Gannon."

"I won't be long," he told her, rising as she left the room.

She closed the door behind her.

"Sit down," Christiane said coldly.

"Don't order me about." He stayed on his feet, belligerent.

"*You* brought her here. You entrusted her to our care."

"Which should be proof enough I'm not some pig-headed numskull who believes women should be kept barefooted and pregnant. I admire you, dammit. I did in Paris, and I do now."

Her anger deflated. "Please sit down," she said, modifying the command. He did. She took a breath. "We are never going to be able to find what's best for Claire if we keep battering like rams."

"I thought you already had. This talent she shows at art—"

"—is only a beginning, Gannon! It is wonderful and wild and exciting, but it only proves—who knows what else she may be capable of?"

He bowed his head and stared at his fingers, laced in his lap. "I have no qualms whatsoever about anything that may lie in the future. But I must ask you—" He paused. "Must beg you. Not to pry into her past."

"I hardly think it's prying to make a few simple inquiries into how she was raised."

"Well, it is!" he countered, veering into anger again because he could sense—could even share—her frustration. "I have already told you that her home life was not particularly happy. Why can't you leave it at that?"

She reached a hand toward him across the table. "Where is it, do you think, that we learn what we know about the roles of men and women in life? It is at the hearth, at our parents' knees."

"People triumph above that." He raised his gaze. She saw something like fear in his gray eyes. "They do so all the time."

"They do," she agreed. "But only when they face it full on—when they confront it, and learn from it, and then push past it. You are tying my hands at my sides when it comes to Claire's past, and I do not know why."

He stared at her, tempted, for a moment, to trust her. She was a renegade, wasn't she? She of all people would understand. . . . The candles flickered in a bit of breeze from the open window. On the ripple, he caught her scent again: *muguets du bois*. He had a sudden overwhelming sense of hopelessness—for himself, for Claire, for the world at large. There was such danger, such terrible danger, hiding everywhere—behind parlor doors, in bedrooms, on the streets, at fancy-dress balls. He must be mad to think that he could conquer it alone.

But he had no choice. He could trust no one, ever. He had made that decision, irrevocably, on the day he had caught up to the carriage carrying his brother and Georgina and Claire. He could not turn back. "Christiane," he said hoarsely. "I can only ask that you believe . . . I do what I do because I think it best."

After a moment she nodded, slowly. "I don't doubt that, Gannon. But is it not possible your vision is clouded by what you know about the situation? If you need a friend . . . someone to talk to . . ."

A friend. He nearly laughed, but caught himself. That was what she'd said to him in Paris: *Gannon, we can always be friends.* It hadn't been enough then. It was not enough now.

"I don't know how you do it," he told her.

She stared. "Do what?"

Make me believe in your honesty, again and again. But he would not say that. He stood. "I must see to Claire."

She rose as well. "As you wish." Unruffled and calm as the hurricane's eye . . .

She extended her hand. He took it, brushed it with his mouth. And then, before he even realized what was happening, he'd grabbed her by the waist, pulled her toward him, crushed her to his coat while he sought her lips with his. Solace . . . oh, God, that there might be solace for him! He tasted it in that instant—before she thrust him away.

"Lord Carew!" she exclaimed in shock.

"Forgive me," he murmured, his color heightening. "Don't—please don't punish Claire for my idiocy."

"I . . ." Christiane began. They looked at one another. He waited, poised on a heartbeat. She did not say anything more.

"I'll go to Claire."

"It's best you do so." She smoothed her gown with her hands.

"Good night."

"Good night, milord."

He withdrew. This time, she left the curtains unparted. She sank back into her chair, raising one finger to her bruised mouth.

Clarisse bustled in to clear. "Madame?" she said uncertainly, seeing her mistress sitting, staring at nothing. "Are you ill? Mrs. Treadwell said she suspected those potatoes may have been old."

Christiane roused herself. "There was naught amiss with the meal." Who would have thought that cabbage and corned beef . . .

She was not exactly sure what this night had proved. But he *had* kissed her. She could not be so aged and decrepit as all that.

Ten

"*There is absolutely* nothing to fret about," Gwen assured Claire, standing behind her classmate to do up her ribbons. "Bess and I have been through this a dozen times. The Countess of Yarlborough's routs are always so packed that it's easy to find a place to stand behind the potted palms and simply be ignored."

"It's a very grand house, isn't it?" Claire said tentatively, twisting her head to take in the room the three girls were sharing. "So much glass. So much light."

"So many useless males," Bess muttered, pulling on her embroidered slippers.

"Don't ruin Claire's first outing here," Gwen chided her gently, tucking back a stray wisp of the Irish girl's black hair. "Just because you and I have been singularly unsuccessful at meeting anyone worthwhile doesn't mean she'll be."

"I shouldn't be seen out at all," Claire murmured nervously, tugging at the pearls around her throat, which had been lent her by Mrs. Treadwell's daughter, Vanessa, their hostess. "It's not fitting. I'm in mourning."

"It's been six months," Bess declared with devastating practicality. "Time to get on with your life."

"I'm quite sure, Claire," Gwen said more gently, "that your mama and papa would not have wanted you to sequester yourself away."

"Papa would have," Claire answered, with the blunt decidedness her fellow students sometimes found so disconcerting. "He would have moved heaven and earth to keep me from showing up at such a place."

"Why?" Bess asked curiously.

Claire wrinkled her nose. "Because all of you—and all the guests—are English."

"That's not strictly true," Bess pointed out. "The countess always has some Continental hangers-on at hand."

"Stop being dreadful, Bessie." Gwen finished with the ribbons, but her fingertips lingered on Claire's shoulder. "Your mother was English, was she not?"

"Aye," Claire said briefly. Gwen started to pursue it, then decided not to. The most important thing was to put Claire at ease. "You look lovely. Doesn't she look lovely, Bess?"

"Of course she looks lovely. She always looks lovely. She has perfect hair, a perfect figure, perfect teeth and eyes." Bess rose from her chair, tossing her wayward red curls. "No doubt she'll attract the devout attentions of some extremely rich earl's son while you and I are lurking behind the potted palms again."

"I hope no one looks at me at all," Claire whispered.

Bess cocked her head. "You make it very difficult to be envious of you, you know, when you are so self-effacing."

"I would not know what to do. I would not know what to say."

"Mrs. Caldburn—" Gwen began encouragingly.

Claire fixed her with her plaintive gray stare. "Mrs. Caldburn doesn't understand life."

Bess laughed out loud. "Truer words were never spoken."

But Gwen was intrigued. "What do you mean by that?"

Claire shrugged her slim shoulders. She was wearing black, at her own insistence, though even Mrs. Treadwell had opined that six months was more than enough time for weeds. The somber, narrow-waisted silk suited her, heightened the alabaster of her skin and its contrast with her lashes and hair. "She lays out all her rules. But life doesn't run according to rules, does it? How could it?"

"There have to be rules," Gwen said dubiously. "Otherwise, everything would just be a chaos."

"Everything *is* a chaos," Claire declared.

"But—" Gwen began.

"Never mind," Bess reassured Claire. "I know exactly what you mean. Gwen clings to rules because she has a scientific bent. This happens, and therefore *this* must happen."

"Natural order," Gwen agreed, nodding.

"If only it were that easy," Claire said longingly.

The Countess of Yarlborough poked her head in through the door just then. "Ready, young ladies?" she asked brightly, her smile as dazzling as the diamonds at her ears and throat.

"As lambs for the slaughter," Bess muttered.

The countess wagged a finger at her. "I have a sentiment, Elizabeth—a premonition. I have a feeling, here"— she tapped her chest—"that tonight will be the night for you."

Bess groaned. "You say that every time you have us to visit."

"I am a perpetual optimist," the Countess of Yarlborough declared grandly. "Now come along downstairs. How very lovely you are, Miss . . ." She was looking at Claire. "I beg your pardon; I've forgotten your name."

"Miss Becker." It had been Madame's idea that she should lie about her identity. Claire had hated the notion at first, but was grateful for it now. It was difficult enough to contemplate confronting the throngs of folk who had been rolling up to Yarlborough Hall in their carriages all evening without the prospect of having every soul to whom she was introduced make pitying remarks about her parents' fate.

"Of course. Miss Becker. Forgive me." The smile flashed again. "And you, Gwen, are as radiant as always. Bess, can you not do something about your hair?"

"Not a thing," Bess announced. "I am what I am. The gentlemen must take me or leave me."

The slightest furrow marred Vanessa's smooth brow. "I do hope, at least, that you have double-checked your ribbons this time."

"At the countess's last ball," Gwen explained to Claire, "Bess was dancing with a viscount when she came undone." Claire unleashed a startled smile.

"So you see," Bess said complacently, taking Claire's hand, "it would be extremely difficult for you to disgrace yourself here more thoroughly than I already have."

Claire's smile turned wry. "I find that rather scant consolation."

"Really? But then, you did not see our Bess standing there on the dance floor in her britches." Gwen grinned wickedly as she took Claire's other hand and tugged her toward the door.

The countess's ballroom simply awed Claire. She stood on the threshold with her mouth forming an O, staring at the glittering chandeliers, the gleaming floor, the grand ladies and gentlemen in their finery—and then tried to spin about on her heels and head back to the stairs. But Gwen and Bess had firm grips on her. "I can't," Claire whispered, aghast at the prospect of setting out into that sea of gay chatter and music.

"You can and you must," Gwen insisted.

Bess leaned in from the opposite side. "If I can show my face again after having unintentionally disrobed on the dance floor, I should think you can summon the courage to dart from here over to those palms!"

It was easier to give in than to fight, and so Claire let

them lead her along the periphery. She kept her eyes
downcast, staring at the twinkling toes of the slippers
Uncle Gannon had bought her in London. Mrs. Treadwell
beamed at the trio from the midst of a bevy of matrons.
"Do bring Miss Fi—I mean Miss Becker—here!" she
called above the clamor.

"Please, no. Not yet," Claire begged. Gwen and Bess
exchanged glances and then acquiesced, veering instead
toward a cluster of gilt chairs set very close to the screen
of palms.

Claire sank eagerly onto a seat. "That was not so bad,
was it?" Gwen asked encouragingly. Claire was about to
answer when a rather stout young man with hair nearly as
red as Bess's caught a glimpse of them, detached himself
from his friends, and hurried over.

"Miss Carstairs! Miss Boggs! What a delight!" he exclaimed, bowing over their hands.

"Good God, Roddy, what is that you've done with your
cravat?" Bess asked, causing Claire to dare a peek at his
chest, which bore a startling cascade of starched silk.

"Invented it myself," he declared happily. "What do
you think I should call it?"

" 'The Grievous Mistake'?" Gwen suggested, making
Bess giggle.

He glanced down at his chest with a touch of uncer-
tainty. "Is it so bad as that?"

"Worse," Bess told him.

The young man looked at Claire. "What do you think of
it, then? Oh, I beg your pardon; we haven't been introduced. Show some manners, Bessie, for God's sake."

Bess sighed. "Miss Fi—Miss Becker. This is my
cousin. My very *distant* cousin, Mr. Farquar. Mr. Farquar,
Miss Becker."

"Charmed," Farquar said, grinning as he reached for
Claire's hand. Gwen had to nudge her before she remembered to offer it. "Are you a student at Mrs. Treadwell's
academy, Miss Becker?"

"Of course she is, you nincompoop," said Bess.

"I was addressing your companion," Farquar declared archly.

"You can tell him to just go away," Gwen suggested to Claire. "We do so all the time."

"We do," Bess agreed. "Go away, Roddy."

"Shan't. I mean to ask Miss Becker to dance with me."

Claire's eyes went wide, like a startled rabbit's. She turned helplessly to Bess, who said, "She means to wait for a better offer. Don't you, Claire?"

Just then, three more young men approached them. "Miss Boggs. Miss Carstairs. What a pleasure," said the one in the lead, who was very tall and thin and had a crop of white-blond hair.

"Mind your step," Roddy Farquar warned the newcomers. "Mrs. Treadwell's ladies are snippish tonight."

"When are they anything else?" the tall one retorted.

"Simpson, tell the truth," Bess said, addressing him. "What do you think of Roddy's cravat?"

"Quite horrendous," he said promptly. "Aren't you going to make introductions?"

Gwen waved a negligent hand. "Miss Becker. Lord Simpson. Lord Granville. Mr. Laverleigh. And vice versa."

"Lovely manners," Farquar sniffed.

"An honor, Miss Becker," Lord Simpson said, bowing. "Are you new to the academy?"

Claire was frozen, tongue-tied. From the way Gwen and Bess had laughingly described their societal failures, she had assumed—she really had—that no young men would so much as speak to them. Yet here came another pair of swains on the heels of the others, calling greetings, grinning, and the lot of them clearly quite familiar to her classmates.

Gwen was nudging her foot. Claire swallowed, daring a glance at Lord Simpson, who was towering over her, waiting patiently. She nodded, then looked back down at her slippers.

"Loquacious, your new friend, isn't she?" Farquar observed.

"Shut up, Roddy," Bess said.

"Are you related, by any chance, to the Berkshire Beckers?" one of the young men asked. This time, Claire shook her head. "I only ask because I am," he explained.

"Mr. Custer," Bess said by way of introduction. "And Mr. Blessingham. What's happened to your arm, Blessingham?" Claire saw that it was in a sling made of dark blue silk.

"War wound," he said briefly.

"The war is over," Gwen said after a pause.

"Not the war between Blessingham and an exceedingly steep set of stairs leading from the back room of Mrs. Devlin's gaming house," Farquar told her, laughing.

"Had you seen the expression on my dear papa's face when he caught me at her faro table," Blessingham said gravely, "you would agree, Miss Carstairs, that it is a wound of war. Could I, perchance, prevail on you to dance with a cripple?"

Gwen cocked her head at him. "It could not make you any *more* awkward, I suppose." All the young men hooted. But she rose to her feet, and he led her toward the floor.

"Bessie?" Farquar asked hopefully.

"Not a chance," she told him.

Lord Simpson had eased his great height into Gwen's vacated chair. Now he hitched it toward Claire slightly. "Is there anything I might fetch you, Miss Becker?" he asked solicitously. "A cup of punch, perhaps?"

"Dance with me, Bessie," Farquar pleaded. "I am trying to attract the attentions of Miss Cavendish, and I'm not likely to do so from here."

"You're not likely to do so from anywhere," Bess retorted, casting a glance at the fashionable young lady in question. "But if you really want to parade that cravat in front of her, I'll not stop you. You'll be all right, Claire?"

Claire felt her head spinning. Lord Simpson was still leaning toward her, waiting for her answer. How could her friends abandon her this way, with all this throng of boys about?

"Claire?" Bess said again, a bit impatiently.

"I'll go and get her a cup of punch," Lord Simpson announced.

"Thank you, Simpson," Bess said gratefully. "Make it the champagne punch. You'll be just fine, Claire. Really you will."

"But—" The word came out as a whisper. Bess and Lord Farquar had already moved away.

Another of the young men—Claire tried hard to recall his name—slid into the chair vacated by Lord Simpson. "He will have my hide for nosing in," he told her, his voice raised above the din of music and conversation, "but would you care to dance?"

Claire shook her head, contemplating the glittering slippers she wore. Then it occurred to her that such an invitation, according to Mrs. Caldburn, required something more. "No, thank you, Mr. Laverleigh. Though you are very kind to ask."

She expected this response to make him go away. Instead, he moved the chair even closer. "You're Irish, aren't you?"

Startled, she raised her gaze to him.

"I can tell it by your voice," he went on.

Claire dared to risk speaking again. "Are you . . . perchance . . . Irish, too?"

He let out a gusty laugh. "Not likely!"

Lord Simpson had returned with two crystalline glasses of punch. "Remove yourself," he ordered Laverleigh, extending one of the glasses to Claire.

"She's all yours," Laverleigh drawled as he arose. "If you want her, that is."

Another of the young men laughed. "I should say he won't!"

Lord Simpson looked puzzled. "Who wouldn't long to sit beside such a lovely lady?"

But the throng was inching away, Claire saw with relief. She took a sip of punch. It tasted cold and tingly and sweet-sour. "Like it?" Simpson asked encouragingly.

"I . . . I do. Very much. Thank you."

He froze, his own cup halfway to his mouth. "Where are you from, Miss Becker?"

Claire felt a twinge of panic. Mrs. Treadwell hadn't mentioned what she was to say to that. But this young man had been so kind to her. . . . "From Galway. In Ireland."

She saw his blue eyes blanken. She *saw* the way the interest clicked closed. "Ireland," he said. She nodded. He leaned back in the delicate gilt chair for a moment. Then he pushed himself to his feet. "Beg pardon," he told her. "I've just noticed someone I simply must greet."

"Thank you for the punch," Claire said.

He barely nodded, moving off to rejoin his friends, who were huddled together a dozen yards off, laughing and casting occasional glances Claire's way.

She hung her head, sensing that for some reason she'd become a failure. What could it be? She'd hardly said a word. They'd only asked her, the boys, whether she was Irish.

In her head, she had a sudden vision of her father, of his black-bearded face, his mouth wide in a roar of outrage as he came at her mother: *Bloody English bitch! Look down your nose at me, will you?* She blinked the image away in fright, but tears had welled up in her eyes. She did not know what to do about that; her hands were on the punch cup, and her handkerchief was in the reticule beside the chair. Gwen and Bess were swirling on the dance floor with their companions. She raised her head to look for Mrs. Treadwell, but could not spot her in the crowd. She felt suddenly ill, overwhelmed. She tried tasting the punch again, but it made her stomach clench in knots. She was hot and flushed. The young men were stealing glances at her, laughing. . . .

"Is this seat taken?" a voice asked quietly.

Claire, staring back down at her slippers, made no response.

"Because if it is not," the voice went on, still soft but insistent, "I would sit here and apologize to thee for their stupidity." Claire's tears began to spill over. "It has been my experience," the voice continued, "that men are like jackals. They'll do things in packs they'd never dare do alone. Would thou care to borrow my handkerchief?" When Claire didn't answer, she found it suddenly laid in her lap. It was a great broad square of snow-white linen, embroidered in one corner with a swirling initial *W.* Then a hand, brown from the sun, with short, square nails atop long fingers, reached in and gently broke her grip on the punch cup. "Go on," he murmured. "Don't give them the satisfaction of seeing thee cry."

Claire darted a glance at Simpson and Laverleigh to make certain their attention had moved elsewhere. Then she grabbed up the handkerchief and swiped at her eyes.

"That's better," the voice told her, and took it back. She had resumed gazing at her slippers; now she let herself peek further to her left, so that she saw his shoes as he eased down onto the seat. They were boots, actually, black ones, and none too well polished. His legs seemed very long as he leaned back in the chair, stretching them out before him. "I haven't seen thee at the countess's before. Are thou one of her mama's students, perchance?"

Claire hesitated. It seemed very rude not to answer him, and so she nodded. "I . . . I only just began there a few months ago. This is my first outing."

"More shame to those fools for trying to spoil it for thee. Let's do something truly shocking, shall we? Let's not let them. What's thy name?"

She started to say "Miss Becker" but suddenly couldn't bear the lying. "Claire," she said instead, though she knew it was a breach of etiquette.

Whoever the man was, he took it in stride. "How do thou do? I'm David. Are thou finished with this?" She looked a little further to her left, saw that he was indicating the nearly full punch cup. She nodded. "Well," he said, and then did the most extraordinary thing. He leaned back even further in the chair, raised his arm, and hurled the contents of the punch cup toward Lord Laverleigh, some

six or eight feet distant. The spray of fruit juice and
sparkling wine spattered across His Lordship's handsome
coat and carefully combed hair. In the same smooth motion, Claire's companion set the cup back on the floor,
caught both of her hands in his, and bent toward her, saying in a slightly louder voice, "Oh, but I disagree! I find the
regent's policies regarding the Welsh tin miners absolutely
deplorable!"

Claire was so utterly astounded that she looked straight
at him at last. She saw a headful of curling chestnut-brown
hair, a pair of laughing hazel eyes, and a wide, handsome
mouth that was already saying, "After all, they are only
asking for the right to earn a living wage. Do thou not
agree?"

From the corner of her eye, Claire could see Laverleigh
turn like a belligerent bull, scanning the room. "Say something," her companion urged in a whisper.

She did. She said the first thing that came into her mind:
"Are you insane?"

"Ah. I see thou has Tory tendencies. Pity. I'm a Whig
myself, through and through."

Claire felt an impossible urge to burst out laughing. The
impulse died instantly, however, as Laverleigh stomped
toward them. "Was it you, Wrede, threw that at me?" he
demanded.

"Although I do admit," Claire's companion continued — and then looked up, blinking, as though startled at
the interruption. "Beg pardon, Laverleigh, what did thou
ask?"

"I—" The raging bull stared him down for a moment,
then shook his head. "Never mind. You wouldn't have the
guts, would you?"

"The guts for what?"

Laverleigh turned away in disgust, making his way toward his friends. "Oh, Laverleigh," the young man, who
still held Claire's hands tightly, called. "There's something
spilled all over the back of thy coat; did thou know that?"

Laverleigh paused, seemed about to say something

more, and then kept moving, muttering to himself. The young man finally released Claire's hands, which had gone rather sweaty. "Now, where were we?" he asked brightly. "Ah, yes. The Welsh tin miners."

Claire stared into those laughing eyes. "I don't know anything about the Welsh tin miners."

"I shall have to teach thee, then."

Just at that moment, however, the music ended, and Gwen and Bess returned from their excursions to the dance floor. Gwen paused upon seeing Claire's companion. "Mr.—Mr. Weed, is it?" she finally asked.

"Wrede," he corrected her easily. "I beg thy pardon. Have I taken thy chair?"

"What has gotten Laverleigh into such a lather?" Bess wondered, as the young lord stomped away from the gathering, going to salvage his coat.

Mr. Wrede stood, graciously, and relinquished his seat to Gwen. "If thou will excuse me, Claire? It was delightful to meet thee."

"Th-thank you," she managed to say, even as she longed for him to stay.

Gwen settled into the chair, and Bess took the one on Claire's opposite side. "Who was that?" the redhead demanded, watching him disappear into the throng. "And why didn't he ask you to dance?"

"He's a Quaker. They don't dance," Gwen explained.

"A Quaker?" Claire echoed in puzzlement.

"It's a religious sect. The Society of Friends is the official name. An odd bunch. They won't swear oaths, and they won't serve in wars. They're pacifists. Fond of social causes—outlawing gin mills, ending prostitution and slavery, that sort of thing."

"Hard to argue with those aims," Bess declared. "Glorious hair he's got, hasn't he? Those curls . . . did you like him, Claire?"

Claire didn't know what to say. "He . . . seemed very nice," she told her friends at last.

"Sorry to have abandoned you," Gwen said then, "but I

do adore a waltz, even if it is with Blessingham. Did Roddy step on your hem, Bess?"

"Only a half dozen times," Bess said distractedly, still staring at Mr. Wrede's retreating back. "I must say, I don't understand why anyone who doesn't dance would come to one of Vanessa's routs."

"Perhaps for the conversation," Gwen offered, contemplating the spots of color high in Claire's cheeks. "What did you and he speak of, Claire?"

"Welsh tin miners," Claire replied, very faintly. Her classmates stared.

"That is certainly an unusual opening gambit," Bess finally declared. "What do you know about Welsh tin miners?"

"Not a thing in the world," said Claire, her cheeks very warm.

Eleven

She did not see Mr. Wrede again until supper was announced. It was then that he appeared out of nowhere beside her chair. "Would thou do me the honor of permitting me to escort thee?" he asked, bending down to her ear.

She glanced at her companions, but Bess was trading jibes with Farquar, and Gwen was just coming off the dance floor with Mr. Blessingham. She looked up at Wrede. "I . . . I'm not certain what to do."

"Well, generally," he said, offering his hand, "one just fills a plate with food, finds a seat, and then consumes the victuals."

"No, no. I mean, I'm not certain of the etiquette."

"Ah. The etiquette." He spoke the word with a tinge of humor. "It seems to me the etiquette depends upon whether one is hungry or not. Are thou hungry?"

Claire, whose stomach had been too full of butterflies to eat either breakfast or dinner, nodded slowly. "I believe I am."

"Well, then." He waited. She stole another glance at Bess, who nodded encouragingly. Then she took Wrede's hand and rose from her seat. He seemed very tall and broad as he walked beside her in his plain black coat and breeches. Her heart was fluttering; the bright lights and noise made her head pound. They started toward the room in which the meal was laid out, but halfway there, she stopped abruptly. Wrede looked down at her questioningly. "Do thou feel faint?" he asked. She nodded again. "A bit of air," he opined, and altered their course, heading to the French doors that led onto the balcony.

The night was warm for April, and others were abroad in the shadowy moonlight—couples speaking in low voices, clinging, kissing. He led her past them, down the stairs to the garden. Claire drew in a deep breath. The night was scented with some delicious fragrance—lilies of the valley, she realized as they approached a fountain surrounded by the sweet little plants. There were benches. He stopped at one. Claire sank onto it gratefully.

He sat down beside her, and was silent. He was quiet for so long, in fact, that Claire began to feel guilty. Uncle Gannon was paying for her tuition at the academy, she knew, solely in the hope that she would attract a suitor to take her off his hands. And here was a kind and sensible young man who seemed, remarkably, to want her company, yet she could not for her life think of anything to say to him. She wracked her mind. Perhaps she should ask him about those Welsh tin miners? She was about to do so when he heaved a contented sigh, stretching out his legs.

"It is a relief, Claire, I must tell thee, to meet a young woman who is not afraid of silence."

"Afraid of silence?" she echoed in surprise.

"Aye. To most folk, it is a frightening thing. They feel compelled to fill up the spaces. I enjoy silence, though. Do thou enjoy silence?"

She thought about it—for so long that he laughed. "I see that thou do!"

She finally thought of something to say that did not seem idiotic. "Why do you speak that way?"

"It is the way of the Friends."

She remembered what Claire had said. "The Society of Friends." He nodded. "Your religion."

"We prefer to think of it as a way of living."

"What sort of way of living?"

"One that sets one apart from the world at large." His voice was low and calm.

"You don't dance."

"No."

"Why not?"

"Because God's call is not to frivolousness, but to serious things."

"God's call," she repeated, and was so curious that she dared to look at him again, into his hazel eyes. "How do you know what God is saying?"

"We listen . . . in the silences."

"I belong to the Church of England," Claire told him.

He nodded easily. "Most folk do."

"Is it hard? Being different, I mean."

"Sometimes it is."

She thought about that, too, for a time. "But it is worth it to you," she said at last. "Why?"

"Because it is easier than being the same." He drew his legs in and bent down, reaching to rub the dust from his lackluster boots. "Easier in the heart, I mean. Take the matter of going to war. It's why Laverleigh taunted me. He thinks me a coward. But to kill a fellow human being for his beliefs . . . to kill anyone, anytime . . . seems to me a clear offense to God, who is the giver of life, and who made it his commandment: Thou shalt not kill."

"But if someone were trying to kill *you* . . . what would you do?"

He grinned. "Talk him out of it. We are great talkers, the Friends."

"When you are not listening to the silences."

That made him laugh. "We fill up much silence that way, aye. More, perhaps, than we should."

"However did you come to know our hostess?" Claire asked in wonderment.

He laughed again. "She is a woman who fills up a host of silences all on her own, is she not? I am a poor relation of her husband, the Earl of Yarlborough. A much-regretted relation, in his view. Yet his wife has proven very kind to us. To the Society, I mean."

Claire contemplated what she had seen of the countess so far, which seemed exceptionally frivolous. "Why would she be, do you think?" she asked in puzzlement.

"It happens sometimes that those magpies who chatter the loudest yearn most for the solace of silence." He glanced at her in the faint moonlight. "A life filled with ease and material wealth is not necessarily that which pleases the soul."

"Do you always talk in aphorisms?" Claire asked, crinkling her nose.

He laughed again. For someone so averse to frivolity, he had a lovely laugh, deep and low and strong. "Was I doing so? I beg thy pardon. I—" Then he paused, with a sudden movement of his head. From somewhere farther down the path in the shadowy garden, Claire heard a girl's voice, faint, protesting:

"No. No, don't, please. Please, sir! I beg ye. I—"

David Wrede was on his feet, moving toward the sound. Intrigued, Claire followed as he strode toward a stand of willows. The girl's voice came again, higher, more urgent: "No! I don't want—please, milord! Please, sir! No! Don't—"

Wrede plunged into the willow branches, saying forcefully yet somehow gently, "What is going on here?"

There was a flurry, a fluster, from the midst of the overhanging branches. Then a girl in a white servant's apron darted out, her hair a wild tangle, her arms crossed over the disheveled bodice of her gown. Her wide eyes met Claire's. She was crying.

"Are you all right?" Claire asked, moving toward her.

"Get back here!" another voice cried, a man's voice, slurred by liquor in a way that made Claire flinch with memories. It was Simpson; the young lord staggered out of the willow thicket with his breeches down to his knees. "Come back here, you little tease!"

The girl darted behind Claire, trying to hide. Simpson saw her, though, and rushed at her, yanking up his pants. He was brought up short by Wrede, who caught hold of the tail of his coat. "Not so fast, milord," the Quaker said, his voice booming now, loud enough to echo in the still night air.

"Let go of me!" Simpson panted. "It's none of your damned affair."

But the strength of Wrede's voice had drawn curious onlookers; they began to appear as if by magic out of the darkness, gathering, murmuring. The sobs of the girl sheltered behind Claire grew softer. Simpson had his breeches buttoned up at last; he whirled on Wrede, fists flailing. "Damn your interfering soul!" he shouted, and Claire flinched as he landed a blow.

Wrede took it in stride. He was as tall as the white-blond lord, and built far more sturdily; the punch landed at his chest but did not so much as rock him. "I'd suggest, Lord Simpson, that thou get thyself some supper." His words rang over the growing babble of the onlookers.

"I'd suggest you get yourself some balls, you nancy-ass traitor!"

There was a gasp from the crowd. The ladies backed away, and the girl behind Claire moaned.

Wrede smiled. Claire saw it very clearly, even in the moonlight. It was not a vicious smile, nor a threatening one. It was the smile of a man who holds the upper hand and is sure of the fact.

"The next time thou takes a lass into the shrubberies, Simpson, thou might at least ascertain aforehand whether her moral vacuousness is as all-pervasive as thine own."

Simpson started to reply, then stopped, befuddled. "Her moral . . ."

"He means, you bloody idiot," another young man in the crowd—Claire recognized him as Blessingham, with whom Gwen had been dancing—"be sure you've got a willing wench. Come on, for God's sake. You're bacon-brained."

But Simpson wasn't done yet. "I'll call him out," he declared, even as Blessingham and another fellow caught his arms to restrain him. "A duel, then! Let's have at it!"

"He won't fight you," Blessingham said disdainfully. "He's a bloody Quaker. Wouldn't fight the Frogs, would he? What makes you think he'll fight you? Come along; he's not worth your time." Simpson went on blustering, shouting taunts and challenges even as his friends tugged him away. Claire turned, meaning to offer to help the serving girl, only to discover that she had already slipped away into the night.

She stood, disconcerted, in the moonlight. The crowd slowly dispersed, drifting back into the shadows, murmuring to one another, occasionally stealing glances at Wrede, who calmly straightened his jacket and ran his hands back through his curling hair.

Finally, it was only she and he, alone beside the willows. This silence seemed too long. "Did it—did it hurt when he hit you?" Claire asked anxiously.

"It hurts when any of God's creatures raises a hand in anger against another. The pain was less to me than to the Creator," Wrede said evenly, brushing dust from his coatfront.

Claire caught her breath. Something about what he'd said had raised a swell of fear within her, a black sea that threatened to swallow her whole. She could not imagine where that fear had come from, but it was so terrifying, so overwhelming, that she started back toward the manor at a desperate run.

"Claire!" he called after her. "Claire, wait!"

She did not dare turn, or that darkness would catch up to her. She kept on running. She ran and ran, up the stairs to the house, through the ballroom, and straight up the stairs. She didn't stop until she found the room she shared with Gwen and Bess, climbed into her bed, and crawled beneath the covers, pulling them up tightly over her head.

Twelve

"*Report, if you* please," the Countess d'Oliveri said matter-of-factly, as Mrs. Treadwell, her charges having dispersed to their quarters in the academy, entered the parlor, looking exhausted.

"Not so bad as last time," Evelyn declared thankfully. "No ribbons unraveling on the dance floor. I wish to God I could report that Gwen and Bess charmed a host of suitors. But they mostly parleyed and jested with Bess's cousin, that Roddy Farquar, and his cohorts."

"What about Roseanne and Mariah?"

"They kept their composure very nicely. Roseanne took several turns on the floor with Mr. Haggarty, among others, and Roddy Farquar asked Mariah for a waltz. Though I suspect that was on Bess's instigation."

"It is reassuring to see our girls looking after their schoolmates. What of Petra?"

"I don't know *what* to do with Petra," the headmistress confessed. "Oh, she is lively enough—and so pretty, when she isn't pulling at her hair. But once she starts in to talking, somehow numbers always seem to come up in the conversation. And then she becomes so excited that the boys shy away."

"How could a conversation at Vanessa's rout possibly turn to numbers?" the countess marveled.

"I'll give you one example. I was present to hear Lord Willoughby approach to ask her to dance. She did not hear him at first; she seemed preoccupied. When he cleared his throat, the poor fellow, and repeated himself, she started and smiled up at him and said, 'I beg your pardon; I was counting the repeats in the parquet pattern. Did you realize the chevrons reverse themselves at intervals of twelve, and that at every repetition the central lozenge switches between maple and cherrywood? I estimate the hall to be one hundred and twenty feet long; if we assume the chevrons to be two inches each in width and the lozenges four inches, that means the entire pattern, with the reversed and then unreversed chevrons and one lozenge each of cherry and maple—' "

"Do stop!" the countess cried, clapping her hands to her ears.

"That is very much the way Lord Willoughby reacted, though he was too polite to show it. Petra was quite nonplussed as he made his excuses and started away. 'Why, I hadn't even gotten to the rosewood border!' was all she said."

The countess laughed, then paused. "And what about Claire?"

Evelyn's hands fluttered. "I wish there were better news to report on that front."

"She proved shy?"

"Extremely so."

"It is only to be expected. She has had no comparable social experiences, from what I can gather."

"It was worse than that. Bess confided to me that Claire said she was taunted—by that dastard Laverleigh, among others—on account of her Irish birth."

Christiane blanched. "Oh, Evelyn. It never occurred to

me to warn her of the possibility. How did she . . . comport herself?"

"Bess said she was reduced to tears. The good news, I suppose, is that she had a champion."

"You don't sound overly delighted about it," the countess noted.

"It was Mr. Wrede," Mrs. Treadwell confessed.

"Wrede?" Christiane reflected. "I don't recognize the name."

"He is one of Vanessa's husband's cousins. A *distant* cousin," the headmistress said with emphasis.

"Dear me. I gather the distance is welcome, from Vanessa's point of view."

"Not so much from Vanessa's as from the earl's. The Wredes are tried-and-true Friends."

"Friends are a marvelous thing to have in this world," said the countess, somewhat puzzled.

"No, no. The Society of Friends. The Quakers," Mrs. Treadwell elaborated.

"Oh!" the countess declared, and took a sip of her wine. "I don't know much about the movement. Fond of abstinence and prayer, isn't it? Seems harmless enough."

"They are an utter abhorrence to the ton," said Evelyn.

"Really? I can't understand why." Christiane's mouth curved downward. "Abstinence and prayer were all those ladies ever spoke to me."

"They are pacifists," Mrs. Treadwell explained. "They refuse to go to war. As such, they were roundly condemned as traitors during the Napoleonic mess."

"Pacifists even in the face of Napoleon? What an intriguing notion. I'm quite sure I've never met a Quaker. What other traits do they bear?"

"They denounce all frivolity—and count music and dancing as frivolous."

"So Claire did not dance with her Quaker swain. What exactly *did* she do?"

"It is sometimes difficult to re-create an exact sequence of affairs from the reports of the girls."

Christiane burst out laughing. "I love it, Evelyn, when you are subtle. You mean, I take it, that what came back to you was a mess of rumor and innuendo?"

"It seems quite clear," Mrs. Treadwell said crisply, "that there was some sort of altercation in Vanessa's gardens between Lord Simpson and Mr. Wrede."

"I thought you said Quakers were pacifists."

"Mr. Wrede apparently intervened when Lord Simpson's attentions to a serving girl were less than reciprocated."

"Well, God bless him! If only more such stalwartness went on! How did he intervene, pray tell, if he is such a pacifist?"

"He . . . spoke up."

"He what?"

Mrs. Treadwell waved an apologetic hand. "I know. It doesn't seem likely. But it's what Bess and Gwen could glean. Apparently he overheard some fuss in the shrubberies, ascertained that the young lady in question was less than amenable to what Lord Simpson was attempting, and . . . spoke up. Quite roundly. Enough so that a crowd gathered, and the young lady escaped."

"How marvelous," the countess breathed. "How terribly brave."

Mrs. Treadwell did not seem so enthralled. "Christiane. For heaven's sake. He's utterly unsuitable."

"Why?"

"He is not *de bon ton*! He doesn't fit in!"

"What is his family?"

"Respectable—for Quakers," the headmistress said darkly. "David assists his father in running a highly profitable shipping company that trades with the New World. They're quite well-to-do. There are three younger sons and a daughter or two."

"And Vanessa's husband invites him to routs simply because of the family connection?"

"It's Vanessa that invites him, actually. She has taken

David under her wing. She told me once that he makes her conscious of her soul."

"Impressive, considering Vanessa. But why would he attend her parties, if he looks down on gaiety?"

"The Quakers are, above all else, a practical sect," Mrs. Treadwell noted. "He talks business with the gentlemen, and he intrigues the ladies; he is said to be an adept conversationalist on nearly any topic at hand. Meanwhile, he observes what fripperies the mighty are leaning toward, what wines and liqueurs they're serving, what delicacies line their tables. Then he places his orders for his father's firm for more of the same."

The countess laughed. "How very clever! And what has Claire to say of him?"

Mrs. Treadwell frowned. "It is hard to tell. At first, Bess and Gwen told me, she seemed to like his company very much. But after the incident in the garden, she apparently ran away. Bess and Gwen reported that they found her in bed afterward, completely shaken. She was scarcely coherent. She could not even descend to breakfast the next day."

The countess thought on this. "It's possible that the violent scene between Simpson and Wrede rekindled unpleasant memories for her. Have you spoken to her?"

"You know how difficult a time I have forming any sort of discourse with her," Mrs. Treadwell said apologetically. "She keeps so much to herself." She put her hands to her forehead. "I am quite depleted, Christiane. Being the keeper of six tender young things for the course of an entire weekend—it does make me wish you were more acceptable to society!"

"I'm so very sorry," Christiane said wryly.

"Not," the headmistress said swiftly, "that the fault is your own."

"Nor does it seem to be in Mr. Wrede's case," murmured the countess.

"And I suppose it is our duty to inform Lord Carew that

his niece is consorting with renegades," Mrs. Treadwell said heavily.

Christiane, who had not seen or spoken to Gannon Finn since that kiss, nodded. "I shall see to that," she offered.

"Thanks," the headmistress told her, sincerely grateful.

"But first, I think," the countess noted, "I must speak with Claire."

Christiane waited until after supper the following day; then, as the maids were clearing, she mentioned to Claire that she would like to see her in the parlor. The Irish girl nodded briefly and joined her there. She sat on the settee at the countess's invitation, her head lowered, color bright in her cheeks.

"I owe you an apology," said Christiane.

Claire's head jerked up; her gray eyes were startled. "Oh, no! I owe you one—and Mrs. Treadwell, too."

"Why is that?" Christiane asked gently.

"Because I did not make a success at the Countess of Yarlborough's fete."

"There are many ways to measure success. But the apology I owe you is because I did not warn you that some members of society might be prejudiced against you due to your homeland."

Claire's head sank back down. "Papa warned me," she whispered. "He said it over and over again. It was why he did not want me schooled in England. 'They'll just look down on you,' he told me." She flushed. "I did not believe him. And Mama said he was exaggerating. That's what she always said."

Christiane took a seat beside her on the settee. "The ton," she began, and paused. God, this was difficult! "The ton is such a very small thing," she began again. "So very few members, I mean, in terms of the nation, not to mention the world at large. They have a way of life. They become frightened when they feel it is threatened by any difference, any deviation. It's pathetic, really, when you think of it. In order to feel themselves superior, its members must denigrate others. And that denigration takes a host of forms. National distinctions are only one."

Claire, unexpectedly, nodded. "They mocked at Mr. Wrede as well, because he is different. They were perfectly *beastly* toward him. Far more so than toward me."

"Do you understand why they jested at him?"

"Gwen explained it. A little. He has a different religion."

"Not exactly. He is a Christian, just as they are. But he practices differently."

"He practices better, if you ask me," the girl said heatedly. "Even when they mocked him to his face, he was so composed, so gentle. And if he had not come to the rescue of that poor girl, who knows what might have happened? Yet she never so much as thanked him. Can you imagine that?"

Christiane, somewhat astonished at Claire's vehemence, smiled. "It seems he made a fond impression on you."

"I think he is the most wonderful person I have ever met." Those gray eyes sought the countess's, held them. "I think he might *be* God."

"Good heavens. That would embarrass him mightily, from what Mrs. Treadwell tells me of the Quakers. They seem to be very self-effacing folk. But tell me, Claire, why you ran from him in the garden. And why you did not come down to breakfast."

"I had a headache."

"When? In the garden, or in the morning?"

"Both." But that straightforward gaze had glanced away.

"Would you care to see him again?"

The girl's small, piquant face showed a tug-of-war between fear and yearning. After a moment, she answered: "No."

Christiane nodded. "Then you partake of the general sentiment that he is a shirker. A coward."

"No! That's not it at all; I already said as much!"

"Then why would you not wish to see him?"

"Because . . . because . . ." Abruptly, Claire rose to her feet and began pacing across the small parlor. "He is too good for me."

"Most folk would say he isn't good enough," the countess observed.

"That only shows how little most folk know."

"I've never met Mr. Wrede," the countess noted, rising as well, going to her desk. "What does he look like, can you tell me?"

"He is tall—so very tall," Claire said promptly. "He has hazel eyes, and curling chestnut hair. Magnificent hair, Bess said of him. And well built. Not thin, not heavy. Strong."

Christiane hid a smile. "What of his dress?"

"Very plain. Sober. Gwen said that was a hallmark of the Quakers." Claire paused. "I wonder . . . do you suppose he might have come to my rescue in the first place because I was also wearing black? Perhaps he thought me a Quaker."

"Perhaps he did. I suppose, Claire, what most concerns me is this: Will you be willing to attend another of Vanessa's balls?"

"No," the girl said definitively.

"If you do not mingle with society—"

"I don't care."

Christiane crossed to her, reached for her hands. "If you allow small-minded people to quell you, defeat you—"

"They were horrible. Wretched. All of them. Except for him, of course."

Christiane nodded, squeezing the girl's hands and then releasing them. "It is so new and raw to you. Perhaps, upon further reflection, you'll—"

"I won't change my mind. I am not going back."

"How do you expect to find a husband if you sequester yourself?"

"Why do I need a husband? Gwen and Bess seem happy enough without suitors," Claire said defiantly.

"Do you honestly think so?"

"Don't you? Where is it written in stone that a woman needs a man to complete her? Especially those like Bess and Gwen, who are so smart and accomplished? Isn't that the entire point of this academy?"

The countess sighed. "Not every girl—every woman—requires marriage to be happy. But it suits the needs of most very admirably. Marriage, after all, provides children. If every miss took your scornful view of it, how would the world go on? And when it comes to that, why do you think Gwen and Bess continue to attend the Countess of Yarlborough's routs despite the fact that they have yet to meet young men they consider worthy of them?" Claire started to say something, then stopped. "If you ask them," Christiane continued gently, "I think you'll find that even though they are intelligent and accomplished, they long very much to wed. The human soul yearns for companionship, Claire. It seems to be woven into our sinew and bone."

"Isn't the company of women enough?" the girl asked plaintively. "Neither you nor Mrs. Treadwell has wed again since you were widowed."

"But each of us experienced the joys of marriage." Christiane suppressed a qualm; Mrs. Treadwell's had been none too happy, and her own had been not much more than a matter of convenience, the only option she could envision after Jean-Baptiste's death. Into her mind, unbidden, there came the memory of Gannon Finn bending his mouth to hers. That one swift kiss had reawakened an ache in her heart she had never thought to feel again.

But Gannon was beside the point, which was Claire. *I am old,* Christiane told herself. *What becomes of me is of little account.* Claire was just embarking on the grand voyage that was life. And the countess was determined not to allow her to run from it, shun it. She gathered her thoughts, and was about to speak again when there came a knock at the door.

"What is it?" Christiane said in exasperation.

Clarisse poked her head in. "Begging yer pardon, mum, but there's a caller for Miss Finn."

"Uncle Gannon!" The girl rose from her seat in delight.

"No, miss. A Mr. Wrede. He didn't have a card. And he asked for 'Miss Claire.'" The maid's prim expression showed precisely what she thought of these social deviations.

Christiane raised her brows. "Well! He doesn't waste time, does he?"

Claire had gone ghost-pale. "I cannot see him."

"Why not?"

"I don't know! Because . . ." She drew in a deep breath. "He frightens me. Make my excuses, Clarisse, please. Say I have already gone to bed."

"It's not yet eight o'clock," the maid said dubiously.

"Say I'm ill! Say anything at all!"

"Clarisse," the countess declared, taking charge, "please show Mr. Wrede in."

Claire stared at her as though she'd been struck. "I thought you were on *our* side," she whispered.

"I am," the countess retorted, smoothing her skirts and checking the state of her hair. Then she looked at Claire. "Always. Forever. But sometimes, you must trust me."

"Mr. Wrede," Clarissa announced.

Christiane rose from her chair, taking her first look at the man.

Tall indeed, she thought, going toward him with her hand extended. And his hair *was* splendid, rich and deep red-brown, though his clothing was peculiar, very dark and drab. All in all, though, he was a fine-looking man despite his lack of fashionableness—or perhaps because of it. He was the farthest thing from a fop. "How do you do, Mr. Wrede? I am the Countess d'Oliveri. It is kind of you to call."

His gold-brown eyes met hers. "I am sorry for the intrusion." His voice was bold and strong—thrilling, really. Then his gaze went to Claire. "I worried about thee, when I did not see thee again. I feared I had offended thee somehow."

"No," Claire said, the word a wisp. "No. Not at all."

He nodded slowly. Everything he did seemed slow and strong, self-assured but with no trace of boasting—and markedly unlike the tulips of the ton. "Yet thou ran away," he noted.

Claire seemed to be shrinking back against the settee, to be visibly diminishing. Christiane contemplated stepping in, but resolved to allow the two to play the scene out themselves.

David Wrede waited. There was a long silence. Christiane had to bite her tongue; why didn't Claire say something, anything? Yet Wrede seemed patient enough; he simply stood in his black coat, hat held in his hands, and waited. Just as Christiane was thinking his patience would never be rewarded, Claire spoke up, in a burst:

"I admire very much what you did for that poor girl in the gardens. And I appreciate your kind attentions to me. But I wish—" There, finally, she faltered.

"Wish what, Claire?" he asked in his deep, echoing voice.

"That you had not come."

He nodded thoughtfully. "I can go away again, if thou wish it."

"I do." He started to turn. "No, that's not true. I don't!" Claire looked plaintively at the countess.

David Wrede might not be prone to impatience, but Christiane was, especially in the face of such an apparently admirable swain. "Make up your mind, Claire," she said, with a hint of pique.

Wrede let out a low, rich, rolling laugh. "It is a woman's prerogative, is it not, to change it?"

Christiane liked him more than ever for that laugh. "They do say so. But when you have gone to so much bother as to come here—"

"I never asked him to!" Claire declared, somewhat wildly.

"Perhaps I should not have called unexpectedly," Wrede said, and smiled. He had, the countess noted, a very winning smile. "If thou like, I could go away, write thee a proper letter, and wait for thy answer." Claire said nothing. He pressed it: "Would thou answer?"

Nothing but silence. "Would you care to sit down, Mr. Wrede, while Miss Finn ponders her reply?" Christiane said, a tad caustically.

Claire threw her a desperate glance. "Not Miss Finn," she hissed, but the damage was done. Christiane saw Wrede register the name like a knife-thrust.

"Miss Finn." He paused, taking it in. "Are thou—but thou must be. Dear God in heaven. Please accept my apologies—and my sympathies for the loss of thy parents. I had no idea."

Claire was as pale as moonlight, all her color fled. "No doubt," she said shakily, "you think it . . . frivolous of me, to have attended that ball."

Wrede's gaze sought the countess's. Then, "Not a bit," he told Claire stoutly. "I think thy teachers gave thee good counsel. Grief such as thine must be nigh unbearable. To seek escape, any escape, in such tragic circumstances—I only wish I had known before."

"Why?" Claire flared up, suddenly blazing.

"Claire," the countess began, remonstrating.

But David Wrede was not in the least disconcerted. "So that I might have tried to comfort thee," he said.

Claire was crying. "I don't want comfort. I want—oh, God, I don't know what I want!"

Christiane started toward her, but Wrede was faster. He caught Claire up from the settee, gathered her into his strong arms, held her to his broad chest. "There, there," he murmured, smoothing her black hair as though she were a child crying over a skinned knee. "How could thou know what to feel? What could prepare thee for this?"

"I hate him!" Claire cried viciously, pounding her fists against Wrede's coat. "I hate him! Hate him, hate him!"

Christiane, looking on in a sort of suspended horror, saw Wrede raise his gaze to the ceiling. "If thou hate him," he said quietly, "thou compound the killer's crime. His viciousness becomes thine. Thou must strive with all thy heart, Claire, to hate the sin and yet love the sinner."

She turned on him. "What would you know of it?" She fought to free herself from his embrace. "What would you know about it? You are nothing but a coward, just as they said!"

"Claire!" Christiane said, appalled.

But Wrede took it in stride. He caught Claire's wrists, held them fast, and stared straight into her eyes. "I will not comfort thee with false hopes. There are reasons behind all things, though the reasons are not all God's doing. Thou must listen to the silence, and seek the peace that lies inside thee. The answers are there."

Claire drew back from him, with such an expression of desperation that Christiane caught her breath. "There is nothing inside me but darkness."

"Look deeper. Seek the Inner Light."

"There is no light!" Claire cried in anguish.

"The Light is there." He put his hand to her cheek, cupped it gently. "The Light is *always* there."

"You speak in aphorisms," she said disdainfully.

He smiled at her, faintly. "An aphorism is only an over-worked truth."

"See? There you go!"

He released her at last, stepping back. "I would like to call on thee again, Claire. I would like to walk out with thee."

"Walk out?" Christiane said faintly.

"A Quaker's poor excuse for courting," David Wrede explained. "Since we do not dance. May I call on thee, Claire?"

"No."

"Please?"

"No!"

"Will thou not walk out with me?"

"Never."

Christiane, looking on, was about to interject angrily—
was the girl mad? Did she think suitors like this were so
easily found? But Wrede remained sanguine. "Should thou
change thy mind," he said softly, huskily, "the invitation
stands."

Claire was crying quietly. "I'll not change my mind,"
she declared.

"If thou should, I will be there for thee."

Claire raised her tear-stained face. "Don't say that.
Don't make me believe that."

"It is God's truth." Wrede nodded, to her and then to the
countess. "I'll take my leave. Claire . . ."

But Claire was shaking her head, wringing her hands.
Wrede hesitated, then left them. There was silence in the
parlor—an unhappy, uncertain silence, punctuated by
Claire's breathy sobs.

"He seems a most decent young man," the countess
began.

"Exactly," Claire whispered, dabbing at her eyes. "He
deserves far better than me." And then she ran from the
parlor, leaving the countess to wonder what on earth could
have caused the girl to behave that way.

Thirteen

She sent for Gannon, of course. She felt she had no choice. But she did not bother with planning a private supper; she simply asked him to call ahead of his regular Sunday visit, writing that she had to speak to him on a matter of great urgency. She sent the letter on Tuesday morning. He arrived on Wednesday, just at dusk.

"You are prompt," she noted, as Clarisse showed him into the parlor. She was trying very hard not to notice how splendidly virile he looked, with his hair and clothes disheveled from what must have been a hard ride.

"You alarmed me with that note." He took her hand, pressed the briefest kiss to it. "What is amiss?"

"You'd best have a whiskey." She poured it for him as he settled into a chair.

He took the glass, tipped it toward her. "Cheers." His eyes were the gray-green of a storm-ridden ocean.

"It's Claire," she said, and saw him register some brief emotion — it might have been disappointment — before he nodded acknowledgment.

"She has . . . misbehaved?"

"No, no. Nothing like that. Quite the contrary, really. She has attracted a suitor."

He stared. "You're jesting."

The countess found herself offended, for Claire's sake. "I don't see why you should say that. She is extraordinarily lovely. That rich black hair . . . those eyes . . ." *His eyes.*

"Of course she is. I did not mean it that way. I am only . . . surprised. She seems so shy and withdrawn. I cannot imagine her encouraging a young man."

"That's precisely why I asked you to call. She isn't encouraging him—not at all. In fact, she has said she never wants to see him again."

"Why not? Is he unsuitable?"

"That depends, I suppose, upon one's definition of the term. He comes of good enough stock. As a matter of fact, he is a relative of Mrs. Treadwell's daughter's husband."

"Of the Earl of Yarlborough? Well, I daresay he must be suitable!"

"He has one count against him—and one only, so far as I can ascertain, having met him."

"And what is that?"

"He is a Quaker."

Gannon Finn nodded slowly, taking that in. "I see. And Claire finds that objectionable?"

"Oh, no. I don't think it's that. Well, in a way. Perhaps."

His smile flashed at her, devastating as ever. "You are talking in riddles, you know."

Christiane went to pour herself a whiskey. "Forgive me. I don't mean to. But in truth, I find it rather perplexing myself. Here is what went on—or what I can gather, from the reports of Mrs. Treadwell and the other girls, and of Claire herself." She related to him what she knew about Vanessa's rout, the young men who had scorned Claire, and how David Wrede had come to her rescue, along with his later aid to Simpson's victim in the garden at Yarlborough Hall. Gannon listened closely, carefully.

"So you met him there—at the countess's?" he inquired as she paused in her recounting.

Christiane blushed. "I was not present. You must remember, I have no public profile with regard to the academy. Owing to the . . . the irregularities of my past life."

"Poor Christiane. Still suffering from that moment of madness with Lord Weatherston. How many years has it been now since the ton cast you out?"

"Damn you," she whispered.

"I was quite sincere." Silence hung between them for a long moment. He broke it first. "Where did you encounter Mr. Wrede, then?"

"He came here, to the academy. To call on her. To ask her to walk out with him."

"What did you make of him?"

"I found him enchanting," Christiane said truthfully. "He seems honest, plainspoken, courageous, sensitive—"

"And not much of a looker." Gannon nodded in understanding. "We all know the sort."

"Not at all!" Christiane said, bristling. "He is a fine figure of a man! Very handsome, in my opinion—and in those of the girls and Mrs. Treadwell, too! Not to mention Claire's. She spoke most rapturously about his hair and figure."

"Claire did?" He sounded astonished again.

"She did."

"Then what was her objection to him, if not his religion or his appearance or his manners?"

"I was hoping you might shed some light on that," Christiane said. "It certainly escapes me."

He leaned back in the chair, extending his long, booted legs. And then he said something remarkable: "Perhaps she likes him too well."

"I beg your pardon?"

"I've seen the sort of thing before. A woman finds herself attracted to a man, is frightened by the attraction, and falls all over herself denying it."

Christiane stared. "If you are insinuating that I was once attracted to *you* in such a way—"

He raised one black brow. "Actually, I wasn't thinking of you at all. Though now that you mention it, the comparison is apt."

"You flatter yourself," she hissed.

Gannon Finn shrugged. "Still denying it, I see."

She rose to her feet in fury. "I have never in my life met so self-centered a man! I said it of you twenty years ago, and I say it still. Here am I, trying my best to see your niece's future settled, and you can do nothing but taunt me and mock me!"

"You invited me to your bedroom," he said implacably, his voice low and harsh. "You inveigled me with your attentions. You led me on."

"I invited you to my bedchamber—once!—because if Jean-Baptiste had found you downstairs alone with me, after hours, he would have slit your throat," Christiane managed to say.

"He would have tried. *Muguets du bois.*"

"What?"

"The scent you wore. You wear it still. It drove me mad then. As it does now." He rose as well, moving toward her. Christiane backed away from him, trembling, until she bumped against the windowsill. She clutched it tightly. "Why would you not tell him?"

"Tell him what?"

"That you loved me. Loved *me,* and not him."

"You're insane."

"Am I, Christiane? What were you hoping for, wishing for, when he and I met that dawn in the Bois de Boulogne?"

"That Jean-Baptiste would win, of course!" And she *had* wished for that, she assured herself. Anything else would have been unthinkable. Why, she remembered even now the jolt to her heart when she'd heard that Gannon Finn had triumphed.

He came closer. "Do you know why I won, Christiane?"

She shook her head, fearful. He whispered in her ear: "Because I loved you more."

She put her hands to his dusty doublet, shoved him away. "I don't know why you would want to torment me this way. To . . . to dishonor a dead man's memory." She stared down at the floor.

"Perhaps because I long so much for you to acknowledge it. I did love you more, Christiane."

"It is ancient history," she whispered.

"Is it?" He leaned toward her again.

"I asked you here to talk about Claire!"

"I know why you asked me here." His mouth closed on hers. His arms gathered her in.

"Gannon," she breathed. "Don't—"

He groaned, tucking her tightly against him. "Oh, God." His kiss was fire. His hands caressed her, his fingertips tracing her cheekbones, smoothing her black hair. "I have longed for this . . ."

"Let me go!" She struggled in his grasp.

"Do you remember?" he breathed against her ear. "That night . . . I remember it all. Every second. Every moment—"

"It was madness! It was a mistake, a terrible mistake!"

"Why do you say that? You cannot tell me you believe that! When you caught me in your arms . . . when I poured myself into you . . ." His hips were hard against her. "The way you sighed for me, clung to me—"

The parlor door burst open. "Uncle Gannon!" Claire cried, and then froze, seeing the room's occupants spring apart. "I . . . I beg your pardon," she whispered. "Gwen told me she saw you arrive from the window. I . . . I thought . . . it must be me you had come to see."

Christiane fought for composure, ran a hand through her tousled curls. "I sent for your uncle, Claire, regarding the matter of Mr. Wrede."

The girl's eyes were wide; she was plainly still trying to make sense of what she'd glimpsed as she entered: the countess in her uncle's arms, their clinging embrace. "You had no right to do that," she declared.

Gannon stepped in. "You must understand, Claire," he said smoothly, "the countess and I are old friends. And—"

"To send for him, I mean." Her gaze was steady now, directed at Madame.

"Claire. Mr. Wrede seems to be a most suitable young man. He—"

"I have told him—*and* you—that I don't wish to see him again."

"But that is precisely why I sent for your uncle. In the hope that he might make you see reason."

"It's clear to me why you sent for him."

"Claire!" Gannon said in shocked surprise.

"You think me such an innocent, don't you, Uncle?" Her voice was disdainful. "Perhaps this is why you suggested I come to the academy. Perhaps your—your shock at finding Madame here was nothing but pretense."

"Claire, you are wrong!" Christiane cried, and Gannon echoed her:

"I swear to you—"

"God, don't swear to me," the girl said heavily, sadly. "You have all of you, every one of you, been swearing to me all my life. Swearing that you know what's best for me. Swearing that you care about me. Swearing that if I only am patient, everything will get better. That's what Papa said. That's what Mama said as well. But they never said it when they were in a room with one another. They only swore it to me when they were alone with me—when the other wasn't there."

"Oh, Claire." Gannon sounded as though his heart was breaking. "Why didn't you tell me how it was for you?"

"Because I did not need one more soul swearing to me that he knew what was best! Forgive my interruption, please, Madame," she said with icy politesse. "Go on with what you were doing. I'll take my leave. Good night, Uncle." She turned on her heel and left them, closing the door with crisp finality.

"Christ," Gannon Finn said, pushing back his black hair. "What have I done?" And he smacked his fist against the wall at his side, so forcefully that the plaster flaked. "Dammit all! Damn it to hell!"

Shaken though she was, Christiane squared her shoulders. "We must help her, Gannon. We must put our own concerns aside—now, once and for all—and help her."

"But how?" he howled, sounding almost animal.

"You might start by telling me the truth. Why did Georgina stay with you, at your estate, while she was carrying Claire?"

"Who told you that?"

"It doesn't matter. Can't you see the time is past for fretting about such inconsequentials? I want to help her, Gannon! I want her to come through this, find happiness somehow. And I cannot do so unless you are honest with me."

He threw himself into a chair, his expression frighteningly grim. "You don't understand. These are family matters."

"Eh bien," Christiane retorted. "Take her with you, then, and deal with them *en famille*. But do not lay her in my lap and expect me to perform wonders without any idea of what has caused her unhappiness."

He reached for his whiskey, frowned at the glass, then took a long, defiant draught. "My brother drank," he said then.

"Most men do."

He glared at her. "To excess."

"Most men do that as well, in my experience."

"You might be just a bit charitable!" he snapped.

"The time for charity is past."

Gannon Finn stared at the floor. "When he drank, he sometimes became . . . unstable."

"Can you be more specific?"

"God, Christiane! What do you want me to say?"

"Did he molest his daughter?"

"Never!" he burst out.

"Did he harm his wife?"

He was silent. Christiane nodded slowly. "That's it, isn't it? He beat Georgina. He beat her, and she had miscarriages because of it. Then, when she was carrying Claire, she came to you for protection."

"I don't want you to get the wrong idea about Hugh."

"What could possibly be the *right* idea, pray tell, about such a man?" Christiane snapped.

"It isn't that clear-cut. She provoked him."

Her black eyes flashed at him. "No provocation justifies such acts!"

He sighed, leaning back in the chair. "No. It doesn't. You're quite right. But they were such a pair . . . he with his Irish pride, she with her English hauteur—it was a morass, I tell you. I was lost as to what to do. I tried to intervene. As God's my witness, I did. I talked to him. I tried to reason with her. But they were caught . . ." He sought her gaze. "Caught together in some devastating game I did not understand. I don't think *they* did."

She found herself pitying him. "And so you took her in."

"I thought—I had hopes. Hugh had always wanted an heir so badly. Perhaps, once he had what he longed for, he would change. Become more gentle with Georgina."

"Did he?"

He shook his head.

"Why didn't she leave him?"

"I don't know. I told her she should. For Claire's sake, if nothing else. She would not listen to me. Do you know what I think, honestly? She was too proud to admit she had made a mistake. Leaving him would have meant admitting that everything her friends in London had warned her of was true—that the Irish are uncivilized beasts." He caught some glimmer of expression as it flitted across her face, and nodded grimly. "There. You would have warned her of the same. You have always been afraid of me."

"Not in that way!" she hastened to explain.

"Admit it. You found me unreasonable in Paris. A madman."

Christiane winced. She *had* used that expression to Evelyn. But he had been honest with her. She owed that much to him. "I found you . . . frustrating. Not—perhaps not frustrating, exactly. But no man in his right mind—"

"There you go," he broke in. "That's it in a nutshell. When we fall, we Finns, we fall hard." He stood up, strode to the window, yanked the drapes aside and stared into the darkened courtyard. "When you do fall so hard, you expect—is it unreasonable to expect, when all your dreams and hopes are pinned on one being, that she should be able to sense your desperation? To at least acknowledge its validity?"

"I . . . you were so young, Gannon," she said falteringly. "You had years and years of wooing ahead of you. And I was settled. I had found my place."

"With a married Frenchman who gadflied off at the slightest opportunity?"

"His nation was at war! There are greater callings—"

He whirled on her. "No! There is no greater calling than one heart to another. There never could be. I knew it, even if you didn't. It was why I won against him in the wood that morning. I tell you, Christiane—I loved you more."

Christiane forced her voice to steadiness. "It was just this sort of wildness that made me spurn your advances."

"Why?" he cried out. "Why should such love, such great *need*, be denied?"

She smiled a little. "Come now, Gannon. You have gone on in the decades since to a grand career as a rogue. You are a first-rate breaker of hearts."

"I should not have been, had you not broken mine."

It was what she had imagined—had dreamed of. But to hear him say it, declare it with such vehemence, shook her to her soul; the responsibility seemed more than she wanted or could bear. "You don't mean that," she whispered.

"God damn me if I don't."

"You were no more than a child. A reckless, feckless child!"

"I was a man," he said with heavy finality. "You made me one."

Christiane took a deep breath. "Gannon. Think a bit. Pause a bit. Have reason. What we shared together—it was no more than the briefest escapade."

"Perhaps to you it was. It meant more to me."

"I asked you here because I am concerned about Claire."

"Do you imagine I am not?"

"If you are, why must you keep bringing the conversation back to matters that are long past?" she asked plaintively.

"Actions have repercussions. You took me into your bed."

"It may shock you to know it, but I took a number of men into my bed." She looked at him in defiance.

"That supper you had prepared for me here. The clothes you wore. Will you deny that you were trying to seduce me?"

She sighed. "Honestly? Yes. Not seduce. Perhaps . . . attract. I felt old, Gannon. Decrepit. I had found gray hairs."

"You never could be old," he said quickly.

Her black eyes slanted toward him, and she smiled. "That is what you said twenty years ago. The difference was even greater then. I won't deny it—when we met again, after so long a time, I was curious. You caught me at a low point. I had some wild notion of discovering whether you might still find me . . . alluring."

"I do." He moved toward her.

"But the time for that is past!" she said briskly.

"Must it be?"

She took a deep breath. "What about Miss Delaney, to whom you are betrothed?"

"She knows—or should—that it will come to naught."

"A man who toys with women's affections isn't the sort I find attractive."

"Even when you yourself are the cause of that behavior?"

"You have no right," she cried, "to put such a burden on me! All I did was make love to you—once! Once! How many women have you slept with in the years since?"

"Dozens," he said frankly. "A hundred, maybe. But in all my life, I only made love to you."

She turned away, turned back, looked straight at him. "Gannon. You don't love *me*. You love what I was twenty years ago, when you came to Paris. You love that unattainable, unfathomable Englishwoman who ran a foreign gambling hell. You love the memory—the chandeliers, the champagne, the silk and satin and feathers—"

"All that, yes," he agreed. "And you, too."

"You don't even know me."

"I know enough."

"You know nothing at all." She wasn't certain where the strength that filled her came from, but she welcomed it, reveled in it. "You never have known me. For if you had, you'd realize that our problems are negligible—are nothing!—beside those of your niece. It is Claire to whom we must devote our attentions—Claire, who has had her entire life overturned by the deaths of her parents. Claire, who is so patently afraid to assay love."

His smile blazed at her. "You say that I don't love you. Yet you say precisely what the woman I *do* love would."

"You are impossible," she said, after a moment.

"All the ladies tell me so. Greer most of all."

"Why—why would you become betrothed to such a woman, Gannon?" she asked tentatively.

"Because there is no danger I'll carry it through."

"Oh, you *are* a dastard."

"If and when I marry, it will be to the woman I love." His eyes bored into her, seemed to reach her soul. She flinched, terrified. Two weeks past, she would have longed for nothing more in the world than to hear him declare his love for her. But now . . . "Of course," he went on calmly, suavely, "that isn't possible until she admits to herself that everything she has called 'love' in the past was only a sham. Until she opens her heart to new possibilities."

"How dare you," she said bitterly. "You know nothing of what went on in my past. Of what my feelings were for my husband, or for Jean-Baptiste."

"How can you be so certain? Here, let's postulate. You are cast out by the ton. You go to Paris. A man, an older man, a married man, takes you under his wing. You agree to his advances, longing for some sense of—"

"Stop," she ordered.

"Settledness. Financial security—"

"I never took Jean-Baptiste's money!" she cried. "I loved him!"

"He was married to another woman," Gannon Finn said implacably. "She had his name. She bore his children. She—"

"I hate you!" Christiane screamed, and burst into tears.

He looked on. When her sobs had diminished, he said, very quietly, "I never would have asked that you share me with another woman. I never would have dishonored you that way."

She had gathered her thoughts. She took a breath, a deep one, and then another. She even managed a laugh. "Gannon. You are just as mad now as you were then."

"Mad about you."

"You don't know me," she said again, a little sadly. "I'm not what I was in Paris, and you knew little enough about me then. Go home, and make your peace with Greer. Marry her. Be happy."

"I don't understand how you can pretend to teach your students about what is real in life when you refuse to recognize it yourself."

Christiane cocked her head. "Is it being Irish that makes you so thick? What does it take to reach you? It was one night—one stupid, heedless moment of weakness on my part."

"It was our destiny."

She laughed. "Do you honestly expect me to believe that you have been pining for me for all these years?"

"That's precisely what I have been."

She drew in a long breath. "Well, then, you are immensely self-deceiving. I found you most unsatisfying as a partner, compared to the others I had had."

She saw a vein flash at his temple. His upper lip curled. "You lie."

She flashed a teasing smile. "You are that sure of your prowess—when you were so young, and a virgin?"

"I wasn't—"

"You were too." She moved from the windowsill, reclaimed her whiskey, took a long sip, feeling much more confident. She had seen how callow he was. She was sure she could make him believe she'd found him lacking. It was, after all, a man's most dreaded fear.

"You . . . I did satisfy you," he insisted. "I could tell."

"Could you?" She half-closed her eyes, ran her tongue around her lips to moisten them, let out a low, soft moan: "Ohhh. Ahhh. Oh! Oh, God, don't stop!" Her voice rose in a crescendo: "Oh, oh, oh! Ohhh! Uhh. Uhh. Yes, yes! *Oh, God, yes!*"

"Stop that!" he ordered, clearly shocked.

"Right *there.* Yes. *Oh,* yes! *Yes!* Oh—dear—God!" Christiane screamed, staring straight at him.

"My God," he whispered. "What sort of woman are you?"

"The sort who knows a man from a boy," she said negligently, pushing back a loose strand of black hair. "Now perhaps we can get back to Claire."

He stood up, abruptly. His face was flushed; his hands were balled into fists. "You are just what they said, all of them. Nothing but a whore."

"I prefer to think of myself as a practical woman. One who does what she has to in order to survive in a world that is ruled by men."

"Is that what you teach your students?"

She faltered a bit. "No. Of course not. We teach them to believe in themselves. Be true to—" He let out a snort. She forced herself to continue: "True to themselves."

"The way *you* are. The way you were." He was furious, she could tell that, but was glad of it. Now, perhaps, they could return to their comfortable old enmity—and to the subject of Claire.

"It occurs to me," she said coolly, "that in your grand career as a rogue, you may not have feigned sexual consummation. But you have surely feigned love. Which is the greater sin?"

He stood looking at her. Christiane felt her every flaw magnified beneath his flint-gray gaze: the white hairs, the crow's-feet, her no-longer-perfect figure and skin. And yet she met his unyielding stare, returned it just as determinedly. She *would* have the upper hand.

Sure enough, he broke the standoff first. "It seems I've been a bloody fool," he noted briefly, and swallowed the last of his whiskey. "Forgive me if I have discomfited you. Though I doubt I have."

She forced a slight smile. "Come, Gannon. You have flattered an old flame immensely this evening. I took no offense. You must not, either. Don't be cross with me."

"Cross . . ." He shook his head slowly. "When did you ever make me anything else?" Then he laughed a little.

Encouraged, she went to the sideboard. "Another drink?"

"No. No, I think that I will speak with Claire now. As for Mr. Wrede, you must do what you feel is best. I begin to think that I am something less than qualified when it comes to matters of the heart."

That stabbed her. For an instant, she contemplated admitting the truth about that night in Paris. But she fought off the impulse. Life belonged to the young. Her time, just as Evelyn had said, was past. "I appreciate your trust in me, under the circumstances," she managed to tell him.

"It seems you have known all along what you were doing," he retorted, heading for the door. "I only wish to hell I hadn't stabbed your man there in the wood that dawn."

Fourteen

Christiane had one more very small whiskey, alone in the parlor. Then she rang for Clarisse. "Is Lord Carew gone?"

"Aye, mum."

"And where is Miss Finn?"

"In her room. She only just returned there."

"Would you bring her to me, please?"

"Aye, mum." The maid bobbed and went.

When the Irish girl entered, her eyes had an odd, veiled expression. "Claire," Christiane began. "I apologize for the way . . . for how you found your uncle and me. I don't want it to upset you."

She shrugged. "He said the same. Said he'd made an ass of himself, and I must not think anything of it."

Christiane winced. "He is hard on himself. It was not that way, precisely. You know that we knew one another, many years ago." The girl nodded. "It seems he harbored a tendresse for me. We discussed it. I was . . . flattered that he still seemed to do so. But I explained to him how impossible it was."

"Why?"

Christiane sighed. "Because we are not now the people we were then. So much time has passed."

"Do you think—" Claire began, then stopped.

"Do I think what?"

"Do you think that when you love someone, you always end up hurting that person?"

"Oh, no!" Christiane rushed to assure her. "Love is the most marvelous thing in the world!"

"It does not seem so to me. Mama and Papa, and you and Uncle Gannon . . ."

"Your world has been so constricted, *chérie*. You have not sufficient basis to judge." And then Christiane caught her breath. "Is that why you don't want Mr. Wrede to call on you? Because you are afraid you will hurt him?"

"He is so very good," the girl whispered, wide-eyed with dread. "He was so very good to me."

Christiane was grateful now for what Gannon had told her about Hugh and Georgina. "You must not think—you must not!—that love always has a tragic finish. Love, true love, endures all things, bears all things—" Then she stopped, remembering Gannon's fierce eyes.

"Bears all things," Claire repeated, and Christiane wondered what horrors she might be remembering from her childhood.

"*True* love," Christiane said again, and took Claire's trembling hands. "True love is a rarity in these times. When you find it—if you are lucky enough to find it— you must hold to it, cling fast. Oh, *chérie*." She gathered the frail girl into her arms, as she'd so often longed to. "Do you think that you could love Mr. Wrede?"

"I cannot! For if I do, I *will* hurt him!"

"No, no," Christiane assured her, smoothing the girl's black hair.

"I fear that I will."

"Mr. Wrede is strong enough, I think, to stand up to the likes of you. He seems a man who knows himself well."

"I cannot comprehend . . . why he should care to call on me."

Christiane laughed, and pressed a quick kiss to Claire's forehead. "Because he is wise and discerning. And because you are beautiful and kind."

"I'm not kind," the girl said, with a sort of dread.

"But of course you are!"

Those stormy eyes, just like Gannon's, sought hers. "Even if I am not, I could try to be."

"If that is how you want to think of it—yes. You can strive to be worthy of him."

Claire raised her chin. It was set with determination. She nodded. "I shall. I shall strive. Because I do find him . . . very dear."

"I'll write to him, then," the countess said with satisfaction. "I'll invite him to call again. Saturday, shall we say?"

"If you would. That would . . . I would . . ." The girl broke off, tongue-tied, blushing.

Christiane smiled. "There, you see? It must be true love, for you are all disconcerted! Now, off to your bed. I'll write tonight, straightaway."

"Thank you," said Claire. And yet she stood unmoving, her gaze very distant. "I don't know what I will say to him."

"I daresay you will discover a world of topics for discourse," the countess assured her.

"He is fond of silence. That is lucky," Claire noted, chewing her lip.

Mr. Wrede presented himself at the academy precisely at three o'clock on Saturday, the hour Christiane had suggested. Bess and Gwen had helped Claire to dress, in a gray silk walking skirt and half-coat, and Gwen had done her form-mate's hair in a very becoming chignon. Claire was shaking, though, as she descended the stairs to the parlor where her suitor was waiting. He was in somber black, and had on a broad-brimmed black hat that hid his chestnut curls. His eyes, though, were dancing.

"Good afternoon, Miss Finn," he said formally as she entered the room.

"Mr. Wrede," she whispered, and cast an anxious glance at Mrs. Treadwell, who was performing matron's honors.

"I've already offered tea," Evelyn said blithely, "and been refused. Off into the courtyard with the two of you."

"I had hoped," Wrede said in his deep voice, "that we might sojourn further afield. I brought my walking stick."

"You will require a chaperone if you are to venture outside the walls," Mrs. Treadwell said briskly. "We insist on propriety, Mr. Wrede. I'm sure you understand."

"Of course. The courtyard it is." He bowed to the headmistress, then took Claire's arm. She tried her best to stop quaking.

"It's this way," she whispered, and led him outside.

In the archway to the courtyard, he paused, drawing in a long breath. "Glorious day, isn't it? We are blessed by such sunshine."

"So we are." Claire looked out onto the square of ivy and grass. It seemed terribly small. She felt her heart constrict. What were they to do, then—pace up and down and up again? She would have to make conversation; otherwise he would be bored to tears. But perhaps it was best he learn the truth about her right at the start.

There was a clatter from the balcony above them. Some of the lower-form girls had come out to stare. "Is that Claire's suitor?" one of them said, very audibly. "Is he an undertaker?"

She blushed scarlet. But Wrede only laughed, her arm tucked into his. "Am I so dreary as that?" he asked.

She looked down at her dove-gray skirts. "I am not exactly in the pink of fashion, either."

"If thou were not in mourning," he asked, looking down at her, "what would thou wear?"

"I've no idea," she confessed. "Fashion is a great mystery to me. The other girls chatter on and on about the cut of a sleeve, the line of a bodice . . . and it is as though they were speaking Chinese. My mama made all my clothes herself. But I can't bear to wear them now. So Uncle Gannon arranged with Madame for me to go to the seamstress in Hartin—Mrs. Tattersall. She is very fond of plaids, it seems. And now and again, he sends me something from London. He sent me this."

"I find it very lovely," David Wrede said gravely.

"It's dull, though. Gray is dull."

"It makes thine eyes go straight green."

Fancy him noticing that. Claire had thought the same herself, when she'd looked in the mirror. "They change color, I'm told," she murmured.

"So they do. I find that curious. Mine are always the same." They'd crossed to the opposite side of the courtyard. Now he turned her about, and started back whence they'd come.

"But your hair changes," she pointed out shyly.

"Does it?"

"Aye. Sometimes it is brown, and sometimes it has a reddish tint." She glanced up at him. "When the sun hits, it is very red."

"At school, the boys used to tease me about my hair. Called me Curly-Top."

"I like your curls. They are . . . like the waves on the sea."

The wall loomed before them. He turned her around again. "Thou are very poetic," he said then.

"Oh, not I. Bess is the poet. She writes the most beautiful verse."

"Do thy teachers encourage verse-writing?"

"They do for Bess. They encourage whatever we are good at. What sort of school did you go to?"

"A Friends school."

"Were the teachers silent?"

He laughed. "Far from it. They had much to say."

"What sorts of subjects did you study?"

"Grammar. Latin. Mathematics." He made a face. "Too much mathematics for my taste."

"I am quite dreadful at any sort of figuring," Claire confessed. "But Petra—that's another of my schoolmates—has the most amazing aptitude at numbers! She can do such long equations—in her head!"

"It is interesting, is it not, how different minds embrace different subjects?"

"It is a mystery to me," she said frankly. "What are you best at?"

"Oh—I have some aptitude with languages."

"Do you really? You can speak other languages?" He nodded. "What ones, then?"

"German. French. Spanish. A bit of Portuguese and Russian. It's useful for our business. I do the correspondence for the firm. And when a problem arises abroad, I am sent to try and fix it."

"You venture abroad? What places have you been to?"

"The Continent. The Caribbean. America. Asia Minor. And to India, once."

"Imagine that!" Claire said, much impressed. "I have never been anywhere. What place did you like best?"

He considered for a moment. "Greece," he said then. "For the monuments." They had almost reached the far wall again, and he turned her around. "So thine instructors encourage whatever thou are good at. What are thou good at, Claire?"

"Nothing much. I am quite hopeless at most of what we study. My parents—" She swallowed. "My father did not favor the education of girls."

"Why not? Do thou know?"

"I think . . ." She glanced at him again, squinting against the late-afternoon sunlight. "I think it was because he feared Mama was more clever than he."

He nodded, taking that in. "And was she?"

"No," she whispered. "She was not clever at all." She looked down again, closing her eyes, remembering the books that had to stay hidden, the gazettes from London that her father would tear to shreds when he found them, the mind-numbing tasks—milking, plucking, carding, weaving—he had insisted that her mother perform. If she'd been clever, Georgina would have run back to England. If she'd been clever, she never would have married him.

They'd reached the opposite wall once more. David Wrede turned her around. His hand on her arm was so gentle, so light. "Thou must be good at many things. What do thine instructors encourage in thee?"

"I told you—I'm not good at anything."

"I don't believe that."

She laughed. "It's true, I'm afraid. I am the despair of all my teachers. Except . . . except for Monsieur Battier."

"And what is his field of expertise?" He'd stopped in the midst of the courtyard, was looking down at her and smiling his broad, slow smile.

"He teaches art," she answered, somewhat reluctantly. His brows lifted.

"He seems to imagine I have a sort of talent," she explained, even more reluctantly. "He likes my caricatures."

He nodded slowly. It occurred to Claire that she was unused to anyone doing things slowly. At home, all the world had always seemed to be in such a rush. And here at the academy, one hurried along from class to class, interspersed with meals, with bells ringing the change of hours, marking the passing of time as though it was something to be hastened through, thrust off, notched on the calendar.

David Wrede, though, did not seem at all affected by such considerations. They had reached the end of the courtyard again. She felt herself itching at the confines of their course, but he merely spun on his heel, ready to start across the yard once more. "Isn't it driving you mad," she could not keep from asking, "to go on stalking back and forth and back and forth again?"

He grinned at her. "No. I would pace this same course interminably, so long as I could pace it with thee."

Claire blushed wholly, totally.

"I could be dissuaded, however," he mentioned, his smile teasing, "if thou would draw me a picture."

At least it would put a halt to their pacing. "I would have to go upstairs to fetch my sketchbook and pencil."

He relinquished her elbow. She ducked through the archway and inside to the staircase, running up to her room. She'd no sooner opened the door than Bess and Gwen confronted her. "How goes it?" Bess hissed.

"I scarcely know. I think he must be bored to tears, yet he does not seem to be. I, however, am ready to stop trudging back and forth. And he suggested that I draw him a picture." She caught up her sketchbook. "Oh, where is a pencil?"

"Here," said Gwen, thrusting one at her. "What are you going to draw?"

Claire blanched. "I haven't any idea."

"Draw him," Bess proposed.

"No, no. I couldn't."

"Why not? It is what you are best at—drawing people."

"Would one of you model for me?"

Gwen shook her head thoughtfully. "I think Bess is right. I think you must draw Mr. Wrede."

"Wouldn't that fall outside Mrs. Caldburn's strictures about intimacy?"

"I can't see how," Gwen told her. "It's only paper and lead."

"I would be too nervous," Claire admitted.

Bess smiled slyly. "So you like him."

"I . . . yes. I suppose I do."

"Well," Gwen began, "if I ever found a man I liked, I should want to demonstrate my best abilities for him. Which unfortunately, in my case, would require him to suffer some near-mortal wound, so that I could heal him."

"All things considered, Claire," Bess said dryly, "you have it better than Gwen. Go and draw Mr. Wrede." Still, Claire hesitated. "Or if you cannot, draw the ivy. Just go and do something; he is looking most forlorn all by himself out there!"

"Very well," Claire whispered faintly, and headed down the stairs and out into the courtyard again.

"There thou are," David Wrede said, smiling as she rejoined him. "I was beginning to think thou had decided I was not worth thy notice."

She stared. "I could never think such a thing."

He nodded toward the sketchbook. "What are thou going to draw for me?"

Claire looked at him as he stood before her in his grave black clothes, in the broad-brimmed hat. "I thought perhaps . . . the ivy on the walls."

"That would be lovely."

Did she imagine it, or did he sound disappointed? "Or I could—"

"Could what?"

She took a breath. "I could try to draw you."

His face registered surprise—no, more than surprise. Shock. "Me? Why would thou want to?"

Claire laughed, reassured; he hadn't been expecting it. "To show what you look like to me."

"I'm not sure I should care to see such a picture," he said, grimacing. But Claire had already sat down on the fountain wall and put her pencil to the page.

"Stand very still," she said.

"*How* shall I stand?"

"Just as you are now."

"But I am not doing anything in particular."

"Yes, I know. It will be better that way." Still sketching, she glanced at him. "Would you prefer, perhaps, to assume some heroic stance?"

"Oh, no. That wouldn't suit me at all."

She smiled, the lead moving swiftly across the page. "That is what I like about you, you know. You are heroic without making a fuss about it."

"I am not a bit heroic."

Claire paused, pushing back a strand of hair that had worked loose from her chignon. "You are to me."

"What, because I hurled punch at Lord Laverleigh? I'll have thee know, I've been besieged by doubt about that ever since. Was it an act of violence? If so, I have sinned."

"You didn't hurt him one bit," she pointed out.

"I offended his dignity."

"He has no dignity," she said, filling in the shadow beneath his chin. "And anyway, I was not thinking of that. I was thinking of the young lady in the garden, whom you spared from such . . ." Her voice trailed away.

"I'm not certain I spared her much," he said frankly, "if she was willing to venture into the shrubs with him in the first place."

"Don't move your head."

He obliged, and stopped talking. Claire went on sketching in a sort of a fever. She nearly had him—his sober coat, the curve of his wide mouth, his merry eyes beneath the brim of the hat. . . .

"For someone who is so holy," she observed, "there is a hint of the devil about you."

"Me?"

"Yes, you."

"There must be some mistake." He moved then, abandoning his pose and coming to her shoulder to see the sketch. "Good heavens!"

"I haven't quite got the mouth right," she apologized, eradicating a line with her india rubber. "The truth is, I can't decide how it should be—grinning, or grim."

"Thy hand is a mirror," he said in wonder. "Only thou have made me altogether too handsome."

She glanced up at him. "It is the way I see you."

"It is very flattering." He paused. "I wish I could draw thee."

She lowered her gaze to the sketchbook. "I'm not certain I would want to see it."

"Thou would be . . . more beautiful than starlight."

"Oh, no. Not I." He had her hand caught in his. She was trembling. Then he bent down and touched his mouth to hers—a slight, sweet graze. She sprang back in surprise. "Forgive me," he apologized, his face contrite but his eyes gleaming with mischief. "I could not restrain myself. It will not happen again."

"It won't?" Claire asked, and was appalled by the disappointment in her voice.

"Well . . . not unless thou wish it to."

Just then, Mrs. Treadwell bustled out from the archway. Claire hoped the headmistress hadn't seen that kiss; she would have liked to hold it to her heart alone for a little while more. "It is nearly time for supper, Claire," Mrs. Treadwell said briskly.

David Wrede took the cue. "I must be going, I'm afraid."

"So soon?" Claire asked plaintively.

Mrs. Treadwell laughed. "It has been nearly two hours!"

Impossible, Claire thought—and then caught Mr. Wrede's gaze. The regret in his eyes—and they were not always the same color at all; just now, they were struck pure gold by the late-day sun—made her knees buckle.

"I'll come back next Saturday, shall I? Or perhaps . . ."

"Yes?" Mrs. Treadwell said encouragingly.

"Do thou suppose Claire might come to meeting with me?"

"What, to a Quaker meeting?" The headmistress nearly laughed, then caught herself. "There are none hereabouts, I'm sure!"

"There is one in Swanley, where I went to school. I still go there often on the Sabbath."

"She would require a chaperone, most assuredly," Mrs. Treadwell noted—then softened. "But perhaps Madame might be free to attend."

"I would not know what to do," Claire faltered. "When to kneel . . . when to stand . . ."

"There's none of that at meeting." He smiled reassuringly.

"I'll discuss it with the countess," Mrs. Treadwell told him. "We'll let you know, either way. Make your good-bye now, Claire."

"Good-bye, Mr. Wrede."

"Good-bye, Miss Finn." But he did not move. "Am I not to have that sketch, then?"

"I . . . I thought to show it to Monsieur Battier," Claire said faintly, wondering if he could tell that she was lying.

He looked straight at her, and she knew he did—but could also tell that he was pleased. "Well, if thou would keep it . . ." He didn't bow; he just inclined his head very slightly before clapping his black hat back on. "I'll take my leave. I hope thou will come to meeting with me. It is at eight o'clock Sunday. Thank thee for letting me call."

"Thank you for coming," Claire said.

Fifteen

"*I've never been* to a Quaker meeting," the countess declared, as Stains drove the carriage toward Swanley the following Sunday—a chilly late-April morning; there had been fingers of frost on the windows of the abbey. "I don't know much about Quakers at all. But I've been reading up on them. Leon—Dr. Caplan—admires them very much indeed. He gave me several books about them, including some writings by William Penn. I'm quite intrigued by Penn. That great experiment he founded in America seems to have proven highly successful."

"What experiment is that?" Claire asked vaguely, remembering the way Mr. Wrede's lips had felt, brushing hers. She pulled the cozy carriage blanket up to her shoulders; it really was very cold.

"Why, his colony there—Pennsylvania. Where one is free to worship God in whatever way one desires."

"There cannot be so many ways as that," Claire noted, frowning.

The countess looked at her. "You would be surprised."

"The servants at home were Papists, mostly. Mama

looked down on them," Claire said thoughtfully. "I could never see why. They seemed much holier than we were. They were always crossing themselves and going to mass and muttering prayers."

"England's record of religious tolerance leaves much to be desired," the countess said, and sighed. "It is difficult to comprehend how God's messages of peace and love could cause so much bloodshed. That is what Dr. Caplan appreciates most about the Quakers—their insistence that 'Thou shalt not kill' means precisely that. Of course, his people—the Jews—have been persecuted dreadfully."

David Wrede had looked so pleased at the sketch she'd done, Claire remembered, feeling her cheeks go warm.

"As have the Quakers," Christiane mentioned.

His hand on her cheek . . . the whisper of his breath . . .

They'd reached the outskirts of Swanley. "Whereabouts is this place?" Stains called from the carriage-box.

"According to the directions Mr. Wrede sent me, we should see the school at any—ah! There it is!"

Claire stared through the window. "Where?"

"That building just ahead."

Claire craned to see the plain brick-red box, which had long windows and white trim and a pitched slate roof. "Where is the church?" she wondered, and then forgot all about that as she glimpsed Mr. Wrede, in his black coat and hat, standing by the white picket fence that surrounded the brick box. "There he is," she breathed. "Oh, Madame. How do I look?"

"Rather drab for my taste," the countess said dryly, contemplating her student's severe gray worsted coat and plain straw villager hat, from which Claire had carefully removed the ribbons. She herself was in black—the plainest gown she had, of slubbed silk, with what she'd thought was a suitably simple black silk cap edged with velvet. "But to judge from Mr. Wrede's fellow meeting-goers, we may be overdressed." The women disembarking from carriages—and even carts—at the school were all in unembellished black or gray or dun, with countrified white bonnets.

"Do you truly think so?" Claire asked anxiously. "I should not wish to embarrass him—not for the world!"

"I don't think you need fear for that," Christiane assured her, having seen Mr. Wrede's broad, handsome face light up as he glimpsed Claire through the carriage window. He strode toward them along the road, his long legs covering the distance quickly, and pulled open the door.

"Thou came," he said, and smiled into Claire's eyes. Christiane felt a pang of something—jealousy, perhaps— at the way he was looking at her. Was there anything so sweet as first love? But she, of course, was far past that.

Claire reached out to him, trembling as he lifted her down. They stood that way for a moment, their hands clasped, their gazes locked. Christiane cleared her throat, a bit petulantly, and Mr. Wrede came to his senses, lifting her down as well. "I thank thee for bringing her," he said fervently.

"I am curious myself, having never attended a Quaker meeting." He offered an arm to each of them, and they started toward the brick building.

"Here, now," Stains called after them, "what am *I* to do?"

"Come along," Mr. Wrede proposed over his shoulder.

"I don't think so," the old stableman said, with an audible sniff.

"There's the Anglican church." Mr. Wrede pointed to its steeple. "Or there's the Five Feathers, just down the High Street. They'll feed thee there."

"That's more like it," Stains declared, somewhat mollified. "What time should I be back?"

"Rather hard to say," Mr. Wrede told him. "We'll come and find thee, shall we?"

"If that's the way ye want it." Stains chucked to the team, slapping the reins, and drove hastily away.

Mr. Wrede looked after him, and then down at the

ladies. "One might think we were very devils," he said, un-
curling his slow smile. "Come this way."

He led them through the gate and into the yard. Everyone seemed to know him; Claire was introduced to more
folk in the space of ten minutes than she could recall
knowing in her entire lifetime. To a soul, they spoke the
way Wrede did, using "thee" and "thou." There were older
people, young couples, and any number of boys, whom
Claire gathered were students at the school, hailing their
host and exchanging pleasantries with him. She did her
best to smile and respond to their greetings, though she felt
terribly shy.

Then, as though at some silent signal — there wasn't
any bell — everyone filed through a set of white doors at
one end of the red brick building. Claire found herself in a
square room lined with wooden benches on all four sides.
There was no altar or organ; there were no red-velvet-pil-
lowed pews or stained-glass windows. Sunlight poured in
through the plain glass, illuminating trails of pale dust
motes. Claire and Madame and Mr. Wrede took their
places on a bench near the center of the square.

And then they sat. Nothing happened, nothing at all. No
priest entered; there were no hymns. The entire assembly,
perhaps fifty strong, simply sat, in silence. The situation
was so very odd that Claire darted a glance past Mr. Wrede
to Madame, who raised her eyebrows in return, with a hint
of a shrug. The silence continued. Claire grew restless,
found herself tapping her toes — and then realized that the
sound was audible. She quickly stilled her feet. At her side,
Mr. Wrede smiled down at her contentedly. She was about
to whisper to him — what were they waiting for? — when
an old man sitting across the room stood up.

"I have been thanking God for this glorious spring-
time," he announced. "I do not believe I have ever seen
one more lovely." There was a murmur of agreement from
the assembly. Then he sat back down.

More silence.

A man with blond hair stood up, just to Claire's left.

"Mrs. Clafton is still sick abed with the ague. Let us remember her to God."

There were nods and murmurs. He took his seat again.

A man in the front row opposite Claire rose. "Our brothers and sisters in Bohemia are faced with such dreadful persecution. May God succor them and give them strength."

"Amen," said David Wrede, nodding his head.

"Amen," Claire whispered, following his lead.

Then there ensued a very long space in which no one said anything at all. Claire fought off that itch to tap. At her side, Mr. Wrede sat amazingly still. The backless bench was far from comfortable. She looked up at the windows across the room, watched the slow dance of dust motes. Just when she was sure she could not keep her feet still one moment longer, another man, older, gray-haired, stood up and sighed.

"I continue to be troubled by our nation importing goods produced by slave labor," he announced. "It is a wrong before God. That any one of His creations should presume to own another is abhorrent. We have prayed and interceded. What more can we do to end this evil?"

To Claire's surprise, Mr. Wrede stood up. "Let those of us with businesses notify our purveyors in the most forceful way that we will not deal in goods tainted by the shame of slavery," he declared, then sat back down, to a general buzz of agreement.

"Let us refuse to buy coffee and cotton and sugar," another man put in, "since commerce in them is built upon human misery."

"Let us petition His Majesty," still another man offered, "that he examine his conscience and pray for guidance on shunning such goods as well."

This elicited an audible hum of comment. "Best not," a young woman across the aisle said tartly. "He is not likely to do so, and such a petition would only place the Friends in jeopardy."

Claire was astonished. She had never heard a woman

speak publicly in a church before. She glanced at Mr.
Wrede, expecting similar surprise at the woman's audacity.
But he was merely shaking his head.

"Miss Stapleton's qualms are certainly valid," he declared, standing again. "Still, does not Our Lord require us
to do all we can?"

Miss Stapleton was still on her feet. "Do thou seek
more martyrs, Mr. Wrede?"

"I seek God's way."

Another woman, an old one, spoke up then. "His ways
are not our ways. Yet not a sparrow falls but He sees it. His
hand guides all."

"How would we cook without sugar?" Miss Stapleton
demanded.

A boy shot up in his seat. "We could cultivate honey-
bees."

Claire was by now utterly bewildered. What sort of
church *was* this, that discussed such matters, and where
everyone, apparently, felt free to venture an opinion?

"An excellent suggestion," Mr. Wrede declared, smiling
at the boy.

"What about tea?" a black-garbed matron demanded.
"What about the poor heathen Chinese, who have no guide
to the Light?"

"There is that also," an old man said gravely.

After that, silence descended again.

It was broken, finally, by a girl no older than Claire,
who stood up in her place, with no apparent self-
consciousness, and said, "Giving up coffee and tea and
sugar seems a great sacrifice. Yet it may be one that God
demands of us. If we do not take a stand, who will?"

"There should be no overall prohibition," a man said
worriedly. "It is a matter of private conscience."

"Afraid thou will miss thy morning cup overmuch,
Josiah?" someone behind Claire murmured, and there was
a ripple of laughter. When, Christiane wondered, had she
ever heard laughter at church?

"If I thought by forgoing it I might lessen suffering,"

Josiah said stoutly, "I would give it up readily. But we have not the numbers among us to effect true change."

"It would be a start," Miss Stapleton noted, and Mr. Wrede nodded approval.

"Even the smallest pebble thrown into the ocean sets off a ripple," he noted. "But as Josiah says, it is a matter of conscience. Let each of us look to his own, and do accordingly. We have no right to dictate to one another, after all."

Claire darted another glance at Madame. She was sitting on the edge of the bench, her back ramrod straight, following the speakers the way one might follow a lawn-tennis match, with utmost attention.

"On that matter of conscience," an elderly man far in the back across the room put in, "I have a concern. Any number of valiant soldiers who fought in His Majesty's wars have come home only to find the pensions promised them lacking. Disappointed they take to the highways; they maraud and do harm."

He paused for breath. The indomitable Miss Stapleton said sharply, "They made their bed when they signed on to murder God's own."

The old man eyed her steadily. "We are all in agreement, I trust, Miss Stapleton, that there is no excuse for taking the life of a fellow human being—not even war. Yet His Majesty has sentenced many of these soldiers convicted of crimes to capital punishment. There are hangings every day at the Tower. Have we not a duty to protest this wrong?"

"What have thou in mind, Silas?" David Wrede asked then.

"I don't know," the speaker admitted. "But my conscience tells me I must do something, or be guilty of their blood by proxy."

"Perhaps a petition to His Majesty?" someone else proposed.

"We might circulate it among the meetings," a broad-faced woman just across from Claire suggested.

"He won't listen. He won't care," Miss Stapleton said scathingly. "He is a sewer of—"

"Please, Miss Stapleton!" Wrede spoke up, with an anxious glance at Claire.

She sat wringing her hands, which had gone suddenly clammy. When she had entered the meetinghouse, she'd thought it very chilly, but now it seemed unbearably warm. She saw the dust motes streaming down in bright waterfalls of sunlight; she heard more voices chiming in, arguing, but it seemed they came from a long way off. She swayed a little on the bench. Her toes were tapping madly, wildly. Her teeth were chattering. She could not decide if she was cold or hot. The sea of faces surrounding her swam in and out of her vision, distorting, shifting, changing. Miss Stapleton stood up to speak again, and her mouth seemed to open and close, open and close soundlessly, like that of a fish. Claire smelled a thousand different smells: boot-blacking, soap, sweat, pomade. She swayed again, saw Mr. Wrede's face swim toward hers, his brown-gold eyes enormous, his mouth a gaping hole. She thought he spoke her name.

She stood up. She groped toward the countess. "I," she started to say, but somehow the word turned into a scream. And now that she had started, she could not stop screaming.

The sea of faces was staring at her, accusatory, blaming.

She shut her eyes tight against the barrage. And then everything went dim.

Sixteen

"I'm so sorry," Christiane told Gannon in a whisper, as they stood beside the bed in the darkened room. "I never imagined . . . who would have imagined? She seemed fine; she seemed gay. She was so glad to see him, and he her."

"There was no hint . . . nothing at all," echoed the black-clad young man who sat holding tightly to Claire's hand.

"What does Dr. Caplan say?" Gannon demanded.

"Some sort of hysteria . . . a delayed reaction to the shock of her parents' death," the countess told him.

"It's not physical?"

"He thinks not. There's no sign of any illness."

Gannon stared down grimly at his niece's motionless form. "What's his prognosis?"

"He doesn't know," Christiane whispered. "I am sorry, Gannon. I feel it is my responsibility."

"Not thine. Mine," Mr. Wrede said resolutely. "It was my suggestion that she come to meeting. It could have been the cold . . . the chill . . ."

Gannon was feeling a chill in his soul. "What precisely happened?"

Wrede shrugged, looking pain-stricken, bewildered. "She just . . . stood up. She moved toward the countess. And then she collapsed."

"Was there incense, perhaps? An overwhelming odor of flowers?"

"We've none of that at meeting."

"Well, what do you have?" Gannon demanded impatiently.

"They only talk," the countess told him, trying to soothe him. "There was only discussion. They spoke of the weather, and who amongst them was unwell, and of social ills."

The sickly sensation in Gannon's bowels intensified. "What social ills?" he managed to say.

"Slavery," Wrede told him. "Whether we should stop buying coffee and sugar to protest it. And—and—" He looked helplessly at the countess. "I cannot even recall."

"Capital punishment. The rogue soldiers," she reminded him.

"Oh, yes. The veterans of the war whom His Majesty has sentenced to die for crimes they say they committed because their pensions have not been paid."

Christiane let out a gasp. "It could have been that—oh, it must have been! Perhaps she was reminded of the monsters who attacked her parents!"

"I never dreamed," Wrede said miserably, holding tight to Claire's small hand. "I never thought—"

Somehow, Gannon managed to push past his own fears and take pity on the young man. "Of course you didn't, Wrede. No one is blaming you. Has she come back to her senses at all?"

"Not really," Christiane said fretfully, biting her lip. "Though she does speak sometimes—says the wildest things."

Oh, Christ. "What sorts of things?" Gannon asked in dread.

She looked to Wrede, who said haltingly, "Horses. Something about white horses. That they'll never be the same again."

Gannon closed his eyes against the image of blood spattered across the white flanks of his brother's team. "Gannon?" Christiane said anxiously, touching his elbow. "Are you all right?" And the brief human contact, her gentleness, brought him close to tears. *Am I all right? No, I am dying. I am being swallowed alive. . . .*

He opened his eyes, looked down at her, tried to smile. When he'd first brought Claire to this place and saw Christiane, he'd thought it the end of the world. Now he could not imagine his niece in anyone else's care.

"No doubt it was only the talk of the brigands," he said reassuringly. "We forget sometimes . . . everyone says how quickly young people heal. But her experience that day was so filled with horror—how can any of us presume to understand what scars it may have left on her mind, or what triggers can reopen the wounds? We will have to move cautiously, do our best to protect her."

"I will protect her," Wrede said stoutly.

"She is fortunate to have you, Mr. Wrede."

The door behind them opened. "Back again," Leon Caplan said softly but cheerfully, entering with his black bag. "How is the patient?"

"Quiet now," Christiane informed him.

"That would be the laudanum." The doctor went to the bedside, took Claire's free hand, felt her pulse, laid his palm on her forehead, gently raised one eyelid first and then the other with his fingertips. She never stirred. "Her breathing is more regular," he announced, "and she's cooled down some. Both good signs. Pupils dilated, but that's to be expected. If she grows restless, you may administer a few more drops of the tincture. No more than four every five hours, however. We don't want her habituated."

"What's that?" Gannon asked.

Christiane stepped in. "I beg your pardon; I've not

made introductions. Dr. Caplan, this is Miss Finn's uncle, Lord Carew."

"How do you do," said Gannon, extending his hand. "Thank you so much for looking after my niece."

"I wish I could do more. Habituation, Lord Carew, is the result of repeated adminstration of a narcotic. The body requires more and more of it to achieve the desired results. And over time—"

"Well, how long do you think she'll need it?"

"Impossible to say. Her reaction to whatever stimulus induced this derangement—"

"Don't," Gannon nearly shouted, and then caught himself as Claire stirred fitfully. "Don't use that word," he said. "She is not deranged."

"I beg your pardon," Dr. Caplan said after a moment's pause. "It is a medical term. I meant no disrespect. The point is, her reaction was extremely strong, from what the countess and Mr. Wrede tell me. Even when they brought her home, she was still unconscious, breathing shallowly, with her heart rate high."

"We took her to an inn there at Swanley," Christiane explained to Gannon, "but when hours and hours had passed with no improvement—and the physician there was an utter idiot—I thought it best to return her here, to Dr. Caplan's care."

"I am not about to quibble with your judgment, Christiane—this once," he told her, with a ghost of a smile.

Just then, Claire sat up in bed, so abruptly that everyone jumped a little; it was like seeing the dead come to life. She opened her eyes, but did not seem to see them. Her mouth opened as well, while she stared straight ahead. "The horses," she whispered. "The pretty, pretty horses. Oh, the poor horses!"

Mr. Wrede leaned toward her, caressing her hand. But she shook him off, clutching at the bedclothes, her knuckles pale. "The horses!" she cried, eyes still staring at nothing. "They will never be the same!" Tears rolled down her cheeks, splashing onto the coverlet. Gannon thought his heart would break.

"Give her more laudanum," he told the doctor.

"I can't. It's too soon since the last dose."

"Oh, God, the horses!" Claire wailed, as Wrede sought to comfort her, hold her to his chest. She collapsed against him, sobbing: "The horses. The pretty white horses. The horses. The horses!"

"Well, do something, dammit!" Gannon begged. Wrede was holding Claire tightly, smoothing her hair, whispering to her, but she flailed against him, straining to break free. Christiane had moved to the bed as well, was attempting to soothe her.

"It's all right, Claire. It's only a dream," she murmured.

"It's not! It's not a dream at all!"

Gannon glared at the doctor. "How can you stand by and see her suffer? You call yourself a physician!"

"I attend to the body," Caplan said helplessly. "I've no sway over the mind."

"The horses." Claire was whispering now, whimpering. "What will become of the horses?"

Wrede spoke up, unexpectedly. "Claire. We have the horses. The horses are fine."

She turned to him. "They are?" she asked breathlessly.

"They are."

"And it doesn't show?"

Wrede glanced at the doctor, who shrugged a little and nodded. "No," Wrede told her. "It doesn't show at all."

For a moment, Claire seemed to approach coherence. "I cannot imagine how you managed that," she murmured in wonder, and let him settle her back onto the pillows. "It's the last thing I would have thought of you."

"Oh, I'm very good with horses," Wrede assured her.

"You must be." She let him draw the coverlet up around her again.

"Sleep now, Claire," he told her. "You must rest. I'll see to the horses."

"Well . . . so long as you are in charge of them . . ."

"I am."

"I'm so tired," Claire whispered.

"Sleep, then, my love." Wrede's eyes flickered to Gannon, as though expecting a rebuke. But Lord Carew was regarding him with a sort of awe. Claire sighed and smiled, and went back to sleep.

Again the door opened. "My turn at the watch," Mrs. Treadwell announced cheerily. "Christiane, you really must get some rest. You, too, Mr. Wrede."

"I'd like to stay," he offered, and looked once more at Gannon. "If Lord Carew doesn't mind, that is."

"Mind? Hell, no, I don't mind," Gannon said, rather explosively. Privately he thought: *I'd get whatever sort of minister marries Quakers in here this moment, if I could. I'd wed her to you in her sleep.*

"It's another two hours still before she can be given more laudanum," Dr. Caplan put in. "I'll stop by first thing in the morning."

"Thank you," Christiane told him. "Can I offer you supper? Tea? Coffee? Or something stronger?"

But he shook his head. "Mrs. Treadwell fed me earlier. And both of Mrs. Lalley's twins in the village have croup. I must stop in there."

Gannon came to his senses, reaching for his wallet. "I must give you something for your trouble, Doctor." He started to peel off notes, but Christiane stayed his hand.

"It's been seen to," she said softly. "Come. *You* need supper—and a whiskey, if I'm not mistaken."

"I don't like to leave her."

"Tut," Mrs. Treadwell declared, smiling at Mr. Wrede. "She is in excellent hands."

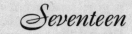

Seventeen

He ate what Clarisse set before him at the table in the parlor, methodically, without appetite. He heard Christiane make various attempts at conversation. He drank three whiskeys as he did. The last one hit him hard; he felt that he could breathe again.

She was apologizing. "I ought to have consulted you, of course, before we went. . . ."

"Stop that," he said, and she stared at him across the table. Her eyes were huge in the candlelight, great pools of grape-black. He sought a more civilized tone. "You did nothing wrong, Christiane. You did what you thought best."

"Yes, but perhaps—"

He had speared a bite of blackberry pie on his fork, had brought it to his mouth. Now he stopped, looking at it, and set the fork down. "He's good for her, isn't he?" he said.

"He seems to be the only thing that is." She hesitated. "Are you . . . I don't want to rush you, but are you finished? I should like to send Clarisse to bed."

"What time is it?"

"Nearly two."

"Good God. Yes. I'm finished. By all means." He pushed his plate away. Christiane rang for the maid, who came in, yawning.

"That will be all for tonight," Christiane told her.

"I'm sorry for the trouble," Gannon chimed in, and gave the maid his best smile. "The pie was very good. On a par, I'd say, with the quince tart." But Clarisse was too weary to muster anything more than a nod.

"Another whiskey?" Christiane offered when the maid had left them.

He shook his head. "I could use a bed, though."

She frowned. "Gentlemen callers put up at the White Fox, in the village."

"You're letting Wrede stay."

"You're damned right I am. For as long as he will."

"You think I should be in there with her."

She sighed. "That wasn't what I meant at all. Mrs. Treadwell will let us know if there is any change."

"Do you mind if I smoke?" She shook her head. He took out a cheroot, contemplated it.

"Gannon," she began, very softly, "you really must—"

"Don't lecture me," he said abruptly. "I couldn't stand it." And he looked at her. "I know I've failed her."

"No, no! You haven't failed her at all! I was going to say you must not be so hard on yourself."

"I have failed her, though."

"I don't see how you can say that. You have been a faithful visitor. She always looks forward to seeing you."

"You don't think today's events are proof she is not . . . happy?"

"I've no notion what today's events are proof of," Christiane confessed. She did not like to see him berating himself this way. She made her tone crisp, lively. "She gets along so well with her form-mates. She is a delight to Mrs. Treadwell and me. And Monsieur Battier is absolutely enthralled at finally having a student with talent."

"Must you try so hard to cheer me up?"

She laughed. "Am I that evident?"

"You are." He glanced down at the cigar he held. "Have you a light?"

"A light. Yes. I have." She went to the corner cabinet, brought matches, struck one and held it up for him. He stared at the little flame.

"Gannon?"

He raised his head. His eyes met hers. She felt a physical jolt as she looked into their gray depths, as though she had bumped up against something hard and inviolable—something that had always been there but that she'd never glimpsed before.

The match in her hand hissed and flared.

He reached toward her, curled his fingers over hers. "You'll burn yourself," he cautioned.

Somehow, she didn't care.

He drew his lips together, pursed them. The motion emphasized the chiseled line of his upper lip, and the pouty, contrasting curve of his lower one, so full and soft. She could not look away.

In a sudden swift motion, he blew out the flame and then pulled her into his lap, pressing those lips to hers.

Her first instinct was to recoil. No—not her first instinct, but the one on which she acted. "Gannon, don't," she said, pushing back from his embrace.

"Why not?" he asked fiercely, his arm circling her shoulder, his fingers stroking the swell of her breast through her black silk gown. He found her nipple, pinched it. Christiane felt desire surge through her, full-blown and furious.

"Because we must not," she began, but his mouth claimed hers again, silencing her. He ran his tongue over her lips with hungry force as he pushed the gown from her shoulder. His fingertips smoothed her skin, lightly, gently. Then he buried his face against her and sighed—a desperate sound.

"Gannon, please!" she hissed, hearing footfalls in the hallway. "Someone will come upon us!"

"Christ, if that's all that worries you—" He reached out and snuffed the candles on the table with his fingertips. Obliterating darkness enfolded them. She struggled in his arms, then froze as in the hallway, the footsteps paused.

"Milady?" Clarisse's voice, sounding puzzled.

Gannon had his palm across Christiane's mouth. She heard his harsh, ragged breathing at her ear, could feel his manhood, hard as rock, pushing at her skirts as she lay across his legs. She hesitated, feeling for all the world like a wicked, wild girl; her every sensation—his rough hand, his breath, the scent of his skin, the brush of his hair on her bare shoulder—was as vividly heightened as the first time she'd been alone in the dark with a man.

He took his hand from her lips. "Just putting out the candles, Clarisse," she heard herself say, and felt his grin stretch against her throat.

"Well . . . good night, then," Clarisse called, a shrug in her tone.

"Good night indeed," Gannon murmured, making Christiane giggle a little, headily. He reached behind her to undo her bodice, kissing her frantically.

She was as wildly eager as he was; she yanked at his cravat, unwinding it and tossing it into the sheltering darkness. Her fingers fumbled as she unbuttoned his shirt, laid his chest bare. He had her gown pushed down to her waist and was fighting with her stays. One hook . . . another . . . another. "Oh, God," he said, covering her breasts with his hands as he freed them at last. He smoothed their curves, cupped them, raised one to his lips, caught the taut nipple and sucked at it, so hard that she gasped. But he only took more of her into his mouth, panting eagerly.

"The . . . the arm of the chair," Christiane began. It was cutting into her bared back.

"Quite right," he said, and shoved the chair away beneath him, tumbling them to the floor. They landed in a tangled heap of hair and disheveled clothing. Christiane could not help but laugh.

"You are behaving like a sex-starved eighteen-year-old!" she whispered, as he fumbled to yank up her skirts.

"I *am* a sex-starved eighteen-year-old, when it comes to you." He'd found the hem at last, fought through a barrage of petticoats to her stockinged calf, caressed it. "Ouch! Damn! Was that your heel you just dug into my groin?"

"I'm afraid so."

"We must lose those boots, or you will castrate me." He knelt beside her and tugged at the laces.

"Stop pulling; you'll only tighten the knots."

"I can't see a damned thing," he said impatiently.

"Here." She sat up, pushing him away, and unlaced the boots. All the while, he was touching her, leaning in to kiss her, putting his hands to her unruly curls. "It would go faster if you'd stop that," she suggested.

"Who's in a rush?" But he was already pulling the boots off, and her stockings, too. He lifted her skirts with a whoosh, laid his hand squarely on her mound of Venus. She felt the heat of his fingers through the sheer cambric of her drawers. He was still kneeling over her, his free hand popping the buttons on his breeches, then yanking them down. She reached up, found his manhood and grasped it. It was as splendid as she'd remembered. He drew his breath in sharply as her hand closed on him.

"Not so fast. Not so fast," he warned. Christiane discovered, however, that she was rife with recklessness, replete with abandon. She began to stroke him, and he had to force her hand away.

"Not yet," he whispered, his voice strained.

"I don't care to wait," she retorted.

"Yet I mean you to." He shifted so that he straddled her, supporting himself with one arm while he untied her drawers and eased them down over her hips.

"That is rather impressive in a man your age," she noted.

He snorted. "I'll show you what a man my age can do."

He did mean to make her wait, though. He dawdled over her breasts, licking trails of kisses from one to the other, teasing their tips with his tongue until her breath grew quick. Then, his lips still caressing her, he slipped his hand between her thighs. "Already wet for me," he noted in satisfaction, running his thumb quickly across her vulva and then deeper, inside her. Christiane let out a short, sharp moan of pleasure. "I recall that you liked that," he told her, and she shivered beneath him: *How could he remember? It had been so very long ago. . . .*

"And this as well." He withdrew his thumb, then pushed inside her more gently with two fingers, their tips softly feathering, tickling her warm, slick sheath. Her moans quickened; her hips began to move, rising to meet his touch, pressing in slow circles, responding to the pressure that was building inside her.

"And this." Even as those long, strong fingers caressed her, his thumb pressed down on the bud of her desire, teased it mercilessly. Christiane arched her back in a long, soundless sigh. She was on fire; he had set rivers, oceans of fire loose inside her. Wild with impatience, she grabbed for his manhood, felt a drop of liquid at its head, spread it with her fingertip across the smooth skin and down over the vein-swollen side. He shuddered bodily, from head to toe.

"Now," she whispered, guiding him toward her.

"No. No. Not yet. There is so much more I long to do to you . . . for you."

"Do this for me. Now." She parted her knees, felt the brush of the carpet on her bared buttocks—God, what would Evelyn say? Just the thought made her laugh.

"What? What is it?" He sounded wary, as though he feared she might be laughing at him.

She put a hand to his face, smoothed his cheek, felt the bristle of beard there. "Nothing," she said fiercely. "Come into me. Come . . . inside me." And then she softened enough to add, "Please."

"Well, since you ask so nicely—" He reared back and plunged into her, reaching straight to her soul.

"Oh!" Christiane gasped as he filled her. *"Oh . . ."* Very

gently, he laid his hand across her mouth to quiet her, even as he withdrew and drove into her again. She bit her lip to stifle her cries, but an anxious, hungry moan escaped.

"You lied when you told me you feigned your pleasure that night, didn't you?" he whispered, withdrawing once more.

She tried to pull him toward her, but he stayed arched above her, unmoving. "Didn't you?" he demanded.

"Yes. Yes!" She would have done anything, said anything, to have him fill her that way just one time more. And anyway, it was the truth.

Satisfied, he lowered himself into her again, settling, exploring, his hips grinding against hers. She echoed his movements, mirrored them, tilting to open herself to him like a flower in the night. Now it was his turn to groan, with frantic longing. "I knew it was a lie," he told her, withdrawing and thrusting. She wrapped her legs around him, seeking to draw him even deeper, further inside her, while he kissed her hair, her neck, her forehead. Then, abruptly, they found the rhythm that suited them both—a wild, headlong pace. He drove into her, and she welcomed him, met him, matched him, urged him on with her frantic, mounting sighs. He hitched her toward him, hands cupping her buttocks in a final adjustment—and then they were both caught up in the motion, the dance, the drive to final ecstasy. She reached her climax an instant before he did; she parted her lips in a wordless cry of joy just as his seed burst into her in a white-hot rush. He grunted, pushing hard at her, staying there, pouring himself out, while she clung to him and buried her face against his shoulder to muffle her gratified sighs.

He fell against her in exhaustion. She kept him there, her hands inside his shirt, holding him fast. *It might be wrong, but it had been marvelous!* she thought, her heart still pounding madly. Even more marvelous than in Paris, because this time he had been so masterful, sure of himself. . . .

He turned his head slightly, licked at her ear. "Mmm,"

she whispered, stretching as well as she could beneath his weight, reaching up to stroke his hair. He nuzzled her throat, and she thanked God for the darkness, that hid from him all the damage two decades had done to her. He could not see the crow's-feet, the white hairs, the laxness of her thighs and breasts. To him, she was just as she had been then, had been ever since in his memory. For a moment, she felt like an imposter. Then she shrugged the thought off. He was becoming rather heavy, but did not seem inclined to move.

"I have dreamed of this," he told her, his mouth still at her ear. "More times than you could imagine." Then he rolled off her onto his side and brought his hand to her face, cupping her chin. "I don't suppose . . . you ever dreamed of me."

What to say to that? She was grateful again for the darkness. "When I saw you again . . ." she began.

"Aye?" he asked quickly.

"It was . . . as though you had not changed at all." That wasn't truth. "I thought you had become even more handsome," she confessed, oddly shy.

"I did not know you thought me handsome at all in Paris," he said huskily, and kissed her. "It might have altered my life if I had."

"I did not treat you well," she said breathlessly. "I am sorry for that."

"You more than made up for it tonight." Suddenly he flopped onto his back, pulling her to his chest. "And what do we do now? Shall I have to wait another two decades for a repeat performance?"

"I—" Christiane froze. There were footsteps in the corridor again. She glanced uncertainly in the direction of the door.

He had heard them as well; he shifted, seeking to pull up his breeches. But even as he did, the door suddenly opened in a crack of light that widened to encompass the room.

"I really think a small glass of sherry, under the circumstances," Mrs. Treadwell said cheerfully, ushering Mr. Wrede in.

On the floor, on the carpet, two guilty figures scrambled wildly to straighten their clothes.

The headmistress paused, hearing the rustle. "Who's there?" she demanded, and bustled to the table, finding the tapers, striking a match. She set the flame to a candle, then stared in horror at what the incipient light revealed. "Good God! Christiane! Lord Carew! Have you no shame?"

If her revels with Gannon had made Christiane feel young again, the headmistress's shock reminded her with a thud of how outrageous her behavior was. "It . . . it isn't what you think," she mumbled, gathering her bodice up frantically.

Evelyn glared at her. "What else *could* it be?"

Mr. Wrede was backing through the door. "I'll get on back to Miss Finn, then—"

Evelyn stood as straight and stiff as a Valkyrie. "And as for you, Lord Carew—with your niece lying helpless and ill—"

"This has nothing to do with Claire," he protested, scrambling to his feet, still buttoning his breeches.

"And that's precisely the point! It's clear she is the farthest thing from your thoughts, either of you! You can think only of your own selfish, craven desires!"

It wasn't like that, Christiane wanted to tell her. *Not at all. It just . . . happened.* But something in Evelyn's fierce stance warned her to keep her mouth shut.

"The fault is all mine." Lord Carew had got his breeches done up, was shrugging back into his coat.

"I very much doubt *that!*" Evelyn declared, her blue gaze skewering Christiane. "I've always been afraid of something like this, you know. Afraid that having you associated with the academy would finally pull it down—"

Oh, that was unfair. "There wouldn't *be* any academy without me!" Christiane cried.

"Perhaps not—but that might be for the best!"

"For heaven's sake, Evelyn! We have been friends for

thirty years." Christiane's attempts at reasonableness were somewhat undercut by the fact that she was trying to do up her stays. "Surely you don't intend for one small lapse in judgment—"

"Is that what it was?" Carew demanded, his voice very cold indeed.

"Oh, Gannon, I didn't mean—Evelyn, don't look at me that way, please!"

But the headmistress had the diamond hardness in her blue eyes with which the tigers of the ton had once faced Christiane down and driven her abroad. "I should prefer not to look at you at all, frankly," she said curtly. "And I cannot—simply *cannot*—imagine what Mr. Wrede must think of the two of you. I must go and try to make amends with him." She turned that skewering gaze on Carew. "Why you would jeopardize your niece's best chance at happiness for the sake of a—a cheap roll in the hay is beyond my comprehension."

"Evelyn," Christiane said pleadingly.

"You make me sick, both of you," the headmistress said in derision, and turned on her heel, slamming shut the door.

Christiane had the stays fastened; now she pulled up her sleeves, fingers trembling.

"A lapse in judgment?" Carew said, glowering down at her.

"Of course it was!" she snapped. "Adults don't fornicate on rugs on the floors of parlors! I can't imagine what I was thinking, to allow you to do that to me."

"To *allow* me to—" He was incredulous. "You begged me for it! 'Come into me—come inside me, please,' " he mimed, in a fair estimation of her breathless entreaty.

"You are a bastard!" Christiane snapped, and swung her palm toward his face. He caught her wrist, though, and held it.

"Why won't you admit what you feel for me?"

"I feel nothing but contempt for you," she said, her voice controlled now, low. "Evelyn is right. What sort of man would have such indecent longings while his closest kin lies at death's door?"

"Oh, so you are siding with the tigers now! How odd, considering that only moments ago, you were welcoming my embraces." She started to speak. "And don't you *dare*," he thundered, "try to tell me you were feigning this time!"

"You caught me off guard. You forced yourself on—" But even she realized how false that sounded. He was laughing, backing away, shaking his head at her.

"I'm beginning to credit Lord Weatherston's story," he said, "when he denounced you as a whore to the ton. I can't be sure about other men, but God knows *I* haven't found your fortifications particularly difficult to breach."

"Oh! Get out of my sight!" Christiane screamed at him. "I hate you! I hate you!"

"Gladly. After all, I got what I came for," Gannon Finn declared with a satisfied smile.

If she had had a weapon, a gun, a knife, she truly would have killed him. She was absolutely dumb with rage.

He hitched his breeches up, straightened his cravat, went to the table and retrieved his cheroot, then drained the last of his wine. "Sleep tight, *milady*," he said with derision. "And by the way, you're starting to go a bit gray. Did you know that?" He headed for the door. "I'll be at the White Fox if Claire should need me. If you should need me as well, of course." He winked at her lasciviously.

She rushed at him, fists raised in fury. But her tangled skirts slowed her, and he slipped through the door with a sly, knowing grin, leaving her flushed and breathless and drenched in shame.

Eighteen

Christiane spent a miserable night in her narrow bed, alternating between horrified memories of that interlude on the parlor floor—oh, God, she really *had* begged for him!—and equally awful anticipation of what the morning would bring. What would—what *could*—she ever say to Evelyn in expiation? Her old friend was right; she had been unspeakably, unforgivably wanton. She had behaved like a schoolgirl—no, that wasn't fair to the girls, none of whom would ever have disgraced themselves that way. *I shall resign,* she thought, though the prospect tore at her heart. But what choice did she have? How could she stay on and face Evelyn's accusing stares? More importantly, how could she ever even pretend to provide counsel to the students who relied on her, looked to her as an example?

I have thrown everything away—everything, she thought cravenly, and felt slow tears slide down her cheeks. She could not remember the last time she had cried. But now that she had begun, she could not seem to stop; the tears just went on flowing, while she buried her head beneath her pillow to stifle her sobs.

After a long time, after what seemed like hours, the flood finally subsided, curtailed by a nascent shoot of righteous anger. She had done wrong, yes, but who was more at fault, she or Gannon? He had begun it all, hadn't he, when he'd pulled her into his lap without a hint of warning? And she was quite sure she knew *why* he had done so—as recompense for the way she had behaved toward him in Paris two decades before. As his petty stab at revenge. Look at how he'd laughed at her as he was leaving, and that cruel jibe he'd made about her hair! He had bided his time for twenty years, waiting for his chance to pay her back for having rejected him. The realization made her shiver. Who in his right mind would hold a grudge for so long a time?

Oddly enough, viewing matters in that light helped to clear her thoughts. She knew now what she must say to Evelyn in the morning. It was the only chance she had at making amends.

She duly presented herself in the parlor before breakfast, knowing she would find her old friend there. "Evelyn."

The headmistress did not even look up, simply went on perusing the bills of account she was tallying. Christiane crossed to her, touched her shoulder. "Evelyn. There is something I must say to you."

"That you are proffering your resignation, I trust," Mrs. Treadwell said briefly, turning over a page in her ledger book.

"I will, if you like."

"Very well. I accept it. I have a cheque made out to you for your share of the profits, negligible though they are, up through the end of the year. Will that be satisfactory?"

"I don't want the money. I want—Evelyn, I have something to confess."

"Something *more*?" the headmistress said acidly. "I don't believe I care to hear it."

Christiane took a breath. "You asked me once whether I had bedded Lord Carew in Paris. I . . . evaded the question in such a way that you were misled. He and I did sleep together there."

"Why am I not astonished?"

"But it is the *circumstances*—"

"Oh, do share all. Let no lascivious detail go untold."

Despite the gravity of the situation, Christiane could not hold back a smile. "I love it when you don your full ton armor, Evelyn."

The headmistress sighed, crossing her arms on her desk. "Better that than to loll about naked on the floor with every Tom, Dick, and—"

"I have been perfectly chaste—up until last night—for nigh on five years!" Christiane said heatedly.

"Well, bully for you. I have been a widow for eight— and it was a good many years before that that I'd last shared Everly's bed."

"Do you never find yourself . . . *lonely*?"

"If I do, I have a glass of sherry," the headmistress said briskly.

"I've tried that. It doesn't work for me."

"Or I divert my energies into my work."

"I work as hard as you do, Evelyn! Can't you have a bit of pity on me?"

"For what? For that shameless display you put on last evening? I hardly see that pity is warranted for such a self-indulgent wallow in venality!"

Christiane sighed. "You are absolutely correct, of course. I'd only hoped that you would let me explain . . . oh, Evelyn, listen to me, do! I've told you how Carew pestered me in Paris. But what I didn't confess was that . . . over the course of time, he wore me down. I found myself flattered by his persistence. And Jean-Baptiste was *always* away, night after night, day after day, busy with the war. And—"

"I'm not at all sure I want to hear this."

"But you must. I need to make you see . . . there was one night, one night only, I swear it. I was low. I felt abandoned by Jean-Baptiste; I felt as though he cared more for

Napoleon than for me. Lord Carew played on my qualms.
He was—he *is*—very clever. I was flirting with him a bit.
I may have led him on." Her friend arched her brows.
"Very well. I *did* lead him on. What can I say? I was young
and foolish. We stayed behind at a table after the house had
closed, after everyone else had gone. We were drinking
champagne. Then Jean-Baptiste arrived, quite unexpect-
edly. Carew announced that he intended to challenge him.
I was trying to prevent it. I spirited him up into my rooms.
I meant only to avoid a confrontation between them, as
God is my witness! But then . . . well . . . one thing led to
another. And we had relations."

Evelyn was saucer-eyed. "With Jean-Baptiste downstairs?"

"I had the maid tell him I was ill and could not be dis-
turbed." Christiane blushed, but met her friend's stare.
"Oh, confess it, Evelyn! Did you never do anything in your
youth that you are now ashamed of?"

"Nothing like that, I can assure you!" There was a moment's pause. Then, "Well? What was it like?" the headmistress demanded.

"He was the finest lover I have ever had."

Evelyn sniffed. "I can hardly match your wealth of experience, having confined my relations to my lawful husband. But I must say, I never found sexual congress with
him so scintillating that I was tempted to seek out more of
it than I had by necessity to accept."

"Did you never climax?"

"Did I never what?"

"Achieve orgasm. You know. *Le petit mort.* 'The little
death.' "

"I was *bored* to death, if that's what you mean."

"Oh, Evelyn!" Christiane was aghast. "You did not
enjoy it? *Ever*?"

"I did not mind the kissing so much. But the rest of it—
all that pushing and shoving and groping and sweating and
grunting on Mr. Treadwell's part—I found it most distasteful, to be frank. Not to mention undignified."

Christiane was beginning to realize, with growing despair, just how incomprehensible her behavior on the previous night had been to her old friend. "You must take my word for it, Evelyn—lovemaking can be the most extraordinary, marvelous, *transporting* experience—"

"Well, that's what men would have us think, isn't it?" Mrs. Treadwell said stiffly.

"But it's true!"

"And that's what your assignation with Lord Carew in Paris proved to be."

"Yes," Christiane said bravely. "It was, as it happens. It went quite beyond anything I had ever experienced with Jean-Baptiste."

"I wonder, then, that you did not throw your soldier over instantly in favor of him," Evelyn noted, her voice very tart.

"Perhaps I should have. But I didn't."

Evelyn turned in her chair. "Why not, Christiane?"

The countess flounced toward the window and drew aside the drapes, staring into the courtyard. "Carew confused me. He flummoxed me. I thought . . . I hoped . . . I only wanted for him to go away, to leave me in peace. Jean-Baptiste and I had been happy before that—before him. And afterward . . . I was so frightened, Evelyn. I was afraid I never would be happy again." She paused. "Last night when he grabbed me, pulled me into his lap—I was not expecting it. Why should I have been? It had been twenty years. And yet he remembered things . . ." She colored again. "I should have been stronger. But he has a way of preying on my weaknesses. He always has had." She straightened her shoulders. "He will not, though, anymore."

"What has caused this sea change?" Mrs. Treadwell inquired, sounding unconvinced.

"When he was holding me . . . making love to me," Christiane said haltingly, "I felt . . . like a reckless, wild girl again. But that was when the candles were extinguished. Once you relit them . . . he mocked me, Evelyn.

After you had gone. He taunted me that I was old, that my hair is gray. It was plain enough that he only seduced me as a form of revenge." And she hung her head. "I know I deserve every harsh word you have to lay on me. I only said as much to myself, and worse, all last night. I've been a dreadful fool."

Evelyn's round face softened a bit. "There, there. So you have, but haven't we all? If I sounded harsh . . . well, perhaps I was just a tad jealous of you. No man has ever pulled *me* down onto a parlor carpet and made love to me. Not, of course, that I would acquiesce if one did. Still, you have had your adventures. You continue to have them. And I . . . never do."

Christiane sensed redemption. Her dark eyes narrowed devilishly. "Lord Carew would no doubt leap at the chance to add you to his list of conquests. If you would like me to put in a word . . ."

"Christiane! You are quite dreadful!" The headmistress simultaneously blushed and giggled. Then her expression turned slightly wistful. "What is it, exactly, that he does that is so marvelous?"

"Exactly?"

"Well . . . within the limits of decent conversation."

"There is nothing I can tell you, then."

Evelyn's mouth formed an O. "But it is all just hands and lips and . . . and unmentionable bodily parts. How different can it be from one man to the next?"

Christiane pondered what to say. Then inspiration struck her. "You have had Cook's chocolate charlotte."

"Only every Thursday for the past three years."

"What do you think of it?"

"It's quite tasty," Evelyn noted, somewhat puzzled. "A trifle heavy, perhaps."

"But have you had the chocolate charlotte they serve at Gaillard's, in London?"

"Of course I have! It is positively *heavenly* the way Gaillard's makes it. Another matter altogether—so rich and dense, and yet as light as . . ." Her eyes were dreamy;

her voice trailed away, and there was a moment's silence. Then, "Oh," she said. "I see."

"It is only cream and sugar and chocolate," Christiane said with a shrug.

"Well! That is a most instructive analogy, I must say. And I shall never again be able to consume chocolate charlotte without thinking of it, more's the rue. Still, I believe I shall confine my experiments to the gustatory realm. And I do wish you would do the same in the future."

"Does that mean you forgive me?"

"I do."

"Oh, Evelyn, you are too good for words!" The countess enveloped her in a grateful hug.

"So long as," the headmistress said sternly, from within her embrace, "I have your absolute assurance that nothing like this will ever happen again!"

"Oh, you do. I swear it! Anyway, I shall never look on Carew without the utmost scorn for his cruelty to me last night."

"Did he really throw your gray hair up at you?"

"In my face!"

"Men are devils." Mrs. Treadwell tsked.

"That they are," Christiane agreed darkly. "And he is Old Scratch himself. I will never, *never* let him take advantage of me again."

"There is still the matter of Mr. Wrede," Evelyn noted fretfully. "I must confess, I did not have the nerve to speak to him last night about what he witnessed there in the parlor."

"Would you like for me to apologize to him?"

"Oh, if you would!"

Christiane hugged her old friend again. "Of course I will. It seems small enough recompense for having you welcome your prodigal partner home!"

Since there seemed nothing to be gained by delaying such an unpleasant mission, Christiane headed directly from the parlor to the room where Claire was ensconced. She pushed the door open quietly and saw the patient lying in her bed, motionless and pale. Mr. Wrede was seated at her side, still holding her hand, with the most amazing expression of rapt concern on his face.

"Excuse me," Christiane murmured, and felt her blush rise.

Mr. Wrede turned to her. "She is better this morning, I think. Her heartbeat seems more steady. And she has not been rambling. Does she not seem better?"

Christiane crossed tentatively to the bed and laid her hand against Claire's forehead. "No fever, is there?"

"No. The worst is over, I think. Praise God."

Christiane gulped a breath. "Indeed. But the worst isn't over for me, Mr. Wrede. I . . . I feel compelled to offer you an apology for what you witnessed in the parlor last evening." He was looking straight at her, his hazel gaze level and direct. Her voice faltered. "I am so ashamed."

"Ashamed?" He smiled a little. "For celebrating God's gift to us of carnal pleasure?"

"Well . . . yes."

"He might have made us dumb and numb as plants. Yet He did not."

Christiane blushed. "You know, of course, that Lord Carew and I have no attachment to one another."

"Thou seemed quite attached to me."

The blush intensified. "I mean, of course, no formal attachment. On the contrary, he is betrothed to another woman."

"Yes. Miss Delaney. Claire doesn't think much of her, I gather. She is very fond of thee, however. She has told me that without thee and Mrs. Treadwell and the friends she has made here, she would have found herself quite lost after her parents' death."

Christiane fought to find her voice. "You weren't . . . shocked by what you witnessed when you and Mrs. Treadwell entered the parlor, Mr. Wrede?"

"What I witnessed was two consenting adults engaged in a consensual act." Then he started. "He did not *force* himself on thee, did he? For if he did—"

She thought it best to nip that in the bud. "No. Not at all. Lord Carew and I are . . ." She stopped; she had started to say "old friends," but that surely wasn't accurate. "It wasn't a question of force," she finished haltingly. "Merely a lapse of reason. On both our parts."

He nodded in understanding. "Love is a most momentous power, is it not?"

"But I don't—" She broke off abruptly. "See here," she said in sudden indignation. "You and Claire haven't—"

"Certainly not!" He drew his shoulders up, affronted. "The situations are not a whit analogous. She is still of tender years."

Christiane winced. "I see. So old folk such as Lord Carew and I have leave, in your opinion, to be as carnal as we like. Is that Quaker teaching?"

"It is common sense, in my opinion," said Mr. Wrede, not a bit abashed. "The sole doctrine of the Friends is to listen to one's heart; that is where God resides, and one must trust in Him."

"What a marvelously adaptive religion."

"Do thou think so? I wonder. I find it very hard indeed."

Christiane paused to consider that. If she listened only to her heart, where would she be now, at this moment?

In Gannon's bed.

"I begin to understand why the Crown has so often considered the Friends dangerous," she said crisply. "In my opinion, the heart is a most unreliable organ."

Mr. Wrede's smile blazed at her. "It is less unreliable, surely, than the brain."

"Whatever do you mean?"

"Only that we know, we sense, deep within us, what is right and what is wrong. Conscience must be our guide. We may employ our faculties to try to wrestle reason to our side, but the fact remains: We know when we are at fault."

"I was certainly at fault in allowing Lord Carew such liberties last evening!"

Claire was stirring on the bed. Mr. Wrede soothed her with a touch of his hand, and after a moment, her restlessness subsided. He pushed a wayward lock of black hair away from her long white neck. Then he glanced up at the countess. "Thou alone can be judge of that."

Christiane chewed her lip. Was she sorry for what she had allowed Gannon to do, or merely that they'd been discovered? She could feel, still, the weight of his thighs on her, the heady sensation of his rod plunging deep inside her. How could she regret such ecstasy? "You are an iconoclast, aren't you, Mr. Wrede?" she asked wryly.

"I believe in being honest. With the world, and with oneself."

"Mrs. Treadwell was concerned you might withdraw your attentions from Claire because of what you witnessed."

He glanced at Christiane sidelong, his hazel eyes teasing. "I should think I'd be more inclined to redouble them."

She bit back a laugh. "You really are dreadful. I shall have to make certain you and she are closely chaperoned."

"Perhaps thou and Lord Carew would care to serve."

"I hardly think so!" And she giggled again.

"Still . . ." He turned thoughtful. "If Mrs. Treadwell expects me to be shocked, I suppose it would be well if I feigned that I am."

"Why, Mr. Wrede! That would hardly reconcile with being true to oneself, would it?"

"Of course it would. My conscience instructs me to cause as little pain to others in this world as I can, both physically and spiritually. So if it eases Mrs. Treadwell to imagine I was outraged, it accords perfectly with my beliefs to oblige her."

She looked at him with a sort of awe. "You're a rare

bird, Mr. Wrede. Claire is unaccountably fortunate to have flushed you out."

He smiled at her, then glanced down at Claire, who was now sleeping peaceably. "On the contrary. I consider myself the fortunate one."

Nineteen

Over the next several days, Christiane took great care to busy herself elsewhere when Lord Carew came to visit his niece. Claire improved steadily, regaining her strength so far as to walk out in the courtyard with Mr. Wrede each morning and afternoon. His steadfast devotion was the cause of much admiring comment from Claire's fellow students, and Mrs. Treadwell was immensely relieved to discover that the scene she and he had stumbled upon in the parlor had not frightened him away. "He told me," she confided to Christiane, "that he feels it more incumbent on him than ever to keep close watch on her, after witnessing such scandalous behavior on your part."

"He told me much the same," Christiane reported, hiding a smile.

Despite her determination to avoid Lord Carew, she did encounter him eventually, inevitably. It was on the road to Hartin. She was returning from a ride, with Stains lagging behind her; Carew was thundering toward the White Fox atop a gorgeous black stallion. Their eyes met as their mounts approached. Determined not to look away first, she stared straight at him. He reined in as he drew near, bringing the black to a stamping halt.

"You found your niece continuing to improve in health, I trust?" she asked coldly.

"I did."

"Good." She started to spur on.

He grabbed for her reins as she passed him. "Christiane—"

"I have nothing more to say to you, Lord Carew."

"If you hadn't—"

"*Nothing* more," she reiterated, yanking the leather from his grasp.

"Bitch," he said softly.

"Bastard," she shot back, and rode on with her head held high.

To her horror, he wheeled the black around and followed her. "Do you know what your trouble is, *milady*?"

She knew it was a mistake, but she answered him. "No, milord. Do, pray tell, enlighten me. What exactly is my 'trouble'?"

"You've got no guts."

That brought her up short. "How dare you say such a thing?"

"You talk about uplifting your girls, teaching them to defy society's mores. But it's nothing more than talk, is it?"

"I don't know what you might mean."

"You're in hiding."

She paused, hands on the pommel, staring at him. "Of course I am in hiding. I have no choice. Were my connection to the academy known—"

"It's known to me."

"And you threatened not to enroll Claire upon discovering it!"

"I did enroll her, though, in the end. And Mr. Wrede seems comfortable enough with your presence there—despite what he glimpsed in the parlor the other night." She flushed, and prayed he would not notice. "I think you lack the courage of your convictions," he went on, maddeningly. "I think you are afraid of the ton."

"I am not afraid of anyone or anything!" *Except, perhaps, you. . . .*

"Prove it," he dared her.

"How?"

"I am hosting a fete in London on Saturday next. A small affair—cards, drinks, that sort of thing. Come to it."

"Why in God's name would I?" she asked, stupefied.

He shrugged. "That is just what I expected you would say. You *are* afraid."

"And you are an idiot!" she snapped. "The parents of the girls at the academy would withdraw them en masse if they ever learned of my involvement here."

"How would anyone coming to play cards at my house learn of your involvement here? Unless, of course, you slipped up and let word of it fall."

"I've been discreet enough till now," Christiane said haughtily.

"Then why not venture out to face the world?"

"I have nothing to prove to the world."

"I think you do."

"How can you possibly imagine that what you think matters at all to me?" And then the dam burst. "And anyway, why would you want me at your fete when I am so old and decrepit and gray?"

"I am sorry for that," he told her, and as she raised a hand to shield her eyes from the lowering sun, she saw he did look contrite. "I was infuriated. How could you tell Mrs. Treadwell that what we'd shared was a lapse of reason?"

"It was."

"I thought it was . . . . extraordinary."

God. Was it possible that he, too . . . but she did not dare allow herself to head down that path. "Besides, I doubt that Miss Delaney would be overdelighted if I were to attend," she said crisply.

"Miss Delaney is in Cornwall, visiting her sister."

"So while the cat's away?" Her voice was plainly sneering. "What sort of woman do you think I am?"

"I told Greer as soon as I returned from Ireland that I could not in good conscience remain betrothed to her. That is why she is in Cornwall, visiting her sister. As to what sort of woman I think you are—I'd say a cowardly sort, if you continue to hide yourself away here." She started to reply, but what he said next made her catch her breath. "And yet the sort I cannot stop thinking of, more's the rue."

She wished that sun were not so bright. "You are only looking for another opportunity to humiliate me."

"How did I humiliate you?"

"You mocked at me! You jested at my hair!"

"I think the gray is quite distinguished." He grinned, reaching out to touch her curls beneath her bonnet. She recoiled from his hand. "For God's sake, Christiane. We are neither of us as young as we were in Paris. The fact remains that I have dreamed of you for two decades." He leaned in further, so that his fingertips caressed her cheek.

"And Miss Delaney?"

"One of a host of poor substitutes."

"Rather a pity for her, isn't it?"

"She didn't care a whit for me."

"You think I do?"

His hand caught in her curls, pulled her mouth to his. "You tell me."

His kiss was hard and unyielding, demanding. Christiane fought him off, tried to push him away. But he went on kissing her, their mounts shifting uneasily beneath them, and at the force of his hungry mouth, her resistance withered; she put her hand to his shoulder tentatively.

He relinquished her briefly, for air. "If you mean somehow to punish me again," she whispered.

"*Punish* you?"

"For what happened in the Bois de Boulogne. For Jean-Baptiste. Isn't that why you did what you did . . . the other night? To take revenge on me?"

"I did what I did the other night because I could not help myself. Because you arouse desire in me . . . as no other woman ever has." His eyes glinted with the sun.

"Heavens, Gannon!" she said breathlessly. But he was kissing her again.

Stains was finally catching up to them; she saw his shocked face over Gannon's shoulder. She started to pull away from Gannon's embrace, then reconsidered. Stains was only the stableman.

"Say you'll come to London," Gannon whispered into her ear.

"I cannot."

"Why not?"

"I have other responsibilities."

"What responsibility could be greater than your redemption in the ton's eyes?"

That made her pull away from him. "There is no chance at all I will ever find redemption there!"

"But you must," he told her.

"Why? I am perfectly contented—"

"I am not, though. I want to stroll through London with you at my side. I want to squire you to Vauxhall. Buy you fripperies at Farringdon's. Dine with you at Gaillard's."

She thought he must be teasing her, but his expression was intensely solemn. "You . . . you don't understand," she whispered, shamed. "No one has ever regained her reputation after such lapses as mine."

"Be a pioneer," he urged her, and grinned, devastatingly. "What have you to lose? Say you'll come on Saturday."

"Who will be there?" she asked suspiciously.

"An elite, well-chosen coterie of open-minded citizens."

She shook her head in disbelief. "There are no such citizens in London. Not when it comes to me."

"You might be surprised."

"What guarantee do I have that this is not some sort of attempt on your part to humiliate me?"

"Why would I want to humiliate you?"

"Because I did so to you. When I told you . . . that I found you inadequate."

"We both know that was a lie." Stains was making harrumphs beyond her shoulder. Gannon Finn caught her hand in his, caressed it. "Christiane. Come. For my sake, yes. But, more, for yours."

"Evelyn will not approve," she said breathlessly.

"Make some excuse. Tell her you are visiting Violet Westin."

"I could say that, I suppose. . . ."

"Good!" He straightened in his saddle. "It is settled, then. Do you know my town house? It's at fifty-four Berkeley Square."

"Fifty-four Berkeley Square," she repeated in a daze.

He stole one last kiss. Then he laughed and cried, "Take her, Stains, you old spoilsport! Christiane, mind you don't disappoint me!"

"I . . ." But he had wheeled about again and was galloping off into the setting sun.

Christiane turned to the grim-faced Stains. "He's an old friend," she said. His expression didn't change. "All the same, Stains, I'd appreciate it very much if you didn't mention to Mrs. Treadwell that you saw what you did."

He spat noisily onto the road. "Should think ye'd have the good sense to leave that sort o' nonsense to them what's young," he muttered. "Should think ye'd know better, I would, at yer age."

"I'm hardly antique," the countess snapped.

"Well, ye ain't no spring chicken neither," he shot back, and dug his heels into tired old Achilles. "Askin' fer trouble, that's what ye be, sneakin' about behind Headmistress's back."

"Oh, mind your own business for once," Christiane told him curtly, flicking the reins and leaving him and Achilles in the dust once more.

Twenty

She **wouldn't** *go,* of course.

Christiane returned to the academy, went to her rooms, took off her jacket and hat, and then crossed to her looking glass, slowly, thoughtfully. Her curls were tousled by the ride, and by his hands; her cheeks were rouged with wind, or with excitement, or with *something*. She considered her reflection critically. She did not look half bad.

Still, what he proposed was insane. She had managed to forge a sort of happiness for herself here, with Evelyn and the girls. She had Leon Caplan to turn to when she needed a male friend to talk to, and for news of London. She would be mad to disturb such equilibrium—and for the sake of what? A few hands of whist at Lord Carew's town house? Why would she do such a thing?

Perhaps, she thought wistfully, unbuttoning her bodice, because what he'd said was true. She *was* in hiding. Despite all the successes in her life, despite her inner certainty that she was a good person, deserving, worthy, the prospect of confronting Mrs. Bartlesbury or Lady Calhoun and having them cut her filled her with terror still, after all these years.

"They have no right to hold such sway over me!" she whispered furiously, staring into the mirror. And yet they did. Why? *Because their attacks came when I was so young, so vulnerable,* she recognized. *And because I had done nothing wrong. I wasn't even guilty.*

But was that true? She may not have had sexual relations with Lord Weatherston, as he'd so callously announced to the world, but she'd been only too willing to agree to meet the man she *had* been enamored of, Harold Hainesworth, in that nondescript inn, when Weatherston dangled the prospect of the elopement before her. Why? What had compelled her to agree, and thus fall victim to Weatherston's vengeful plan?

She perched on the edge of her bed, thinking of her parents—something she did not do often. Her father . . . she had lovely memories of her father, but he had died when she was just twelve. She'd been left with only her mother, a woman whose dreams of social elevation had been hopelessly thwarted when Christiane's country-vicar father had proved less ambitious than she liked. Christiane remembered her father as gentle, inquisitive, kindly, a lover of books, and ungodly handsome. Upon his death, her mother had remarried with what her only child had considered—still considered—unseemly haste, to a military man, Major Thornton, with three grown sons. The meld of families had been most uneasy. The major's brutish sons had clandestinely pursued their new stepsister, cornering her for kisses and fondling so relentlessly that she was desperate to debut.

She'd worked hard at her lessons in comportment and etiquette, but she'd spent every free moment poring over the books that had been in her father's library. She had taught herself to read French, Italian, Latin; she had consumed Dante and Virgil and St. Augustine. She had struggled to understand the scientific tomes and had reveled in the plays and poetry. And then she'd hidden her learning, in her eagerness to escape her wretched home life. She'd latched onto boorish Harold Hainesworth, once he paid her attention, as though he were her lifeline, deluding herself into believing he was sensitive and wise and kind.

What she hadn't understood, what nothing in her experience had prepared her for, was that in the ton's eyes, she was very small fish, and thus ripe for a fry. Emily Madden, the previous recipient of Hainesworth's affections, took offense at the newcomer's encroachments and hatched the vicious plot to ruin her, with the all-too-willing aid of Weatherston, who was so plainly debauched that even Christiane, desperate though she was, had rejected his attentions. And then, in her longing for some sort of life of her own, she had fallen for his trickery like a country fool.

Well. I was *a country fool,* Christiane mused, taking up her brush and starting to pull it through her tangled hair. Even so, she'd been shocked by the repercussions of her trip with Weatherston to the Black Stallion to—so she'd thought—head away with Harold Hainesworth for Gretna Green. Even now, she cringed as she recalled joyously rushing up those rickety wooden stairs to the chamber where, Weatherston had told her, Harold waited.

Instead, Weatherson had followed, locked the door behind them, and done his damnedest to rape her. If she hadn't been so practiced at fighting off her stepbrothers, he might well have succeeded. But her hard-won victory against him—she'd left him on the floor, clutching his privates and bleeding rather profusely from the nose—had been for naught. He instantly told everyone he knew that he'd succeeded in having his way with her, and the ton had believed him. Her mother, in horror, had spurned her; Christiane's memory of their interview when she returned home, bedraggled but triumphant, only to discover that her virtue was unalterably compromised, still sickened her. Disinvited from a host of fetes, with young men snickering at her at every turn, she'd run away from home and taken ship for France.

She'd founded this academy to spare other young

women such turmoil. She believed in her work, and had seen gratifying successes. Nichola Hainesworth, daughter of her old nemesis, happily wed to Lord Boru. Katherine Devereaux, the impossibly proud heiress to the Duke of Marne, joined with such great joy to Alain Montclair. Gwen was worthy of a physician's license, Petra was every day reaching further in her pursuit of mathematics, and the most recent play Bess had penned had been accepted for a tryout by the regent's favored company—anonymously, of course. How dare Gannon accuse her of hiding? Why, she was toiling each and every day to counter the ridiculous strictures of the ton—and doing a fine job of it, too! *Her* girls did not fall victim to the first good-looking man to pay them court. They thought for themselves; they stood up for what they believed in. They faced the future straight on.

And yet they cover for you, a nagging voice inside her said. *They lie for you, pretend you do not exist though they all know your story. When it comes to the ton, you are the perfect proof that one cannot really win.*

Oh, but one could not! Could one? She looked into the mirror and saw nothing but fear in her reflection. *It is only a bunch of pinched old matrons, jealous and warped. . . .*

That is what you teach the girls. But what does it say that you swear them to silence about your existence here?

I have been a dreadful hypocrite, Christiane realized, her heart sinking. *I have asked more of them than I have asked of myself.*

In short, Gannon was right.

Could she face them down? Did she dare to? The prospect made her heart constrict. Yet there was also this that he had said: *I want to stroll through London with you at my side. I want to squire you to Vauxhall. Buy you fripperies at Farringdon's. Dine with you at Gaillard's.*

She tried to imagine it—really tried, clenching her eyes tight shut. She and Gannon, sipping champagne in the Vauxhall gardens. Shopping for hats and gloves at Farringdon's. Sharing an intimate table together at Gaillard's, trading tastes of that marvelous chocolate charlotte from a spoon . . .

Listen to your heart.

David Wrede's words rang in her ears. It must be splendid, she thought ruefully, to be so sure of what one's heart was saying as *he* was.

Listen to your heart.

And what if she did?

She stood very still, felt the anxious pounding in her ears. What was her heart saying?

I did not know you thought me handsome at all in Paris. It might have altered my life if I had.

And what do we do now? Shall I have to wait another two decades for a repeat performance?

Her heart believed him. Her heart trusted him. Her heart belonged to him.

She would go to him.

Now, if her resolve only held until Saturday next.

Twenty-one

As Christiane stepped into the hired coach that Violet
Westin's footman had hailed for her and gave the direction—"Fifty-four Berkeley Square"—she was quaking.
She'd spent hours on her toilette, which was very unlike
her; by now, she knew what suited her and what didn't. Yet
on this night, she had dithered miserably. She'd packed
three options: a severe, unadorned black crêpe sheath; an
ivory batiste that, when she'd donned it before the mirror
in her room at Violet's town house, seemed a tad too di-
aphanous; and a pale-green charmeuse that looked rather
out of fashion, considering the evidence of Violet's new
sleeves. In the end, she settled on the black. It was simple
enough not to occasion comment, she trusted. And the
bodice was rather higher than the others', which she
thought was, all in all, a good thing. She drew her wayward curls into the tightest of chignons, leaving not even a
tendril dangling—then wondered if she looked too severe.
She sought to soften the effect with the pearls the Comte
d'Oliveri had presented her as a wedding gift at her ears
and throat. They were magnificent, and she felt qualms as

she donned them; was she putting on airs? But the maid
lent by Violet admired them so profusely that she was reassured. She did not want, on this evening, to be cowed by
anything or anyone, and the jewels gave her confidence.
That was what jewels were for.

Nonetheless, when the driver neared Berkeley Square
and swore at the sight of a long, slow line of traffic, all her
insecurities resurfaced. So many carriages could not possibly be headed for Gannon's; a neighbor must be hosting as
well. Or several neighbors, more probably, she thought, as
they were admitted to the lengthy crawl. She stared at the
houses they passed—high, elegant places with innumer-
able windows and gaily lit doors. She had not been to a
soirée at such a home in London for more than twenty
years.

"Wot's the number again?" the driver asked, craning to
look at her.

"Fifty-four," she murmured.

"Ah, gad. Look at the line."

And look she did. A few carefully chosen souls, Gannon
had assured her. But the row of carriages waiting to dis-
gorge their occupants in front of 54 Berkeley Square
wound along for two blocks. *He means to trick me,* Christiane realized. *To shame me.* In such a press, there would
be any number of guests who would recognize her, remember her. Revile her. She drew in her breath. "Let's be
gone," she started to tell the driver. Just then, though, the
occupant of the curricle behind them stood in his seat,
waving wildly.

"Lady d'Oliveri?" he called to her. "I say, is that you?"

She saw with astonishment that it was Leon Caplan.
"Doctor!" she called back. "Whatever are you doing?"

He jumped down from his coach, paid the driver, and
walked up to hers. "I scarcely know," he said. "I got an invitation from Lord Carew to a fete this evening. I suppose
it is his way of thanking me for tending to his niece. And
you?"

"I—received the same. For the same reason, I'm sure."

Leon smiled, following along as her driver moved toward the house. "I rather doubt it."

"I don't know why you should say that."

"He and I have been engaged in a correspondence regarding Miss Finn's welfare," the doctor told her. "He's a most interesting man. He has unusual insight into human nature, I believe."

Christiane stared at him, dumbstruck. "You do?"

"Why, yes. Don't you?"

"I did," she said rather grimly, "before tonight."

"Whatever do you mean?"

She hesitated, then decided to bare all. "Lord Carew and I have a bit of a . . . a history, Leon."

"I know. He has told me in his letters."

How *dared* he? "What did he tell you?" she demanded.

Dr. Caplan smiled again. "You must be aware, Christiane, of how he feels about you."

"I know he harbors some delusion that he is in love with me."

"Why do you call it a delusion?"

She waved a hand at the line of coaches. "Because he urged me to subject myself to *this* tonight! He told me it was to be a quiet, intimate affair. Cards and drinks, he said."

"There will no doubt be cards and drinks."

"But I cannot make an appearance in such a throng!"

"Why not?"

"You know why not," she said.

Dr. Caplan scratched his beard absently. "I have gathered from His Lordship's correspondence that he is concerned you are letting life pass you by."

"I'm doing no such thing. I have simply chosen to direct my energies toward the girls entrusted to our care. And you know perfectly well that if my connection to Mrs. Treadwell's academy ever became public, it would mean an end to all we have worked for!"

"Why don't you forget the academy, just for tonight?" the doctor suggested.

"Forget the—do you mean I should *dissemble*?"

"Why the devil not?"

While they discussed it, the carriage had drawn up to the doorstep. Christiane glanced at the brightly lit windows, heard strains of music and laughter from within. Her heart was filled with an enormous longing to step from the coach and join the merrymakers—and, most of all, to see *him* again. And yet—

Dr. Caplan offered his hand. "Shall we?"

"I . . . think not."

"Oh, Christiane." His eyes shone in the lamplight. "I killed the Christ. What are your sins beside that?"

"Are you not afraid?" she whispered.

"That I'll be scorned? Aye. A bit. But I am more afraid that such a chance will not come my way again."

"A chance for what?"

"To make my case. To prove, by my comportment and conversation, that I am not a demon—and that, by extension, my fellow Jews are not." He grinned at her. "You might do the same for jezebels tonight."

The doorman and a pair of boys were waiting on them with mounting impatience. Christiane put a hand to the pearls at her throat and swallowed hard. "Very well," she said, and let the doctor hand her down.

Once they were over the threshold, her wrap was taken by a smiling Irish maid. "Names, if ye please?" she asked, bobbing in a curtsy.

"Dr. Caplan," he told her in a resounding voice, "and the Countess d'Oliveri."

"Very good, sir." She bobbed again and murmured to the butler, who ushered them to the doorway of the packed salon.

"Dr. Caplan," the butler announced to the throng, "and the Countess d'Oliveri!"

Not a single head turned toward them in all that mass of humanity. Christiane dared to breathe again.

The doctor took her elbow and led her into the room. It was so tightly packed that she felt a moment of panic. She searched nervously for the faces she feared: Mrs. Minton, Lady Calhoun, Mrs. Bartlesbury, those terrible ton tigers. She fairly expected women to leap out at her, pointing, sneering, crying her past sins to the world. To her immense surprise, nothing of the sort happened. In fact, no one took the least bit of notice of her. Except . . .

Someone was moving toward her, pushing through the crowd—a tall, chesty woman with waves of gray hair, very patrician indeed. Christiane recoiled; her knees went weak, and she clung to Leon's arm. The gray-haired matron strode forward relentlessly, thrusting fellow guests aside, until she stood squarely in their path. "Is that you, Christiane Roxell?" she demanded, in a voice so loud it seemed to echo to the rafters.

The countess cringed. "Forgive me, but I cannot recall—"

"Lady Custis," the matron said curtly. "And what I want to know is, whatever happened to that brothel you ran in Paris?"

"It wasn't a—"

"Because my Eliot used to always win at your tables, and he never does here in England!" the woman said indignantly. "I wish you'd have a good talk with these poseurs here and tell them how to run a proper gambling hell; there's no decency anywhere anymore!"

Dr. Caplan was sniggering. Christiane elbowed him sharply. "I thank you for the compliment, Lady Custis—I think," she replied.

"Ah, well, nothing's as it was in the old days, is it?" Lady Custis said dolefully.

"No. No, I suppose it isn't. You're looking very trim and lovely, though."

The matron beamed. "D'you think so? I adore your gown. French, I suppose."

"Yes. It is."

"No mistaking a French hand with the needle. Well, we'll all be catching up to you, I suppose, now that this damned war's ended. Who's your giddy friend?"

Christiane glanced at Dr. Caplan, who was still laughing. "Lady Custis, Dr. Caplan," she said by way of introduction, over the chatter and music.

"The Jew who cured Lady Rifallow's nerves?"

The doctor made a bow. "I had the honor to be of some aid to Lady Rifallow."

Lady Custis reached out a crabbed hand, shoving Christiane aside. "I must talk to you, then, about *my* nerves. I've been having the most dreadful stomachaches of late. Happens every time I eat shellfish. What do you think of that, eh?"

"I think perhaps you should give up shellfish," Dr. Caplan said gravely, as a sudden shifting of the press swept Christiane past him and into the center of the room.

That abruptly, she found herself confronting Gannon. "You lied to me," she said.

"How so?"

" 'A small, intimate gathering,' " she reminded him.

"Lord Carew!" A snowy-haired matron had thrust between them. "Such lovely champagne you're serving! And the hors d'oeuvres are delectable. That must be Westfield ham. I'm a Suffolk girl; I'd know a Westfield ham anywhere."

"You're absolutely right, Miss Russ. Miss Russ, have you the acquaintance of the Countess d'Oliveri?"

"Don't know that I do." Miss Russ bobbed her head at the countess. "You're a lovely little thing, aren't you? I adore that hat."

"Th-thank you." Christiane curtsied, coloring faintly. "Yours is ever so handsome as well."

"Miss Russ has recently published a novel," Lord Carew noted.

"Have you?" Christiane asked the woman, surprised.

Miss Russ smiled. "I have. But not under my own name. As Mr. John Russell."

"It was very well received. Got a splendid review in the *Gazette*," said Lord Carew.

"I read that review!" Christiane said in amazement.

"Lord Bertrand penned it, didn't he? Called your book 'witty, trenchant, and—' "

" '—the work of a boy genius,' " Miss Russ finished for her, with a throaty giggle. "If only he knew."

"How in the world do you keep your secret?" Christiane marveled.

"Well, I don't," said Miss Russ. "Except from Lord Bertrand and his sort."

Just then, a tall, gaunt man pushing past them tapped Miss Russ's shoulder with a fingertip. "Splendid review, Joan! Though I should worry a bit if a stick such as Bertrand liked my work."

Miss Russ laughed. "Point taken, Samuel. Still, beggars can't be choosers. I comfort myself by imagining he didn't really read the thing. Did you happen to see Lord Hornsby's diatribe against women poets in the *Post*?"

"Of course. I haven't laughed so hard in ages; have you?" Christiane watched as the woman and the thin man moved off together. "Who is that to whom Miss Russ is speaking?" she asked Gannon.

"Mr. Coleridge, that wrote the drama *Remorse*, that has proven such a hit at Drury Lane this year."

"*Samuel* Coleridge?"

Lord Carew arched a brow. "You know him?"

"No, but I adore his poetry."

Lord Carew looked about, then lowered his voice. "He is not much received in society, owing to his unfortunate opium habit. But he is kind and clever, and I enjoy his company."

"Whom shall I see next—Lord Byron?"

He glanced down at her. "Certainly not. I have *some* standards."

She was not at all sure whether he was funning her or not.

"But his former muse, Lady Lamb, is here somewhere," he noted. "Poor thing. She has found herself quite at sea since he abandoned her so callously."

"What are you—a savior of lost souls?" The question

came out more sharply than she'd intended. Was that what he saw her as—a lost soul?

His blue gaze was cool. "Not a savior. A collector, perhaps."

"Lord Carew!" A good-looking, well-built man with brown mustaches hailed his host. "I've just been through your gardens. Quite splendid, really. A well-thought-out, diverse display. And that folly—remarkable!"

"Thank you, Brown. Can't take a bit of credit for it, I'm afraid. Countess, have you the acquaintance of Mr. Robert Brown, the renowned botanist and librarian to the Linnean Society?"

"How do you do, Mr. Brown?" Christiane extended her hand, and Mr. Brown kissed it distractedly.

"Mr. Brown journeyed to Australia recently and catalogued the flora there," said Lord Carew.

"Did you indeed, sir?"

"It was my great privilege to do so."

"Did you find the flora greatly different from that of England?" Christiane asked politely.

Mr. Brown hesitated, on the verge of a reply. Lord Carew laughed. "Don't get started, Brown!" he cautioned. "He found and described more than four thousand species of new plants there, Lady d'Oliveri. It is a dangerous thing to invite an expert to expound on his expertise."

"I look forward to discussing the subject with you at more length someday, Lady d'Oliveri," Mr. Brown said longingly.

"I anticipate that as well," she told him, smiling, as Lord Carew took her hand and led her away. "Where are we going?" she asked, as more guests hailed him with hallos and waves.

"Somewhere we can talk without shouting."

"Shouldn't you be acting as host?"

"Everything seems to be proceeding of its own accord. That's the value, you know, in a small, closed society. You invite them, and they all know precisely what to do." He edged past the thronged buffet tables toward the French doors.

"It's a very elegant house," Christiane noted, taking in the surroundings.

"What's that?" The musicians had struck up again; the din was outlandish.

"Never mind," she said, and let him lead her outside.

There was a broad terrace there, overlooking a walled garden. Christiane glimpsed a tall hedge at the far end of the lawns, which were marked out with neat brick paths. Just below the staircase, a fish pond shimmered in the moonlight. She glanced back at the velvet-curtained doors. "Have you lived here long?" she asked.

He glanced down at her. "Odd you should ask. I only took possession a fortnight ago. What prompted you?"

"It is so very English. It doesn't look like you at all."

"I was thinking of Claire when I took it. It seemed the sort of place from which she might properly make her debut."

"Where was your London home before?"

"I had a suite in a rather notorious gentlemen's rooming house."

She could not help but smile at his frankness. He took her hand and led her toward the stairs.

"It's quite improper for a host to leave his guests, isn't it?" she asked, staring at the fish pond. Something within it had jumped in a flash of silver, leaving an echoing splash.

"They'll get on well enough without me, so long as the champagne is flowing. And I never could stand a press." He was pulling her further along the brick path.

"Where are we going?" she asked a bit breathlessly.

"Don't you care to see my folly?"

She hung back, clinging to the light that poured from the casements, unwilling to move into the shadows. "I have seen a lot of folly in my time."

"So have I," he said, pausing on the path. "Caused a

good bit of it, too. That makes us well matched, don't you think?"

"Well matched for what?"

"Well, for this, for starters." He kissed her.

"Lord Carew!" she exclaimed, seeking to thrust him away.

"Oh, Christ, Christiane. Don't 'Lord Carew' me. We both know why you came tonight."

She flushed. "It wasn't to be an easy tumble in the rosebushes, if that is what you're thinking!"

"I didn't mean it that way." He'd pulled back, granting her space. "But what's the sense in denying what we feel for one another?"

"You seem a great deal more certain of what that is than I am. You told me this would be an opportunity for me to confront my past. How am I to do so if I am out here frolicking with you?"

" 'Frolicking'?" He arched a brow.

"It's Mrs. Treadwell's influence," she admitted.

"I had in mind something more than a frolic."

"That's what I'm afraid of."

He seized on it. "Why? Why are you afraid?"

Christiane let out a sigh, and took a few steps backward. "I just don't see any point in it."

"In being in love?" he asked incredulously.

"Who is in love?"

"I am." His gaze dropped; he toed a bit of turf with his boot. "Aren't you?"

"Love is for schoolgirls," she said curtly.

"Says who? Mrs. Treadwell?"

"You cannot want to *marry* me."

"Why the devil not?"

She dropped *her* gaze. "I'm of an age . . ." Much as she hated it, she pressed on. "I cannot give you what men marry *for*."

"Do you mean children?" She nodded, shamefaced. "Well, thank God for that!"

"You don't *want* children?"

"Never did. Never will."

"Oh, you say that now. But when you are old and decrepit and alone—"

"Why would I be alone? Won't you be there?"

He really was impossible. "How should I know?" she snapped. "Things happen, Gannon! People die!"

"Not us." He grinned, reaching for her hand once more.

"You should marry Greer. You really should," she told him.

"I don't love Greer. I love you."

"I wish you would stop saying that."

"And I wish you would stop fighting what you know in your heart. You love me, just as I have loved you, ever since Paris." He tugged her along. "Come, let's celebrate. We've lost too much time already. Twenty years, Christiane! Think what we might have done with those twenty years."

"Grown to detest one another, if society is any template," she said tartly.

"When has either of us taken society for our template?" He pulled her on, holding tightly to her hand.

The folly was hidden behind the tall hedge of boxwood. Christiane couldn't help gasping as they turned the corner and she saw it shimmering in the moonlight. She had expected the usual tumble of pseudo Greek ruins that was all the rage. What she saw instead was a rectangular reflecting pool set before a gleaming dome of ghost-white alabaster, adorned with delicately arched entranceways and framed by four tall spires. It was small—no more than twenty feet tall—but astonishingly lovely.

"Built by the previous owner," Gannon told her. "He has a rash of cotton mills in India. Do you know what it is?" She shook her head, drinking in the scene. "The Taj Mahal—to scale, of course, not full-size. The original was raised by the Emperor Shah Jahan as the tomb of his queen. It took him twenty-two years and twenty thousand men to build it."

"Gracious," Christiane said.

"The wife of the man who sold me this house died while he was in India making a great fortune," Gannon added. "He came home and erected the miniature in her memory."

"How terribly sad."

He glanced at her. "Yes. It is sad, isn't it, when we let love pass us by? When there is nothing left to do but raise monuments in its memory? But he didn't recognize that until it was too late. I have wondered, often, whether Shah Jahan did—or whether his masterpiece was meant as expiation for some secret sin of betrayal or neglect toward his wife." The moon hung above them, twinned by its mirrored companion in the wind-swept pool. Gannon's hand touched her waist. "Christiane, there is more to society than the women at Almack's. There are my friends, for instance. You *might* grow to like my friends."

"You don't understand," she said quietly. "It isn't just society. It is Evelyn as well, and the responsibilities I have."

"If you believe in what you teach those girls—"

"Of course I do!"

"Then isn't it time you stood up for what you believe? Besides—" He stroked her cheek, laid his palm there. "You won't be alone. You will have me at your side."

She looked past him at the glistening alabaster dome, and she bowed her head. "I am afraid."

"Do you think I'm not? But you're a risk on which I'll gamble everything. I must; I have no choice. I've had no peace without you since the first time I saw you. If I've any chance for happiness at all, it is with you."

"What if," she began, and then stopped.

"Go on," he urged her.

She sighed hopelessly. "What if it is only the *dream* of me that you have been in love with? I'm not—not perfect, you know. I am not even as close to it as when I was three-and-twenty. I cannot help but think that you don't see me as I am—that you see only some mirage from the past on which you've pegged your dreams."

"That's ridiculous."

"It is not. Look at me, Gannon." He did, and smiled. "No, really, truly, *look* at me! I have crow's-feet! I am going gray! I am growing *old!*"

"And I want only the honor of watching you do so. Perpetually."

"You say that now. But in ten, in another twenty years—"

"God willing, you and Mrs. Treadwell will still be raising Cain at your academy. But at night, you will come home to me."

She shook her head. "There's just no talking to you, is there?"

"No. And so I'm forced to ask myself—why are we wasting time at it?" Grinning, he drew her tight against him and tilted her chin up gently with his fingertips. Then he kissed her, with a quiet, solemn urgency that turned her knees to cotton. His tongue pushed at her lips, seeking entrance, sliding into her mouth even as she started to protest. He groaned; she could feel the hard swell of his manhood at her skirts. He reached for her bodice, cupping her breast in his hand, fondling the tip through the cocoon of smooth black silk. Christiane felt that irresistible fire kindle deep inside her belly, and fought to cling to reason.

"No," she whispered—in a voice that was none too steady.

To her amazement, he drew back. "Quite right. We have our guests to attend to first. But after that—" He caught her to him one last time, planting a kiss at the side of her bared neck so passionately that she shivered in delight. "After that, I'll have my way with you." While she was still catching her breath—why *did* he have that effect on her? She felt heady and weak, and there was a moistness between her thighs—he laughed and caught her up in his arms, her long skirts trailing, and bore her triumphantly back to his house.

The rest of that evening was a whirlwind of surprise and pleasure. He tucked her close to his side and kept her there, proudly presenting her to everyone they encountered: a host of writers, musicians, artists of every sort, the occasional odd businessman or military figure or actress—some of these last very lovely indeed. A few of the guests seemed to recognize her name, but only a few, and when Gannon would mention that she had only recently returned to England from France, everyone pressed her eagerly about French ways and fashions; though Napoleon had been a deadly enemy, he was a much admired one.

Her worst moment came at supper, where she was seated next to Lord Cobblesby, whose redoubtable consort had been one of the loudest of the tigers, according to Mrs. Treadwell, in condemning Christiane for her adventures abroad. Lord Cobblesby, who had been a frequent guest at La Maison Touton while he was on the regent's business in Paris, was perfectly delighted with his proximity to his old acquaintance, and made a point of leaning across the table to his wife to declare, "Didn't I tell you she always was a perfect lady? It's the likes of you that forced her to France in the first place; how dare you then complain of how she got along there?"

Seeing Lady Cobblesby stiffen, Christiane hastily put in: "But, milord, Lady Cobblesby had every reason to condemn me. I was a silly, headstrong girl."

"Quite right," Lady Cobblesby sniffed. Then, to Christiane's amazement, she leaned close and whispered, "You were dead on, though, m'dear, about that devious Weatherston. Everyone knows it now; didn't he get Amanda Feathers in the family way? And she was as pure as driven snow before she met up with him. So it's no wonder the likes of *you* would have fallen prey."

At her side, Christiane heard Gannon choke on his laughter. She maintained her composure, with an effort. "It's disgraceful, isn't it, milady, how men will take advantage of women?"

"Positively," the old woman agreed, clucking her tongue and folding her napkin as she rose from her chair. "Now, where the devil is the whist?"

"Right that way." Gannon indicated the doorway to the card room.

"Come along, sir," she ordered her husband. "Let's see if we can get a table."

"Lovely to see you again, Lord Cobblesby!" Christiane called as he was firmly marched off by his wife. "How they've all mellowed!" she marveled, after the couple was out of earshot.

Gannon's grip on her elbow tightened. "Perhaps not quite all." They were being approached by a fading blonde who was practically dragging a tall, stout man with a monocle. Christiane's heart sank, but she put a good face on it. "Why, Lord and Lady Hainesworth," she said. "How do you do!"

Harold Hainesworth, for whom she'd been so desperate at eighteen, flushed and murmured something unintelligible. His wife was more forthright. "Hello, Lord Carew, Christiane. Tell me, Christiane, are you still involved in that academy of Mrs. Treadwell's?" Christiane opened her mouth, then couldn't think of what to say. Fortunately, the baroness plunged right on. "Because I must tell you, I continue to recommend it ever so highly to all my friends. You would not believe what a perfect dream our Nichola is these days—and those twins! The most beautiful babies that ever were born, isn't that right, Harold?"

"Mmph," the baron mumbled.

"We were up to visit them at Christmas, and they'll be down to Bath with us in August. I am looking forward to it so! Granted, I did not think Lord Boru much of a catch at first, but now that I see how wonderfully he treats her— just as though she were a princess—" She shot a pointed glance at her husband, then lowered her voice, leaning in again. "He gave her a ruby neckpiece that had been in his family for five hundred years. The thing must be worth ten thousand pounds. And she wears it when they go hunting! There are dogs all over the house . . . oh, she's such a renegade, our Nichola. Still, they are so happy together. . . ."

Her voice trailed away wistfully. The baron was polishing his monocle with his handkerchief.

"I am delighted to hear it," Christiane said warmly.

"I'm not so small a woman, I hope, as not to admit when I was wrong," the baroness declared. "Of course, I only mention Mrs. Treadwell when I make my recommendations to the ladies—never you!"

"I appreciate that very much indeed."

The baroness winked. "It is our little secret. Isn't that so, milord?"

"Mmph," said the baron. "Could use a drink, eh?"

"I should say you'd had enough for tonight." But he was sidling away. The baroness leaned in one last time. "I said it before, Christiane, and I'll say it again—I should have let you have him while you wanted him. *Five* sons, not to mention Nichola, and he pays me no more mind than he does the kitchen door. Must go and stop him before he gets falling-down drunk and makes a spectacle. Do take care." And to Christiane's astonishment, the baroness pecked her cheek before hurrying off after her husband.

Gannon burst out laughing and took her by the arm. "So much for the past you were so fearful of confronting. I believe you owe me a dance, milady." And he led Christiane out onto the crowded floor.

Twenty-two

It was nearly three in the morning before the last stragglers headed to the door and out to their carriages. Christiane should have been exhausted, but instead she felt impossibly alive, invigorated, as though her every nerve had been stretched to its end. She stood beside Gannon in the doorway and waved the final guests off. He had his arm around her, and nuzzled her throat as the footmen handed a ruddy-faced Lady Cobblesby and her husband in. "You have brought me luck, Christiane!" the old dragon called gaily. "I won nearly two hundred pounds! Do be sure, Lord Carew, that you have her here next time you throw a fete!"

"Oh, I intend to," Gannon assured her. Then the horses pounded away, leaving only the empty street. "Dammit all," he muttered.

"What is wrong?"

"She's not supposed to *win*. I only have her here so my friends who are badly in need of money can take home some of hers. She has more than enough—and she usually plays dreadfully."

"You invite her here simply to provide your friends with income?" she demanded.

"Well, it's not because she's decorative."

"Why does she come, though, if she loses?"

"She is one of those women who like to think themselves savvy when it comes to the arts. She is always trying to show poor Coleridge her poetry."

Christiane laughed, then evaded him as he reached for her. "I must be going. Violet will be frantic with worry."

"You're a grown woman."

"Yes. But it is unkind to leave her in doubt as to where I might be."

"One last glass of champagne," he urged. "She's with Prinny, didn't you say that? He'll not be done yet with his carryings-on." He drew her inside, closing the handsome door, and signaled to the weary butler. "Just bring us a bottle of the Veuve Clicquot, O'Malley, and two glasses, and you may go on to bed. Tell the kitchen so as well."

"But the tidying-up, milord—"

"Will wait until the morning. Go on, then."

"Very good, milord." The man yawned hugely as he headed for the kitchens. Gannon led Christiane into the vast, deserted drawing room, and settled beside her on an upholstered chaise.

O'Malley came in with a tray bearing the glasses and bottle. "I'll open it," Gannon told him. "You did splendid work tonight. I'm grateful for it."

"My pleasure, milord." The butler bowed and was gone.

Gannon had a satisfied gleam in his gray eyes as he popped the cork and filled the flutes. "I think I've had more than enough," she demurred.

"Pity. I'd hoped you might care to revisit my folly." He tipped his glass to hers with a gentle clink.

"I should be going," she said again.

"Why are you so afraid of me?"

"I am not afraid of you." But she heard her voice quaver, and knew he'd heard it, too.

He'd taken her hand in his; he was stroking the soft

white skin of her inner wrist. "I want to make love to you, Christiane. I want more of what we shared that night at the academy. I want to hear you sigh, and feel you quiver, and quiver in return as you reach for me."

"That was a mistake," she said firmly.

"A mistake? I don't think so." He put his hand to her thigh, his fingers firm against the sleek silk. "I dream about you. Every night," he whispered. "I dream of coming into you, of filling you, and of your sweet surrender." He trailed his fingertips across her bare shoulder, let them slide to her bodice, slip inside the cool black silk, until he touched . . .

She jumped to her feet. "Thank you ever so much for having me here tonight," she said, knowing she was babbling. "It's been simply lovely. Now if you'll just hail me a carriage—"

"Not a chance."

"I can't imagine what you have in mind!"

"Oh, I think you can."

She put her hands on her hips, glaring at him. "How am I ever to regain my reputation if I misbehave again?"

"Ah," he said, and reached to stroke her cheek. "That's the beauty of it. You are old enough to know your own mind now. And you have no one checking up that you are in your bed."

"Violet will certainly—"

"Violet will come home from Prinny's with a dreadful headache and go straight to her rooms."

"But the servants—"

"Ah. I see. You are willing to be curtailed by a house-maid's scorn."

She sighed in exasperation. "It is different for you! You are a man!"

"That I am," he said evenly. "A man who aches to have you in his bed. Not on the parlor floor of the academy. Not in those rooms you shared with Jean-Baptiste in Paris. But here, on my own turf. On my own terms."

"You imagine that will make a difference?" she demanded with a hint of defiance.

"I think it will make all the difference in the world."

She stared at him. He looked back at her. There was a bulge at the front of his breeches. She started to turn for the door.

"If you leave now, I won't trouble you again."

His words were perfectly tranquil, polite, but she heard the steel in them, and knew he meant it. She stood, hesitating, trying to make up her mind. What did she want? That was canard; she knew what she wanted. It was simply a question of whether she was brave enough to say so. And he meant to have her say so; he wasn't about to make it easy.

"Gannon," she said, and then faltered.

He was merciless. "Yes?"

"I do want you," she whispered, shamefaced.

His stern face creased in a huge smile. "Well, thanks be to God," he said, and rose from the settee to take her hand.

Together, they climbed the darkened stairs.

He opened the door to his chambers. She caught her breath. There was a fire in the grate, flinging shadows across a huge postered bed draped in rich ivory silk. He sat on the bed and pulled off his boots and stockings. He removed his jacket, flung it over an upholstered chair. She set her reticule down on a bureau, very tentatively.

He stood and unbuttoned his breeches.

"I think a bit of foreplay," she murmured.

"Forgive my impatience." He removed the breeches entirely.

"Gannon," she protested.

He threw aside his cravat and began to unbutton his linen shirt.

"You are supposed to seduce me!"

"I am seducing you."

"You are not. You're undressing. You—" He'd removed his drawers. He was naked. His manhood stood straight and hard, at the ready. She averted her gaze—and then let her eyes sidle back, remembering. . . .

He smiled, went to the bed, drew back the covers, and climbed in, stretching out against the linens with his arms behind his head.

He really was the most impossible man. If he expected her to come crawling to him like some sort of trollop—"What *do* you think you're doing?" she demanded hotly.

"Giving you ample time to reason it out, of course. So there can be no question of a lapse of judgment on this go-round."

Her gaze dropped to the rug. "You mean to shame me," she whispered.

"No. Never, Christiane. I mean only to make certain the choice is yours."

"Do you expect me to climb in there with you just like that? You are supposed to kiss me, and fondle me, and undress me. To whisper that you love me."

"I love you!" he shouted, so suddenly that she recoiled. "Why should I whisper it?" He bounded up from the bed and crossed to the window, pulling the drapes aside, throwing open the casement. "I love the Countess d'Oliveri!" he bellowed into the night.

"For God's sake, Gannon!" Horrified, she rushed to close the window. "Whatever will your neighbors think?"

He stared down at her. "You're really no different from the tigers, are you? You are bound by the same rules they are. You believe in the same things they do."

"I believe in—in proper comportment, yes! In decency."

His smile was slow and winning. "Then why do you find yourself in my bedchamber, and with me naked?"

"Because you turn everything around!" she wailed. "You make the world topsy-turvy. I cannot think straight when I am with you!"

He went for the window again, wound it out even as she clawed at his arm. "I love the Countess d'Oliveri," he announced to all of Berkeley Square once more, "even though she is a bit of a stick!"

"Would you stop that?" A dog had started barking; light suddenly shone in the second floor across the way. Christiane shrank back from the window, yanking the drapes closed.

"There's one sure way to shut me up." His eyes were dancing.

"Are you mad?"

A shadow crossed his face, so briefly she wasn't certain it had truly been there. Then he laughed. "Mad for you." He bounced back onto the bed. "Take me or leave me."

"You frighten me."

"Good. You should be frightened. It is recompense for all the suffering you've caused me. Are you coming to bed?"

"Do you love me, or . . . do you hate me?" she asked in trepidation.

"Will you marry me?"

"Must you keep changing the subject?"

"I'm not changing the subject at all! Why would I want to wed you if I hated you?" He leaned toward her, stretching out his hand. "What do you say?"

She didn't know whether to laugh or run from him. "Is that an earnest proposal?"

"As earnest as you'll ever get from me."

She looked at him. His long, virile body gleamed in the firelight. She could feel her heartbeat quicken; she remembered the sensation of that rod he was so shamelessly flaunting thrusting deep inside her, heard the echo of her own cries. "Gannon," she said, her voice faltering. "Gannon. I *am* afraid."

"I know," he said.

"With Jean-Baptiste . . . and with the comte . . . I still had something of myself. They never asked for everything. For all of me. But you—"

"All or nothing, Christiane. I will not help you hide. But I will always be at your side."

"Always?"

"Always." And then he grinned. "Even, I think, when you'd prefer I was not."

"Claire's suitor—Mr. Wrede—"

"Yes?"

"He says the Quakers believe one must listen not to the world, but only to one's heart."

"I am growing more and more fond of the Quakers. What does your heart say?"

"That I . . ." She stopped, swallowed. "That I love you."

He rose from the bed. He crossed to her. He kissed her, his hand soft against her hair. She returned the kiss, her lips parting beneath his. He unfastened the pearls at her throat, removed the studs from her ears with practiced ease, and laid them carefully on the bedside table. "Lovely pearls," he murmured, reaching for her ribbons. "A gift from some other man?"

"From my husband." She fought the urge to cringe, said it proudly.

"He had excellent taste. In more ways than one." He raised the black silk over her head. Beneath it, she wore black as well—a sheer black corset, tightly laced, and matching drawers, made for her in Paris. It had been many years since she'd donned them. "Oh, my." Gannon whistled, drinking in the sight. "Christmas Day is here. Mind if I unwrap my gift?" She could not help but giggle at the gleam in his eyes. He loosened the corset slowly, his thumbs tracing the mounds of her breasts above the silky cloth, then slipping inside to rim her nipples. They went instantly hard to his touch. "Ahh," he breathed, letting the corset slide to the floor. He reached down, eased the drawers over her hips; they fell in a soft flutter as he smoothed her buttocks with his palms. Then he knelt and rolled down her stockings, removed them and her elegant high-heeled shoes. He paused to plant a kiss against the thatch of black curls between her thighs as he stood again. He was much taller now that she was barefoot; he towered over her. She crossed her arms over her chest.

"Almost perfect," he whispered, and withdrew a pin from her hair, then another and another, until it fell from its tight chignon in bright black waves. "There," he said with satisfaction, running his hands up and through the mass of it, shaking it loose as though in liberation. "Don't wear it that way again." She nearly bristled at the order—before he softened it with a "Please" so gently wistful that instead she smiled.

"Am I to be allowed to dictate as to your grooming as well?" she inquired.

"Absolutely."

She ran her hand along his cheek. "You could use a shave."

"I'll go and see to it now." And he started off from her, in all earnestness.

"Gannon! I was jesting!"

He turned back, abashed. "Some women don't care to kiss a man with a stubble."

"I like the feel of it," she assured him, even as she recognized: He might pretend to be cocksure, but he was as nervous as she. She proved her words by standing on her tiptoes to kiss the cheek.

He grinned. "If you told me to shave my head, I'd do it, you know. You hold that power over me."

The thought made her a little giddy—or maybe the champagne was finally asserting itself. The fire in the grate sparked, throwing sprays of light and shadow over them both. He held out his hand. "Come to bed."

She climbed in first. The sheets were silken-smooth; the pillows were clouds of down. He stretched out beside her, turned to her, smiling, and drew the covers up over them. The sensation of his naked limbs against hers in that billow of softness was devastating. She put her hands to his shoulders, felt the strength of his muscles. Iron and silk . . . He lowered his mouth to her breast, suckling so sweetly, so marvelously gently, while his hands glided over her waist and thighs. Then he grew more intense, pulling at her nipples with heightened passion until she writhed to his ministrations and flung her leg over his, so that she could feel his manhood at her belly. He let his fingers slip inside her, stroking her, fanning the flames until her breath came in gasps. One long finger found the bud of her desire, plucked at it, twirled against it, teasing mercilessly, releasing a flood of longing in her soul. And still he did not stop; he was pulling at her breast with his mouth and tantalizing her with his hand, and she was all on fire. She clung to him, desperate to have him inside her—

And then he was, that suddenly—arching over her, his long, hard rod pushing deep within her. She was awash in desperate pleasure. His loins pushed against her, in frantic desire. She opened to him eagerly, wholly; her senses were a muddle of firelight and moonlight and that other, that miraculous light that seared her eyelids even as she clenched her eyes shut. "God. Oh, God. Christiane," he grunted, each word a slamming thrust of his groin against her. He had his head thrown back; his teeth were bared, and his hair was loose and wild.

"Now! Now!" she begged him, clinging to him, following him, answering him thrust for thrust. His loins unleashed their bright tide of fire; she felt it surge into her, sear her, engulf her, just as her own pleasure crested. "Oh!" she cried, in awed wonder. She felt she must be visibly ablaze, incandescent. His seed poured into her, and they collapsed together, panting, his body heavy atop hers.

For a long time, they said nothing. Then he raised himself on his elbow. "I'm famished," he announced, smiling down at her. "Are you hungry?"

As a matter of fact, she was; she'd been too full of nerves to eat the handsome supper to which he'd escorted her. But then she thought of what admitting it would involve—servants tramping in with platters, poor O'Malley roused from his bed—and shook her head. "No. I couldn't eat a thing."

"Pity," said Gannon, climbing from the bed and reaching for a robe. "I really must have something to eat." He started for the door.

"Where are you going?" she asked in dismay.

"To the kitchens."

"You mean—you're going down there yourself? You're not sending for a servant?"

"Christ, no! Why would I trouble them? I'll be back in a bit."

"Wait!" she cried suddenly. He turned, his brows raised. "I'll come with you. If you have a robe I might borrow."

Looking very pleased, he searched in the wardrobe and brought one forth. "Probably too long," he said apologetically.

She put it on. It was knit of soft, creamy Irish wool, cozy and warm, but so huge on her that he laughed as she fastened it up. "You look very fetching," he told her, holding out his hand.

Together they went out into the corridor and moved toward the stairs. Christiane heard a sudden stirring in the darkness below. "What was that?" she whispered, clutching his arm.

"Homer, no doubt." He let out a low whistle, and something huge bounded toward them up the staircase. Christiane stifled a scream as it lunged for her—and then drew itself up, complacently sniffing the hem of her robe. It was only an Irish wolfhound—immense, but eminently docile.

"Do you like dogs?" Gannon inquired, scratching Homer's ears.

"I like *some* dogs." This one's flanks reached all the way to her waist.

"He knows I have a habit of making late-night raids on the kitchens—and that there's usually something in it for him."

"Good doggie," Christiane murmured nervously, reaching out to pat the creature. It promptly reared up and gave her a slathering lick across the cheek.

"He likes you," Gannon observed happily. "He doesn't like everybody."

"God help those he doesn't," she murmured, pushing

his paws from her chest. "I'd forgotten—Claire told me your brother raised wolfhounds."

"Hugh cared a great deal for his dogs."

She shot a glance at him in the flickering lamplight. "And you don't care for yours?"

"There's a vast difference between having one good dog and having a stable of them."

Homer was wagging his tail madly, insinuating himself between them. "You have just the one, then," Christiane said hopefully.

"There's also Chlöe."

"Chlöe?"

"His mate. It wouldn't serve for him to be lonely, would it? And here comes Chlöe now!" Another gargantuan beast was thundering up the stairs. "She's a bit more touchy than Homer," Gannon explained, as the new arrival stared at Christiane with glittering gold eyes, then let out what was an unmistakable growl. "You have to humor Chlöe."

"Humor her *how*?"

"Well, the best way is to feed her. But we have to get you downstairs for that. Hey, Chlöe!" He let out an ear-splitting whistle that reverberated wildly against the stone walls. The bitch gathered herself in expectantly. Gannon pulled something out of his robe and hurled it down the stairs. Both dogs set off after it in a mad cascade of thundering paws. "Shall we?" asked Gannon, offering Christiane his arm.

Very tentatively, she took it, and let him lead her downstairs. "What was that you threw?"

"Nothing at all. Just the motion is enough to set them off. Wolfhounds aren't particularly bright. But it ought to give us just enough time to clear it to the kitchens, if we hurry." They reached the entranceway; the dogs were still rooting about in the half-darkness. "Come on!" he urged, laughing, and they ran across the cold marble in their bare feet. They ducked through a doorway and down another corridor before the dogs realized they'd been tricked and came hurtling after them. "Safe home!" Gannon cried, pushing the door to the kitchens open with his shoulder. Chlöe and Homer were already upon them, slavering and panting. Chlöe, Christiane thought, was looking at her as though contemplating how tender she might be.

Gannon hurried to light a lamp atop a long, wide table, then looked about. "Oh, see here! Cook has saved them the bouillon bones!" he announced, and pulled a pair of hocks from a pot in the sink. The dogs instantly froze, frothing a bit at their muzzles. Gannon glanced at Christiane. "Would you prefer I let them out into the garden?"

"Actually, I would," she admitted.

"Not everyone is fond of wolfhounds," he acknowledged, and opened the rear door, tossing the bones onto the lawn. Homer bounded after them eagerly, but Chlöe waited, gazing at her master suspiciously.

"I wouldn't fool you twice, lady," he assured her, with a rub of her broad flanks and a caress of her nose. She sniffed, let out a single bark, and then followed Homer outside. Gannon closed the door behind them, and Christiane let out a sigh of relief. "They're very well behaved, you know," Gannon mentioned.

"I'm sure they do you honor," she said dubiously.

He grinned in the lamplight and lifted the silver dome atop a platter on the table. "Oh! The crab cakes—they were delightful. Did you take any at supper?" She shook her head, and he set one to her mouth. She obligingly opened for it. It was very good indeed.

He popped three into his own mouth before moving to the next dome. "Asparagus tart! I didn't think there was any of that left. Do you recall our discussion with Claire regarding asparagus?" He cut her a wedge, and himself a larger one.

"Don't you think we might have plates?" she asked tentatively.

"What's the fun in raiding the kitchen if you use proper manners? I say, what would you like to drink? We've got all manner of wines in the cellars. Or there's ale, or cider—or I could make chocolate."

"*You* would make it?"

"Of course. It's not difficult in the least. That's what we'll have, then—chocolate." He headed for the hearth, where a fire was still barely flickering. "Unless you'd prefer champagne."

"Chocolate would be lovely," she said.

She watched as he blew up the fire, added wood, selected a copper pot from the myriad the maids had left to dry on the sideboard, and measured milk, cocoa, sugar, and vanilla into it. "I never would have imagined you were so domesticated," she noted as he replaced the cocoa cannister in a cabinet.

"I'm quite a decent cook, actually. I spent a lot of time in the kitchens when I was a boy." He paused, let his gaze glance off hers. "Our parents didn't have a lot of time for us. We were more or less raised by the help."

She took a bite of the tart that lay in her hand. "I never learned to cook," she confessed. "My mama thought it beneath a lady to do anything more than give orders in a kitchen. And our cook was an untalented bully. As a consequence, I ate perfectly dreadful food the entire time I was growing up."

"No wonder you loved France."

"It was a revelation. I do appreciate England, of course. But the French are so much our superiors in gustatory matters."

"What is Claire learning at the academy regarding cookery?" he inquired, stirring the contents of his pot.

"Regrettably, Mrs. Treadwell hews to the 'lady in the kitchen' line. But I've noticed a good number of the girls congregate with Cook when they have a bit of free time. She is quite splendid at her craft, as you know. And Mrs. Caldburn makes sure they have the basics—bread, ale, roast mutton, Yorkshire pudding. Proper British stuff."

"Only the basics? Pity. It can be very creative, cooking, don't you think?" The firelight shone on his black hair as he withdrew the spoon from the chocolate and licked it. Christiane watched, fascinated, as his tongue lapped at the bowl. "Almost ready now. I like it with a bit of brandy. What do you say?"

"Brandy can't hurt."

He grinned at her. "A girl after my own heart." He took a bottle from a sideboard and poured a dollop in.

The dogs were banging at the door. "Monsters," he muttered, and cast about for something to placate them, lifting the silver domes on the dishes left along the table. "Ah! The roast beef!" He stabbed a huge hunk with a fork, went to the door, and opened it. Christiane braced herself for the onslaught. But Homer and Chlöe apparently were more than familiar with this midnight-raid routine; they just stood, drooling, until he tossed them the meat.

"Won't they fight over it?" she asked.

"No, no. They're life-mates; they never fight. Homer will take what he likes, and Chlöe will get the rest."

"That doesn't seem exactly equitable."

He raised his head. "I suppose it isn't, come to think of it."

"But it is a rather fair summation of an Englishwoman's lot in life."

"Oh, you are bitter, aren't you?" He tasted the chocolate once more, nodded, and used a folded towel to lift the pot off the fire and pour its contents into two mugs. "This is ready, I think."

"Thank you." She took the mug he handed her, blew across the top, and sipped. It was very good chocolate. "You have talents I never would have dreamed of," she admitted, taking a more hearty swallow.

But he was lifting domes again. "What I really want are those pastries Cook makes with the chocolate icing and the custard-cream filling. Though I don't suppose any are left." He looked extremely mournful.

Christiane lifted the dome nearest her. "Oh, look here. It is your lucky day."

She had to smile at the way he brightened, wholly, instantly. "I'll be damned! No, you first. They really are very fine."

She plucked one up and tasted it. "Mmm," she agreed, starting to lick the icing from her fingers.

"I'll do that," he offered—and did, while gazing into her eyes.

Christiane was utterly disarmed. "You aren't a rogue at all, are you?" she whispered, as he helped himself to half a dozen of the pastries, one right after another.

"Not so. I'm a terrible rogue," he insisted, through a mouthful of custard cream.

"A terrible bluffer is more like it."

"You have found me out," he confessed in a stage whisper. "All my dissolute life, I've wanted nothing more than to settle down with the right girl."

Girl. His choice of word chilled her gay mood. She set her half-eaten pastry aside. "If that is so," she said carefully, "then you must have been longing for all that goes along with that domestic dream."

"Meaning?"

"Children." He started to speak, but she cut him off impatiently. "Be honest, Gannon. Every man wants children. A scion—an heir to continue the line. It is human nature."

He swung himself up to sit atop the long table, between the domes. "I never have."

"I cannot believe that."

"Perhaps if your childhood had been as . . . as awful as mine was . . ."

"But you would make such a marvelous father!"

"No. I wouldn't," he said decisively.

"You don't know that."

"I know—and you do, as well—that we learn how to be a parent from watching our own. We have no other example. What they teach us is deeper than bone." He reached for another pastry, weighed it in his hand. "Do you know what I think? I think all this palaver about *my* wanting children is only proof that you do."

"I regret not having had them, sometimes," she admitted bravely. "Don't you?"

"No. Let Claire continue the line—with David Wrede,

if he'll have her. He *will* be a good father. I wouldn't. I
wouldn't know how."

She stared down at her bare feet. The stone floor was
cold. "What did he do to you?" she asked, very softly.

"Not to me. To my mother."

"To her, then."

He took a long swallow of chocolate, then shook his
head. "Family secrets. Not fit for disclosure."

"You asked me to marry you tonight," she reminded
him.

"And you said no." He glanced up with heart-stopping
quickness. "Would you say yes if I told you?"

"I won't know unless you do."

He looked away and let out a sigh. "It was really nothing more than the usual sort of extreme beastliness, I suppose. You know. Beatings. Belittlings. If you read about it
in a book, you would say, 'Oh. That.' But when you are living it, watching it, frightened and wanting to help but not
knowing how . . ."

"Was Hugh like him?"

His eyes were sharp. "Why would you say that?"

"Things that Claire has said."

"Hugh was cut from the same cloth," he said grimly.

"Thank God you are not."

"Yes," he said after a moment. "Thank God." He
grinned at her as she leaned against the table. "You do look
a vision in that robe. A bit more sustenance, and I daresay
I'll be bolstered enough to ravish you again."

"It's a marvel you're not the size of a house," she noted,
watching him begin on a sandwich of deviled ham.

"I make certain I get plenty of exercise," he said slyly,
making her laugh. "Are you sure you don't want some of
this ham?" She shook her head. "A bit of cold pigeon?
Some of the melon compote?"

"I haven't been getting as much . . . exercise as you."

"Yes, but I intend to remedy that from now on. You
need to keep up your strength."

"I will let you know if I am feeling faint."

She wrapped her hands around her mug of chocolate and sipped, watching him pick happily through the remnants of the feast. As she did, the strangest sensation coursed through her. The emotion was so unfamiliar that it took her several minutes to assign it a name. She felt *contented,* straight to her soul. When had she last felt that way? When she was with the comte? No. Deep inside, she'd always known with him that she was settling for something less than complete contentment. He'd recognized it as well, of course; their marriage had been *très à la mode,* convenient for both, more a joining of minds than of hearts. As for Jean-Baptiste—oh, contentment had played little part in that crazed, hectic dalliance, with his wife and children and duty to his country always standing like walls between them. There had been passion there, but not much peace. It took a young heart to endure the bruises such an affair entailed.

And when one's heart was no longer young?

Then there might be nothing more satisfying in the world than to stand in your bare feet on a chill stone floor and watch the man with whom you'd just made love eat bits of pigeon breast with his fingers.

To her shock, she felt tears rise in her eyes.

He held a scrap of the meat out to her. "Sure I can't tempt you with—Christiane. Are you crying?"

"Of course not," she said hastily, rubbing her eyes with her fists. "I am sleepy, that's all." But the tears would not stop.

He set the pigeon breast aside and hopped down from the table. "Liar. You *are* crying." He moved to embrace her, frowned at his sauce-covered fingers, wiped them on his robe. "Here, now, what's the matter? Did I say something? Do something?"

What had he done? He had opened a window and dared her to look through it onto a life she hadn't let herself imagine since she was eighteen years old. She didn't know, though, how to tell him that.

He pulled her into his arms, stroked her loose, wild hair.

"You mustn't cry," he told her, sounding alarmed. "I won't have it. I only want you to be happy. It is all I ever have wanted. Even back in France. I didn't think he was making you happy enough—as happy as you deserved. And I knew that I could. Because I loved you so."

"Idiot," Christiane said, her voice muffled against his chest. "I am crying because I *am* happy."

"Are you?" He drew away to stare down at her. "Are you certain?" She nodded, more tears spilling over even as she started to laugh; Homer and Chlöe were pounding at the door again.

"I suppose they've finished the roast beef," she said, and sniffled.

"They're used to sleeping with me." He put his hand to her cheek and brushed it dry. His own eyes were suspiciously bright. "But it's a very mild night." He released her abruptly and turned to the table, upending all the domes and heaping everything that lay beneath them onto a single tray. He needed both hands to lift it. "Could you . . ." He nodded toward the door. She obligingly opened it, taking care to stand well to the side. "Here you go, you beasts! Christmas has come early!" He hurled the contents of the tray through the doorway. The dogs stared for a moment in wonder, then fell on the bounty as though they hadn't eaten in days.

"I wonder," mused Christiane, watching Chlöe chomp down half of an asparagus tart, "what effect that might have on wolfhound urine?"

"We're certain to find out; she will anoint the whole garden." He kicked the door shut, tossed the tray back onto the table, and held out his hand to her. "Mind if I take you back to bed now, milady?"

"Are you sure you're fortified enough?"

For answer, he pulled her upstairs.

Twenty-three

Mrs. Treadwell eyed Christiane over the rim of her glass of sherry. "Your weekend in London seems to have done wonders for you, I must say," she noted. "You are positively aglow. Whatever did you do?"

Christiane blushed. "Oh, nothing much, really."

"Is Violet well?"

"Very well. She sends her regards."

"And Peter and Martha?"

"I didn't have a chance to see them, actually."

"Pity. Did Violet entertain?"

Christiane shook her head, taking a seat on the settee. "No. We had a quiet evening together on Friday. But on Saturday, she was invited to Prinny's, and of course I couldn't go along. I say, how is Claire?"

"Well enough." But the headmistress was still eyeing her suspiciously. Then her face brightened. "I know! You've had your hair dyed!"

Christiane laughed. "Not likely."

"Visited one of those spas, then, where they treat you with massages and mineral waters and facial creams."

Christiane shook her head, biting down on her lip. "Well, whatever you've done, I must say, it—" She broke off sharply, drew in her breath. "Good God. Don't tell me you saw *him.*"

"Him who?" Christiane inquired, even as she recalled their parting—his ardent kisses, the winsome way he'd begged her to stay.

"Lord Carew, of course. That's it, isn't it?" Mrs. Treadwell's round face was aghast. "And you promised me you wouldn't! You swore it! Have you no thought for our girls? For this academy?"

Christiane sighed. She had rather hoped for more time to prepare for the inevitable showdown. Now that it had come, though, she'd just as soon be finished with it. "If you must know, Evelyn, yes. I did see Lord Carew. He invited me to a soirée at his home."

"And you never said a word of it to me! How could you be so duplicitous?" Mrs. Treadwell wailed. "A soirée! A public soirée!"

"If I had spoken of it to you, you would have done your best to dissuade me from going," Christiane said briskly. "And not to have gone would have been a graver mistake than any I have ever made in my life."

"Why?" Mrs. Treadwell breathed.

"Because . . . it was perfectly splendid. Unimaginably splendid."

Mrs. Treadwell stared. Her partner's dark eyes were shining even more brightly. "I think you must be daft," she declared. "How could you do such a thing?"

"Well, Lord Carew pointed out to me, quite rightly, that no one there would be aware of my connection with the academy. Sure enough, no one was—except for Emily Hainesworth, who took pains to assure me that she continues to recommend us roundly to the mamas of her acquaintance. Without mentioning my name, naturally."

"Who else was there?"

"Lord and Lady Cobblesby attended. A Miss Russ, who writes books. The poet, Mr. Coleridge. Oh, and Dr. Caplan came. It was all very gay and amusing." Mrs. Treadwell nearly swooned. "I must say, everyone was perfectly civil to me. Emily told me how devoutly she wished she'd let me have Harold when I wanted him. And Lady Custis expressed hopes that I would open a gaming hell on this side of the Channel."

The headmistress took a long swig of sherry. "I cannot imagine what society is coming to."

Christiane smiled at her. "It isn't what society is coming to. It is, rather, what Lady Cobblesby and Lady Custis and Emily—and I—have become."

"And what is that?"

"Why, women of a certain age, of course! Who are past the sorts of jealous, petty squabbles that occupied us when we were younger." She reached for her friend's hand. "I think that when we are in the glow of youth, we consider other women our enemies. But as we grow older, we recognize that we were fighting the wrong foes. Men—men are the enemy! It is because of them that we make fools of ourselves, constrict our lives, lose our figures in childbirth, and then sit by in impotence while they chase after younger skirts."

"Men are not our *enemy*," Mrs. Treadwell said slowly. "They are our protectors! Our knights in shining armor!"

"And that's why Mr. Treadwell died in his mistress's bed?"

Mrs. Treadwell drew her breath in sharply. "You have no right—"

"Oh, Evelyn, you told me that the very first time we discussed founding this academy! And you also told me how distraught you were that Vanessa had wed Yarlborough—that she was silly and flighty to consider his title and riches more than his personality. And then you said you could not blame her, because you had been a wretched model for her, letting your husband dally and never standing up for yourself. Don't deny that you did!"

"We agreed, I believe, that we would pursue our goals in private!" the headmistress shot back. "That the time was not ripe for England to consider women worthy! That we would mount a *secret* rebellion. And yet I find that you have taken the battle to the streets, as it were."

Christiane looked her squarely in the eye. "Perhaps we were wrong. Perhaps we were too timid."

"Don't be absurd. If any man alive were to discover that Gwen has been slicing up piglets—"

"What about Mr. Wrede?" Christiane demanded. "He certainly is well enough acquainted with our curriculum by now, and it has not caused him to relinquish his suit for Claire's hand."

"Mr. Wrede is a social pariah."

Christiane restrained herself. "Times change, Evelyn," she said, mildly enough. "Manners change. It just may be that our time has come."

Evelyn had her mouth drawn up tight. "So. You have a new lover. You must be very proud of yourself."

Christiane bit back the tart reply her friend's prudery prompted. "I have agreed to marry Lord Carew," she said instead.

Mrs. Treadwell clutched her heart. "Are you *both* mad?"

"On the contrary. We are both very happy. At last."

There was a brief pause. Then the headmistress said, "Forgive me for not rejoicing at your news, Christiane. It is only that I am sure you are making a dreadful mistake."

Christiane laughed. "Perhaps I am. But at least I am doing *something*—not simply sitting and sipping sherry while I wait for old age and death to claim me. He says he loves me, and I believe him."

"Perhaps you ought to speak to Greer Delaney," Mrs. Treadwell snipped.

"He explained all that," Christiane assured her. "He has been in the habit of taking up with young ladies he didn't care for, simply because he was pining for me all these years."

"That's what he told you."

The countess lifted her chin. "Yes. That *is* what he told me."

"Oh, it's true, isn't it—there's no fool like an old fool," said Mrs. Treadwell, wagging her head.

"I'm not old!"

"Perhaps not, but I am—too old to listen to such nonsense. Love—at your age!"

"I was not aware there was a limit."

"Women of decent sensibilities recognize the fact."

"Are you calling me indecent, Evelyn?"

"I believe your behavior calls your common sense into question."

"What exactly are you getting at?" the countess demanded.

"Well, if you insist on pursuing this crazed infatuation with Lord Carew—" The headmistress paused.

"Yes?" Christiane asked, a dangerous edge to her tone.

"I'm afraid I simply must insist that you relinquish your duties here."

Christiane bit back a laugh. "Evelyn, he wants to wed me!"

"I'll believe that when the invitation arrives. Nay, not even then—when I see you with the ring on your finger." And she shook her head balefully. "It's the same thing he said to get Greer Delaney into his bed, for heaven's sake."

But Christiane was blithe. "Oh, be reasonable. You've said yourself I'm not young anymore. What would he have to gain by feigning affection for me?"

"I don't know," the headmistress muttered. "But I don't trust the man."

For an instant, looking into her old friend's troubled eyes, Christiane felt a qualm. But then she remembered how Gannon had gone to the window of his town house, thrown the shutters open, and shouted into the street: "I love the Countess d'Oliveri!" It was only the perfidy of her own husband that made Evelyn so suspicious. Christiane felt sorry for her.

"It may be," she said thoughtfully, "that I am deceived

by Lord Carew—though I very much doubt it. But even if I am . . . oh, Evelyn, listen, do! Love has come back into my life when I least expected it! And it has made me feel like a girl again."

"You are certainly behaving like one. He is after something. Mark my words."

The headmistress's stubborn pessimism was beginning to grate. "I have a right to be loved!" Christiane declared angrily. "I have a right to happiness! And you have no right to try to spoil it for me!"

"How public do you and Lord Carew intend to make your affair?" Evelyn inquired acidly.

Christiane counted to ten, very slowly, in her head. "Perhaps it would be best," she offered then, "if I removed myself from the school until you are convinced that Lord Carew's intentions toward me are honorable."

"If you are going to gad about making such an idiot of yourself, I really think it would be best if you do."

Christiane smiled thinly. "I believe you are jealous of me, Evelyn. I honestly do. After all our years of friendship, for you to turn on me this way—I can only conclude that you wish you had *some* sort of passion in your own life."

The headmistress stood, her feathers clearly ruffled, and pointed to the door. "I'd suggest you leave now, before you say something more that you will come to regret!"

"Did that touch too close to home?"

"On the contrary—it merely provided additional proof of how decadent and shameless you've become! I won't have the girls exposed to you for one more day."

"You're as bad as the tigers!" Christiane said accusingly. "Worse, because I supposed you my friend! To turn on me simply because I have this chance at happiness—"

"If that is what you choose to call it," Mrs. Treadwell said darkly.

Christiane laughed. "Well, I *shall* go, then!" she declared. "I'll go to London and be happy with Lord Carew. But don't come crying to *me* when one of the girls decides to run away, or attempts suicide, or falls head-over-heels for the wrong sort, or any of the other scrapes I've pulled you out of. Because I will be far too busy being in love to care!"

"You always were self-centered!" the headmistress shrilled as Christiane started toward the door. "You never did think of anyone but yourself. I might have expected just this sort of thing when you came begging to me for help in setting up this school!"

But Christiane refused to listen; she was running up the stairs to her rooms.

On the landing, she nearly bowled over Gwen and Bess, who were lurking, looking guilty and anxious all at once. "You're not *really* leaving, are you?" Gwen demanded.

And Bess chimed in: "You wouldn't leave, would you? The academy would not be the same—it would not be *special*—without you!"

The countess put an arm around each of them. "It appears I must, ladies. The headmistress has declared me unfit to educate you."

"But that is so unfair!" Bess wailed. "You are only doing what you and she always impressed upon us as the most important thing in life—following your heart!"

Christiane gave their shoulders a squeeze. "It seems my heart has led me to a decision Mrs. Treadwell cannot stomach. But there's no reason why anything here should change. You will still have your courses of study, your teachers, your friends."

Gwen was near tears. "If you go, this will be naught but another prissy finishing school. Do you imagine Mrs. T would ever have allowed Dr. Caplan to bring me that piglet? Or championed Petra against her father's wishes?"

"I will hear nothing morning till night," Bess put in glumly, "except, 'You simply must lose weight, my dear!' "

Christiane stopped on the stairs and smiled at them. "No matter what you hear," she whispered, "don't believe it. I've learned a secret, you see. The ton tigers aren't nearly as formidable as they would have you think."

"They're not?" Bess asked dubiously.

"Not a bit. Do you know what those women are? They are simply girls with hopeful hearts who have seen life pass them by. Their power resides only in their determination to make sure that others share their misery. And Mrs. T . . ." She hesitated, then forged on. "Mrs. T is one of them. I did not think so, always. But I know it now."

"Then you are leaving us here with no hope!" Bess cried.

"Don't you see, pet?" She smoothed back the redhead's wayward curls. "I am going out into the fray ahead of you; that is all. When you come up to London this autumn, I will be at all the best events—in the company of Lord Carew. I shall be much better situated to ensure your futures than I have been while sequestered here. I'll take care to speak to the young men who are your potential swains. I'll discover which ones might harbor a tendresse for poetry, or be infatuated with the internal workings of the human body. I shall be the advance guard, as it were."

"No more wasted time," Gwen murmured thoughtfully. "No more dancing with louts like Lord Simpson. It isn't such a bad notion, Bess."

"But we will be so miserable in the meantime!" the redhead protested.

"It's not so long a meantime," Christiane said soothingly. "Only a few more months—months in which," she added, more sternly, "you must pay heed to what Mrs. Treadwell and Mrs. Caldburn and all the others here teach you. When I do make introductions for you to the young men I've scouted, I expect to find your manners beyond reproach. No snorting or scratching, Bess!" The young lady in question, who had just reached to remedy an itch, stopped herself hurriedly. "And as for you, Gwen, you really must learn not to bring conversation to a dead halt by counting down the stages of decrepitude of the liver in those who indulge in hard spirits. It simply isn't party fare."

Gwen let out a giggle. After a moment, Bess joined in,

then gamely straightened her shoulders. "Very well," she declared. "So long as it is only a few months . . . I suppose we can cope. Don't you think so, Gwen?"

"I begin to think it the best possible situation," the dark-haired girl noted. "So far, Bess, you must admit our sojourns into society have been less than fruitful. But with Madame working as our spy—"

"Precisely," Christiane said, and smiled at them warmly. "You'll see. It is all for the best."

"Oh, but what about Claire?" Gwen cried suddenly. "You know that Mrs. T and she have never truly been sympathetic, one to the other."

"Don't be an idiot, Gwen," Bess told her. "Out in the world, Madame will be a far more effective champion for Mr. Wrede's suit than she would be hidden away here."

"I assure you, I will be most conscious of Claire's welfare—and of Petra's, and of yours, both of you." The countess hugged them to her tightly. "Oh, do wish me well, you two! Mrs. Treadwell is so full of dire predictions that I have nearly lost my nerve."

"But you must go to him," Gwen said solemnly. "If you don't, then all you've taught us is in vain."

"Absolutely," Bess agreed, brushing away her tears. Then her blue eyes brimmed over again. "Still, we will miss you so!"

"It is only a little while," the countess assured them, "until I will be inviting you up to London to stay with Lord Carew and me. And we shall see the sights, and make the rounds, and discover at long last whether there are any men in England worthy of the two of you. And if there are not—then we will venture abroad!" She released them then, with a quick kiss to each girl's forehead. "Now get along to bed."

"Good-bye, Madame." Gwen came to her for one last hug. "If you see my father there in London, urge him to send in my tuition on time. Mrs. Treadwell does keep harping that he forgets."

"Until we meet again, *chérie,*" Christiane said, a catch

in her voice. She had not, when she'd bickered with Evelyn, quite computed the cost of all she was leaving behind.

"I think he is outstandingly handsome," Bess hissed, and giggled.

"My father?" Gwen teased.

"Of course not! Lord Carew!"

"Well, naturally! What other sort of man would suit our Madame?"

"*Au revoir,* Gwen, Bess." Christiane kissed them, then hurried to her rooms before her tears spilled over. She packed in a reckless lather, stuffing gowns and shoes and hats helter-skelter into her trunks. She heard Evelyn come up the stairs, heard her hesitate in the corridor outside, and could not decide what she wanted her old friend to do.

Finally, the footsteps moved on.

Christiane crawled into bed and spent a restless night balancing the ecstasy she felt in Gannon's arms against the girls' distraught faces. At dawn she rose, and sent Clarisse to rouse Stains and have him hitch the carriage. He and the stableboy hefted her trunks down the stairs. If Evelyn was awake, she gave no sign, made no attempt at peace.

So. Christiane stood on the drive in the thin, chill light and stared at the old abbey, with its stout, ivy-covered walls and mullioned windows. Then she shivered, shrugged, and let Stains step her into the coach. "Fifty-four Berkeley Square, London," she told him resolutely, and took care not to look back.

They made good time. It was only half-past eleven when they rolled up to Lord Carew's town house. It was the feast day of St. George, and church bells were sounding in the air.

Stains handed her down. She climbed the stairs, let the knocker drop, and was suddenly seized by such a rush of doubt that she fell to her knees. She forced herself to rise as the door swung open, not wanting the butler to find her that way.

But it wasn't the butler. It was Gannon, a half-gnawed

turkey drumstick in his hand, and Homer and Chlöe raising holy hell behind him.

His gray eyes ignited. He reached for her.

"You've come home," he said.

Twenty-four

"Three of spades," Christiane declared, laying it upon the discard pile with negligent grace. "And I am out, as it happens. Again. Tally them up, you poor devils! How many points against you, my love?"

Gannon made a mock scowl and threw his cards to the table. "Eight."

"Jot that down, Mr. Wrede. And you, Claire?"

"Only three this time. I am luckier than you, Uncle!" Claire's eyes danced devilishly as she laid down her hand.

"And three for Claire, Mr. Wrede. Shall we play again?" The countess swept the cards toward her across the gleaming table.

"I daresay we are boring Mr. Wrede to tears," Gannon growled.

"Oh, quite the contrary," his guest assured him. "Since I have never learned to play hearts, I find observing the game most interesting."

"And he never cheats at scorekeeping," Christiane mentioned, with a sidelong glance at Gannon. "Unlike certain other folk."

"That was an honest mathematical error, I assure you!" His Lordship retorted.

"He can't abide losing, you know," the countess whispered to the young folk.

"Perhaps," Mr. Wrede ventured, "it is just that he is constitutionally unsuited to a game in which the object is to *avoid* capturing hearts."

Christiane and Claire stared at him for a moment, then burst out laughing. "Why, David," Claire gasped through her giggles, "how uncharacteristically unchivalrous of you!"

"I meant it as a compliment," David assured his host.

"Aye, well, I'll take it as one, then," Gannon replied, a hint of a grin breaking his stern expression. "It is only God's truth."

"You are unspeakably vain," Christiane told him, leaning toward him for a kiss, which he readily provided.

David glanced at Claire. "Should we withdraw, and leave them to it?"

"Not a chance," she said severely. "We are their chaperones, do you forget? Without our steady influence, imagine what they might get up to!"

"Imagine," murmured Gannon, stroking Christiane's wrist with his fingertips, making her blush.

"One more hand," she decreed, pulling away from him to take up the deck. "And do see, Gannon, if you can remedy your frightful score." She commenced to shuffle, then passed the cards to Claire to cut. "What did you think to wear, Claire, to Lady Cobblesby's fete tomorrow?"

A shadow fell across the girl's face. "Must we go? It is so pleasant here with you and Uncle . . . and David, of course. Can we not just pass the evening as we are now, in the comfort of family?"

Christiane looked at her with sympathy. "It *is* pleasant, isn't it? But don't forget—even though *your* affections are happily settled, we must do our best still to see to Bess and Gwen and Petra."

Claire exhaled a sigh. "You are right, of course. David,

don't you know three more stalwart Quakers who are suitable for them?"

"Surely thou would not want the academy branded as a hothouse for bad marriages," he teased her.

"Which reminds me," Gannon put in. "How about choosing a date, you two?"

Claire's color rose, but David only laughed. "We are waiting for thee to do so first, sir," he announced. "Age has its perquisites."

"The way you harp," Christiane said, clucking her tongue.

He grinned at her. "Only because thou put the lie to it."

She shook her head at him. "He *is* a charmer, Claire."

"Isn't he?" the girl said happily, tucking her arm through his.

"What about a double wedding?" Gannon said suddenly. They looked at him. "Well, why the devil not? Save me a ton of money."

"Ever the Irishman," Christiane said dryly.

Gannon stuck out his tongue at her.

"It would, though," David noted thoughtfully.

"Every bride wants her own day," Christiane objected, smiling at Claire, "when she can be the sole object of attention."

"I don't," the girl replied promptly. "I should be only too grateful to share."

"Do thou mean that?" David asked her. She nodded vigorously.

"It would have to be a Quaker wedding, though," Gannon pointed out. "Do your minister-sorts perform marriages for renegades and ne'er-do-wells, Wrede?"

"We pledge only to one another, with no intermediary," he explained.

"I like that notion," said Christiane.

"But you do so in a plain fashion, surely," Claire noted, "which would hardly suit Madame."

"How do you presume to know what would suit me, whippersnapper?" Christiane retorted. "I happen to think black flatters me very well."

"It does," Gannon affirmed, his gray gaze raking over the low-cut black sheath she wore.

"Do Quaker *brides* wear black?" Claire asked, her eyes wide.

"No, no," David assured her. "White and ivory and blue and beige are all considered proper."

"Do they carry flowers?"

"Aye." He smiled, smoothing her black hair back from her brow. "That matters to thee, does it?"

"More than the color of the gown."

"Would the ton attend?" Christiane wondered aloud.

"Most likely not," David conceded.

"Then let's do it, by all means!" Claire begged.

Christiane looked at Gannon. "Are you in earnest?"

"Absolutely."

"And you, Mr. Wrede — you would not object to sharing your wedding with a pair of old scoundrels such as us?"

"I'd be honored. Thou championed my courtship of Claire. Without thy help . . ."

"Who knows where we would be?" Claire finished the thought, smiling up at him.

Gannon alone seemed unconvinced. "It's not what I envisioned, Christiane. I thought St. Paul's — the entire spectacle."

"A fig for spectacle. This *is* my second wedding, after all," Christiane reminded him. "A big to-do would only assure Evelyn I am a hopeless cause."

His eyes met hers. "Will you invite her?"

"Of course I will. But she won't come." The thought intruded slightly on Christiane's happiness. "She wouldn't at St. Paul's, either, though, so there's no point in fussing over that."

Claire reached across the table for the countess's hand. "Your oldest, dearest friend," she murmured. "Surely she will want to be there."

But Christiane shook her head vehemently. "No. She

won't. She is convinced I'm quite mad." Then she shrugged off her sadness and kissed Gannon's cheek.

"June?" David proposed.

"What, a scant month hence? Too soon," Christiane demurred. "Too much to do between now and then."

"And too ordinary, anyway," Gannon added.

"We lose July and August," Christiane noted, "to the season at Bath."

"I have always liked autumn best of all seasons," David mentioned.

"You and I," Gannon reminded the countess, "were reacquainted then. I vote for October. I'm very fond of October. Ale-making weather."

"It could not be this October," Claire said with a frown of concern. "That would be unseemly. Too hasty, considering . . ." She faltered.

"It would be more than a year after your parents' deaths," Christiane said gently. "Time enough for proper mourning, I think."

Gannon was restless, she noticed; he sprang up from his chair and went to the sideboard for more whiskey, made a production of fussing with the seltzer cannister. Why would he be uneasy at the conversation? *Perhaps it is less the conversation than the reality of a wedding,* she registered. She had been so pleased by his abrupt, businesslike dismissal of his betrothal to Miss Delaney. Should she have been concerned instead? Had he and Greer ever discussed potential dates for their wedding? They must have. She pictured the enormous ruby ring the blonde had twined on her finger. Women longed for such concreteness, reveled in endless talk of gowns and flowers and invitations. Yet he had let Greer pass out of his life without a hint of regret.

As he had, according to Claire, the fiancée before that . . . and the one before that. . . .

Would she prove next in that long line of discarded lovers? There were men for whom the chase was everything, who lost interest once they had attained the object of their desire. He could be such a man.

She would not let such doubts bedevil her, she resolved, reaching for her own whiskey-and-water. It was not worthy of her . . . or of him.

Finally he turned back from the sideboard, and Christiane released her breath, not having known that she was holding it in. His brow was clear of care; his gray eyes shone like old silver, patinated with hope, rich and warm.

"Claire," he said, his voice deep and still and firm. "You must believe me. Your happiness was your mother's foremost concern in life. If you were to wed Mr. Wrede tomorrow, against all ton stricture, she would beam down at you from heaven. I am sure of it."

Claire was holding tightly to David's hand. "I don't know. I just don't know."

"I will make thee happy," David vowed breathlessly.

The girl was silent for a long moment. From the expression on her face, she might have been fighting demons. Then she shrugged off whatever mood had seized her. "October would suit me well," she whispered.

David Wrede enveloped her in his strong arms. Gannon crossed the room to Christiane and kissed her, swift and hard.

"October it is," he decreed. "Deal those cards, my love."

"I wonder," *Christiane* mused, sitting at Gannon's dressing table, pulling a brush through her loose curls.

He was already in bed, arms clasped behind his head, the linens made a tent by his erection. "Wonder what?"

"Whether we might be rushing Claire a bit."

"Nonsense," he said gruffly. "Best thing in the world for her, to be married. He's the perfect man for her."

"Oh, I've no doubt of that." She set the brush aside and started a braid.

"Leave it loose," he commanded, and then softened it: "Please."

"If you like." She untied her dressing gown, let it fall back against the chair. The chemise she wore beneath was of sheer oyster dimity. In the looking glass, she saw raw hunger in his gaze. It made her shiver in anticipation. Still, she lingered at the glass. He must have hungered for Greer as well, for her cool blond beauty and bounteous bosom. What she wanted proof of was his love.

She decided on a teasing tack. "Folk will be sure to talk, you know, if after so long a string of unresolved betrothals you rush to the altar with me."

"Let them talk," he growled. "They always do. Come to bed."

She reached to unfasten her earrings. As she did, she had an uncanny sense that she and he had enacted this same scene before—what the French called *déjà vu*. Why should she feel that?

She took up the bottle of eau de toilette on the table before her and unstoppered it. The familiar, ethereal scent of *muguets du bois* filled the air, made her head swim. She put the crystal stopper to her throat and shivered at its chill. She raised her gaze slowly to the mirror, saw his reflection—his tousled black hair, the covetousness in his eyes—and remembered: He had looked just that way in Paris, on the night she'd taken him into her bed. She had sat this same way, made these same ministrations, tensed just so at the prospect of what she was about to do. . . .

And had known, had sensed, that it was a mistake. That in rising from her seat, in going to him, she was betraying not only Jean-Baptiste, but herself as well. That moment, that instant when she'd regarded him lying in her bed, had set all this in motion. If she had resisted the temptation . . . if she'd been true to her lover . . . where might they all be now? Jean-Baptiste, unhampered by the wound Gannon had yet to deal him, might not have perished in the war. He might have left his wife for her. She might not have married the Comte d'Oliveri. And Gannon—Gannon might have left off his mad infatuation with her, finished his grand tour of Europe, returned to England, and wed Georgina.

In which case Claire would never have been born.

"What is keeping you?" he demanded impatiently.

She shook her head to clear her muddled thoughts. "Forgive me. I don't know." She rose from her seat— again. She went to him. As she did, she felt her heart beating in her throat, keeping time, tolling its passing.

Something inside her was terribly afraid. There was a darkness there that his welcoming arms could not quell, an emptiness his kisses did not fill. Damn Evelyn, anyway, for her predictions of woe! She put a brave face on it, responded to his caresses as he would expect, moaned at the proper times as he thrust inside her.

But when he rolled from atop her in contentment, kissed her throat and then her mouth, turned on his side, and began to snore, she hugged herself tightly and lay in the darkness, listening to the uncertain pounding of her heart.

Twenty-five

"*That was not* so bad, now, was it?" David Wrede asked earnestly, settling in beside Claire as Lord Cobblesby's footman clicked the carriage door shut behind them.

She shook her bowed head, staring at her gloved hands. "No. Not so bad, I suppose."

"I thought it was simply marvelous," Christiane declared, leaning back against the seat. "I won fifty pounds from Lord Trelawny at whist. That will teach him to bet against me. What was it he said, love?" she applied to Gannon.

"That one can always read a woman's hand from her expression. Hell, I could have told him that was idiocy."

Sean, the coachman, called, "Where to, m'lord?"

Gannon raised a brow at Christiane. "We must see Mr. Wrede home first, I suppose," she ventured. "Unless he'd care to come back with us for a . . . oh. I continue to forget that you don't drink, David. It takes a rare soul who doesn't to provide such fine company. Still, you can watch *us* drink."

He laughed. "I appreciate the invitation. But I have an early meeting with a new client of my father's."

"Pity. To Mr. Wrede's, then, Sean!" she called. "What's the direction again, David?"

"Burtons Court," Wrede reminded her. "Number ten."

Sean grunted acknowledgment and whistled the team on.

"We're to dine with your family this weekend, Wrede, aren't we?" Gannon inquired.

"On Friday at seven." He winked. "An unfashionable hour, I know. That's the trouble with Quakers."

"You've met David's parents before, have you not?" Christiane asked Claire.

"I visited them at Easter."

"They adore her," David told Christiane. "As do my sisters."

"They were very kind to me," Claire said softly. But she seemed distracted, oddly edgy.

Christiane exchanged glances with Gannon, who shrugged a bit. The countess made her voice light and gay. "I know it is difficult for you, Claire, this sudden rush of attention. So many new faces, so many names to remember! You are doing very well, though. Gannon, don't you agree?"

"Absolutely."

Claire acknowledged the compliment with the briefest nod. Christiane smiled reassuringly despite her own qualms. The evening had not been an unqualified success. While Gannon's set had proven very kind to the countess, seeming to take some sort of convoluted pride in welcoming a renegade home, Claire had a harder time of it. She did not make conversation easily. And any slight to David cut her to the quick. Tonight, for instance, one of the men had mimicked his speech, slyly "thee-ing" and "thou-ing" fellow guests at the dinner table. It was in good fun, and David had laughed. But Claire simmered; Christiane saw it, and ached for her wounded pride.

Or was it pride? In the shadowy coach, she shot a

glance at Gannon's niece. Christiane had not forgotten what Gannon had told her of Claire's childhood, and while it wasn't exactly surprising that Hugh Finn's ferocious possessiveness should resurface in his daughter, gentle David Wrede seemed the perfect foil for such emotions. Except that Claire always *felt* things to such extremes. Christiane dearly wished she could convey to her the wisdom that four decades–plus on the planet had instilled: *The world's attention is not always on you!*

"Miss Delaney was beastly to me," Claire whispered, her head still lowered.

Christiane started. "I did not know she was there!"

"Thy uncle's disappointed sweethearts," David told Claire, with a ghost of a smile, "are not likely to pay thee compliments."

"She said things, though . . ."

"What things?" Gannon demanded, straightening in his seat.

They passed beneath a gas-lamp that ignited Claire's enormous gray eyes and made them gleam green as a cat's. "I don't want to discuss it," she whispered, and leaned into Mr. Wrede, closing those chatoyant eyes.

The carriage rolled to a halt. "Mr. Wrede's residence," Sean announced.

"Good night, milord, Madame. Claire, my heart—" He exited the carriage with a final kiss for her, then shut the door behind him.

"Home?" Sean asked hopefully.

Claire had her head bowed. She must be tired, Christiane thought. "Home, Sean," she declared, loving the sound of the command, Gannon's hand holding tight to hers.

The carriage rolled on. The long line of coaches piled up outside Ranelagh elicited a burst of curses from Sean, who chose to make a detour. This new route led close to the docks; Christiane, glancing up at a gaslight, saw a sign for Meekin Lane. They could not be far from the home of Matthew Darby's *Guardian*. For a moment, she contemplated proposing that they stop in to see her old friend. He had been scrupulous in trumpeting her presence at social occasions in the pages of his gazette, clearly attempting to ease her return to respectability—and he hadn't made a single mention of her involvement in Mrs. Treadwell's academy, bless his soul. She really did owe him . . .

Gannon's fingers closed over hers, and he moved his thigh tight against her skirts, rubbing gently back and forth.

All thoughts of Matthew Darby vanished from Christiane's mind.

When they arrived at the town house, Christiane accompanied Claire to her rooms, ostensibly to retrieve a book she had left there, and made idle chitchat while the maid undressed the girl and took down her hair. She was still concerned about what Greer Delaney might have said to upset her. "Brush it out for ye, shall I, miss?" the smiling, round-faced Irish maid offered, pulling out the last of the pins.

"Not tonight, Bridey; I'm too tired. Just braid it."

"Very good, miss." Bridey nimbly made three long ropes of the black tresses and wove them up. "Anything else, then?"

"Are you cold, Claire?" the countess mentioned, seeing her shiver a little in her filmy nightdress. "We could lay a fire."

Claire laughed at that. "In May? Folk would think me daft. No, Bridey, you can go."

"I can't wait until Bess and Gwen and Petra come up next weekend," Christiane said as the maid left them alone. "I found out tonight that that nice young Lord Riverton writes poetry—*and* is mad about the theater."

"Which one was Lord Riverton?" Claire asked, stifling a yawn.

"The sandy-haired fellow who tripped on the rug on the way to supper. Very tall and thin? Blue eyes? A little awkward?"

"I can't recall him. But he does sound perfect for Bess."

"Do you remember Mr. Gouvernour, then?"

"I can't say I do."

"I was thinking of him for Gwen," Christiane said thoughtfully. "Dr. Caplan tells me the young man is studying chemistry over the vehement objections of his parents."

"Why would they object?"

"It seems he keeps blowing things up with homemade gunpowder that he concocts."

Claire giggled through another yawn. "You see? There truly is somebody for everyone, just as they say."

"So there is, it seems." Christiane found the book she wanted—it was Voltaire's *La Pucelle*—lying on Claire's desk, atop a sketchbook. Idly, she smiled at the sketch on the open page: a caricature of Sean that caught his surly air perfectly. Turning the page over, she next saw a handsome sketch of Gannon and Homer, with the hound looking at his master adoringly. She flipped that as well, to find a drawing of two horses hitched to a wagon or carriage of some sort; only its staves showed. They were piebald, white with black blotches on the flanks, done in charcoal, and extremely lifelike.

"Oh, I like this sketch you've done of the horses," she mentioned.

"Of what?"

"Horses." Christiane turned the page toward Claire.

"I didn't draw that," the girl said.

"You must have, *chérie*. It is in your sketchbook."

Claire stared at it. "If I did, I don't remember."

"You don't remember because you are exhausted, no doubt." Christiane kissed her cheek, then laid her palm across the girl's forehead. "I wonder if you are coming down with a fever. How do you feel?"

"Fine," Claire assured her, and smiled.

Christiane tucked the covers up around her. "I'm not going to ask what Greer Delaney said to you, because whatever it was, it was only meant to be cruel and cause trouble. I am sorry she was ugly to you, though. I feel it is my fault." She bent and kissed the girl's cheek.

"Of course it isn't," Claire murmured, her eyes already closed.

"Goodnight, *chérie*."

Claire mumbled something that might have been "Good night" and snuggled into the pillows. Christiane smiled, blew out the lamps, and went out, closing the door very gently. As she turned from doing so, she felt Gannon's hands on her shoulders. "Shh," she started to warn him—and then realized the hands were paws. "Dammit, get down!" she hissed at Homer, pushing him away. Not a bit offended, he wagged his tail and delivered a loving, slobbering kiss, straight on her lips. "I can't decide which is worse—having Chlöe hate me or having you adore me," she said ruefully, wiping her mouth with her sleeve. "Where's your master?" He let out a short bark and loped ahead of her down the corridor. On the way, she saw Claire's maid coming toward her with an armload of freshly pressed linens. "Let her get good and settled, Bridey, and then lay a bit of a fire for her, will you?" Christiane asked. "There's a damp in the air, and she looks so peaked."

"Aye, mum. Thought so myself, I did. His Lordship's in the kitchens."

"It's a wonder that man isn't fatter than the regent, the way he stuffs himself," Christiane muttered, making Bridey giggle. Homer had paused at the top of the stairs, looking back anxiously. "Yes, yes, I'm coming. Get on, you monster." She nudged him with her hip, and he bounded down the steps and across the vestibule, nails clicking on the marble floor.

She paused in the kitchen doorway, watching Gannon offer Chlöe a bite of the chunk of Gloucestershire cheese he held and then take one himself. "That is disgusting," she observed.

"Why? We saved some for you." He held the cheese out to her, then laughed at her expression. Chlöe bared her teeth and growled. "I was only teasing," he assured the dog, and tossed it to her instead. She caught it with a snap of her jaws that made Christiane blanch.

"Anyone would think you hadn't just consumed a five-course meal."

"That was hours ago. And anyway, it wasn't very good. Lady Cobblesby needs a new cook." He opened a crock, sniffed it hopefully, and grinned. "Pickled beets, Homer!"

"Dogs don't eat—"

Gannon speared one with a fork and flipped it to Homer, who caught it and gobbled it up, magenta juice trickling from his massive chops. Christiane shuddered and poured herself a brandy. "Claire all settled in?" Gannon asked.

She nodded as she sipped. "I think she may be hatching a fever, though. Her eyes seemed rather glassy, and she was shivering. Whatever do you suppose Greer might have said to make her so upset?"

"No idea," he said through a beet, and sent another Homer's way.

Sensing that he didn't care to pursue it, Christiane changed the subject. "What do you think about Lord Riverton for Bess?"

"Which one was Riverton?"

"He tripped on the way in to dinner."

"Was it that alone suggested the match to you?"

She made a moue. "As it happens, he writes poetry."

"Everyone writes poetry. The question is, is his worth reading?"

"You don't write poetry." She looked at him. "Do you?"

"I did when I was younger."

"Was it worth reading?"

He shook his head emphatically. "None of it." She laughed and came a few steps closer. Chlöe's growl deepened.

"You'd think she would be used to me by now," Christiane said nervously.

"She knows a rival when she sees one. Don't forget—

you turned her out of my bed. Come along, you two." He seized a couple of dried sausages from the table and lured the dogs to the back door. She expected him to fling them the meat and then slam the door, but instead he paused. "Fireworks! Come and see," he said.

She approached cautiously, one eye on Chlöe, but the bitch's attention was riveted on the sausages. "I don't see any fireworks."

He grabbed her and kissed her. "Let's make some." He threw the sausages back into the kitchen and pulled the door to, shutting the dogs inside.

The night was warm, and the air was rich with the sweet scent of lilacs. The moon was yellow and full-ripe, just rising over the back wall. "What have you got in mind?" Christiane asked suspiciously.

"Just a stroll through the garden."

"Well . . . if you wish. But I must warn you, I find love-making *en plein air* vastly overrated. There always seem to be sticks and stones—not to mention bugs." She swatted at something that had dived toward her hair.

"Odd. Most of the women of my acquaintance have taken great pleasure in being ravished in gardens."

"They were only pretending. It's different for the man; he's on top. *He* isn't the one who winds up with rocks and prickles in his derrière."

"What about at the seaside?" he asked curiously, taking her hand as they went along the path.

She grimaced. "Even worse. All that sand in crevices."

"You are sorely lacking in romantic imagination, aren't you?"

"Tell the truth. After their first experience of being ravished in a garden, didn't those women of your acquaintance strongly suggest that you retire to your rooms instead?"

He laughed. "Come to think of it, they did. Excuse me." He'd paused on the path; now he stepped off it, toward a lovely little hawthorn, and fumbled with his breeches' buttons. A moment later, she heard a streaming hiss. "Ah. That's better." He rebuttoned and rejoined her.

"Why *do* men enjoy pissing out-of-doors so?" she demanded.

"No need to aim."

"That makes sense."

Arm in arm, they followed the curve of the path past the tall, screening hedgerow that hid the folly. Suddenly, Christiane caught her breath: "Oh!" The miniature Taj Mahal glittered in the moonlight; its reflection shimmered in the dark pool. And just in front of the pool lay . . .

"What *is* that?" she asked in wonder, pausing on the path, trying to make out the shape.

"A bed."

"A *bed*?"

"Mm-hmm. It just so happens I share all your qualms about lovemaking out-of-doors."

She turned, scanning the garden walls. "Surely somebody will see us."

"I'm fairly certain not. But come and test the sight lines for yourself, if you like." He led her forward.

Hesitantly, she followed, craning her neck. "Your next-door neighbor, there—"

"Is away in Dorset on business. I had the servants ask."

"And on that side?"

"Gone for holiday in the Lake Country. He's dreadfully keen on bird-watching, and he heard there were some sort of African swallows passing through." He plunked himself down on the mattress and began to pull off his boots.

Still she hesitated, torn between shock and laughter. "Whatever put such a notion into your head? All this trouble—" She contemplated the luxe bedclothes, the piles of bolsters and cushions and pillows.

"I wanted to make love to you in moonlight."

She watched as he peeled off his clothes. "Aren't you concerned—"

"No. I'm not." He patted the bed.

She perched on the very corner of the mattress, still

scanning the garden walls. "The masters of those houses may be gone," she pointed out, "but the servants are there."

He smiled in the moonlight, bemused. "I believe Mrs. Treadwell's influence has worn off on you in a most distressing manner. You have already admitted to being no stranger to outdoor pleasure."

"That was always furtive," she hissed. "This is so . . . anticipated!"

He laughed, rolling toward her. "You cannot have it both ways. I've gone to great lengths to spare you rocks and prickles. Now, won't you oblige me?"

She sat, unmoving, as he drew her sleeve down to bare her shoulder, as his hand stroked her breastbone, caressed the nape of her neck, found the pins that held her hair in its tight chignon and drew them out. The black curls fell in a tumble; he caught them in his hands, buried his face in them. "I love you so," he whispered.

Christiane hesitated. Then she reached for her ribbons and undid them slowly, as he watched. The bodice of her black gown fell, and then the sleeves. He caught his breath admiringly.

"Look at you," he whispered, fingers fumbling for her stays. "How beautiful you are."

Her mind was filled with Evelyn's cautions that she was old and foolish. But her body was alive with an exquisite longing; when he put his fingers to her bared breast, she thought she would die of pleasure. He followed with his mouth, as his hands pushed the gown down over her hips. He was suckling against her, his tongue circling her nipple, which was taut in the night air. She felt the first inklings of that familiar fire low in her belly, and suddenly she no longer cared whether he might notice gray hairs or sagging flesh or freckles. She wanted him. He wanted her. Let the neighbors be damned.

Slowly she drew up on her knees, letting the gown slide downward. He kissed her navel, pushed his tongue into its cavity. She shifted so that she straddled him. He lunged for the tip of her breast, caught it in his teeth as he yanked her drawers down. She rose up, felt his manhood pierce her, heard his quick-drawn breath. "Oh, God," he whispered, hands splayed across her bared buttocks. "Oh. Oh. Ohhh—"

She lowered herself slowly until she sheathed him completely, and felt him shudder. He arched against her, eager, his breathing more rapid. Beyond her shoulders, she could feel the moon and stars egging her on.

He'd clenched his eyes shut as she covered him; now he opened them slowly. "I want to see . . . every moment of this," he told her, the moon caught in his gaze. No longer ashamed or afraid, she wanted only to please him. She slid back, rising above him, and plunged down again. He groaned his gratification. She hung above him, teasing his rod, moving in slow circles so that its head flicked across the core of her desire and then away again, there and away again . . . there and—

Ahh. The fire blazed up inside her, astonishing, as always, in its brightness. She tucked her knees to him, set her palms against his chest. He moaned with longing, pawing at her thighs, trying to draw her in. But still she waited, tantalizing him, provoking him, until at last he seized the tip of her breast in his lips and pulled so hard that she could not help but fall to him, her hips landing against him, that hard rod sunk inside her to its depth.

"Mmm," he murmured, kissing her hair, her ear. She had thrown her head back in abandon; she was riding him for all she was worth. "Yes!" he cried, trying to gather her into him even as she fought to maintain her rhythm. "Yes, yes. Oh, my love—" She stopped driving onto him and instead swirled, ground against him, dazed by bliss, not wanting the ecstasy to end, not able to bear that it should go on. The garden was a mad muddle of moonlight and shadow and scent and sound. And then his loins exploded against her; she felt the burst of his seed and the answering release of her own juices, and she cried out his name—

Her cry subsided. He held her tightly. And another

sound, one that had been drowned out by their shared plea-sure, rang out in the quiet night air. They paused, still breathless, trying to place it—a strange, shrill, incoherent noise. A prayer? A scream?

Gannon sat up abruptly, nearly tumbling Christiane onto the gravel. "My God," he said, and grabbed for his discarded breeches. "My God. That's Claire."

Twenty-six

He managed to dress before she did, but she was only a dozen paces behind him when he reached the door to Claire's room and thrust it open. She heard the Irish maid, Bridey, sounding terribly frightened: "I don't know what's wrong with her, m'lord!"

"Claire?" Christiane heard Gannon say sharply. There was no response. "Claire!" he cried again, so anxiously that Christiane was almost afraid to venture inside. Yet she did, and saw him kneeling beside the bed where his niece lay huddled, hugging herself tightly, the covers thrown off. Her eyes were wide open, but she did not seem to see him; she stared into space, her lips moving almost imperceptibly.

"I just came in to light the fire, mum, like ye told me—" the maid stammered.

"Hush, Bridey. You've done nothing wrong." Christiane was thinking rapidly. Leon Caplan was in London; she'd seen him at the Cobblesbys' fete. She grabbed the maid, who was blubbering in fright. "Send Sean to fetch Dr. Caplan at this address." She went to Claire's desk, scribbled the direction for Mrs. Mordecai's rooming house on a bit of paper. "Have Sean tell him Miss Finn is taken ill." The maid hesitated, eyeing Claire with fascinated horror. "Dammit, go!" Christiane commanded, and Bridey backed out of the room uncertainly.

"What is she saying?" Christiane asked, coming closer to Gannon. Then she heard the whispered words for herself:

"The horses. Oh, God, the pretty, pretty horses!"

"Claire," Gannon said, taking her shoulders, shaking her gently. "Claire, it is just a dream."

"Whatever will I do about the horses?" Claire's voice rose in a screech. The hubbub had attracted more servants; they'd gathered at the door. Christiane whirled on them. "Someone go and fetch Mr. Wrede," she ordered. "He lives at Number Ten Burtons Court."

Gannon looked at her. "No."

"But he always has been able to comfort her!"

"How often," he broke in, his voice tight, "do you expect him to see her in such straits and still be willing to wed her?"

She stared. "Surely he would not abandon her!"

"It's a chance I'd rather not take. Have them bring the laudanum."

"Shouldn't we wait for Dr. Caplan?"

"I know the dosage."

Christiane hesitated, then turned to the servants. "Seamus, fetch the laudanum."

"I don't know where it is, mum."

"In my office," Gannon said shortly. "Top left drawer of my desk."

Seamus rushed off. "I still think that sending for David . . ." Christiane began.

"No," Gannon said, quite definitely. "I'll not have him see her this way." He was seeking to force Claire's tensed body to uncoil, pulling her legs away from her chest.

"Be gentle!" Christiane cried.

"The horses," Claire whispered in horror.

"Forget the bloody horses," her uncle hissed.

"Gannon, please. You'll hurt her." Christiane sought to pull him from her.

"I know what I'm doing. I've dealt with her before when she was this way."

Just then, Claire shuddered, and her eyes blinked open. "Is he dead?" she whispered.

"Hush, Claire," Gannon told her.

"Oh, Christ!" the girl screeched, pushing frantically at his restraining arms, fighting to rise from the bed. "Oh, sweet Mary and Jesus—"

Seamus hurried through the doorway, a bottle clenched in his fist. "The laudanum, m'lord—"

"Give it here," Gannon commanded, and unstoppered the bottle with his teeth. "Claire. Drink this. Down it goes." He put the bottle to her lips.

For an instant, she ceased struggling; her gray eyes met his. "No," she whimpered.

"You must. It will calm you."

"No! No more forgetting!" she raged, trying to knock the bottle from his hand. "I want to remember."

"You need to sleep," he said, with preternatural calm. "You must rest, Claire. Rest."

"Rest." She repeated the word, her gaze locked on his.

"That's right. Rest." He held the bottle up again. It seemed for an instant she'd take it; then she wrenched free of his grasp.

"I'll dream!" she wailed, in so forlorn a voice that Christiane felt her blood go cold.

Gannon gathered his niece to him. "No dreams. No more dreams. I promise," he crooned, the way a mother might sing to a baby. "Take this, now; there's a good girl." He held the bottle to her lips. And this time, she took a sip of the drug. "That's the way," he whispered. "Rest. Sleep. No more dreams. . . ."

"I'm so tired," Claire murmured, swaying in his grasp.

"I know you are. Here, then." He laid her back against her pillows, pulled the covers up over her with such gentleness. He smoothed her brow, ran his hand across her hair. She relaxed visibly, the tension flowing from her limbs. The servants in the doorway let out a collective sigh of relief. Silence descended on the room, broken only by the soft crackle of the fire in the hearth. Gannon leaned forward to kiss Claire's cheek.

As he did, her eyes opened once more. "I can't help but fret about those horses," she announced very clearly.

"I've taken care of the horses," he told her. "I swear it to you." She nodded, and he smiled at her. Her eyelids drooped, closed, fluttered, and then stayed closed. Gannon remained motionless at her side, waiting until her shallow breaths turned deeper, more even. When he seemed assured she would not awaken, he turned to Christiane. "I'm sorry I was short with you. I—I hate seeing her that way."

"What horses does she mean?" she asked, bewildered.

"Who knows?" He smiled winningly.

The sketchbook Christiane had seen earlier was on the floor beside Claire's bed, with a pencil atop it. She moved toward it, reached to pick it up.

"Leave it be," Gannon ordered sharply.

"She drew a picture of horses—"

"I'm sick to death of horses!"

Christiane felt tired and dispirited. All the magic of that interlude in the garden had vanished; she had the sense she'd sometimes had in Paris, at the racetrack—that she had backed the wrong horse. Damn horses, anyway! She longed intensely to be back at the academy among the girls, to be sipping sherry with Mrs. Treadwell, to be anyplace except where she was now.

Gannon seemed to sense her thoughts. "Forgive me," he apologized formally, and bent to kiss her. Christiane felt herself flinch at the motion. He stopped, looking at her. "Christiane," he said then. "Don't you give up on me. Don't you ever give up on me. If you do, I'll be lost."

Bridey popped up in the doorway. "Dr. Caplan," she announced, giving a little curtsy and letting him precede her.

"Thank you for coming, Doctor," Gannon said politely.

"But I'm afraid the countess has brought you out to no purpose. As you can see, Claire is resting comfortably."

"What propelled you to send for me?" Leon asked Christiane.

"It was a nightmare," Gannon answered for her. "Nothing but a dream. A bit of laudanum, and the terror is gone."

The doctor moved to the bed, checked Claire's pulse, put a hand to her forehead. "There's no fever," he mentioned. "Did she seem delirious?" The question was, again, addressed to Christiane.

She knew instinctively what Gannon wanted her to say. She longed as much as he did to see Claire married to David Wrede. But if something was amiss with the girl . . . if she needed help . . .

"She was talking about the horses again," she confessed.

Leon's bearded face creased with concern. "That's not a good sign."

Gannon was frowning. "She's tired, that's all," he told the doctor. "We've had a busy week."

"How much laudanum did you give her?"

Gannon shrugged. "A bit. A sip."

"You do understand it isn't a drug to be administered lightly."

"I'm not an idiot," Gannon snapped, so harshly that Christiane stared.

"He is only trying to help," she protested—then cringed as Gannon whirled on her:

"I don't need his help." He picked up the doctor's black bag, snapped it shut, and thrust it at him. "I can see to her."

"I have a duty to my patient," Dr. Caplan said, calmly but firmly. "So long as Miss Finn is a student at the academy—"

"Well, she isn't any longer!" Gannon said curtly. "I withdraw her as of now. As of this moment. She is no longer your responsibility."

"Gannon, you can't mean that!" Christiane said in shock.

Leon didn't back down. "Whatever it is you think you're doing, milord, it isn't in Miss Finn's best interests. She needs the care of a physician."

"I know what's best for her."

The doctor hesitated, looking to Christiane, whose gaze darted to Gannon. His Lordship was clearly simmering with rage. "I'll sit with her tonight," she told Leon. "If there is any change, I'll send for you immediately."

He nodded then, still holding his black bag against his chest. "Very well."

"And thank you for coming. We're grateful. Aren't we, Gannon?" Gannon muttered something unintelligible. She glared at him. "Bridey, would you kindly show the doctor out?"

"I can see myself out. Good night, Your Lordship. Good night, Christiane."

She waited until she heard the clatter of his horse's hooves on the cobblestones. Then she went and shut the bedchamber door against the lingering servants. "Could you possibly have been more rude to him?" she asked icily.

"I? Rude to him? He treated *me* as though he thought me an idiot," Gannon shot back. " 'How much laudanum did you give her?'—does he think I am trying to poison her?"

"That isn't what he meant. He is worried about her, that's all."

"So am I." There was a hint of hollowness to his tone. "I only want to help her." He looked at her, and his eyes, his beautiful gray eyes, were haunted. "She'll be better tomorrow. You'll see."

Faced with his evident pain, Christiane relented. "Of course she will be." She kissed him. "You go on to bed. I'll sit with her."

"Bridey can do that."

"I told Leon I would."

"I'll sit with her as well, then."

"There's no need for both of us to lose our sleep."

"Is it that you don't trust me around her?"

She stared at him, astonished. "Of course not!"

"Maybe you think I'm out to poison her as well."

"Don't be absurd. It only shows how weary you are, that you would propose such nonsense. Go to bed."

"Come with me."

"I gave Leon my word."

The muscles of his mouth tightened. "As you wish," he said, and went out, closing the door with an exaggerated click.

Christiane looked to the bed. Claire was sleeping soundly, lulled by the laudanum. It had worked, what Gannon had done; he had taken care of her, just as he'd told Leon. Still, what had Claire said? *No more forgetting. I want to remember. . . .* Gannon, clearly, did not want the girl to remember whatever it was that teased at the corners of her mind about the pretty white horses. And why had he refused to send for David Wrede?

She drew a chair up to Claire's bed, leaned back in it, and shut her eyes, closed them tight against the maelstrom of questions. But nothing could quell the commotion in her head. She sat and stared into the darkness, into the future, with the sense that something irrevocable had happened, and that the world—her world, their world—would never be the same.

Twenty-seven

She awoke still hunched in the chair, exhausted, befogged, with a wretched headache. Someone was knocking at the bedchamber door, very softly. Christiane glanced at the bed. Claire was pale, but sleeping; her breath was deep and even. She tiptoed to the door and opened it. Bridey stood there with a letter in her hand. "For ye, mum," she whispered.

Christiane took the envelope and slid a fingernail beneath the seal. She knew the handwriting; it was Matthew Darby's. What now?

The message was brief: "Can you meet me behind the little pavilion in Ranelagh Gardens at noon? It is a matter of the utmost importance."

Christiane glanced at the clock on Claire's mantel. It was nearly eleven now.

What a bother. She couldn't imagine why the editor of the *Guardian* would suddenly want to see her. She considered not going, sending a boy with a note in reply instead. She could plead that Claire was ill, which was true enough, and that she had to stay at her bedside.

Besides . . . nagging at the back of her mind was how furious Gannon had been when he'd accosted her in the street months before, after she'd been to visit the publisher—how he'd threatened her, and so terrified the driver with his wrath that the man had called the watch on him. Gannon, she'd come to realize, was an intensely private man, particularly when it came to his family. He was desperate to protect what he loved. That was why he hadn't wanted to send for David Wrede the night before, when Claire took ill. It was the same impulse, she recognized abruptly, that had been behind his behavior in Paris two decades before, when he'd made such a to-do about rescuing her, about saving her from her life as the mistress of Jean-Baptiste, marrying her and taking care of her.

In Paris, Christiane had resented, fiercely, the notion that she needed to be taken care of. Now she found it the most appealing idea in the world. Falling in love with Gannon, living here for these few weeks with him, had made her see that when you gave yourself to another human being fully, wholly, it didn't take away one iota of what you were; it only made you more complete.

But then she remembered how good Matthew had been about keeping the secrets she *had* told him. She owed him this. Besides, Claire looked to be recovered from whatever had caused her such distress the night before.

She folded the note back up and tucked it in the envelope. "Could you sit with her, Bridey, until I get back? I've an errand I must run."

"Aye, mum," the young maid agreed, bobbing her head.

Should she tell Gannon she was going out? Christiane hesitated. "Do you know where His Lordship is?"

"In his office, mum; Cook just sent coffee up." The maid winked conspiratorially. "I see he has been to look in on ye, though."

"What?"

Bridey nodded toward the chair where Christiane had been curled up. In a little bud vase on the floor beside it was a single fat green stalk of asparagus, tied with a jaunty red-ribbon bow.

Christiane laughed out loud at the unexpected conciliatory gesture. If he'd been in to see her and Claire, he'd be at work for a bit longer—enough time for her to slip out to see Matthew and then return without him noticing. She preferred it that way. She picked up the vase and its unorthodox contents and went to her rooms, where she dressed quickly before hurrying downstairs.

Chlöe, lounging on the floor of the front vestibule, bared her teeth and growled as Christiane descended. "To hell with you, too," Christiane murmured amiably.

The bitch rose to her feet with an unnerving snarl. "Down, girl!" the butler, O'Malley, ordered sharply, appearing from the kitchens. "Goin' out are ye, mum? Shall I have Sean bring the carriage 'round?"

"No need to bother Sean; could you hail a hired carriage for me?"

"Of course, mum." The butler moved toward the door.

Chlöe tensed, the ruff of hair between her shoulder blades rising. O'Malley lunged for her collar: "I said down!"

"I believe I'll wait out on the stoop," Christiane noted, and slipped gingerly through the front door.

How odd it seemed to see Matthew Darby in broad daylight, she thought as she hurried toward him on the path behind the pretty little pavilion. "Hello, Matthew!" she greeted him, extending her hand for a kiss. "Lord Carew and I nearly stopped in to see you the other night; we were in your neighborhood."

"Roughing it, were you?"

She laughed. "No, no. His niece's fiancé has rooms near there. I say, Matthew, I do appreciate how kind you've been to all of us in the paper."

"Don't mention it."

Her old friend seemed ill at ease, the countess noted. "Is there something I can do for you?" she inquired.

His dark gaze met hers and then veered away. "You had asked me to inform you if I heard any news regarding the deaths of Claire Finn's parents," he said very quietly.

"Dear God! Have the culprits been identified? Arrested?"

"Nothing so certain as that. Just the wisp of a rumor . . ."

"What rumor?"

His gaze sidled back, with a hint of pity in it. "That it was Lord Carew killed them."

She stared for a moment in shock. Then she laughed. "How absurd!"

"I'm just passing it on," Matthew said, tugging at his haphazard cravat.

"Where *did* you hear such drivel?"

"From Lord Fitch. He had it from Lady Fitch, who had it from the horse's mouth." Horses again. "Greer Delaney."

"Good heavens, Matthew. A discarded fiancée? What sort of source is that?"

"Laugh if you like," he said stubbornly. "The tale makes sense. He was there on the spot; he's admitted as much. He told the law he rode off in pursuit of his brother and Georgina after he called at their hotel and was informed they'd left to return to Ireland. He was the first to come upon the scene." Strange, Christiane thought—he had never mentioned that to her. And neither had Claire. "The only witness was the girl, who never has been able to give any sort of coherent account to the authorities beyond saying that the coach was attacked by some men and a drover frightened them away."

"*Why* would he kill them?" Christiane demanded.

"Miss Delaney has her ideas on that as well. The way she tells it, Carew had been having an affair with his sister-in-law and was trying to convince her to leave Hugh for him. Hugh found out and came to London to confront his brother, and Georgina picked Hugh over Gannon in the end. *Again.* That's why they were headed back to Ireland without having told him they were leaving London. They were sneaking away, but he caught up to them."

"Rather odd, don't you think, that Miss Delaney remained betrothed for a number of months afterward to a man she knew was a murderer?"

"The way she tells it—and she's been telling it all over town—she was afraid he'd kill her as well."

"Surely you aren't going to print such nonsense."

He looked straight at her. "I would, if you weren't involved."

Christiane stood with her pretty buttercup-yellow parasol above her head, as irate as she had ever been in all her life. "You've known me such a long time, Matthew. Do you think I could love a man who was a murderer?"

"I think you could if you didn't know him for what he was. Greer Delaney says *she* did."

"Greer is an idiot."

"And you're not. We both know that. It's why I asked you to meet me." The gazetteer appeared profoundly uncomfortable. "I suppose what I'm asking for is your assurance . . . that it's not true."

She opened her mouth to give him that assurance—and then remembered how quick Gannon had been to reach for the laudanum the night before. *I want to remember,* Claire had cried. But he hadn't allowed her to; he'd made her swallow the drug. What if Claire *did* know he had killed her parents, and that was what she was trying to remember? What if that was what Gannon was so afraid Claire would recall?

But that was silly. The girl had never shown the slightest sign she was afraid of him. On the contrary, she had pined when he hadn't come to visit her at the academy, and she relied on his counsel now. Christiane felt a flush of shame; how could she even think such thoughts? She remembered what he'd told her the night before: *Don't you give up on me. . . . If you do, I'll be lost.*

Her smile blazed. "Well, you have it, then," she told
Matthew Darby. "My assurance. It is simply not true."

"You know that for a fact?"

"Of course I do. Greer Delaney is only out to discredit
Gannon because he threw her over."

He looked grim. "That's what I thought as well, when I
heard what she'd been saying. But there's also talk—I
haven't pinned it down yet—that Dr. Driscoll of the Royal
Academy spoke out of turn about Georgina at a dinner
with his fellow physicians. As much as told them that the
girl—Claire—is Gannon's daughter, not Hugh's. Apparently, Hugh and Georgina were estranged at the time of the
girl's birth, and Georgina was living with Gannon."

Christiane remembered how she had jumped to just that
conclusion when Dr. Caplan had told her that Hugh's wife
had spent her pregnancy on Gannon's estate. She sighed
and nodded. "That's true—that Georgina was living with
Gannon. But it wasn't because they were lovers."

"Why was it, then?"

Christiane hesitated. Even though she knew she could
rely on Matthew's discretion, she found herself reluctant to
tell poor Georgina's secrets, out of pity for Claire. The
girl's past was already being thoroughly scrutinized by the
ton, evidently. "You must take my word on it," she finally
said. "It wasn't that at all."

"He *was* first on the scene," Matthew said stubbornly.
"That's not rumor; that's true. I had it from the sheriff of
the shire where it happened."

Why, she wondered, had Gannon never told her that?
But then, they'd never talked much about what had happened to his brother and Georgina; he was so reluctant to
discuss "family matters." "It doesn't prove anything," she
told Matthew in exasperation.

"It looks a bit suspicious, though, doesn't it? Why
would he follow them as they were leaving unless it was
because he wanted to prevent his brother from taking
Georgina back to Ireland?"

"What did he tell the sheriff?"

"That he'd called at their hotel that morning and found they'd left unexpectedly. That much was confirmed by the hotel staff. He claims he rode out after them because he wanted to say good-bye."

"Isn't it perfectly natural that he would want to do so?"

"Christiane. I'm not just here as the editor of the *Guardian*. I'm also here as your friend."

She laughed. "A fine sort of friend, who would insinuate that the man I am to marry cuckolded his brother and then killed him in cold blood! I've never in my life heard anything so ridiculous. If the Crown has any proof Gannon is guilty of those murders—or if anyone besides Greer Delaney claims to—let the matter be put before the law. But no more of these damnable rumors. They ruin lives. Believe me. I know."

"I'll hold my peace, then. I was sure you'd say as much." He grinned crookedly. "You can't blame me, though, for wondering. It would be a sensational story, if it only were true."

"You'll just have to dig up some other scandal," she told him, and smiled.

"Never fear; there are always plenty of them out there. Thanks for coming to meet me. I don't suppose you've any dirt to toss my way?"

She hesitated, glanced both ways along the path, then leaned her head toward his. "Here is a tidbit for you—but mind you keep it close to your chest. The Countess d'Oliveri is happier than she has ever been before in her life."

Matthew Darby laughed. "Don't you know there's no profit to be made in good news?" he said.

She was gay as she rode back to 54 Berkeley Square. Hearing Matthew articulate Greer's theory of why and how Gannon might have killed his brother and sister-in-law had made her realize how ridiculous such notions were. It was despicable of that woman to be whispering such calumnies—and to Claire! No wonder the poor girl had been so upset last night. She would speak to her at once, of course, and try again to impress on her that she must not be so influenced by the opinions of others. Should she tell Gannon what Greer was up to? He would be furious when he heard. It would be even worse, though, if he got wind of it from someone else; at least she could break it to him gently. Perhaps she would even be able to make him see the humor in it. . . .

"Mum?" The carriage driver was standing ready to help her down outside the town house.

"Already?" she asked in surprise. "What do I owe you, then?"

"A shilling sixpence."

She dug it out of her reticule, and, feeling generous, added another shilling as a tip. "Thanks kindly!" the driver told her. She gave him a little wave, climbing the steps to the front door.

The butler, O'Malley, opened it to her. "M'lady. If ye will permit me—"

"What, no Chlöe ready to rip my throat out?" Christiane asked, not hearing the familiar growl of the wolfhound in the front hall.

"No, m'lady. If ye will forgive me—"

She started up the stairs. "We have an invitation to dinner and the opera with the Ormsby-Smiths this evening, O'Malley. With His Lordship's permission, I should like to send our regrets."

"I've already done so on his orders, m'lady."

"Really?" Christiane said in surprise. "I wonder why he cancelled. Miss Finn isn't worse off, is she?" She reached the landing and headed for Claire's rooms, intending to look in on her.

"If ye would just permit me—"

Christiane rapped on Claire's door, got no response, and pushed it open. "With His Lordship, then, is she? She must be feeling better."

"With His Lordship, aye, m'lady. But—"

Christiane reversed direction. "In the office?"

"No, m'lady."

"His sitting room?" She bustled off along the corridor, while the butler trailed behind her.

"No, m'lady."

"I know—my rooms!" She turned and made for them, with O'Malley still at her heels. She pushed open the door, and saw a blotch of dark on the Oriental carpet. Had Homer or Chlöe—but no. It hadn't been the dogs, for there lay the beribboned stalk of asparagus as well, and the shattered shards of a crystal vase. . . .

And beside them was a crumpled ball of parchment. A letter. Matthew's letter. "Oh, God," she whispered, and whirled toward O'Malley, her eyes fearful. "What happened?"

"That's what I was trying to tell ye, m'lady. Bridey told me he came to Miss Claire's rooms askin' where ye was. She told him she didn't know where ye'd gone—just that ye'd had a letter 'n' gone out. So he asked who the letter was from, 'n' Bridey said she didn't know, that ye'd taken it away to yer rooms. She followed him in here, 'n' said he picked the letter up 'n' read it, 'n' then cursed a blue streak 'n' smashed down the vase. Then he told her to get Miss Claire's things packed up straightaway. He packed his up as well."

"But where has he gone?"

"Aerfailly, mum."

"Aerfailly?" Christiane heard her voice crack in amazement. "To Ireland, you mean?"

"Aye. Taken Miss Claire, he has."

She felt as though the butler had struck her, punched the breath straight out of her. Why hadn't she thought to toss Matthew's note in the grate? She recalled again, with a dreadful sense of foreboding, how furious Gannon had been when he'd confronted her in her carriage on her visit to London months ago, after he'd followed her about all day. "The greatest gossipmonger in all of England," he'd called Matthew. *I have a right to protect my niece,* he'd said.

"What else did he take with him besides Miss Claire?" she asked, in a cloud of dread.

"The hounds. Oh, and Bridey. That's all."

"He must have left a message for me." The butler shook his head slowly. "But there must be some message—some explanation!" she said wildly.

O'Malley looked at her with pity. "He left no word."

She didn't believe him. She went to Gannon's office, searched the top of his desk, the bureau. She went back to the room they'd shared, looked on the bed, in her wardrobe, in her jewel box, even her hatboxes. She searched the mantel, and her writing desk. Nothing.

How could he be so cold?

Unless . . .

Was it possible that what Greer Delaney was saying about him—that he'd murdered his brother and Georgina—was true?

Christiane stepped back against the bedroom wall, the blood pounding in her head. She tried to shake the notion off, brush it away, to think of something, anything, else. But the idea, tiny, unbidden, had slipped into her mind and would not budge—just stayed there for her to chew over like some hard, indigestible bit of gristle.

Ridiculous, she told herself.

Utterly absurd.

Completely out of the question. It simply wasn't possible that he could have committed that crime.

Still, that nugget stayed put. He had vanished, left her without a word of explanation. Why? Why should her meeting with Matthew Darby upset him so? She'd told him the man was an old friend. His reaction was illogical, incomprehensible.

Unless—

Oh, God. He had been right in what he'd said about doubting him. Her suspicions were like a tiny stream of water trickling over the hard rock that was her faith in him. Given time enough, that trickle could wear even bedrock away.

What in the world was she to do now? One moment, she felt heartsick for doubting him. In the next, she felt a fool for ever having believed in him at all. Should she go after him? Forget him? How could she even decide, with her heart in such upheaval? She needed a safe, calm place in which to sort out her thoughts. A sanctuary. But where could she go?

In her mind, there rose up a vision of a tall iron gate, and moss- and ivy-covered stone walls, and leaded casements wound out to catch a summer breeze that bore hints of bright, girlish laughter. . . .

More than anything in the world, she longed to be back at the academy.

Twenty-eight

"*So. Thrown you* over, has he?" Evelyn said, hands on her hips. "Just as I warned you."

"He hasn't thrown me over." Christiane poured herself a whiskey with shaking hands. It was just after suppertime at the academy, and she had only just arrived, having left the London town house as quickly as she could after discovering that Claire and Gannon were gone. Now she was wondering whether her decision to seek refuge here had been wise.

The headmistress paid no heed to her denial. "I don't take any pleasure in having been proven right, mind you. But if you'd listened to me—well, that's neither here nor there. What matters is that you're rid of him, and for good this time. I always did say he was out to pay you back for having spurned him in Paris."

Paris. The way the city shone at night, reflected through the mullioned windows that the maid wound out to catch the breeze from the Seine. The savor of rich bordeaux, and the sweet, unearthly scent of muguets du bois *in the vase at the side of the—*

Christiane was not feeling up to trying to explain to a woman who had only ever made love to one man—and had detested it—what had drawn her to Gannon. It didn't matter now. She needed a haven, and what other choice did she have? "It's very kind of you to take me in, Evelyn," she said humbly.

"You are still my oldest and dearest friend." The headmistress's smug smile was humiliating. "I'm happy to put you up in your hour of need."

"I had thought perhaps . . ." *That I might return for good.* But the expression on Evelyn's face precluded even asking. "A week?"

"Oh, two weeks, if need be," Mrs. Treadwell said grandly. "I only wish it could be longer. But you understand, I have the academy's reputation to protect. We make our own choices in this life. And you made yours."

The girls were more welcoming, and more tentative. "What happened?" Bess whispered when the countess visited their rooms to greet them the next day.

"I'm not certain," Christiane said frankly. "He—we had a bit of a quarrel, though not much of one, really. And he took off back to Ireland with Claire—without so much as a word of farewell to me."

"I can't believe it!" Bess declared, tossing her red curls. "There has to be some sort of mistake. A misunderstanding."

"I'm afraid not," Christiane told her.

"What will you do now?" Gwen asked anxiously. "Will you go after him?"

"Not likely."

"But if you love him," Bess began.

"Love doesn't answer everything in this world, you know," the countess said a bit tartly. "Love doesn't straighten your cravat and sweeten your tea and keep your new boots from giving you blisters. Merciful heavens, I don't know where you girls get some of your notions about love."

There was silence for a moment. Then Gwen asked gently, "Will Mrs. Treadwell let you stay?"

"Actually, I have been thinking of traveling," the countess told her. "To the New World, perhaps. Or India."

"She *won't* let you stay, will she?" Bess cried.

"I don't know that I'd care to," the countess admitted, "when the price would be hearing her say ten times a day, 'I told you so about that man!' "

The girls laughed, shakily. "Have you . . . sufficient resources?" Gwen wanted to know.

"To get there, yes. And once I do, I can always open a gambling hell. Don't fret over me, *chérie*. I am like a cat; I always land on my feet. Tell me about your studies."

"I have had a poem accepted for publication. In Scotland, granted. But still," Bess burbled.

" 'But still' indeed!" the countess said in delight. "What is the poem? May I read it?"

"I don't know that you'll want to. It's a love poem."

"Inspired by whom?"

"She won't tell," Gwen reported. "I've tried every which way to worm it from her. It must be serious this time."

Christiane laughed. "And what have you been up to, Gwen?"

"Dr. Caplan brought me a shark to dissect."

"A shark? Why on earth a shark?"

"Because their physiology—"

"Ooo, there's a grand word," Bess teased. Gwen stuck out her tongue at her just as Clarisse bobbed in the doorway.

"Visitor for ye, mum."

Christiane rose involuntarily from her seat; her heart had careened into her throat. "Is it—"

"Mr. Wrede, mum."

"Oh. Oh!" The countess put her hand to her mouth. "My God. Poor Mr. Wrede. I never gave a thought to what he must be—heavens, Clarisse, do show him into the parlor."

"We'll wait here," Gwen announced. The redhead shot her a glance that clearly said: *Are you daft?* "It isn't any of our business, is it?" Gwen pointed out firmly.

"Spoilsport," Bess hissed.

The countess smiled. "No, both of you, come along. It will serve to make you more wary in matters of the heart. God knows I wish I'd been." She led the way to the parlor.

Clarisse showed Mr. Wrede in. The countess crossed to him quickly, took his hands in hers. "David, I'm so terribly sorry."

"Sorry? For what?"

"He doesn't look a bit damaged, do you think?" Bess muttered to Gwen. The countess had to concede it; if his fiancée's sudden disappearance had thrown David Wrede into a funk, he was hiding it well. He was dressed in traveling clothes—a well-made and well-worn black cape, black hat, his black boots.

"Bring tea, Clarisse, if you please," the countess ordered.

"Miss Boggs, Miss Carstairs. How do thou do?" David greeted them warmly.

"Do you know that Lord Carew has taken Claire back to Ireland?" Bess burst out.

"Oh, yes. I called at the house this afternoon, and O'Malley told me as much. He also told me how distraught the countess had become when she heard, and that she'd rushed off here." His calm hazel gaze met Christiane's. "I am on my way to Aerfailly. I've never seen Ireland, though Claire spoke of it often enough. I thought to surprise her there. Perhaps thou might care to come along?"

"Do you know *why* Gannon has taken Claire to Ireland?" Christiane inquired.

He shook his head. "I assume it was business."

"Business!" she said in disbelief.

"Folk get called away abruptly on business all the time. I do," he noted, looking puzzled. "What else would it be?"

The countess paled. "Oh, David. I am so sorry to be the

one to have to tell you this. The night before last, Claire had . . . another of her bouts. The horses, all of that."

His forehead creased in concern. "Why did thou not send for me?"

"It was my first thought to do so. But Gannon wouldn't allow it."

"I don't understand."

Clarisse had brought in the tea tray; she was trailed by Mrs. Treadwell, who patted David's shoulder kindly. "Poor young man. But chin up, chin up—there are plenty of fish in the sea!"

"Have I offended Lord Carew in some way?" David appealed to the countess.

"I don't think it was that. I think it's more likely—"

"I can't recall—is it one or two sugars, Mr. Wrede?" asked Mrs. Treadwell, who was handing cups around.

Anyone but a Quaker would have cursed at the interruption. As it was, Christiane thought even David might let slip an oath. But he gathered himself in, drew a breath, and posed the question: "Why would Lord Carew not send for me?"

"He said he was afraid that if you saw her—that way— too many times, you would not want to wed her." There— she'd said it.

Wrede was appalled. "How could he believe such a thing?"

"Oh, that isn't why he left," said Mrs. Treadwell, extending a cup and saucer to him.

"You weren't even there, Evelyn," the countess said with some exasperation.

"Are you telling me the fact that there are rumors all over London claiming Lord Carew killed his brother and Georgina has nothing to do with his abrupt return to Ireland?"

The girls, wide-eyed, gasped. Christiane blanched. And David Wrede . . . laughed.

"Lord Carew? Ridiculous," he declared. He looked to Christiane. "Surely thou do not think him capable of such a thing."

"N-no . . ."

"I don't see why you say that, Christiane," Mrs. Treadwell put in helpfully. "You thought he was a madman twenty years ago in Paris. That's the precise term you used when you wrote me of him—'a madman.' And nothing that has happened since you met up with him again would seem likely to change your mind in the least."

"It's more vital than I thought that I go to Aerfailly," David Wrede declared. "My father's firm has a number of ships at dock in Dover. I'll have one take me to Ireland tonight. Come with me," he urged the countess.

"I don't think you understand, David," she said gently. "Lord Carew doesn't want you there. And he certainly does not want me."

"It is thou who do not understand," he responded, politely but firmly. "Claire needs me. What else would I do but go to her? The only question is whether thou will come along."

"Don't so much as suggest it!" Mrs. Treadwell shuddered.

"I am not about to go chasing after a man who left the *country* without so much as a word of good-bye—a man to whom I was engaged!" Christiane declared.

"I can see how thou could decide that he was rude to thee."

"And so he was—unspeakably!"

"I can also see how thou could conclude he was so distraught over Claire's illness and the rumors Mrs. Treadwell spoke of that he could not think clearly. In which case he needs thee more than even he can know."

Mrs. Treadwell set down her teacup with a clatter. "I do hope, Christiane, you won't credit such nonsense!"

"It could be that as well as the other," Gwen spoke up.

"Oh, I'm sure that it is!" Bess cried eagerly.

"Do hush, both of you!" the headmistress scolded. "You are nothing but silly schoolgirls. What do you know about the world?"

"I know the glass is as likely to be half full as it is to be half empty," Bess retorted.

"It is all over the ton that the man is a cold-blooded killer," Mrs. Treadwell declared.

"It was all over the ton once upon a time that Lord Weatherston had had his way with me," Christiane said thoughtfully, "but that didn't make it so."

The headmistress was beside herself. "I will wash my hands of you *forever,* Christiane, *once and for all,* if you elect to go on such a wild-goose chase. It is shocking to run after a man! It is utterly undignified!"

The countess glanced at Gwen and Bess, saw their faces blurred with desperate hope. But wishing for a thing didn't make it so; she knew that well enough. She tried listening to her heart, but could not tell what it was saying; it was pounding too loudly in her head.

David Wrede was waiting for her answer, waiting patiently.

"Go. Go. Go," Gwen and Claire were chanting beneath their breaths.

"Don't be a *damned fool,* Christiane!" Evelyn burst out.

The countess looked at her. "Twenty years, Evelyn. Twenty years, and all those women . . . and yet he remembered things . . ." She blushed, but held her chin up. "I owe him this." Then she turned to David. "When did you wish to leave?"

"As soon as you can."

"I haven't unpacked my baggage. How fortunate," Christiane said.

Mrs. Treadwell stood, seemed about to say more, then merely shook her head and left the parlor without a word.

Christiane didn't see her again, though Gwen and Bess and Petra came to watch as Stains loaded her baggage into David's phaeton. Gwen put her hand on the countess's arm and drew her back toward the gate. "I don't know what you will find," the young woman said, "but I will feel better if you have this with you." She handed Christiane a small red felt sack. It was surprisingly heavy for its size.

"What is this?"

"A pistol. Mrs. Treadwell bought one for each of us, and we have target practice with Stains every Thursday and Saturday. Mrs. T has never forgotten what good use Katherine made of hers when that highwayman attacked her a few years back. Do you need me to teach you to use it?"

"I know how to shoot. But I'm sure I won't need such a thing."

Gwen glanced to where David Wrede was helping Stains load the countess's bags. "Well, we know *he* isn't armed, don't we?" she said in her practical way. "And I'm not at all sure a Quaker pacifist is what you want at your side when you head off on an adventure like this."

The countess was touched—in a way. "Why, Gwen. How very thoughtful of you."

"I'm sure you won't use it," Gwen said stoutly. "But I feel better knowing that you have it. If anything *should* happen—" She paused, then burst out: "Oh, Madame. Do take care."

"I will." The countess gave her a quick hug. They walked back toward the phaeton, and Christiane embraced Bess and Petra as well. She glanced at the academy windows, and thought she saw a flicker of movement at the drapes of the parlor. But it could have been a trick of the twilight that was falling fast.

"Isn't it just so romantic?" Bess asked, and sighed. "Setting off on a pilgrimage of love."

"Oh, it is," Petra agreed breathlessly.

Christiane slipped the red felt sack into her reticule.

"I daresay we'll be dancing at your wedding after all, Mr. Wrede," Bess burbled.

"If it is my wedding, thou won't be dancing," he said with a grin.

Christiane let him hand her up into the carriage and waved farewell to the girls. She found the weight of the gun in her reticule more comforting than she cared to admit.

Twenty-nine

"Ever been t' Ireland before, then?" the loquacious driver engaged by David Wrede at the Ballynakill docks inquired, sending a plume of spittle to the side of the road.

"Never," Christiane murmured.

"Ah, then, ye're in for a rare treat. Lovely country, bain't it?"

Sitting on the stiff wooden seat of the open wagon, a chill drizzle falling around her, surrounded by a vista of gray, rocky cliffs, gray-green fields dotted with white-washed cottages, and the endless gray expanse of fog-wrapped sea to the west, the countess shivered. "Lovely," she agreed politely. "How much farther to Aerfailly?"

"An hour, mebbe. Mebbe three hours. I'll have ye there in nae time at all." The driver cleared his throat and spat again.

"Thou must take my cloak to sit on," David Wrede offered from beside the countess on the uncomfortable seat.

The driver cast a curious glance back at him. "Ye've an odd way o' speakin', haen't ye? In the way t' becomin' a priest or somethin', are ye?"

Wrede and Christiane exchanged glances. "Or something," he acknowledged, and gave her a rueful grin.

She turned her gaze back to the surrounding countryside. For a woman of her time, Christiane had seen much of the world. But she had never been anywhere that felt so distinctly foreign as the west coast of Ireland. Its jagged ridges and stark heights and unkempt fields were completely unlike the tamed, coddled landscapes of England and France and Italy.

Then the clouds and fog lifted, and slanting shafts of sunlight poured down onto the drenched fields, making them glow a green so rich, it was like napped velvet. "Ah," their driver said with sublime satisfaction. "A gorgeous day." He smiled happily, then raised a hand to point at a tiny hut in the distance. "Right there's where Jenny Riordan was murdered by her husband. Ye read about that even back in England, I expect."

"I don't believe I did," Christiane said faintly, not daring to look at David Wrede.

"No? Surprisin', that. What she did was kill their babies. Smothered all four of 'em, one after the next, before any reached the age o' one. Convinced the husband the first three was natural, but he took umbrage with the fourth."

"Merciful heavens," Wrede muttered.

"D'ye see that outcrop o' white rock there? Up on the hillside?" their intrepid guide inquired. "That's where th' High Rourke did *his* firstborn son in, after th' boy challenged his authority by killin' the Red Roan o' Raenessy. Ah, a beautiful sad tale that be. And on that mountain behind it—ye can just see the top there—is where the enchantress Sorcha Shannon imprisoned the hero Riordan until he went mad and plucked his own eyes out. Another old, sad tale."

"Are there any happy tales told hereabouts?" the countess asked a trifle tartly.

Their guide pondered this for a moment. Then, "None come t' mind," he said.

They thudded on along the pitted roadway. "What are we going to do when we get there?" Christiane asked David. She'd been much impressed by the way he had handled all their travel arrangements, from engaging the ship to plotting its course to hiring this drover, and it seemed only natural to apply to him for advice.

"That depends on what we find."

"What do you think we will find?"

He glanced at her. "What do you?"

"Off that way there," the driver interjected, "in that patch o' bare brown dirt along the hillside, is where Eoghan Mulder raped 'n' murdered Maisey Kennerly. Slit her throat, he did, 'n' left her t' bleed t' death. Nae grass will grow there ever since."

Christiane fought back a shudder, then looked at David. "Is there nothing at all that you can imagine spurring you to violence against another human being?" she asked curiously.

"Nay," he said, with great certainty. "I could not do harm knowingly to any man."

"Have Quakers no duty to see that right triumphs and wrong is punished?"

"Punishment is God's business, none of ours. He alone can see what lies within the heart."

Christiane's hand curled over her reticule, which contained the red felt bag Gwen had given her. "I begin to see why dealing with you people drives the government daft."

He grinned at her. As he did, the sunlight abruptly vanished, and the faint, misty rain resumed. The wagon pushed on along its bumpy path.

"Just there is where Cadmus Farnally pushed his Aenwyn off the cliffs 'n' then dived in after her to his own death," the driver mentioned, pointing to an outcrop above the cloud-shrouded sea.

"Why would he do such a thing?" the countess demanded irritably.

He turned on the seat. "Done him wrong, she did," he said, as though she were a simpleton.

After another hour or so of such bone-chilling small talk, the wagon cleared a steep hill and rounded a bend. In the distance, gray and grim against a backdrop of skittering dark clouds, a lone tower loomed up. "Aerfailly," the driver said with satisfaction. "Nearly there."

The castle was *ancient,* Christiane saw as they approached. It consisted of no more than that round stone keep and a brief, blunt extension, though there was evidence someone had tried to plant the grounds; spindly rosebushes climbed against the tower, and a parade of ferns marked the path from the road to the front doors. She stared at the blank, black windows, wondering whether Gannon might be watching them as they approached. Just ahead, the road curved away from the keep, leading back toward the cliffs.

The driver reined in at the head of the drive. "Nae sign o' smoke," he said, and spat onto the peat. "It don't look to me as though a soul's alive in the place."

"Don't say that!" Christiane cried.

The man shot her a quick, appraising look. His eyes were bloodshot, but beautifully blue. "Before we unload, why don't ye go 'n' see if anyone be at home?" he proposed.

David and Christiane peered at the lonely keep and then exchanged glances. "Not a bad idea," David noted. He paused, then added a five-pound note on top of the fare he'd already paid the man. "Will thou wait here until we let thee know?"

"Aye, so I will." The man leaned against a wheel, pulled out a clay pipe, and began to pack it with tobacco, whistling faintly.

David took the countess's elbow and led her toward the door. "I have the distinct impression," Christiane hissed, "that he is hoping we will find another gruesome tragedy for him to add to his guided tour."

Wrede laughed. "He is a bit macabre, isn't he?"

"A *bit*?" She rolled her eyes.

The scree of rain became steadier as they crossed the

turf, and the heavy air was stirred by a swirling of wind. A sheet of crumpled parchment blew toward them in a sudden gust, flapping against David's thigh. He caught it, flattened it out, and stared down at it. "Great heavens."

Blocking the rain with her sleeve, Christiane contemplated the image on the page: two horses rigged to a carriage, very neatly sketched out. "That looks like Claire's work, doesn't it?"

"It is. I am sure of it." They moved on. Another burst of wind sent old, dead leaves skittering—and one more parchment page tumbling along the path. David snatched it up and scanned it, while Christiane peered over his shoulder. It was the horses again, but this time they were rearing in alarm.

"Horses," he muttered. There was a rumble of thunder, and then a flash of lightning crackled low in the sky. The rain redoubled, became a drenching downpour. Wrede drew his cloak up over Christiane's head, and together they ran for the doors—a hardy set of weather-beaten oak, overlaid with much iron ornament. There was a lion's-head knocker. Wrede rapped with it. Nothing happened. He tried again. No answer. Tentatively, Christiane reached for one scroll-shaped knob, turned it, and pushed. The door swung inward, with a faint, creaking rasp of the hinges. She hesitated. David stepped inside.

"There's no one here," he told her, and she followed him into a drafty, circular room so dim that it took several moments for her eyes to adjust. Just as they did, though, a door cracked open at the far side of the hall, and a pale face appeared. "Bridey?" Christiane called, recognizing the maid. The face vanished. Christiane ran across the flagstone floor, found the door shut, and pounded on it above the rising racket of the storm. "Bridey! Open up to me!"

She shoved at the door, and it burst open, revealing a stone-walled kitchen and Bridey, huddled beside the hearth, her eyes frightened and wide.

"Hello, Bridey," the countess said evenly. "Are Lord Carew and Miss Finn here?"

The maid nodded slowly.

There was another sheet of parchment on the floor by Bridey's feet. "Is this thine?" David inquired, nodding toward it. Bridey shook her head, backing away. He crossed the room, drew it up, stared at it. "Christiane," he said urgently. She hurried toward him, contemplating the sketch in the faint light. It was painfully detailed and precise. It showed a short, stout man in neat livery. The man was in the act of climbing back from the box into an open carriage. He had a knife thrust into his chest. His eyes were wide and staring, with an expertly captured expression of disbelief.

"Bridey, what's this about?" Christiane demanded, turning the picture toward her.

"I don't know, mum. I don't have no notion what be goin' on here anymore," the maid declared, and crumpled into tears.

"Where are Lord Carew and Miss Finn?" David asked urgently. The maid hesitated, then nodded toward an arched doorway.

"Upstairs," she whispered.

"And there's no one else in the house?"

She shook her head.

"When's the last time thou saw them?"

"An hour ago, mayhaps."

"What were they doing?"

"He brought her down for food. I'd made a rasher of bacon and fresh bread at noon—eggs, too. There they be." She nodded toward the stout oak table, on which two places were laid, the plates still piled with food. "She would not eat then, so he brought her down again later to try. But the minute he lifted his fork and knife, she took off, back up the stairs."

"Why would she run off upstairs, Bridey?" David asked.

"Runnin' away from him, she was. That's what I think."

David went to the archway and peered up the staircase. "Where's the nearest officer of the law, Bridey?"

"In the village, sir. Constable Larkin."

"How far off is the village?"

"Just a mile or so."

David glanced at Christiane, who nodded. "There's a wagon and driver outside," he told the maid. "Could thou ask him to take thee to fetch the constable and bring him back here? Could thou do it quickly?"

"Aye, sir." The maid seemed much relieved to be taking orders. "What'll I tell the constable ye want him for?"

"Just say his presence is needed." The girl headed past them toward the front doors.

"Bridey!" the countess said suddenly. "Where are the dogs?"

"They followed 'em up there, mum." The maid hurried out, glad to be gone.

Christiane began ransacking the kitchen. Inside a stout wooden cooler, she found the remains of a haunch of venison, and picked it up by the bone.

"What in the world—" Wrede began.

"That Chlöe detests me," the countess said grimly. "If I am going to encounter her on a dark staircase, I intend to be pre—" She froze as a distant scream pierced the air.

"Claire," David Wrede said, and tore up the stairs, with Christiane at his heels.

They reached the first landing, and he hesitated, listening. All was still again, eerily still. Christiane had a sudden terrible, dark foreboding. Why would Claire be afraid of Gannon? Why would she have tried to run away from him? She could think of only one answer: that the girl, in drawing those chilling pictures, had recalled how her parents had died in their carriage that day—and remembered who had killed them as well.

"Take this," she said impatiently, thrusting the haunch at David. She withdrew Gwen's pistol from her reticule, and then the bullets.

"No," David said, reaching to stay her hand.

"You follow your conscience," she told him, slamming a bullet home, "and I'll follow mine." There came another scream, from higher up in the tower. They ran to the second landing and paused, close together, hearts pounding in the silence. "It was higher yet, I think," Christiane murmured.

"Are thou sure? I thought—"

The calm was broken by a sudden burst of cries: "No! No! Let me go, I tell you! Let me go! Oh, let me *go*—"

They ran upward, and the cries grew louder. Now they could hear Gannon's voice, oddly firm and calm, interspersed with Claire's: "It's for the best," he was telling her. "You'll see. It will be for the best."

"No! *No!*"

The staircase ended abruptly at a low wooden door. Through the crack at its bottom came a thin veil of light . . . and a low, unmistakable growl. Inside, the voices were still going, Claire's in a rising crescendo, Gannon's unnaturally composed. David tried the door handle. It turned. "Give me the meat," Christiane hissed. "And stand back." He flattened himself against the wall. Christiane thrust the door open and was met by Chlöe's snapping jaws. "Get out, bitch!" she screamed, smacking the huge hound's snout with the venison and flinging the bone into the darkness below. The dog skittered on the worn stones, her momentum carrying her downward. Christiane reached back to yank David in, then slammed the door shut.

The clamor in the room had broken off abruptly. In the sudden silence, Christiane raised her gaze. Gannon stood at one of the high, wide windows, his body braced behind Claire, who was standing on the sill, holding on, white-knuckled, to the edges of the open abyss.

"Let her go," Christiane said evenly, leveling the pistol at him.

"I can't," he replied, a haunted wildness to his gray eyes. "I—" But whatever else he said was drowned out by a sudden burst of barks from Chlöe, who was thudding against the closed door. Homer, who'd started toward Christiane with his tail wagging, hesitated, glanced back at his master, and then joined in the furious melee of noise his mate was making from the stairwell.

"Let her go!" Christiane tried to shout above the clamor. Gannon shook his head. Claire had begun screaming again, was writhing in his grip. David stood at the countess's side. "Go and grab him!" Christiane cried, but he didn't move. Impatient, she glanced at him, saw him mouthing something that she could not understand for all the ruckus the dogs were raising. To hell with him, she thought bitterly, cocking the hammer. She spread her feet solidly, aimed the gun at Gannon's head, and fired.

As she did, David lunged for her, catching her sleeve, drawing her arm to the right. The shot rang out, but the bullet struck the wall, ricocheting wildly while the explosion reverberated against the stones. The cacophony of the dogs halted, sliced off as though by a knife. Homer stared at her in confusion, tail lowered, head bowed.

"Oh, God, Christiane!" Gannon cried into the waves of harsh echoes. "I'm trying—"

Grimly, she started to reload. But David Wrede was wrestling for the gun. "Let me go, let me go!" she raged, clawing at him with her free hand, leaving a faint streak of red down his cheek.

The sight of the blood seemed to ignite something in Claire; she shoved past Gannon and charged the countess, screaming: "Don't you hurt him! Don't you dare hurt him!" Chlöe had redoubled her mad yelps from the stairwell. David put a hand to his wounded cheek in surprise. And Gannon—instead of pursuing his niece, Gannon simply stood silhouetted against the dull gray sky beyond the window, his chest heaving as though he could not catch his breath—or as though he might cry.

Homer, smelling the venison on Christiane's hands as she struggled with David for the gun, gave her a lick from his enormous tongue. Startled, she relaxed her grip on the weapon, afraid it would go off in his face. David wrenched the pistol free just as Claire reached them, careening into his arms.

"Chlöe!" Gannon roared, in the voice of a madman. "Be still!" The wolfhound's barks cut off instantly. Homer sidled toward Christiane and took another greedy swipe at her fingers.

"Kill him," Christiane panted, as David contemplated the gun he now held. "Kill him, for God's sake! Can't you see he was trying to murder Claire?"

"Bloody hell," Gannon said angrily.

"Kill him before he adds more murders to his list!"

But instead, David hurled the gun toward the open window. It sailed past Gannon, who made no effort at all to reach for it as it flew over the sill. Christiane felt her heart buckle. "Oh, God," she whispered, as Gannon took a step toward them. "He is going to kill us all."

"Of course he won't," David declared, clinging to Claire every bit as tightly as her uncle had. "He wasn't trying to push her out of the window. Could thou not see that?"

"What *was* he doing, then?" Christiane demanded.

David held Claire even more closely. "He was trying to keep her in."

Thirty

The dogs were in the courtyard, thank God, gnawing more bones that Gannon had found for them in the kitchen. Christiane was sitting in a rocking chair there, a glass of Irish whiskey in her hand. David Wrede was still holding Claire; she'd fainted in the tower, and he'd carried her all the way down. Gannon was waving hartshorn under his niece's nose.

"I think she's coming around," David said, as Claire stirred in his arms. Her eyes fluttered open. He smiled at her, but she flinched and turned away.

"Claire?" Christiane rose, moving toward her. "Claire, why on earth would you try to do such a dreadful thing? To kill yourself—"

"She was afraid she would lose Mr. Wrede's affections," Gannon said curtly.

"I wonder where she might have gotten that notion," Christiane shot back.

"How could thou ever fear that, Claire?" David asked.

"You don't know," she mumbled, tears rolling down her pale cheeks.

"What don't we know, *chérie*?" Christiane asked, very gently. But the girl buried her face against David's black coat. Christiane reached toward the table, for the sketch of the man with the knife in his chest. "What is this picture you've drawn?"

"Let me go," the girl pleaded to David, who obligingly set her on her feet. Faster than lightning, she whirled for the staircase.

"Stop her!" Gannon bellowed.

David already had. He was stern-faced as he dragged her back. "This has gone far enough," he declared. "It is time for the truth, Claire."

"No! I can't . . ."

"Oh, Claire." He looked down at her earnestly. "Thou must tell the truth. This house has seen too many lies."

"He's right about that," Gannon said, sounding weary.

Claire's fearful gray eyes went to her uncle. "You told me . . . that I must *not* remember. Must not think of it."

"I was wrong. I didn't know . . ." He glanced to Christiane, and then to David. "She didn't seem to recall anything by the time the sheriff got there. She drew an utter blank. It was . . . so awful—the carriage and the horses and . . ." His voice trailed away. "I thought she would be safe so long as she didn't remember. I thought we would fare well enough together, she and I." He shook his head. "But then the nightmares began."

Claire was trembling in David's arms, her face averted. "I took her to the academy," Gannon said. "I thought perhaps that without me near to remind her, she'd keep the memory locked away. But then you got her started drawing pictures. She kept on drawing pictures." He picked up the one on the table, stared at it a moment, set it back down. "And now she remembers it all."

David tapped a finger against the picture. "Who is this in the sketch, love?"

Claire glanced at it sidelong. "The coachman."

"And who has stabbed the coachman?"

"Papa." The word was a wisp.

"Why?"

Claire seemed to shrink into herself. "He was trying to stop Papa from hitting Mama."

"Why was thy papa hitting her?"

"They argued . . . in the carriage. She did not want to return to Ireland. The doctor had told her she was dying. That she hadn't much time left. She said—" Her voice caught in a sob. "She told him she hated him, and she hated Ireland. That all her life since she'd met him had been a waste."

"What did he answer?"

"That she'd bloody damned well come back with him. She shouted that she wouldn't. And then he—hit her. Again and again."

The countess felt as though some infinite weight lay across her heart. David Wrede was ashen, but he pressed on. "So the driver tried to stop him?"

Claire nodded. "He had a knife in his boot. He pulled it out. He reined the horses in and came back over the box, shouting at Papa to leave Mama be. But Papa wrested the knife from him and stabbed him." She curled her fist around the hilt of an imaginary knife and jabbed the air twice, quickly. "Like that. That."

"What happened then?" David asked, even more softly.

"Mama caught at me to pull me out of the coach. She was screaming at Papa, screaming such dreadful things. I'd seen him angry before, and her, too, but never like that. He lunged at her with the knife. Then she stumbled and fell down to the floor of the coach, and I saw that the knife was inside her. Just—here." She touched the front of her bodice. "I wanted to take it out of her. I thought it must be hurting her, to have it inside her, so I pulled it out. And then there came such blood . . . oh, the blood just went everywhere, everywhere! All over the horses, and Papa, and the carriage . . ." Her voice had become a low, soft wail.

David Wrede had her wrapped in his arms, would not

relinquish her. He was smoothing her black hair with his hand. "What did thou do then, Claire?"

She shook her head. "I can't tell. I can't say."

"Oh, Claire. You must."

Again she shook her head, wildly. There was a clatter of carriage wheels on the drive outside. Claire's eyes went wide. "They are coming for me, aren't they?"

David wrenched her around to face him. "Listen to me. The Light—"

"There is no Light in me!" she wailed hopelessly.

Someone banged at the doors to Aerfailly. "Constable Larkin here!"

"Tell me what thou did, Claire."

She met David's gaze reluctantly, and something she saw there, some aspect of love that could not be moved or deterred, pushed her on, in a whisper: "I did not *mean* to hurt him. I was not trying to hurt him. But the carriage floor was all slick with blood. And he came at me just as I took the knife out of Mama. His boot went . . . *whoosh*. He fell. He fell *at* me. Onto me. Onto the—" She squeezed her eyes shut, her hands raised as though to ward her father off, and a long shudder wracked her.

"Aye, just so," said David, and pulled her close.

Christiane looked to Gannon. "Any judge in England would consider it justified. After she had seen Hugh kill the coachman and her mother—"

"But it never *can* be justified, can it?" Claire cried.

"I'm comin' in!" the constable roared.

"Claire, listen to me!" David said desperately. She had squirmed free of him, was heading for the stairs. He caught her from behind. "The Inner Light is only what God tells each soul, each private soul, to do."

"I killed my *father*. 'Thou shalt not kill.' 'Honor thy father and thy mother.' Don't you understand, David? Don't you see what I've done?"

"It was an accident, love. As much his fault as thine. Do thou feel in thy heart thou did wrong?"

The question rang out into momentary silence.

Claire stopped fighting him. "I—"

"Did thou mean to kill him?"

"No. No! I never, *ever* meant to hurt him."

"Listen to the Light, then!" David urged her. "Fight the darkness!"

"*You* would never hurt anyone. You would never kill anyone—"

"Oh, Claire." He smiled at her sadly. "It's easy enough to see the Light when the most one faces is rudeness from the likes of Lord Simpson. But thou—thou have managed to keep it burning within thee against such a flood tide of shadow—and for so long! Thou are . . . so bright. I could never hope to be so radiant as thee."

There was a thud of footsteps in the front hall; then Constable Larkin, beefy and broad-shouldered and red-faced with hurry, appeared in the doorway, a shotgun at the ready. Bridey trailed behind him, an expression of antici-pated horror on her face. Behind her was the driver, eager with the prospect of the mayhem they might find.

"What's all the fuss, then?" the constable demanded.

Christiane went toward him, summoning charm. "I'm ter-ribly sorry you've been called out here on no account, Con-stable Larkin. We feared there was an intruder in the house, you see, and sent Bridey to fetch you. But we have made a thorough search, and it turns out it was only . . ." God. She could not think of an excuse; her mind had gone blank.

"The hounds," David Wrede supplied, so readily that Gannon choked on his whiskey. "Lord Carew's wolfhounds. They'd gotten down into the cellars some-how."

"Ah. After rats, no doubt." Constable Larkin nodded sagely.

"There are rats in this house, certainly," Gannon said, with a thunderous glance at Christiane.

After they had apologized a dozen more times to the con-stable and sent him and the driver packing, Gannon and

Christiane and Claire and David sat at the kitchen table, while Bridey made tea and served up fresh eggs and toast. "I wish I had remembered what happened to Papa and Mama sooner," Claire announced. "I want to go back to England. I want to tell the authorities what I did." She looked less ethereal, more sure of herself, than in all the time Christiane had known her.

"You cannot go back, pet," Gannon argued. "I agree with the countess that the courts will likely hold you blameless. But the scandal would be immense. You would never be able to show your face in society."

Claire let out a giggle. "Society . . ."

And Wrede joined in, with his low, rich laugh. "How could she show it anyway," he asked Gannon, "after she marries me?"

"You maintain a certain respectability," Gannon argued. "You move in the Countess of Yarlborough's circle—"

"I am nothing but a poor relation—a hanger-on," David said with admirable dignity.

Claire looked to her uncle. "I *have* to go back. If I don't admit to what I did, there is the possibility someone else will be arrested for the crime—some poor soldier or such. I could never live with that prospect."

"I'd rather confess to it myself than have you do so," Gannon said, bitterness in his voice. "Most of the ton thinks I'm guilty anyway."

Claire shot a sidelong glance at Christiane. "I doubt Madame would forgive me if I let you go away to jail."

"Madame has proven that she sides with the ton. Quite emphatically."

David cleared his throat. "Thou must be tired, Claire. Let Bridey come up with me and put thee to bed. Will thou do that, Bridey?"

The maid nodded. "Aye, sir."

"I don't know that I can sleep," Claire fretted.

"I will sit with thee, then," he promised, taking her by the hand.

The three of them went up the staircase, their voices

slowly fading. Christiane and Gannon were left sitting across from one another at the kitchen table. "What did you mean by that last remark?" she demanded.

"Just what I said. You came here toting a pistol because you thought me a murderous maniac. It's not exactly what one hopes for in the woman one loves."

"The pistol was Gwen's. She gave it to me. I never would have thought of it on my own."

"You were ready enough to use it."

If he was angry, she was, too. "You won't deny there was some basis for my suspicions. You did leave me there in London without a word of explanation."

"I found that note from Darby. I knew damned well what he'd be telling you about me. I'd heard about Greer's whisperings."

"Why didn't you ever tell me you were there? That you found Claire after it happened?"

"The story doesn't exactly do my family credit, does it?" he demanded, his stormy eyes flashing. "What would you have had me admit to you? 'First my brother killed the coachman and Georgina, and then Claire killed him—' "

"It was an accident!"

"The ton doesn't care about that. All it lives for is gossip and whisperings—tiger fodder." He glared at her. "It's all you care about as well. Why else would you have met with Darby?"

"Because he is an old, dear friend?"

"Fuck you," he told her.

"He is, though, Gannon," she said levelly. "I won't deny he wanted to print the story Greer was telling. But he came to me as a friend, first, to ask if it was true. I told him he was crazy. I told him it was nonsense. I defended you to him. I told him if he wanted some *on-dit,* he could tell the world that the Countess d'Oliveri had never been so happy in her life." She looked at him. "Then I returned home to find that you were gone."

"Was that when you jumped to the conclusion that I was a murderer?"

"No. That was when I jumped to the conclusion that you were a bastard. It was Evelyn who insisted you must be a murderer."

Gannon pushed his hair back from his forehead with both his hands. "Listen to us. Will you listen to us? You were right in what you said to me once. We are too old, both of us. Too old for love, too old for trust, too old ever to believe in one another unquestioningly. It takes a young heart to be so naïve. We are past that, you and I."

She had her hands clasped in her lap and was staring down at them. She said, very softly, "Is that what you told Greer? That you were too old?"

"What I told Greer *when*?"

"When you broke it off with her."

"No," he said. "I just told her about you. Told her that I loved you."

Slowly she raised her head, looked straight at him. "You always had me, didn't you, to use as a convenient excuse? 'I cannot marry you; I cannot truly love you. My heart belongs to the woman I loved and fought a duel for in France, long, long ago.' Only now, with me, you can't use that excuse, and you need another. So you've *chosen* another—that I don't believe in you."

"You *did* fire that gun," he growled.

"Well, if you had heard the litany of heinous crimes that driver regaled us with all the way from Ballynakill—lovers, offspring, spouses, all murdered in the most gruesome ways—"

"Be honest, Christiane. You were only too ready to ascribe my brother's and Georgina's murders to me. Why not? It's no more than the English expect of the uncouth Irish."

Christiane nodded her head. "You're right."

"Of course I am. To you English, there's no crime an Irishman isn't secretly longing to commit: buggery, bestiality, sacrilege—preferably while in a drunken stupor—"

"Not about that."

"*And* while playing a harp and dancing a jig." He paused. "About what, then?"

"We *are* too old. Too old for the sort of blind, unquestioning love that David and Claire share."

He got to his feet, strode over to the hearth, and stood staring into the embers, his back to her. His broad shoulders rose in a sigh. "Yes. We are."

"But there is also the kind of love St. Paul talks of," she said quietly. "A wise sort of love. The kind that can't be hoodwinked, or turned by society's scorn. That bears all things, hopes all things, endures all things."

He raised his head. "Endures all things . . ." His eyes met hers. "We are both awfully fond of flight, aren't we?"

Christiane nodded. She was thinking of her mother rushing to wed her stepfather, and of her stepbrothers' unwanted attentions, and of her mad eagerness to debut. She was thinking of how readily she had agreed to elope with Harold Hainesworth to escape her family—and how quickly she had run off to Paris once the ton turned on her. "So we are."

He must have known her better than she thought. "Running away is easy," he said. "Staying the course is what's hard. But that isn't why I didn't marry Greer, or any of the others. I didn't marry them because I knew in my heart it would not be fair to them. Because I loved you from the first moment I saw you. I know it isn't rational. It may not even be sane. But there you have it. Love at first sight." He smiled a little, looking abashed. "When you hear about that sort of love in stories, it always is reciprocal. Maybe that's why I was so certain you loved me, too."

"I'm not sure I didn't," she confessed.

He glanced up quickly. "Jean-Baptiste—"

"I . . . thought I loved him. But he never . . ." She drew a breath. "He never frightened me. From the first, you did. You wanted more than I thought I could give. Than I was willing to give."

"I wanted all of you," he confirmed. "I did." A pause. "I do."

She shook her head wistfully. "You said yourself we are too old. Just look at how quick we were to distrust each other."

"It's no wonder if it takes us some time to get it right," he pointed out. "We're neither of us used to being honest with those we love." His gray eyes were somber. "I . . . did not have the right teachers in how a man and a woman should behave toward each other."

"No. Nor I."

"But here is the trouble. Just when I am ready to give up," he went on haltingly, "I look at you. And every time I look at you, I fall in love all over again."

"Oh, Gannon."

"I don't know what to do about it, except to keep on asking you to marry me."

Christiane listened to her heart. It was roaring at her. She smiled. "And I don't know what to do except—say yes."

He caught her to him, pressed his mouth to hers. His kiss was long and hard and delectable, and when he finally released her, there were tears in his eyes. "I would do anything for you," he whispered. "Anything. You could ask me to climb up to heaven and bring you down the stars, and by God, I would try."

The wolfhounds, bored with the courtyard, expecting their usual late-night goodies, were banging at the back door. Christiane opened her mouth as one request occurred to her. "Anything, you say. Do you suppose you might—"

Gannon drew back abruptly: "Anything except that."

"But she hates me so!"

"Chlöe doesn't hate you," he scoffed. "She's just jealous. She'll come around in time."

"She hasn't so far."

He laughed, going to unlatch the door. "You worry too much about her. She's only a dog. It's not as though—" He broke off as Homer pranced in, wagging his tail eagerly as he approached Christiane, who had one wary eye still on the door. After a moment, Chlöe loomed up there.

"What's that she's got?" she demanded sharply, seeing something shiny clenched between the bitch's bared teeth.

"Drop it, Chlöe!" her master ordered. The dog showed no inclination to obey. "I said drop it!" he thundered, in a voice that made Homer cower. Chlöe met Gannon's gaze with defiance, turned her head to glance at the countess, and then acquiesced, albeit gracelessly.

"Only a dog?" Christiane shrieked, as the pistol Gwen had lent her, which David Wrede had hurled from the tower window, clattered onto the floor.

Gannon could not help himself; he burst out laughing. "Oh, good girl, Chlöe! You've never retrieved *anything* for me before!"

Thirty-one

"There's Irish in you. I'm sure of it," Gannon whispered, his mouth brushing hers in the darkness.

"There's Irish in me *now*," Christiane said, and giggled. He laughed and ducked to kiss her breasts even as his hips hitched more tightly against her. "Quite a bit of Irish," she said breathlessly, smoothing his buttocks with her hands.

"And I find myself surrounded by English," he murmured, moving in slow, devastating circles against her. "A typical situation for my kind, more's the rue."

"You could beat a retreat."

"Perhaps I shall." He started to, but she clung to him. "Or perhaps I'll make a mad, brash advance."

"Oh, I'd advise that!"

"You know what they say, though, about hasty warriors."

"What do they say?"

"They come to quick ends. And we would not want that."

"No?"

"No. What we want is a protracted combat, a lengthy

battle with plenty of hard-fought skirmishes." He reared up suddenly, catching her breasts in his hands and plying their taut buds with his fingertips until she moaned with pleasure, her muscles tightening, the light shimmering through her in bright waves. He relaxed, pulling back onto his haunches. "And interludes of deceptive lull, in which both sides regroup."

"Another death on the English side, I fear," Christiane said, when she could speak again.

"That's certainly what the Irish hoped for." He reached down and brushed the curls of her mound of Venus, then shifted on the bed until his mouth was at her thigh.

"You show no mercy, do you?"

"And take no prisoners." His tongue flicked against the bud of her desire, moved deeper, savoring her secret places.

"Oh, Gannon—"

He pressed on relentlessly, relishing the tightening of her muscles, the rhythm of her movements as he sucked and lapped and licked at her, the way her hands abruptly clenched on the sheets and her back arched, the quickening of her breathing, the crescendo of small, lovely cries as she moved toward—

"Surrender," he whispered, raising his head, meeting her gaze.

"Never! The English don't—oh!" she gasped, as he rose and thrust his manhood into her, straight to the hilt.

"Surrender to me," he said again, catching her by the shoulders, pulling her to him, raising her straight off the bed. He held her that way for a moment, hard against him, before he lowered her again to the soft linen sheets. He withdrew his long rod, waited—

She lay beneath him, lips parted, drenched in the moonlight that poured through the ancient casements and lent her pale skin and midnight hair an unearthly sheen. "Ah, Christiane," he murmured, and touched the wild curls that framed her face. "It's no use, is it, with you? It never was. Very well. I surrender instead."

He plunged into her frantically, rode her wildly, and she felt his tension mounting, heard his hitching groans, sensed that he could not hold out much longer. Accordingly, she matched the movements of her hips to his, thrusting at him, tucking her heels up against his shoulder blades. *"Oh,"* he groaned, sinking even deeper inside her. "Oh, my love—"

"Now," she whispered, smoothing her hands along the bands of taut muscles at his back. "I want you so. I want . . . I want . . ." And there it was: the magical, mystical rhythm, the two of them swept up in it, helpless in its thrall. The surrender was mutual; there were only victors in the mad race to the finish, in the jumble of cries and sighs and the sweet, longed-for release of juices that mingled at the point where they were joined as one. He came in a long, shuddering rush; she came whimpering with wonder. He collapsed atop her; she lay beneath his weight perfectly willingly, her pulse pounding in her head.

When he could move again, he shifted to his side, pulling her along with him, holding her tight against him. "What think you of my rooms, then?" he asked.

"I hadn't much opportunity to look about as we came in."

"Complaining?"

"Not at all." Her mouth curved in a smile when she thought of their frantic haste to reach the bed. "The linens are supremely soft."

"Irish," he said in satisfaction, then swung his legs over the side of the high canopied bed, getting up to piss, at rather astonishing length, into the chamber pot. "Racehorses and Irishmen," he noted, seeing her arched brows.

"Racehorses and Irishmen *what?*"

"Have big bladders."

"Have bigger opinions of themselves."

He grinned, coming back toward the bed. "Have even bigger pricks." He bounced down beside her and stretched out, his hand moving in a proprietary fashion toward her thigh. "What think you of Aerfailly in general?"

She paused. While she did not want to offend him, neither did she wish to spend any more time in this crumbling ruin than was necessary. "I'm sure it has a great deal of historical significance," she finally said.

"Oh, no, not really. It's your standard thirteenth-century Irish keep, not much improved since. I hate the place."

"You do?" she asked in surprise.

"God, yes. As soon as I came into my inheritance, I bought a gorgeous brick Tudor outside Cork. You'd like Cork; I truly think you would. It's not London or Paris, of course, but it's lively in its way. And I've found that in general, the English are insatiably curious about us Irish. Makes it easy to throw great big parties. They're all dying to come down on the ferry to see the wild Gaels at play."

Christiane blushed. "You've not much respect for my countrymen, Gannon."

"You've little enough for mine," he countered, and laughed when she bristled. "What the hell, then? It's true. Anyway, you'll have to come to terms with Ireland; might as well do it sooner rather than later."

"Why will I?"

"Why will you what?"

"Have to come to terms with Ireland?"

"We can't very well settle in England, can we? Once we take Claire back and she admits to what happened, we will all be complete social pariahs. And with *no* hope of redemption this time."

"Evelyn will cut me dead," she said mournfully.

"Surely she will understand what happened. Surely she won't blame Claire."

"Not—not blame her, exactly. But I know exactly what she'll say." Christiane pitched her voice higher, mimicking the headmistress. "'I have a duty to the other girls—can't afford the risk of scandal—it would frighten the mamas away.'"

Gannon laughed and propped his head on his elbow, looking down at her in the moonlight. "I don't understand you or her. I cannot decide whether you are best friends or worst enemies."

"We are both, I think." She shrugged. "What we feel for each other isn't so different from what I feel for you, I suppose."

"With certain significant differences, I hope." He let his fingertips trail down her throat to her breast.

"Certain ones," she agreed. "But she is the only person on earth who can make me as angry as I get at you."

"She won't come to the wedding?"

She shook her head. "Not a chance in the world. It's a pity. I *was* looking forward to seeing Gwen and Bess and Petra settled, at the very least."

"Perhaps if I were to talk to her . . . explain about Hugh . . ."

Christiane shuddered. "As if she doesn't harbor enough prejudice against the Irish as is! If she ever learned how beastly your brother was to poor Georgina—"

Gannon's hand, which had been exploring eagerly, paused.

She waited.

"Hmm," Gannon said.

"Hmm what?"

He resumed his attentions, and planted a kiss at her breast. "Nothing. I thought I heard the dogs."

"I didn't hear anything." She snuggled closer to him. "It is good we have each other, since no one else is likely ever to receive us again."

"Does that prospect disturb you?"

She considered it. "Pleases me, rather. A lifetime alone, just you and I . . ."

Satisfied, he made love to her again.

Thirty-two

"*I can't imagine* why you'd come all the way from London to see me," Mrs. Treadwell protested to her visitor, a rather shortish fellow with a thatch of undistinguished brown hair, spectacles, and a peculiar streak of blue-black across the right cuff of his well-worn coat.

"You are the countess's oldest friend, are you not?" he asked agreeably, taking a sip of the tea she had poured him.

"I *was*," the headmistress noted. "But I am not now."

"Dear me." Her guest blinked behind the spectacles. "I'm so sorry to hear it. Would it be indelicate of me to inquire as to the cause of the rift between you?"

"It would indeed, Mr. Darby."

"Forgive me, then. It is only that . . . the countess always spoke of you in such glowing terms. It is difficult to imagine that anything could destroy the deep affection she held for you."

Mrs. Treadwell stirred a bit of cream into her tea, worrying her lip. Matthew Darby waited patiently. He had three decades of experience in providing reluctant gossips with the irresistible opening for what they were *dying* to proclaim to the world.

"I don't believe her affection is *destroyed*," the headmistress allowed finally. "We have quarreled before, she and I. Only never so—so vehemently." Her blue eyes swam suddenly with tears. "It is just that it was so deucedly difficult to watch her making such a *fool* out of herself over him."

"You mean Lord Carew."

Evelyn nodded, swiping her eyes with a kerchief. "And when we had our last row, she threw it up at me that she had never wanted to accept Claire as a student in the first place. It's true enough she spat nails at Carew when she saw him again, after so many years. But I remember wondering even then why she should be so provoked. I confronted her that very night. And she admitted—" The headmistress seemed to catch herself. "Well, that's neither here nor there. I took her in, didn't I, even after he'd gone off and left her? Even then! But she *insisted* on heading for Ireland and chasing after him." She glanced up, meeting Matthew Darby's gaze with defiance. "If there is one thing I cannot abide, sir, it is a woman without dignity."

"I could not agree more," he assured her.

"And where is the dignity," Mrs. Treadwell went on plaintively, "in running after a man who has abandoned you without a word of explanation?"

"Where indeed?"

Evelyn's eyes narrowed. "See here, Mr. Darby. Are you here in some professional capacity, or merely as Christiane's friend?"

"Well, both, as it happens. There's been a dreadful buzz in London in the past few days about all this business— the countess and Carew and the girl—and I did hope you might help me sort it through."

"For publication?"

"If at all possible," Darby said.

"Oh, I couldn't do that," Mrs. Treadwell said. "I wouldn't ever do that to the countess. Not in a million years."

"She is going ahead with her wedding to Lord Carew, I believe?"

Mrs. Treadwell nodded. "And she knows what I think about that! I won't be attending, but the girls are going. They begged and begged until they made my head spin. They are so fond of her." She picked up her teacup and stared at it. "I really had no choice but to ask her to relinquish her position, though, don't you agree, Mr. Darby? She had not turned over the new leaf she'd promised. She set a wretched example for the girls with her goings-on with Lord Carew. Only think how appalled the mamas of my students would be if they ever learned of her involvement here."

"I believe you are quite correct," Mr. Darby intoned. "Indeed, it is my opinion you could not be more fortunate that the countess and Miss Finn left here when they did. Any further association with them would have resulted in your school's utter ruin."

She stared at him in trepidation. "Why should you say that?"

Mr. Darby hitched his chair toward hers. "Haven't you heard? Miss Finn returned to the city two days past in order to confess to having murdered her father."

Evelyn went ghost-white. "No! That can't be true! Claire isn't capable of such a thing!"

"There's no question, I'm afraid. The authorities have it all in writing. She admitted that she stabbed him."

"I can't believe it. I won't believe it. Did she kill her mother as well?" the headmistress asked in horror. "*And* the coachman?"

"Ah." Mr. Darby stroked his nose thoughtfully. "That's where the tale grows interesting." He paused. "I trust I can rely on your discretion, Mrs. Treadwell?"

"Oh, absolutely!" she breathed.

The publisher of the *Guardian* smiled slowly. "Well. Suppose I tell you what I heard."

"My agent has an offer on the place already," Gannon told Christiane as they took a stroll through the garden of the Berkeley Square town house, on a September morning when the rest of London was busy paying calls. "I was afraid I'd take a bath on it, but the market's heated up just at the moment. So we're in fairly good stead."

"I never felt this house was truly yours," she mused, glancing back at its looming bulk.

"I only meant it as a pied-à-terre from which to launch Claire's debut."

"The Crown's been quite decent in its treatment of her, don't you think?" She took his hand as they approached the boxwood hedge.

"*Damned* decent," he said, with feeling. "Makes me wish I'd brought her in to them six months past."

"She hadn't remembered what happened six months past," she pointed out. "And it helped that they were desperate to lay the case to rest after so long a time."

"There's more to it than just avoiding criminal charges, though." He looked down at her. "Can she put it behind her, Christiane?"

"I think so. With David's help."

"Something's troubling you," he noted, seeing a shadow in her dark eyes.

She shrugged dismissively, shaking her head. "She and I were at Madame Descoux's shop yesterday for the final fittings on our wedding gowns. Who do you suppose was there?"

He let out a groan. "Not Greer."

"None other. She was having a marvelous time whispering to everyone she could collar about how the law might have forgiven Claire, but the ton never would."

He paused, holding both her hands, the tiny Taj Mahal glistening in the sunlight just beyond her shoulder. "Claire doesn't care about that, does she?"

"Oh, no. She's such a homebody. She never did enjoy going to balls and fetes with the other girls. She'll be perfectly happy looking after David, keeping house for him."

Gannon leaned in to kiss her. "And what will keep you perfectly happy, after we are married?"

"Why—looking after you, of course."

"I don't require much looking after," he noted wryly. "One of the drawbacks of marrying a man of my advanced years."

"Well, we always can travel, I suppose."

"You don't sound altogether enthusiastic."

"I must confess, I was perfectly exhausted when we got back from Ireland. All that changing of coaches and riding on ships and packing and unpacking . . . one of the drawbacks of marrying a woman of my advanced years. I intend to advise all our girls: 'Mind you travel while you're young!' " Then she caught herself, and laughed a little. "What am I saying? They're not mine any longer, are they? Silly of me."

"You put so much into your work at the academy," Gannon said softly. "I imagine you'll miss it."

"I think it's all for the best, Gannon, really. I was mad to think it ever had a chance at changing anything." Beyond his shoulder, she saw O'Malley coming toward them.

"Forgive me, m'lord," the butler said briskly, "but Madame has a caller."

"Have I, O'Malley? I can't imagine who—" Christiane reached for the card on his tray. She stared at it for a moment. "There must be some mistake."

"I don't know about mistake, m'lady, but she's waitin' for ye in the drawing roo—" Before he even finished, the countess had grabbed up her skirts and was running toward the house.

She paused once she reached the doors, though, and took a moment to smooth her curls and straighten her sleeves. Then she squared her shoulders and entered the drawing room with her head held high. "Why, Evelyn, what a delightful surprise," she said archly.

"I doubt that," the headmistress said.

"Come to warn me again not to go ahead and marry a murderer?"

"Oh, no. Not a bit. I declare, when Mr. Darby told me what had really happened in the coach that day—"

"Mr. Darby? Mr. *Matthew* Darby?" Christiane was incredulous. "Where did you come across him?"

"He came to call on me at the academy. He was rooting about for more fodder for that scandalous gazette he puts out, I imagine."

"Darby came to the academy?" Christiane still could not quite grasp this; it seemed a most unlikely thing for him to do.

"Oh, yes. He was asking all sorts of questions about you and Claire. I didn't give a thing away, of course. Not a thing. You and I may have our differences, heaven knows, but I'm not the sort to spread tittle-tattle. I turned the tables on him!" She seemed quite pleased with herself.

"How did you do that?" the countess asked in trepidation.

"Why, I wormed the entire story out of him."

"The story of . . . ?"

"Claire killing her father, of course."

"And Darby told you all about that, did he?" Christiane was beginning to wonder whether her long-held trust in the publisher had been misplaced.

"He certainly did." Mrs. Treadwell bobbed her gray head. "And I must say, it puts a different color on matters. That is why I'm here."

"Is that so," said Christiane, who was by now thoroughly nonplussed. "Would you mind telling me just what Mr. Darby said?"

"He explained all about how Hugh Finn killed the coachman when the poor man tried to stop him from beating Georgina, and how Hugh killed Georgina, and then how Claire stabbed Hugh to death when he came at her in a rage."

"True enough," the countess confirmed.

"And what's more, he told me how Lord Carew took Georgina in when she was in the family way with dear Claire, to keep Hugh from beating her until she lost that baby, too. I don't mind saying, I cried like a baby myself at the tale. Poor Georgina, married to such a monster! I declare, when I remember how lovely and lively she was, once upon a time . . ." Evelyn broke off, rummaged in her reticule, and dabbed her eyes with a lacy kerchief. "You just never know what is going on behind someone else's window-shutters, do you?"

"No, you don't," the countess agreed.

The headmistress raised her chin. "Hearing that horrible tale from Mr. Darby convinced me of one thing, Christiane."

"And what is that, Evelyn?"

"The work of the academy *must* go on. It is absolutely *vital*. Why, Mr. Darby himself said it: Imagine how different Georgina's life might have been if someone, anyone, had taught her to stand up for herself—to believe in herself."

"It was my understanding that you intended to carry on with the academy."

Mrs. Treadwell's pale blue eyes searched the countess's face. "That's the trouble, you see. I'm not the academy. We both know that. I am just . . . the administrator. You were always its heart and soul."

"Goodness, Evelyn, that's not so. The girls rely on you in so many ways. You teach them so much—"

"I teach them to curtsy and pick up the right fork, yes, but not the most important things. They learn those from you. How to follow their hearts. How to stand up for what they believe in. How to treasure the friendship of women. I can't teach them such stuff." Her eyes were swimming with tears again. "How will I, when I've never learned it myself?"

"Evelyn, please don't cry."

"I can't help it," the headmistress sniffled. "I feel like such a fool. I am so ashamed of myself! That I would care more for the good opinion of Mrs. Minton or Lady Calhoun than for you, after all we have shared—" She drew a deep breath. "I won't ask your forgiveness, for I don't deserve it. I simply wanted to say that I am sorry, and to wish you every happiness with Lord Carew. There, now. I'm done. I'll be on my way." She started for the door.

"Just one moment," the countess said.

"I daresay you'll give me an earful. Very well, go ahead," the headmistress told her bravely.

"What I wanted to give you was this." Christiane crossed the rug and caught her in an embrace.

Evelyn let out a sob and returned the hug. "I have missed you so, Christiane! You cannot imagine—"

"Oh, but I can. Every time I thought of my wedding day, I was sick with misery that you would not be there."

"I've been a jealous old shrew, that's what I've been."

"And I have been an utter idiot—too proud to come to you and tell you how I felt, and how terribly I missed you." Christiane took her old friend's hands and squeezed them tightly. "Thank God you came to me."

A bit embarrassed by the release of so much emotion, Evelyn took the opportunity to glance around the handsome drawing room. "It's a most impressive home you and he have taken," she said admiringly. "And on such a fine block."

"Oh, we're not staying. He has a buyer for the house. We don't much care for London."

"So you'll be leaving the city." Christiane nodded. "And going . . . where?"

"Gannon has an estate outside Cork."

"Cork?"

"In Ireland."

"Oh." Mrs. Treadwell appeared quite crestfallen. "All the way in Ireland . . ."

"I was thinking, though—"

"Yes?"

"It's odd, I know, but I have grown very fond of Kent."

The headmistress's eyes widened. "Do you mean you would come back?"

"In an instant, if you'd have me."

"Oh, Christiane!" Mrs. Treadwell was so excited that she did a little dance, still holding the countess's hands.

"On one condition, that is."

"Anything. Anything!"

"You have got to come to my wedding."

"You couldn't keep me away for the world." Mrs. Treadwell pulled her back toward the settee. "You must tell me everything about it. What sort of flowers will you have? Who is making your dress?"

"Would you like a bit of sherry, Evelyn?" Christiane offered.

"I wouldn't say no to it. We *are* celebrating, after all."

Christiane poured two glasses.

"To old friends," Evelyn declared, clinking hers to the countess's.

"No matter how old we get!" Christiane agreed.

Thirty-three

"This is where thou kiss the bride, David, I believe," Silas Brown declared roundly, his voice booming.

David Wrede was only too glad to comply, to laughter and a burst of applause from the assembly gathered in the courtyard of Mrs. Treadwell's Academy for the Elevation of Young Women. Gannon followed suit, so enthusiastically that Christiane had to push him away and gasp for breath. "Please, Gannon! You are setting a bad example for David and Claire."

"David and Claire are setting a bad example for us, rather," he noted.

Christiane glanced at that couple's fervent embrace. "Or a good example," she amended, and threw her arms around Gannon's neck again, much to his delight. The bridesmaids for the double wedding—Bess, Gwen, and Petra—were counting off the seconds of David and Claire's kiss: "Thirty-seven! Thirty-eight! Thirty-nine . . ."

Someone tapped Gannon's shoulder. "Go 'way," he muttered, his mouth on Christiane's. "We are out to best

the youngsters." Then he glanced to see who it was. "Oh!
Sorry, Mrs. Treadwell."

"Mrs. T," she insisted. "You must call me that, as the
girls do. And I only wanted to give the bride a kiss as
well."

Christiane returned her embrace joyfully. "Thank you
so much for suggesting that we have the wedding here,
Evelyn. It is perfect, absolutely perfect."

"Where else would you have held it? This is your home,
after all, and always will be."

"I hope Cook isn't put out with such a press to feed,"
Gannon put in.

"Cook loves to show off, and you know it," the headmistress said complacently.

"One hundred!" the young folk crowed, as David reluctantly released a blushing Claire from his embrace.

"Gracious, David," she murmured in embarrassment—
but her gray eyes glowed.

He promptly started in again, to a chorus of hoots from
the guests.

Christiane stood watching them, one arm through Mrs.
Treadwell's, the other through Gannon's. "I envy them
their night tonight," she said softly.

The headmistress gave a shudder. "I don't."

"If they had any sense," Gannon murmured, "they
would envy us ours."

She thought about that for a moment. "You're right,"
she said then, with a wink.

"You lost, you know," Bess declared, bouncing up beside them.

"We let them beat us," the countess countered. "It
seemed the noble thing to do. You young folk *will* insist
you have a corner on the market in passion, but we know
better, don't we, Gannon?"

"That we do."

"Bess, your hair is coming all undone," Mrs. Treadwell
fussed, motioning to smooth the girl's unruly red locks.

Bess jerked out of reach. "Don't touch it! Not a single strand!"

"But—"

"Lord Riverton," Bess announced grandly, "only just told me he finds my hair 'a glorious flood of bright fire.' " They stared. "Well, you needn't all look so surprised!" she said in mock outrage.

"Young Neville Riverton?" Mrs. Treadwell asked, sounding dazed. "Heir to Lord Rawnleigh? However did you make his acquaintance?"

"Madame introduced me to him at the theater in London. He is a friend of Lord Carew's friend Mr. Coleridge. *And* he writes plays!"

The headmistress whirled on Christiane. "You keep close counsel, don't you?"

"I wasn't sure he would please Bess," the countess said modestly.

"Not please her? With a fortune that size?"

"Oh, I don't give a fig about his fortune," Bess declared, as the gentleman in question approached and invited her to go with him for a glass of champagne. "Did I mention that he writes plays?" she threw over her shoulder as she let Riverton lead her away.

Gwen was heading toward them. "I've been wracking my brain as to what Mrs. Caldburn taught us," she teased, contemplating the newlyweds. "Do I congratulate you, Your Lordship, and wish Madame good luck? Or is it the other way around?"

"Congratulate us both," Gannon said promptly, just as the countess answered:

"Wish *me* good luck!"

Gannon arched a brow at his bride. "Do you think you'll need it?"

"I'm sure I will."

Gwen laughed. "Well, then, I do!"

A sturdily built young man with long, fair hair and spectacles came up beside her and bowed smartly to Gannon:

"My sincere felicitations, milord. And the best of luck to you, milady." He bowed over Christiane's hand.

"Show-off," Gwen sniffed.

His blue eyes widened in amazement. "What, I got it right, then?"

Christiane laughed. "To tell the truth, we are none of us sure. We shall have to apply to Mrs. Caldburn."

Mrs. Treadwell cleared her throat meaningfully. Gwen looked at her askance, then recollected herself. "Oh, I beg your pardon; I haven't made introductions, have I? I am a social failure all around, I fear. Mrs. Treadwell, permit me to present Mr. Gouvernour. Mr. Gouvernour, this is the academy's beloved headmistress, Mrs. Treadwell."

"Then I have you to thank, dear lady!" Mr. Gouvernour declared, pumping Mrs. T's hand.

"For what?" she asked, beaming.

"For the first young lady I have ever met who is willing to take notes—not to mention plunge in with the occasional scalpel—while I examine cada—"

"*Do* you know, Mr. Gouvernour," Gwen interrupted, gaily but firmly, "I am simply dying for a glass of champagne. Could we please go and get some?"

He pushed his spectacles up on his nose. "Of course, sweetheart, if you wish. An honor to have met you, Mrs. Treadwell. Lord and Lady Carew, all felicitations."

"Thank you," Christiane said gravely, since Gannon was trying too hard not to laugh to be able to speak.

Mrs. Treadwell was looking unmistakably cross. "Let me guess. You introduced them in London."

"They did seem perfect for each other," Christiane said helplessly.

"I declare, I feel as though you have gone ahead and settled everyone's future without me!"

"There's still Petra," Gannon pointed out.

"Not to mention all the younger girls," the countess reminded her friend. "And a new crop beginning just a week from now."

"Are you sure you don't want more than a week of honeymoon?" the headmistress inquired.

"Why, Mrs. T," Gannon said, sounding scandalized. "You salacious thing!"

She promptly rapped him with her fan.

"How can I revel in my own happiness," Christiane asked the headmistress, "when I haven't yet seen those I care for settled?"

"Petra *is* going to prove problematical, I fear," Mrs. Treadwell allowed, glancing at the girl across the courtyard.

"I wasn't thinking of Petra."

The headmistress blinked. "No? I can't imagine who else . . ." She broke off. Gannon was grinning, and Christiane's dark eyes glinted devilishly. Mrs. Treadwell held up both her hands, warding them off. "Oh, no. No, no, no. Don't even think of it, Christiane. I am much too old to be concerned with such things."

"I think if you are bold enough to have it known that you are looking, Mrs. T," Gannon said, "you'll find more men than you might imagine are in the market for a mature woman such as yourself — one who is worldly and sophisticated, rich with experience. . . ."

The headmistress snorted. "It's beyond me what you see in him, Christiane. He's such a dreadful liar."

Clarisse had popped up beside them. "Beggin' yer pardon, Mrs. Treadwell, mum." She bobbed a curtsy toward Christiane and Gannon. "I'm ever so happy for ye, m'lord, Madame."

"Thank you, Clarisse. Would you happen to know if Cook has made her quince tart for the festivities?" Gannon asked.

"A whole tableful," the maid declared, eyes sparkling. "But there's someone to see you, mum."

"To see me?" Mrs. Treadwell echoed in dismay. "Now?"

"Aye, mum. She said it was an emergency."

"Oh, for gracious' sake. Had she a card?"

Clarisse crunched her nose up. "I asked her, right enough, and what did she say but, 'I'd rather not.' Very grand manner she puts on, if you ask me."

"Wouldn't present a card? How terribly intriguing," the headmistress noted. "Where have you installed this creature of mystery?"

"In yer parlor, mum."

"Excuse me, won't you, please? I won't be but a moment." Clearly intrigued, Mrs. Treadwell bustled off inside.

"Kiss me again," Christiane commanded Gannon.

"I had thought perhaps that quince tart . . ."

She stared at him, aghast.

"I was only jesting," he insisted, bending his mouth to hers.

"Evelyn is right," she grumbled. "You *are* a dreadful liar!"

It was half an hour before Mrs. Treadwell finally reappeared and beckoned to Christiane across the courtyard. "Do come here!" she called, waving frantically.

"There is rather a wild look in her eye," Gannon observed as he and Christiane made their way through the well-wishing crowd.

"You'll never guess who my caller was," Evelyn announced when they reached her side.

"The regent, enrolling Princess Charlotte?" Gannon ventured.

"Too late already for that one," Christiane muttered.

Evelyn shook her head, tight-lipped, looking as pleased with herself as a cat that had got the canary.

"Don't tease, Evelyn!" Christiane chided.

She needn't have troubled; the headmistress clearly couldn't keep the news to herself a moment longer. "Lady Calhoun!" she said triumphantly.

"The Lady Calhoun who holds the keys to Almack's?" Gannon asked, his curiosity pricked.

"The very one," Evelyn confirmed.

"Ooh, how I hate that woman!" Christiane declared.

"She is the very worst of the tigers! What in the world could have brought her here?"

"The chickens," the headmistress declared.

"*What* chickens?"

"The ones that always come home to roost. In particular, her youngest daughter, Isabella. Sixteen years old, Theodora says, and as wild as a hellcat. Has already tried to elope with the stableboy—twice. Made it so far as Newcastle this last time, before her father and brothers caught up to her and dragged her home."

"Imagine that," said Christiane, adopting a not-very-convincing expression of sympathy.

Evelyn didn't even pretend. "Theodora was crying," she declared with immense satisfaction. "She sat there in the parlor with the tears streaming down her face, begging me to take Isabella on. 'You are my last hope, Evelyn,' she told me."

"And what did you say?" Christiane asked avidly.

"Well, considering the circumstances, I felt it only right to disclose that you are my partner."

"To which Lady Calhoun replied . . . ?" Gannon prompted.

"To which Lady Calhoun replied, 'Oh, for glory's sake, Evelyn, we all know that.' Then she paid for two terms in advance."

Christiane stared for a moment in disbelief, then burst out laughing. "Lady Calhoun has enrolled her daughter here?"

"I never would have believed it," Evelyn declared, "if I hadn't been there myself."

Gannon tucked his new bride close to his side. "If this renegade academy of yours teaches any lesson, ladies, it is that one should never be so brazen as to say 'never.' "

"Never," Christiane agreed breathlessly, and turned to meet his kiss.

Berkley Books proudly introduces

Berkley Sensation

a **brand-new** romance line
featuring today's **best-loved** authors—
and tomorrow's **hottest** up-and-comers!

Every month...
Four sensational writers

Every month...
Four sensational new romances
from historical to contemporary,
suspense to cozy.

With Berkley Sensation launching in June 2003,

**This summer is going to
be a scorcher!**